THE AUTHOR

THE AUTHOR

— A NOVEL BY —

THE AUTHOR

BOOK I

META LIT

Copyright © 2025 Meta Lit LLC
Presented by Daniel Thomas Hind
All rights reserved.

THE AUTHOR by The Author

FIRST EDITION

ISBN 978-1-5445-4737-4 Hardcover
    978-1-5445-4736-7 Paperback
    978-1-5445-4862-3 Ebook

This book is dedicated to you.

"*There comes a time when you realize that everything is a dream, and only those things preserved in writing have any possibility of being real.*"

—James Salter

Disclaimer

This foreword is not an endorsement of the book that follows. It is more of a disclaimer. You do not have to read this novel. Throw it on your bookshelf and let it gather dust. Keep it on your coffee table to impress someone who comes over for drinks.

I, however, am not so easily impressed by literature. My client, the author of this novel, knows that intimately. It's been screamed at him through phone lines across continents, whispered in his ear in the corners of movie premiere afterparties, but I should have known better than to think he'd take my advice on this one.

As much as I tried to treat it like a joke when he first pitched it, this book is not a joke.

We were drinking bourbon on my backyard patio. The kids had gone to sleep. It was a fine night to drink with a dear friend who's made you boatloads of money. I'd invited him over to pitch a big reboot of a major franchise, an idea he'd already rejected twice. The studio was relentless in its pursuit. The money, it goes without saying, was astronomical. My client had just come off two majorly successful motion pictures. The reboot wasn't the only project he'd been offered in the wake of these triumphs, but it was the one I wanted him to grab by the balls. I started softly. Innocently. I asked him what he wanted to do next.

To my great surprise, he said he was going to throw his hat into the ring of literary giants and write the first great novel for Millennials, Gen Z, and whatever cyborgs come after. Not some fantasy horseshit, he said, *real* literary fiction. Highbrow written for the lowbrow. Yada, yada, yada, I couldn't believe what I was hearing. I hoped it was the bourbon talking.

I had to remind my client, gracefully, as I bit my tongue, that he's not an author, he's an actor. A very famous actor at that. Writing a novel could only hurt him. If it's not incredible, he'd be murdered as a hack. He stopped me right there. He wasn't worried about that, he said, desire in his eyes. You know the look exactly. He was worried it would be so fucking good and, still, no one would read it.

So, we agreed! I tried to make him see that even if the book *is* the next great American novel, whatever that means, no one will care. Nobody reads novels anymore, especially young people. Why waste your time? It's a lose–lose proposition.

We had another glass of bourbon, he turned down the reboot, and with great charity I saw him out without slamming the door.

Sure enough, eighteen months later, my office received a package in the mail. It was a manuscript accompanied by a handwritten note.

> Your whole life you tell yourself you want to be seen and heard.
> Then you are and you realize you were dead wrong. You just want to be read.
> Sorry for the radio silence. Been holed up in a cabin.
> …Do you still love me today?

I held the very thick (too thick) bundle of pages in my hands. For a moment I was inconsolable. I tried to coach myself through it. Some of my older clients *had* written memoirs before, this wasn't exactly new territory. Yes, but they had all employed ghostwriters, and their books were mostly factual accounts to elicit sympathy for their traumatic pasts, not disdain.

Still, how bad could this be?

A few pages in, I knew we had a real problem here.

These are dangerous times for public figures. I often advise my A-list clients to say as little as possible when interviewed, allow the audience to project onto you. Stay off social media, leave it to the imitators. And under *no* circumstances should you *ever* put any sensitive information—that is, colorful opinions that could be misinterpreted or weaponized by the media, sexual solicitations to anyone no matter how much you think you trust them, admissions of transgressions that could be held against you in the court of public opinion or, worse, the court of law, basically *anything* that has the slightest chance of reflecting badly on you—in writing!

You can imagine my horror, then, as I read the first-person account of my client whizzing through early 2010s Hollywood as he lied, stole, degraded, and intoxicated himself on his way to fame. This was all news to me.

I want to state for the record—on behalf of my agency and its board, in defense of myself and my better judgment, and for the sake of my client—this is a work of fiction. Nothing that follows is historical fact and any resemblance to real people or events is purely coincidental. Because if anyone thought for one second that any of it was true, this book would be career suicide for my client. The following pages would end him. And, if not for this disclaimer, would end me too.

I'm left with no other option than to protect all those implicated.

To be clear, I possess no knowledge of what actually happened and what is imagined. What's fact, what's fiction. This is a novel, after all, *not* a memoir. I've let Legal handle the provisos, I'm sure they had a field day.

Here's what I do know: My client is a good man, a brilliant artist, someone whose success has been built on eccentric habits and obsessively strict routines. He is a man of stoic principles, who treats himself like a scholar and an athlete, meditates daily, abstains from drugs, and cares deeply about his work and loved ones. He's someone who quietly heads multiple companies and nonprofits, contributes *generously* to philanthropic organizations, and makes appearances for charitable causes when asked. He's someone whose admiration spans continents, whose name blows up the box office, and whose talent on screen is once in a generation. That is who he is, how you will remember him. It's his destiny and legacy.

Part of my legacy is to ensure it all plays out that way. Which brings me full circle to why I am the one introducing this work of mostly, I hope, fiction.

Upon learning of my client's intent to publish, I immediately went into damage control and identified two protections:

Anonymity

Our agency has demanded my client remain anonymous. We've worked overtime to bury all, and I do mean *all*, associations between our client and the contents of this book, including names, dates, locations, timelines, et cetera. While my client promises that artistic integrity reigns supreme, nothing written happened exactly as described. Good luck trying to figure out his real identity. You can try, but you will fail.

For reasons sufficient to my client, he is quite happy with this arrangement and wants the merit of his literary achievement to stand on its own legs, free from the shadow of his celebrity. More importantly, we don't want him to get sued or canceled.

Hence, you'll know him only by his pseudonym, "The Author."

Representation

Considering the risk, no matter how remote, that my client's identity is somehow revealed, in good faith, our agency has chosen not to represent this project. Therefore, legally speaking, we have nothing to do with this book or its contents; my client has chosen to self-publish under his own volition. I am doing my client a courtesy by explaining all of this in writing.

And with that, my work here is done.

—"Harrison" (The Agent)

(And if after this preamble you decide to ignore my advice and continue reading? Enjoy. It's what my client wants. And I always make sure he gets what he wants.)

several years earlier...

CHAPTER I

wet hot famous

The car ahead signaled toward the shoulder and parked halfway onto the dirt. Reflexively I followed, nerves hopped and hacked, and didn't look to my right and didn't turn around. Horns honking but I didn't hear them. Time had dilated to an impractical expanse, so big I was sure the whole world had died like one great big engine death and left us here in this stillborn disappointment. Is that what happens when time grows? Not passes but grows. Everything hushes to a pause. Like the breath between a laugh.

I could not move. The car was doing the work for me, maneuvering to the side of the road, parking itself just behind the one I'd hit. Another narrator might describe these few seconds as the shape of panic, but I'd never read that fucking guy's story. And perhaps the world had not died; perhaps I was just experiencing some sort of systemic vasoconstriction due to the excessive cocktail of party drugs administered over the past twenty hours.

My cheeks burned hot. Sweat cried from my forehead. I tried to open the door, my hand making to grip the handle, but looking down I was still clutching the wheel. If a camera were on my face, and I always imagined there was, it might have caught the yawn of a smile. Through the windshield I saw a woman emerge from a silver Volkswagen hybrid under a big green road sign that read *No Exit*. She was a greying brunette with kind unassuming eyebrows; I guessed late forties. Her body inoffensively chubby, she exuded a sort of middle-class ordinariness that invites carnage.

I muttered something unfair and horrible which I would later repeat when describing her to the people I called my friends.

She walked to the back of her car and bent over to inspect the area I'd driven into seconds ago. Apple bottom. Too many apple pies. I could feel myself getting hard and with a newfound vigor shucked myself free from the wheel, accidentally sounding the horn, which sent the woman down on her ass like some frightened rabbit fat with babies. No, it is not safe to litter here.

I was outside of the car now, delivered from its routineness. Instinctively I heard myself wrangling with the Hertz representative: I have no fucking idea, what dent? An armada of vehicles slowed to avoid me, a mere arm's length away, teasing at the inevitable. Hair blowing in the exhaust, California dreamin'. For a moment I considered taking a selfie and posting it on Instagram, counting by the thousands the number of *likes* this sort of perspective would award me while simultaneously lambasting each and every moron behind the thumbtap for contributing to the devaluation of an artform. If I died right then I'd be a celebrity by morning sun. A digital monument, no filter. I imagined the photo's composition: the light-shadow a premonition kissing through the background, a life described in retro vintage, the racing ghost of a Buick inches from sending me to that nowhere-destined place, the sunspot halo above my eyes. I wouldn't blink, I told myself. What would my eyes say? What would you say seeing them?

I imagined my face posted across the internet, all the friends I'd posthumously accumulate—come with me, I want to take you with me—and at once understood the psychology of a ghost: it's not the sticking around that's attractive. I considered living forever in a digital medium, celebrated exclusively for my death, almost like James Dean but without the proof; the wistful clichés —*He had so much potential*—redressing the failure I'd been while alive. Then I imagined an old beaten truck operated by a deadbeat degenerate driving fuck-all-to-hell down the 405 swerve to barely miss me and slam into this poor woman, a victim of my narration, effectively terminating both the claimant and witness of a crime that had surely been imagined but not yet proven.

But a horn blasted. I'd nearly wandered beyond the white divider line. You too buddy, I thought and waved at the honking. The seizure of recycled air, the exhaust tornadoing like junk hollow tribal music. Dizzy. I was dizzy. I steadied myself, peering into the tinted car window to see whether my appearance might pass for sober, my starry details eclipsed by an epic comedown of nuclear proportions. I promised my reflection not to lose my shit.

I then proceeded to lose my shit. Tears tasted in my mouth as I hustled toward the woman, feigning a noticeable limp for no reason other than to elicit sympathy. My legs were fine. In fact I was in tremendous shape and, despite indulging in a daily regimen of prescription amphetamines prescribed for someone else, never got sick. I shouted or half-attempted language or cried like the doleful pilgrim I was and took the woman by her hands.

"Your leg," she said. "Are you all right? Are you hurt? Should I call 9-1-1?"

Absolutely not!

I winced and rubbed my knee just like I did that time in second grade when Randy Hicks slide-tackled me from behind, cleats up, to stop my breakaway. One goal away from scoring a hattrick. Head down, I gingerly walked off the soccer field, sucking my cheeks, crushed that I couldn't win your adulation. Who were you? I didn't know then but I always felt your presence. Like an imaginary friend always keeping score.

Exasperated, I said—was surprised to hear myself say—my mother had just been in a terrible car accident near her home in Santa Monica, right next to the Hotel Shangri-La. I paused in disbelief. I hadn't prepared for such a lie, and, anxious I'd now have to commit to this undeveloped plot I was wildly unfit to narrate, I managed to shut myself up to see where this woman might take it. Her eyes softened.

"Oh dear. Oh no. Are you serious?"

Just look at me!

"I'm rushing over now," I said. "She's barely breathing, they said." Who *they* were was immaterial. What mattered was that this woman's experience of my experience of my mother's life hanging by a fucking thread—an Oscar-worthy performance, I might add—should conjure the pretense of armies, doctors, religious heads, and Christ almighty rushing to her aid.

These were real tears.

That my mother lived in Long Island and had never even visited California was immaterial. In fact Mom hated the very idea of my moving to Los Angeles, an idea I'd recently floated multiple times while training at the Stella Adler Studio of Acting —if you count railing lines of adderall in the bathroom prior to scene study class *training*. No question, Mom's dying in Santa Monica would be profoundly ironic because in a little over an hour I was to fly home to New York to celebrate her birthday and surprise everyone with the big news that I'd just been signed by my new agent Harrison at WME. Mom, I'm going to need your help (money) to ship my belongings across the country—Happy birthday!

I think I passed out. I must have because the woman grabbed me as I fell into the honking horns. The smell of gasoline was profound. Confessions, imitations, assurances spat from my mouth with a frazzled urgency that only infants appreciate, my gaze sufficiently schizophrenic.

She was at my side, the woman was literally at my side, propping me up for balance. My poor leg, I didn't know how I'd hurt it. As I sobbed and mewed I noticed myself confusing the two accidents, my mother's imagined crash and the actual consequence of the *tiny bump*, I'd call it, playing out before me, thereby assuming blame for the false tragedy of my mother's car-flipping inferno, severity escalating, blood on my hands. My mother's blood! The woman gasped in horror as if I'd just stabbed myself, *or* her—which, give me the knife, I thought—and pulled me into her fat bosom as would my own mother, petting my hair and whispering a lullaby of hushes. I was in a tizzy, she said. I needed to get my head straight. Everything's okay. Nothing's my fault. Okay?

Okay!

The totality of this exchange all but eclipsed my responsibility for the one true thing of this elaborate spectacle: that at eighty miles per hour I'd driven my rental Mazda right into the back of some innocent woman's Volkswagen while jacked up on an indiscernible amount of cocaine to keep last night's roll going so I could get on a plane that was leaving for New York in less than an hour with or without me. These were real tears.

"Calm down," the woman said. She touched my face.

I looked into her eyes and experienced her experiencing me as the object of her future fantasies and how today's scene would play in her mind repeatedly, indefinitely, with illimitable alternate endings and intimations of sequels to come. I rubbed her shoulder. She kissed my forehead. I kissed her cheek. "Go, your mother needs you," she said and kissed me again. To you I dedicate this, my second attempt at a novel, I wanted to say but didn't know how. She hugged me goodbye, slight pause before release. "Call me if you need anything." She recited her number, perhaps expecting I'd take out my phone to save it, and dumpily made her way back to her car.

"Only a few scratches on the bumper. You can't even notice!"

Did she say that or did I?

Day three in Los Angeles: put it in the books.

X X X

The day before the accident, my second day in Los Angeles, was a celebration.

I rolled face for hours. Dipped, licked, and snorted nearly an entire gram of mdma all by myself. It was Saturday. I arrived at The Standard Hotel twenty-five minutes late. The valet attendant tapped the window of my rental Mazda and waved to roll it down. I did a keybump of coke and opened the door, expecting him to escort me into the belligerently cool hotel.

"Sorry, sir, but you'll have to take your car to the valet down the block. This area is for private use only." I glanced over at the Ferrari, the G-Wagon, the Porsche, and lit a cigarette.

Nothing a free baggie of high-grade amphetamines can't solve, *am-I-right*?

He paused, checked to see if anyone was looking, and took the keys.

Inside danced with purple electric lights. The lobby gave the impression of an early James Bond film. Groovy but boutique, eccentric but sophisticated, museum-like: look but don't touch. Several guests stood queued behind the large black laminated kiosk counters, boxed and framed by silver edging. A cool springtime funk played lightly overhead, synths and slappy bass. A man dressed in a white suit and black turtleneck, German-looking with cropped hair, pointed me in the direction of the obnoxiously yellow restaurant with 1960s-inspired seating. There I spotted Harrison's very attractive assistant, who to my dismay must have been a lesbian, maybe some sort of activist. She said her name was Woolf.

"Two Os like Virginia and never forget it."

"How could I? It's nice to officially meet," I said, attempting to hug her hello, which she did not reciprocate.

"You must have huge fucking balls," she said, pride warming over me. "If you ever stand me up again, I'll cut you out of your own dream. Do not kiss me," she deflected as I kissed her European.

I asked if she had a contract, which only made her laugh.

"Being a raging liar does not make you an actor. Don't you people get that?"

I wanted to quote Alan Watts and say, "One's life is an act with no actor, and thus it has always been recognized that the insane man that has lost his mind is a parody of the sage who has transcended his ego"—but I couldn't remember the quote exactly and instead said nothing, imbuing my silence with an air of incredulity, the truth so obvious that to respond would be insulting.

"Whatever. Let me know when you're back from New York," she said before giving me her number. "Never text me unless you have news. And never call me, period." I was not invited to her table upstairs, she made sure to mention, because we were not friends and I'd already made her late. "The bullshit you pulled yesterday got you this meeting. I don't know what Harrison sees in you, but it's my job to develop you into something marketable. We have a long way to go."

I blew kisses at her tanned slender back as she walked away. Then reached into my pocket and half-emptied the baggie of mdma straight into my mouth.

Showtime.

Today's event was "Invite Only," a private show for WME employees, celebrity clients, and industry scenesters featuring young DJs newly represented by the agency.

A group of pretty strangers were already in the elevator when I shouted to hold the door. "WME event?" I asked, marveling at the blood-orange ceiling.

The fashionable Italian dude in cotton button-down and Prada shades nodded.

"I like your vibe," said the black chick with long braided hair. "What's your sign?"

"Me? I'm straight."

Everyone cracked up. I had no idea what she was talking about.

"No, your astrological sign."

"Sorry, I'm from New York." I told her my birthday.

"Sagittarius. Thought so." She smirked. "I'm Pisces."

She proceeded to educate me about myself, speaking passionately about my horoscope with the wild confidence of someone deeply confused, which, thanks to generous helpings of coke and molly, I found endearing. I gave her a hug as the elevator opened onto the rooftop, the day preternaturally bright and blue. I told these people I'd just been signed by WME, how my acting career was going to do wonders for my writing career. After many congratulations the older gent gave me his business card and said to the heavyset Latino dude with clipboard, "We're all together."

Just like that, I was in.

The Rooftop at The Standard consists of a giant swimming pool centering an expansive outdoor lounge: tiki bars and dance floors, that sort of thing. It was early yet, none of the featured DJs had started spinning. At that moment the pool was the party, not the music.

"We're going to put our stuff in a locker," the black chick said. I nodded along but lost them in the bathroom. They could have been anyone.

I spent the early part of the day walking laps around the pool. No one was swimming. Just a sea of translucent plastic cups pumping discordantly to the chimeric rhythm of shadowed bass seemingly sounding from some far-off place, as if another party was happening simultaneously on a different roof and we were listening to the residue of better fun.

There was no other party. This was the fun.

A cacophony of voices lily-padded among the participants, the loudest very obviously coming from the group of tourists splashing around below my feet. Interchangeable agents-in-training, I imagined, or worse, *lawyers*, and their posse of skinny fat girls who drank with unparalleled aggression. Now we're one of the boys, now we can be loved. And would you believe it, they were my friends! I noticed a girl who worked in the mailroom at the New York office and knelt down to ask if she had a light; seamlessly, someone handed me a joint, already lit.

My roll kicked up nice and clean as I cocktailed the molly with the coke I'd scouted from Craigslist the night before. A cool synthetic mist hovered in the air, a whiff of coconut. I bobbed my head and pretended to enjoy myself, my body relaxed with the conviction of a predator, Ray Bans on, locked and loaded. I took off my shirt, wrapped my phone inside, placed the bundle along with the pack of American Spirits on the ledge, and jumped in. Immediately I felt the confluence of stares, a phenomenon I'd grown accustomed to since losing all the weight. Or maybe it was the coke talking. I laughed idiotically, high-fived whomever, and made sure to acknowledge all the pretty people. Someone handed me a cup from which I drank indiscriminately, finishing its contents in one undergraduate chug. Then I helped some chick onto her boyfriend's shoulders and, exaggerating how much fun I was having—fist pumps and shoulder shrugs—casually floated back to the ledge. I'd successfully established a presence. I'd been absorbed.

There I perched and proceeded to smoke cigarette after cigarette, making sure not to get my hands wet, and spoke avidly if not fanatically to whomever would listen about my writing and the "State of Literature," as it were, a bleak devolution toward dissolution in which the novel had been rendered obsolete in an age of digital reproducibility where social media was in the process of supplanting mass media which was in the process of supplanting the news.

"Culturally we're fucked but everyone knows that," I said. "What no one's talking about is the over-commodification of language thanks to a digital commons underwritten by massive corporations that surreptitiously marketize its content and steal your data." To no one in particular I gave what I thought was a rather brilliant, albeit damning, criticism of the unregulated capitalization of the internet and its devices, a prophesy of the world to come: how we'll soon bear witness to an emergent phenomena of consumption addicts and broadcast sluts for whom everything's shareable, sellable, and made to seem unbelievably urgent; how already there's no longer clear distinctions between art and advertisement, news and opinion, journalism and capitalism, public and private; how by collapsing modes of communication we're promoting the dumbing down of language to nothing more than beanie baby hieroglyphics. "It's fucking retarded!" I shouted with real anger, moved by my feeling moved. "Worst of all we've divested the novel of cultural impact. The novel no longer influences culture because you can't stream it, tweet it, or scroll through it. Does anyone even *read* anymore?"

The guy to my left drank from his cup and slowly bobbed away.

I lit another cigarette and imagined fleeing into a romantic past to reengage an archaic artform, the novel, that one day with my pioneering, *if I dared*, could be invested with a new negative power that restored Literature's maximal, albeit presently dormant, value. "Like a luxury good," I heard myself say, exhaling the blue gorgeous smoke. "I just can't find the time to write. Or

I let myself get distracted. I've been thinking of going to creative writing school, whatever that is, to commit to a routine…"

The guy to my right asked what I was on and if he could have any. I let him dip into the sealed plastic baggie of mdma I'd carefully secured in the small velcro inner pocket of my spandex capris. He threw up a high-five and said, "Epic," and told me he knew some chicks who would give us some coke. I followed him out of the pool.

Over the course of the next however many hours I smoked the entire pack of cigarettes, telling myself as I lit each one that I'd quit at the beginning of the new month, and at some point noticed I'd finished most of the molly in the little baggie. This seemed improbable, certainly precarious. One hundred milligrams is enough to chrysalis, two hundred to butterfly—at nearly seven hundred milligrams, save for what I'd shared, I wasn't sure what I was in for, but I knew it'd be *Epic*.

I proceeded to make out with two lesbians, tell three girls I loved them, and promise so many guys we'd hang out tomorrow, saving their numbers and labeling them by the shared experience: Coke Dude, STandared Hotl, and so on. Eventually I bought Woolf a drink with money I did not have, hoping to catch her around, but drank half of it before realizing I wouldn't find her anyway. Everything was excruciatingly happy, burning livid under big baby sun reflecting white noise off the dark mirrored buildings just beyond the rooftop: tall commercial properties, the financial centers of Downtown Los Angeles. I imagined how my life would have turned out if I had been hired by one of the banks I'd peer-pressured myself into interviewing with before graduation. I pictured this alternate version of me in the building across the way looking down at the party, seeing my present self looking up, and, bemused, turning away in shame.

I must have looked lost, or gay, or both, because an older guy, a fag, came up to me and said, "Here baby, take these. Get you straightened out."

"What are they?"

"They're gre-eaaaatttt!"

I pushed him aside or lapped his palm and saw a plush sofa nearby and floated over to talk to a group of strangers, realizing I'd forgotten my drinks. I kissed the nearest girl goodbye and found a large group of bikinis dancing in front of the DJ booth and fell into them and disappeared.

The day unraveled with intense disregard for personal space and private property. I ingratiated myself with everyone I encountered, taking each stranger by the shoulders as if we'd been friends forever, pouring myself drinks from their expensive tables behind the velvet ropes, encouraged to have more.

I told everyone I was a writer, acting was more like my day job. I'd never acted in anything legitimate before, not unless you counted my entire life, and hadn't written a single paragraph since college but emphasized that I was hard at work on a novel. Saying it made it half true. In those moments of soul-swelling euphoria I believed myself capable of tremendous profundity, of writing works as timeless as Tolstoy's, as radical as Nabokov's, creating for myself a cult of personality like Hemingway's, and writing with such elegance and aplomb that F. Scott would shudder in his grave. Everyone thought my writing a novel was the "dopest" thing they'd ever heard because "who the fuck writes novels?" I must be "way smart" was their conclusion, and

I encouraged more of that sort of talk. Then, in what seemed like practiced succession, the middle-aged Persian gentleman handed me a flute of champagne while the woman I interpreted to be his mistress, half his age, sporting ludicrously colossal sunglasses, fed me a keybump of coke. I kissed her forehead as she touched my chest as the girl to my left put a cigarette in my mouth while the girl from behind kissed my neck and, turning around, I discovered the girl was a man.

X X X

I found myself sprawled across a white soft waterbed encased by red plastic hollow. I didn't know where I was relative to the rest of the party nor how I had gotten there. All I could discern was that I was inside a pod, which to the best of my ability I'll describe as a plastic igloo that from the outside looked like a spade. The smell of coconut was profound. I didn't know if I had just woken up or gone down, but the shade suggested of sleep and I gave in to the suggestion, my body liquefying into lazy currents of wow.

Three girls shared the pod bed with me, some towels thrown about. I blinked and smiled in appreciation of my fortune. Two of them were turned away and asleep or feigning to be, their thong bikinis dispelling imagination altogether, and I imagined them very much awake and trembling at the thought of me waking to find them. The third, the girl facing me, looked up and smiled. She kissed me hello in a manner that suggested I'd known her my entire life and that we were in love wasn't out of the question. I was positive I did not know her, positive we'd never met, though circumstance indicated otherwise. She looked down at the phone in her hand and began to read, piercing her brows in concentration as if my stirring had interrupted a prior engagement. Instinctively I reached for my phone, but it wasn't on my person, and I was seized by an animal terror, panic accumulating in my throat, my eyes. If I'd lost it I would have no hope of finding my way back to the Airbnb, no proof of my whereabouts whatsoever; my presence in Los Angeles could only be verified by the virtual. Then I realized she was holding it, and now I knew exactly what was going on here. She was reading selections from my undergraduate novel, which a few years prior I'd turned in as my senior honors thesis like the pretentious shit I was. While studying abroad my junior year I had the idea— as if I were the first aspiring author who had this idea—to write a contemporary version of *The Sun Also Rises*, which had had a profound effect on me. My protagonist would flee his former life, including his education, and find himself anew in an old world bereft of standardized expectations, a romanticized Europe suited to an artist. The novel would be autobiographical but fictionalized—"autofiction" is a genre now popularized by the likes of Karl Ove Knausgaard, Ben Lerner, and Rachel Cusk that at the time I believed, mistakenly (retardedly), I was pioneering —and contain a series of slightly veiled transpositions. Instead of suffering physical castration like Hemingway's Jake Barnes, my protagonist's castration would be psychological, an overt nod to contemporary institutions' gelding of modern man. I'd change names of friends: my roommate Scott would become Justin; my best friend Doug would become Andrew; my new girlfriend, truly the love of my life, would become "you," the second-person singular who, I hoped, would scale into the second-person plural, a poetic dedication to all my future readers; and so on. I worked on the novel for a year, almost fanatically, and submitted the fifty-five-thousand-word manuscript a few weeks before graduation, my proudest moment to date. But instead of acknowledging my naivete and tossing the novel in the proverbial can, chalking it up to a good experience to learn from its extreme failures, I leaned into my naivete and spent the following two years post-graduation reworking it, earnestly believing I had something publishable. I ended up rewriting the novel so many times I eventually lost all sense of direction, then taste, then one sad sober morning I realized I'd only made it worse.

"You?" the girl said distractedly, reading the words on the screen.

I'd pulled this sort of stunt before, made myself "vulnerable," something I "never did"—playing to my reader's whims, typically a beautiful woman I wanted to bed but couldn't because I was in a "committed" relationship—and reluctantly shared my "work," which conveniently I kept saved on my smartphone.

I nodded with feigned embarrassment.

Say that it worked, was working, because unprovoked she began to read aloud, auratic and serious she was, selected lines of a Spanish woman featured in the story:

"'The heart divines its own spirit. It is the creator and the created. The heart decides but it does not choose. It sees the truth that the head cannot and the head often betrays the heart for its own fascination. The head allows many ugly promises to enter the body but they are false prophets and forgotten just as easily if allowed to disappear and if not allowed then they are devoured and digested by the heart which is immune to such ugliness.'"

As I listened I could hear myself in her voice and to my surprise gripped her leg as if to say I was proud of her recitation, when actually I was proud of myself.

"'The head makes reasons against the heart,'" she continued as I inched closer, feeling myself getting hard. "'The head is selfish and fractured and interested by what is not there, and the heart holds no capacity for imagination because its yearning is real and claimable and must be taken, to distinguish the loneliness from what's not there, it must be taken, it must.'" Suddenly she threw down the phone with superfluous intensity and told me I was brilliant, that my words described her thoughts, thoughts she'd never shared with anyone, thoughts I'd articulated better than she herself ever could, and she kissed me in a way I could not possibly write but would attempt to anyway, just like I'm doing now. She kept reading aloud and thereafter I couldn't tell if she was speaking as the woman in the story or as herself, whoever she was, a broken mix of Spanish and English underscored by demonstratives. I experienced the girl experiencing herself captured in the present tense of the story's action, even though it was written in the past tense, suffusing herself with romantic idealizations of the moments to come as if already they'd been written (they had), her fate already determined—similar to an actress viewing a performance of herself. There was nothing to do but take it in. The potential for total transfiguration was a grant each moment could draw upon, we were imbued with a power of suggestion beyond ourselves, the immediacy of which rendered us powerless. We had to have it.

She fed me a lick of mdma, which I sucked clean off her finger, and I reciprocated the drug as she sucked mine. She looked

Portuguese but could have been Persian or Greek or indeed Spanish, her dark hair streaked gold and her skin of the same denomination, which I touched and held and again kissed deeply. Pulling away, drawn into the iceblue frost of her eyes frantically searching into the depths of my own for what I did not know, frostbitten I was.

She pushed me down and straddled me like a murderer, and I held on, held her at the fold of her hip, the soft tissue over taut fabric, my fingers tucking under the elastic of her bikini. I half sat up onto my elbows and cupped her mouth and asked who she was, perhaps a model or actress, someone recognizable, someone celebrated for being recognized. She brushed away my hand and laughed like I'd already asked, and just then I remembered I had. You've seen this girl while driving down Sunset Boulevard, her giant face postered alongside the Andaz. You've seen her in magazines. You've jerked off to her Google images, if you're anything like me.

She told me my words were more beautiful than her face and my face more beautiful than my words. I had no reciprocal compliment prepared and asked, audibly this time, if she were real. She didn't know what I meant. I told her she looked like the woman I had written in my undergraduate novel, the one she was reading. "As if I had written this woman with you in mind before I knew who you were, before I knew you were real."

Real? she asked but only with her eyes as she took my hand and placed it over her heart, my cock cramping inside my unconscionably tight, unconscionably expensive Lululemon spandex—for which I have no explanation other than my ass looked good and my legs long.

What I actually wanted to say but didn't know how was that I was creating her for *you*, a reader who by reading is participating in the creation of a fiction that, in the act of reading, comes alive, steps off the page. How do I say it? How can I explain that I'm imagining her just as you are now? Bound by the constraints of narration, how can I communicate that we're all in this story together? I did not know how to describe it. And I don't, still.

I told her she was the muse of my dreams, the fantasy delivered. Just ridiculous. Then she kissed me as if never again would it happen and we lay put like that, crouched and fetal, for I don't know how long.

One of the other girls woke, or pretended to wake, and lit a joint. Would you believe it, it was Woolf! I wanted to thank her for inviting me into her circle, wanted to say something profound or disarming, to say anything at all—but I couldn't. It was dark now as my girl passed me the joint and the consideration of night seemed impossible. Time was shrinking, not speeding up, that was what we were doing. I was about to hand the joint back to its originator but already it was gone, in fact it had been extinguished long ago. The girl took my hand outwardly extended to no one and led us from the pod. I waved goodbye to Woolf, who smiled at me with affection in her eyes. But no, she was laughing. And then I saw why. It was my erection, ballooning through the spandex like a Hess Truck, despite all odds, despite all the amphetamines. I emptied the rest of the mdma from the baggie onto my tongue.

Outside was warm under the lights, Downtown lit up around our spinning top so many stories high. The party had transitioned into night, bad electronic music playing from somewhere above or beyond—loud, hollow, synthesized. I ran over to a group of girls smoking cigarettes and, unable to control the volume of my voice, asked if I could have one. They had obviously just arrived, their short skirts and heels showing off night attire, whereas I was still in my bathing suit or whatever you'd call it. One of them made a joke about my wardrobe or lack thereof, and I said I'd take off my spandex and run ass naked into the pool if she gave me a smoke, which she did, then I asked for another, only to be shooed off. I stumbled away and found my girl, who didn't say anything, just sort of frowned and looked away from the skirts. Just then I considered the possibility that she might not speak English after all, at least not fluently; her performance earlier might have been just that, a performance. First striking me as preposterous, this indulgence of the imagination quickly ingratiated itself into the realm of possibility and presented like a winning lottery ticket. I didn't have to say anything, I thought. Her initial experience of my writing formed her impression of me as an author—*The Author*—someone only capable of marvelous speech that swelled with profundity with every utterance and non-utterance. Now my silence was an investment made for her imagination to appreciate. I didn't have to speak a word.

    I communicated this thought with a kiss which, lacking all depth of feeling, felt amazing. She laughed and grabbed my hand and implored me to follow her to the bar. Flashes of impossible orange turned to flame and drizzle and then nothing all at once, color dissolving into a kaleidoscope of sepia and crawling zygotes, and with another flash orange returned. I opened my eyes and now I was sitting on, or sliding down, a rubber lounge chair. I didn't feel panicked so much as retarded, incapable of making choices for myself. The girl pointed to the bar and made drinking gestures.

"Water. You wait," she said.

I nodded, annihilated by her attempted English, and tried to say it was a good idea, I would be here, wherever this was, a big lounge chair, a submariner amongst a company of handsome strangers, experiencing the symptom of myself.

It was then that I got the call from New York. It was my girlfriend, the love of my life. (Please forgive me.)

I answered the call, but this is where narration gets tricky, I have to admit, because my brain was having a hard time registering my body attached to it, or my body was having a hard time registering my brain at the head of it, but actually I was face-planted on the ground. The muscular stranger helping me back up to the chair said his name was Brad or Brett, but I'm probably making it up.

"Thanks. Want some molly?" I said, handing him the baggie. "Never mind, it's all gone."

He looked at me, blinked, and walked mournfully back to his friends. I dropped the plastic baggie, watching it half-flutter like a dead butterfly, and remembered the phone.

"Where are you? Where are you?" She sounded like a starving baby. She'd been calling all day, all night—it was already 9:00 p.m.!—and was about to involve the police. "I've been so scared. Oh my god. Thank god you're all right. Your mom is freaking out. Why haven't you called? Where *are* you?"

"Why would you call my mom!" I said, truly terrified. Then I tried to catch her up to the plotline involving Harrison, the agent at WME who'd agreed to sign me. She let out a horrible breathless toll, a souvenir of love; I could feel her transitioning from living inside one nightmare where I'd died and gone to hell to another nightmare where I'd abandoned her to sign with some big agency in Los Angeles.

"How cliché a storyline!" I said, trying to calm her down. "Who'd ever believe it!"

After much convincing I told her I loved her, don't worry, no character in a story, not even my own, could take me from her. I'm flying back to New York tomorrow, my flight leaves in the morning. Tell Mom I'm sorry for lying at her expense; I can't explain, you'll understand when you read it.

I grabbed my personals from the locker, god knows how I remembered the combination or if I'd even used a locker, and didn't say goodbye to anyone. On the way out I realized I didn't have a shirt and took the first one I saw bunched on the ground next to a lounge chair. I put it on, skintight, barely making it over my shoulders, and in the elevator mirror was surprised to see Miley Cyrus on my chest, tongue protruding, the light of the world wishing me well. Then I realized I hadn't gotten the girl from my novel's number and laughed psychotically because, since I wrote her, I could just make it up—not that I'd call her anyway. The elevator doors closed as my eyes melted down my face, my vision littering into yesterday's story, tomorrow's sadness. With hesitation a voice asked if I had been to the day party and, what the fuck, I hadn't noticed the manicured couple behind me; they scared the spit out of me. Sorry, I said, attempting to wipe down her dress. I thought I might vomit and might've said as much as the woman nervously studied her iPhone, which I couldn't afford, as if engaged in a serious task while the guy vocally fumbled some rushed incoherent remark about how excellent their dinner had been, a subject they had not been discussing. The door opened, another couple entered, and hysterically I exited in search of a water fountain or trash bin but soon gave up and just vomited on the expensively carpeted floor. Relieved, sort of, the taste of hot metal shrieking in my mouth, I continued on. A set of doors led into a swanky billiards room. I ran through them to the bartender and begged for relief.

"Water, do you have?"

Two large men grabbed me by the shoulders and brutally escorted me out a different set of doors, informing me with awesome contempt that I had not been invited to Ms. Cyrus's private reception—which, looking down at my shirt, amazed, I could not believe.

Outside at last, under purple velvet lights, a red carpet ushered my deliverance. I tipped the valet attendant sixty bucks because money didn't mean anything and played it cool as I waited for my rental car, smoking a cigarette procured (stolen) from the bum passed out against the stairwell. The car door opened, the valet holding it like a cape. I rushed over, tripped inside, my Ray Bans falling off my face. What the hell, not to worry, I told the attendant as he reached down to grab them, slamming the door shut, barely missing his head. I was off to save the day, tomorrow.

Waiting at a red light I saw a baggie of coke and pack of American Spirits in the cupholder, which meant I *had* planned on telling my girlfriend about signing with WME. I felt proud, if that's the word, and rolled down the windows to endorse the shitty hip-hop blasting from my stereo, Rick Ross grunting he's a boss, a siren for all to hear. I lit a cigarette and inhaled, the navigation on my phone would lead me home, wherever that was, I didn't even have to touch the wheel.

X X X

Kill shot. Oh god, protect me.

I told her I loved her, I would protect her. I didn't know from what. Four years *is* a long time. I was pleading on my knees, some pathetic rendition of a movie I'd seen. Wolves howling, candles flickering. The candleflame that flickered and bent.

What sounds the best? I said. Read it aloud and tell me what sounds the best.

No, this is not your fiction, said through blond hair weeping in the shadows, her shoulders heaving. Inside our room played like a movie. Some minor chords to underscore the element of dread I felt while packing up my belongings.

Come close to me, I said. Come close.

She squirmed and begged and fucked my ears to deaf. So I threw her the drugs and let her go ballistic. Which never actually happened, I wish; it would have been so much easier if it had.

Why can't you write me as a real person? she said, attempting to walk off the page. Why do all the hard things get brushed away into poetry or whatever this is you have me saying? I'm on rotation in the morning. Patients, real people, actually depend on me. How could you be so selfish?

Because poetry doesn't mean anything, I tried to explain. Because on the page, one step removed, I don't have to look at you. This is all that I have, my delusions.

If you want to write then write! Just stop talking about it, for god's sake.

This is me doing that now, I could not explain.

I've always supported you. Put up with your apocalypse moods. Crying, she pleaded with me not to leave, not to write her out.

I won't write you out, I didn't say, I'll just blend your story with many others. Make you a composite, anonymous. I'll never share your name.

But residency is in two years, she said. We can look into LA programs if that's what you want. I'll do whatever I can. Please. I know you. You'll regret this.

I pressed my mouth to her mouth-cheek-hair, a sopping wet coalition of sympathy to drown in. I heard myself promise I'd never leave—I was just moving.

She slapped my chest, my cheek, and emptied the coke onto the dresser top, cutting four enormous lines with indiscrimination other than to cannonball. Actually that was me in the bathroom, alone. Death-starved lover. Star-crossed starving. In less than one minute, three lines were gone. She put down the straw, but it wasn't her hand, and out of the bathroom I walked with no words written worth sharing, at least not yet.

Tank on the floor before me. Bra on the floor before me. Bend over. Here's the part where you seduce me to stay. But no, you wouldn't do that, you never did, which drove me insane. I needed you to show me what you wanted, needed to know I'm wanted. I wanted you to rip my heart out and throw it on the bed and straddle my bleeding corpse and tell me I'm the one, you'd rather kill me than let me leave. But you didn't, which I'm sure was my fault.

Then you cried something whispered and sounded like my mother when I was momma's baby boy sick in stupid hospital with pneumonia, the doctors unsure why the antibiotics wouldn't take. Love that has no name, only sound. I felt tired. I felt hungry. Remember all the late nights we'd smoke weed and eat Pinkberry? You hated how thin I'd got. I'm sorry if it made you self-conscious; I loved how powerful looking good felt. You thought I might be bulimic, remember asking me at Alta on Valentine's Day, our final one? No, it wasn't bulimia, that sounds so embarrassing, it was much worse.

Help me count the number of nights I spent in a bathroom stall sniffing for an inspiration I could not find inside myself. You can't because I never told you about the drugs. I wasn't an addict, just a loser. If you're reading, now you know.

On top of the bed you twisted some thinly infantile love ritual under moonlit morning, the moon smiling through the half-wall window before us, the only window in our shoebox apartment, a New York bookmark. You and the window naked and the moon tooth-crooked and the cigarette eating itself on the tray reserved for fights like these, no hand to hold it, no hand to hold.

I had her on her back now, legs squeezing to throttle, and she gasped, begging to take me in, absolutely needing to take me in. Slap me all you want, I said. I won't write you out so much as read ahead. I heard myself promise I'd never leave.

For the last time, stop with the poetry and fucking look at me, she said. You fraud. What are you saying?

What am I saying? Can I say?

So many years later I want you to know I was proud of you for being a doctor, even though you thought I wanted you to be someone else. These throwaway moments, those only I can share, they're not what I remember, they're what I've made up. In truth I could write an entire book about you, and I have, which no one will ever read—unless you've handled my phone. I'll save you forever, will never press delete. Just turn the page. The author is not your friend. No matter how close you get. That's why I have to leave.

She came twice, or faked it, and I didn't even.

Afterward I fed her three xanax and she laughed because she'd just taken two in the bathroom, she said. But that was a different time, someone else. I always looked up to you for being happy without the help, like a character in a book I could never touch. And so you'll remain.

I took a few pills myself and managed to get some shuteye as the morning moon hung stupid and out of place.

Tomorrow I was moving to Los Angeles because, baby, I was famous.

CHAPTER II

the talent

The door opened and the man bleeding hot money from his mouth said he was looking at Hollywood's next great talent.

It was my first day in Los Angeles. If I had not been entirely at ease racing around town with a stomach full of edibles, unfortunately late for the most important meeting of my life with supremely powerful agents that I'd arranged under fraudulent pretenses, I could now relax. After all, I'd written it to go like this—apart from all the drugs.

I swiveled in the elegant office chair as the other agents stood to greet Hot Money, bearded, tall, a superficial mix of European genteel and country Western. Analog of cool.

"Sit down, you clowns," he said. "Sit." I rose as the others sat.

"We've just been getting to know each other," one of the agents said.

Hot Money walked into the light-filled conference room—high tech, modern, unusually glamorous. He took my outstretched hand and gripped it with enthusiasm. Impulsively I threw my arms around him. Maison Francis Kurkdjian Baccarat Rouge 540 wafted from his collar. He kindly pushed me away, smiling his gorgeous money smile, and said, "That's nice." He looked to the other agents. "Who has my Red Bull?"

A sugar-free Red Bull shot across the smooth black marble tabletop like a pinball.

"Bingo!"

"Bullseye!"

"Bitch, *please*."

The agents laughed a many-headed laughter. Forkfuls of jelly. I followed along, managing to hold my tongue inside my mouth. In another telling of this story I'm on all fours crawling across the table. Somehow I knew to keep it together.

It was the blue and white WME logo on the wall. I couldn't believe what I'd pulled off. All the relevant departments were present, a representational dream team: Motion Pictures, Motion Pictures—Literary, Television, Digital Media, Talent. The influence was palpable. Fruit platters, steel coffee carafes, granola bars, bagels, carbonated beverages, bottled water—all prearranged for me, screaming of endorsement. I thought I might be hallucinating. Or maybe I'd executed myself, a death by a thousand lies, which shot me through a wormhole into the alternate enviable universe you're now reading.

"We were just saying," the female agent said. She was a middle-aged brunette, an industry titan, representing the MoPic-Lit department. "We saw the reel and loved it."

"Reminds me of River Phoenix right before he died," Television said, talking about me as if I wasn't there.

"I totally see it," Talent said.

"Darker, like his brother," said Digital Media, "but feminine and angular."

"*Androgynous* is the word," Hot Money said, representing Motion Pictures. The aluminum can clacked open; he drank. "Don't insult the kid." He slapped my back. "He's got more balls than that." He walked to the head of the room.

"Still just enough baby fat in his face. There's a softness. He'll age very well."

"I'm getting Freddie Prinze Jr. circa 2000 vibes, only more dangerous."

"More tortured artist."

"Thanks," I said, hoping these were compliments. "Can I get some ice for this?" I asked, referring to my water.

Hot Money clicked a button on the desk. "Woolf, please bring in some ice." He looked up. "For our guest."

"You know there'd be no Leo if River hadn't died," Digital Media said, looking proud. "You know that, right?"

"Of course I know that!" Talent said.

"I was talking to the *talent*," Digital Media said.

"Me?" I asked.

"I was there with Leo the night River died!" Talent said.

"No, you were not!"

"*Lord*. Now you're going to tell us how close you were to signing them both," Hot Money said. The room erupted in laughter. Imagine sword swallowers, gullets wide open. Chickens being burned alive. I had no idea what was going on, could not decipher this strange Hollywood speak.

"Could you imagine River playing Leo's doppelgänger in *The Departed*?" I said, wanting to appear conversant, a student of the *work*. "Or *Inception*? Now that would be a trip."

"Is it too late to say he's got kind of a Johnny Depp vibe?" Talent said, studying me. "If he could grow some facial hair?"

"Definitely Orlando Bloom," said Television.

"Why don't you tell us what you've been up to," Hot Money said, ignoring his colleagues. He stared at his reflection in the big-screen monitor and adjusted his tie. "Mike says you've been doing some Off-Broadway stuff over in New York?"

"More like Off-Off-Broadway," I mumbled; a lie, but not entirely untrue: the evening graduate program at the Stella Adler Studio of Acting was simply a few more steps removed from Broadway than I'd let on. "But yes."

"Good for you," Hot Money said as he sized up the digital smartboard.

A stylish assistant with auburn hair and shaved sides walked into the room and handed me a tall glass topped with ice. I filled it with water from the plastic bottle and drank and filled it some more.

"Which plays, kid?" MoPic-Lit asked.

"*Blue Room*."

"Never heard of it," said Television. "How's that Off-Broadway stuff pay?"

Again, the laughter.

"I know it," MoPic-Lit said, her hand at her chest, calming herself down. "David Hare. Nicole played the female lead back in the nineties. She's a friend."

"Yes, exactly," I said, eager to engage someone about something I could at least pretend to care about. "I played the actor and the model."

"Of course you did."

"In our production we reversed the genders of each character."

"Very *woke*," said Digital Media, his choice of words indiscernible as intentional or ironic; I determined I did not like him.

"Sounds interesting," Hot Money said, barely paying attention. He took hold of the remote. The big-screen monitor signaled on. *Bee-Boop* in C major. Suddenly we were staring at ourselves on the screen. I don't know why but I smiled and waved. "What I'm about to share with you is strictly confidential," Hot Money said, staring into the dead black of my eyes. "Got it?"

"To be kept inside this room," said Talent.

"For *esteemed* ears only," punctuated Television, the angularity of his face magnificently thin.

"Think of this as our in-house strategy for someone like you," said MoPic-Lit.

"Someone with star power," said Television.

"Mega potential," said Digital Media.

"*Major*," Hot Money emphasized.

"We hope…our *intention*," said MoPic-Lit, "is that after hearing what we have in store for you—"

"You'll *appreciate* the sort of four-dimensional chess we're playing."

"—you'll sign with us."

"I'm going to film this," Hot Money said, handling the remote. "I like to get a raw look at the talent. You'll thank me one day." He smiled.

"Whatever you want," I said, so turned on I could barely see straight. I had to stop myself from offering him head. "Yes."

Just then the door opened. The same stylish assistant leaned in. "I have Rob Lowe on the line," she said. "Says it's urgent."

"Not now, Woolf," Hot Money said. "Tell Rob I'm—" he paused and looked at his colleagues, "making history."

MoPic-Lit bit her lower lip. Talent had to excuse himself. Chairs pivoted, bodies repositioned. A tremendous energy took hold.

"You really want me to say that?"

"No. I want you to do your fucking job."

The assistant disappeared and the door slipped shut. Talent came back to his chair. The agents set their devices on the table face down. Hot Money proceeded to tell me how a development deal works.

He said that to kick things off Digital would work with me to establish myself online and build my following. In today's landscape, having a strong presence on social media is *essential*. If I wasn't on this new platform called Instagram, I needed to be. WME has an in-house team of geeks who know how to game the algorithm using bots, whatever those are, to quickly explode my following in a way that appears "organic," said with air quotes. He went on to use terms like "target audiences," "A/B testing," "psychographics," and "avatar" as if I had the slightest idea what any of it meant. It sounded terribly important. I wanted to interrupt—

First of all, what the fuck is *Instagram*?

Second of all, don't you see that if we encourage the artist, teacher, or activist to come alive in every asshole on the internet, we're in for an age of universal deafness and lack of understanding?

—but said nothing. Instead I nodded along with inordinate enthusiasm.

Digital Media took the stage next, leaning back in his chair with his hands in front of him in the shape of a tepee. He said he'd be aligning strategic partnerships for me with in-house brands and social media *creators*, a new type of digital artist I already wanted to wipe from the record books. "WME reps both sides of the money," he continued. "We're pioneering packaged deals in the digital space with the same ferocity Ovitz once did in entertainment." He looked at Hot Money, whose eyes widened. "But fuck CAA," he said. "Point is, there's lots of money to be made. Stupid amounts of money. Fuck CAA."

I immediately reconsidered my issues with social media.

Then someone mentioned something about a mansion in the Hills and the first social media reality show, perhaps they'd place me there for a quick hit of, again using air quotes, "organic virality" while Hot Money laughed and said the mansion was a throw-in if I wanted some easy pussy, it wouldn't even be fair. I nodded along like this was my normal life.

Hot Money said Digital would work with Television to set me up for a co-starring role on a new type of streaming show with a built-in audience that matched the ideal fan profile they'd already manufactured, tested, and validated on social media.

"An easy sell," Talent said.

"The future of marketing," Digital Media said, kissing his fingertips like he'd drained the game-winning three.

You have to remember this was the early 2010s before any of this shit was common. These people represented a significant slice of the brain trust responsible for engineering a new digital landscape that would soon scale beyond traditional legacy media and commodify all "content," drug of the decade, distributed on the web.

Hot Money told me to think "Hulu" or "Amazon Prime," which would soon be entering the media game in a big way. I'd be a new character in one of its first original series who wins over a fanbase where lots of dollars were already being spent, a supporting lead who doesn't quite steal the show but makes a name for himself while the platform eats up market share. Once again I had no idea what any of it meant, but it sounded valid.

"Leverage," Television said.

"*Lev-er-age*," Digital Media echoed.

"Once you land the show, you're in the door. Then we go *major*," Hot Money said.

"Major?" I repeated.

"By this point I'll be working on landing you a co-star in a *major* film. Keep this between you and me but Pacino is considering playing Picasso, or Dali, I can't remember which. Something artsy like that is sure to get the Academy's attention. The only problem is that Al's not a client. Besides him, it's going to be a packaged deal." He stretched across the table and grabbed another Red Bull, zero sugar. "Which fucking kills me."

"There's really no one better than Al for it," said MoPic-Lit over the clacking of can. "He's perfect for the role."

"I know, I know," Hot Money said, downing the caffeine, taurine, B-12, aspartame, whatever other chemicals. "There really isn't. Fuck."

"We're a year or two out from that deal anyway," MoPic-Lit said in a reassuring way.

Hot Money wiped his lips. "Point is, this will be a big win for you." He pump-faked and lobbed the empty can across the room. It missed the wastebin by yards.

Talent jumped in. "Perhaps young Picasso, or young Dali. Like in *The Godfather Part II*." He raised two fingers.

"That's it," Hot Money said. "That's it!"

"I see it!"

"Ka-pow!"

"Bang!"

"Zoom!"

What was happening?

"Landing a gig like that, you'll be in an elite cast of Hollywood untouchables who've transcended the network television phony baloney," MoPic-Lit said. "Which, I have to tell you, ends up killing more careers than it launches."

Television glanced at her and squinted. "Once news breaks of you landing the feature," he said, holding her gaze before turning his pencil head toward me, "that's when I'll line you up for generational wealth. A shapeshifting deal."

"The shifter!" screamed Digital Media, banging the desk.

"We haven't even talked about the publicity angles we'll be orchestrating," said Talent, cutting in. "A narrative that has everyone asking, 'Who is this guy?' and 'Where did he come from?'"

"A meteoric rise," said Hot Money.

"An overnight success."

"The shifter, son!"

"A monster role," Television continued. "A leading role. Think HBO or Netflix original series. The walls separating movies and TV are about to come tumbling down."

"We're talking *Mad Men* big. *Sopranos* big," Hot Money said. "B-I-G."

"But you have to be *good*," said Television. "That goes without saying."

"Our whole strategy hinges on your ability to deliver," Talent said.

"Can you deliver?" Hot Money asked.

I took a sip of water and pierced my eyes in such a way as to indicate the answer to the question was so obvious that only a poser would respond—a *choice*, I hoped, that would showcase my unutterable confidence, not to mention my mastery of the craft; of course I was capable of hitting your lobs out the park; let me get a swish of that Red Bull, *dude*; where do I fucking sign?—then noticed the water dribbling down my shirt. Distractedly I mumbled something cliché about my entire life having prepared me for this moment, patting down the wetness.

"How can we know for sure?" Hot Money said.

"I also acted in *Zoo Story*," was all I could think to say, mortified, hoping, I guess, the play would showcase my *range*.

"Edward Albee," MoPic-Lit responded, reengaging the game of ping-pong we'd earlier established.

"I played both parts in different runs," I said, as if scene study class represented a "run."

"Which did you like playing more?" she asked. "The killer or the killed?"

"I never thought of it that way," I said, deflecting the weirdly sinister look in her eye. "I thought of it more as an absurdist meditation on miscommunication as anathematization, social disparity, and dehumanization in a materialistic world."

She smiled, nodding in a way that indicated I was merely a child.

"Right," Hot Money said. "Clearly what we have here is a student of the *work*."

"Craft," I said.

Hot Money smiled. "Right." He smiled wider. "Right!"

"In a high-leverage development deal like the one we're

discussing, we'll be your point office," Talent said. "Consider us your home base. Where you'll be safe."

"By the time we get to this phase of your development—"

"Which will take about three to four years," Hot Money added.

"Merely a college education," said MoPic-Lit.

"You'll have millions of followers," Digital Media punctuated.

"Millions of fans," Television confirmed.

"Can you handle that?" asked Talent.

I held his gaze, felt my life pass before my eyes.

"Not to mention the hundreds of thousands if not *millions* of dollars in sponsorship deals and influencer marketing royalties I'll be landing you," Digital Media continued. "Thank you and you're very welcome."

Hot Money was pacing the room. "Loop in Jan's office. We'll see if we can get him a Super Bowl spot in a Mercedes commercial, something *luxurious*. A nice money play before we go mega."

"Mega?" I repeated.

"Mega."

I was engorged, my cock throbbing through my skinny jeans; I did not care to hide it.

"At this point in your development you'll be ready to star in your first major film," MoPic-Lit added. "I'll be on the lookout for a historical adaptation piece."

"Think *Saving Private Ryan*," said Talent.

"Or *Gangs of New York*," said Hot Money.

"Something that will perfectly suit your look, artistry, and brand," MoPic-Lit confirmed in a way that made me feel like I *had* a look, artistry, and brand. "You'll be known as a *serious* actor. This is your Oscar moment."

"An international movie star," Hot Money said as he walked up behind me and massaged my shoulders, his Richard Mille watch worth more than my entire life.

"All by your early thirties," said Talent.

"The total package," from the hot breath above. "And then, after that, you can do anything you want. And I mean *anything*."

"Can anyone say 'Marvel'?" said Digital Media. "Who's your favorite superhero?"

"I'm not sure." I paused to consider. "Ace Ventura?"

"Only if you *want*, of course," said Talent. "You'll have your pick."

"A sweet and simple play to net you multigenerational wealth," Hot Money said. "And our agency a shit ton of money."

"And then you can *really* do whatever the fuck you want!" MoPic-Lit said in fiery tone, turning me on even more.

"Producing. Directing. Whatever," said Talent.

"I also write," I said, finding my notebook in my bag, absorbed in the role I was playing: an actor shopping agencies, weighing his options. "With my fame I'd love to try and make literature cool again," I had the audacity to say.

"That's nice," Hot Money said as he walked toward the front of the room, his hands draped behind his back.

"I've got lots of ideas," I said before incoherently rushing through the working idea for this novel you're reading.

"I hope it's clear," Hot Money said, ignoring me, "we're here to take care of you. So long as you perform." He smiled. "We're very good at caring for our performers."

But I was off in a dream. I couldn't narrate myself to respond. All I can remember is Talent saying, "Hey, why don't we loop in Mike from New York? We'll inform his office of the *plan*."

Then came the laughter. Some sort of glitch in the programming. A tightness of breath.

"We can get Mike on video," said Digital Media.

"That's right!" said Hot Money, banging the table. "We nearly forgot about Mike, didn't we?" Again that delicious smile, rich and beautiful. A death weapon.

From outside the crystal ballroom, its glass walls, eyeballs slotted and shot like pinballs. Assistants, floaters, mailroom clerks eager to conquer the world with their soft stupid fingers. Headsets on. Watching them look back at me from their desks, I could see I was totally fucked.

"Looping in Mike from New York."

X X X

The day began with a lie.

"I'm going to the gym," I said when she asked why I was up so early. "All-company volunteer day at some rundown park." I dropped my bag and kissed her forehead hot from sleep. "I want to get a workout in before the torture. Go back to bed."

"Okay. Love you," she said.

"Love you too."

New York. Outside, the rain spat from all directions. I stopped under the sloped doorway awning and watched a Dominican woman scurry by, laughing or lachrymose, leaning into it. I bundled myself and ran.

My plane would depart from JFK in three hours.

Turning left onto Fort Washington Avenue, I headed north past the vision center, Vazquez Optical, the sky so grey as to blur the divide between cloud and infinity. The timeworn pre-War buildings of Washington Heights arched like tombstones. The stink of garbage, hot with wet, rose from the streets. I traversed the grid cemetery and passed the entrance of J. Hood Wright Park when a stray dog ran out and startled me. My heart sank for the dog, I'd drink his tears that night. But the dog was fine; he couldn't even look at me. The gravel strewn with debris, I stepped over pens I imagined were needles, pebbles that crunched like broken glass—any evidence to fuel my demented drive to obliterate myself from the current draft of my life's story and start anew.

For two years I'd been living with my girlfriend, honestly the most beautiful creature I'd ever known. We'd been together for four years and made love on Saturday mornings, made love only then. Medical school had taken something vital from her. I felt betrayed, even if I understood. It was how hard she worked: I hated myself because of it. Our kitchen window saw out onto the George Washington Bridge that connected Manhattan to New Jersey, all lit up and jeweled at night. New York Presbyterian Hospital and its patients right around the corner.

That morning I could have told her what I was about to do, where I was really going. I could have spilled my guts and turned myself in before any of this ever happened. But there had been a fight. Not between her and me—I had divided myself in two.

I descended the subway stairwell at 175th Street, where the A Express hustled through the dark, screeching its wheels. It would take me to Forty-Second Street, Port Authority, I rehearsed, where I'd transfer to the E Train, ride it to Sutphin Boulevard, walk through the friendly breezeways guarded by soldiers with M-16s and into Jamaica Station to get the AirTrain to John F.

Kennedy International Airport. The entire trip should take no more than ninety minutes. The doors closed.

Two hours and forty-five minutes until takeoff.

It was early yet. Few passengers donned the chalk-blue benches of the subway car, their dumpy uptown shoes insulting the black rubber floor. I grabbed the pole's smudged silver. A homeless man sat dead in the corner, taking up the entire bench. He wore one shoe, his right foot so fat and swollen with sickness it seemed healthier to amputate. Here's a man who is truly fucked, I thought, whereas the rest of us are merely pretending. I didn't know what he made me feel but for a moment I began to doubt myself, doubt the credibility of my misery. I reached inside my pocket for an adderall and bit my tongue to produce enough saliva to swallow. At 125th Street a parade of commuters entered and blocked my view of the homeless man. Young girls pinched their noses. No one paid him any attention other than to communicate to another passenger a shared disdain for his imposition. The inconvenience. In New York we bond and feud over territory like anywhere else, only our interests are mapped in square inches.

"You ain't listening to me," the black woman with heroic hips said to the man in hoodie, presumably her partner, as they entered the train. He moved through the car clenching his eyes so tightly I thought he might disappear into himself. "You think being in public is going to save your ass? *Shit!*" Students in uniforms and construction workers bumped through, grabbing the railing, clogging the noise.

The train started. Outside on the platform the people of our mutant city disappeared like phantoms, faceless memories I'd let linger for later editing. A Dominican kid pushed up next to me and started rapping the lyrics of a song I'd never heard. His passion made me embarrassed. I plugged headphones into my ears, rolled my eyes, and looked down at my iPod to drown him out. But I didn't press play; I loved his voice so much I nearly had the nerve to offer backing vocals.

But there was a problem. The train slowed to a rumble and then ceased altogether. In the dead dark tunnel, the white static was deafening. The incandescent lights exposed everyone's shared frustration. Passengers looked at their watches, checked their phones, some studied the subway map to see how far they had to go. There was a moment of minor protest punctuated by long and extended breaths. Then nothing.

After five or so minutes, a voice crackled from overhead. "Ladies and…men," it puked, skipping every few words. "It would appear… jumped…on the track…death…tragic…New York…Police…for more information…behalf of the MTA…inconvenience."

In one morbid and syncopated downstroke, a communal revulsion sounded from within the train. Grunts and cursing and "this sorry motherfucker" and so forth.

Two hours and twenty minutes until takeoff.

Panic had taken hold of me. Hot metal tasted in my molars. I wanted to bite the throats of the Mexican girls screeching to my left. The fat stinking homeless man with the dead foot did not stir. Somehow this was calming. I told myself to relax, practiced deep breathing. Two minutes later I was the asshole audibly demanding an explanation. Did anyone know how we could contact the conductor? No one paid me any attention apart from the old Jewish man who sat against the railing, balding but for his scraggly hair. "This always happens," he said, not looking up. "Bet we'll be stuck here for an hour. What can you do?"

"Someone has to call the police," the jerkoff next to me said. But looking over, there was no one there; in the window's black reflection, the jerkoff was me.

I considered and reconsidered swallowing the five adderall pills in my possession and making a run for it through the ancient tunnels filled with how many rats. Finally the speaker mumbled something about "Eighty-First Street" and "track signaling" and "emergency platform," and after another ten minutes or so the train muscled forward.

Two hours until takeoff.

At Eighty-First Street I fled through the opening doors and up the steps outside the Museum of Natural History. To my delight the rain had intensified. My Chelsea boots were already soaking wet, my hair pissing in my eyes. Those were my hands flagging for one of the yellow taxis motoring south down Central Park West, my body positioned in the middle of oncoming traffic. None stopped. I started running downtown but realized this was absurd. What was I going to do, run to JFK? Outrun the rain? Across the street a cabby pulled against the curb. Out rose a well-dressed passenger and his Burberry child.

"Thank god," I said, sprinting over, stiff-arming the kid's cute little umbrella. The door slammed shut. "JFK please!"

"No good. Traffic no good at this time."

"Sir, you will make it good. You will make it good, sir."

"No, I go Manhattan only. Where you going?"

"JFK!" I told him I would tip him one hundred dollars I did not have.

"Cash or credit?"
"Credit."
"No, no. I go opposite way."
"I will report you!"
"Get out, sir. You block business."

Wet with fury, wetter than clothes can handle, I slammed the door hoping to break it. Leaves clotted against the curb. Another cab pulled up behind the one I was cursing. I waved my hands like a windmill. Sir! Sir! I pleaded with the Cameroonian driver to do his job. Save me from epic fail.

One hour and forty-five minutes until takeoff.

Cresting the Triborough Bridge, lurching the Grand Central Parkway into Queens, and painting the edges of the Van Wyck down Long Island, we somehow made it to JFK with enough time to board, but I'd have to be quick. I paid the untoward total with my mom's credit card I was only to use in emergencies. Inside Terminal 4, thank god no luggage to check, I ran like revolution toward the Virgin gate, wildly through the heavily crowded public space filled with oblivious itinerants, and ducked under the roped-off entrance. Fuck my life, the security line! One massive marvelous maze longer than the eye could stretch, moving with the grace and speed of a paraplegic. I stood at the back, huffing and puffing loudly enough to elicit some sort of sympathy from my fellow travelers, finding none, and felt annihilated.

Thirty minutes until takeoff.

With nothing to lose except all my dignity, which luckily had ditched me long ago, I flagged down the TSA attendant holding the empty clipboard. I was waving at her to look my way, but she was busy staring off into the infinite void of this sad and wasted life. Finally I just cut the line and tapped her shoulder. She looked at me without turning her body, only the fat of her neck, and asked what did I think I was doing? Excuse me ma'am, but I'm going to miss my flight! Get back in line, she said, fierce Latino flare. But that I could not do! I had a last-minute *audition* in LA I'd just been called in for—which was not entirely untrue—and the opportunity could be *life changing*—which was definitely true! Could you help a brother out? *Please?*

"No shit!" she said, checking my ticket. "Really? Are you an actor or something?"

Mortified, I replied I was. "And an author," I threw in for good measure, accidentally brushing her breast with my hand. I blushed.

"Damn! That's tight!" she said, magnificent smile, chubby cheeks painted pink. "Have I seen you in anything?"

The worst question.

"A few bit parts on sitcoms," I lied, mumbling something about TNT or TBS. I held her by the shoulder, intimating a comradery we'd never share, and said, "After today you might be seeing a lot of me." I smiled. "But I need your help. My plane is about to leave without me."

"I got you, Mister Celebrity. Hey Tonya!" she screamed at her colleague, loud enough for the entire airport to hear. "This guy's an actor! He's got a big audition in Hollywood." She winked at me. "Let him through!"

The travelers queued in the inscrutably long line cursed me under and over their breaths, through morning papers that crinkled in dispute, into their phones—just imagine what their texts read, what horrible truths they typed. Sunglasses on to avoid the absurdity of my privilege, I handed the superobese security attendant my license; she confirmed my actuality.

"Well, go on now."

Things were looking up as I approached the front of the final security checkpoint.

"Please remove your shoes, place them inside a bin," said the blue uniformed attendant standing behind the table. "Remove all laptops, electronics, iPods, and devices from your bags and place them in their own bins. Any liquids under three ounces in a bin, otherwise they gotta go. Don't ask, just do. Keep it moving. Thank you very much."

The line shuffled forward. Faint violin Muzak played overhead, a specific sort of public art that underscores how sterile and packaged your life has become. Like a good civilian, I took my laptop out of my backpack, placed it in a tray, and unzipped the secondary pocket to ensure I hadn't missed anything, any liquids or electronics, god forbid any drugs, I laughed to myself.

Which is when I saw the ziplock bags stuffed with drugs.

I did a double take.

Inside my backpack I found multitudes of edible marijuana snacks and candies, fat nuggets of purple- and red-striped weed, a few pills of molly—or maybe were they xanax?

I started vibrating like a mental patient, like a beeper all juiced up. With deep regret I realized I'd brought this backpack to the Governor's Ball music festival last weekend. My friends and I were too high to remember where we put the drugs; I figured we ate them all.

Nope. Here's where we put the drugs!

"Sir, please keep moving forward," the security guard said. "All items in the tray. Everything out of your pockets. Wallets, keys, coins, tissues, condoms—hey, not my business—cellphones, headphones, whatever you got, take it out. Place your pocket items in a separate tray."

I had my head so deep inside my backpack I looked like a dog blowing a Skippy jar. I let the hissing asshole behind me take a bin and stepped aside.

Twenty minutes until takeoff.

There was no choice to make: I had to get rid of the drugs. But if I abandoned the line I'd surely miss my flight. That was not an option.

I'll just throw them out, I decided, determining I'd have to be very careful not to draw anyone's attention on my way to the single wastebasket in the middle of a floor populated by security guards and hundreds of triggered and highly suspicious travelers, to say nothing of whatever state-of-the-art surveillance system was being monitored by a police force with canine support ready to swarm.

Only I decided this *after* I began stuffing my face with heroic amounts of edibles and drugs, so panicked I couldn't risk the chance of being charged with possession!

As I practically inhaled the four or five homemade brownies, two designer snack packs of cannabis-infused cookies, packet of sour weed gummies, three pills of whatever, and at least half an ounce of straight grass—aggressively swallowing many thousands of milligrams of THC, an ungodly figure, not to mention several grams of gluten, an unfortunate tradeoff—I assured myself that one day I'd laugh while telling this story to my fans, laughing because of the positive outcome of today's fortuitous, if not iconic, events: I was about to be signed! If this was the price to pay, so be it.

Chewing myself stupid, I realized I was about to get on a plane and fly twenty-five hundred miles across the country alongside many strangers where my only responsibility was to keep cool and not cause a riot. They would be tough miles. Very soon I'd be twisted in a way that only Hunter S. Thompson could appreciate. And then there was the meeting, of course.

Oh my god, the meeting! At WME! Which my entire life depended on.

There was no going back and no time to waste. I'd have to ride this one out.

"What's the opportunity here?" I imagined Dr. Armand, the therapist with the radio show and messy office whom my mother insisted I talk to, asking.

"Today I'll project myself into a scorching epochal hero's journey and position myself alongside the greats," I would say. "I'll write myself into the history books. One heroic act to burn the loser from my DNA."

Only instead of a wise old man, my supernatural aid came packaged and sealed as Skywalker Kush. Passing the threshold of guardians, I was in the belly of the whale now, hurling myself forward into the future.

Inside the full body scanner that surely causes cancer, farting contraband out my ass, I raised my hands above my head.

"Do you have anything in your pockets?" the young black security guard asked.

I made sure not to smile as I shook my head. The overwhelming taste of oil coated my mouth; there were enough drugs stuck between my teeth to put me in prison. The roving contraption spun around me. "Please step forward. Raise your arms," the security guard said. I have no chance, I thought as he patted me down.

"What do we have here?"

The adderall! In my terror, I forgot to remove the stray pills from my pocket.

"Oh, those," I said, horrified. "That's embarrassing. I get nervous when I fly. I have a prescription. The container is in my bag."

"Yeah, okay." He smiled, looked off to the side, and assented. "You're good to go."

I nearly fainted, but not before running like hell through the terminal and stopping at a kiosk to buy gallons of bottled water—Of course I'll need a fucking bag, you think I'm going to juggle these?—and boarded the plane with the grace of a bull elk, the last passenger to Los Angeles.

Seven minutes until takeoff.

We were somewhere above Pittsburgh when the drugs began to take hold.

I'd smoked plenty of weed in college and frequently enjoyed the evening spliff, but this was something else entirely. When smoking marijuana you get high from delta-9 tetrahydrocannabinol. But when you ingest THC, the drug has a much more potent psychoactive effect once it passes the liver, I later confirmed on Reddit. For even the experienced pothead (which I was not; I was addicted to many substances but weed was not one of them), one measly edible is all it can take to annihilate your ego and so too your relationships with time and space. That's why it's very important to dose responsibly.

My eyes grew heavy as I fingered the pages of the Cormac McCarthy novel I was reading, rereading, not taking anything in. The text blurred and bent as I mistook the cold blowing from the air conditioner tickling my ear for the tongue of the Korean American passenger seated to my right. "Take it easy!" I said, holding on for dear life.

"Ma'am?" I called for the attendant. "I'm going to need lots of alcohol to sleep through this." I handed her my mother's credit card and told her to keep my tab open. Only I attempted this ridiculous exchange while simultaneously unbuttoning my pants in the middle of the aisle, preparing to eject whatever mutant was clawing in my stomach. The nearby passengers laughed at the inebriated idiot dethroning his belt, pulling down his pants in public, while the sympathetic flight attendant escorted me to the bathroom.

Los Angeles, coming in hot.

X X X

Earlier that week I'd executed Phase II of a many-month project.

Homie! I want to set you up with this kid, I copied from my personal email in Firefox and pasted into the draft I was composing in Outlook. He'll be in LA end of week. You should meet. Have had my eye on him for years. Take my word for it?

I triple-checked that Mike, my boss, a television agent in WME's New York office, early forties, engaged in this sort of undergraduate banter when communicating with colleagues, cross-referencing various threads of correspondence in his sent box. Call it confidence, call it training—I'd been writing emails, memos, press releases, and coverage for agents across WME's Literary and Television departments for nearly two years—forgery was an assistant's primary job.

I clicked Send to Harrison Stone, one of the head agents in Beverly Hills' Motion Pictures department, and immediately deleted the message from Mike's sent box. I stood up, tidied some files on Mike's desk, and checked his inbox. The phone rang.

"Mike Ma—"

"Shut up, it's me."

"Mike," I said, terrified. "Yes. What's up? How are you?"

"Updates please."

"Right," I said, gathering myself. "Sloane called. She's upset we took our ten percent on the Amazon job. She said she'd only notified our office as a courtesy and for tax accounting. She doesn't think it's fair we earn out since she basically brokered the deal herself."

"Shit, she's right. Can you draft an email and apologize? Have Accounting cut a new check."

"Already drafted. Ready to send with your go ahead," I said. "I left word with Accounting to hold until further notice. Will circle back after our call."

"Good boy. Fire away."

"How's your wife holding up?"

I wanted to demonstrate a soft sympathy by acknowledging the gravity of his situation: his wife's father had just died after a long battle with cancer. Some assistants might consider this out of line, a quick-draw attempt to establish intimacy; most don't dare beyond an operant relationship with their bosses until they've proven themselves, and I'd only been working Mike's desk as a floater for the past three weeks after requesting out of the Literary department. Originally my plan was to leverage connections in the publishing world to get my undergraduate novel into the right hands. But I wasn't writing and working for established authors only made me hate myself.

Mike had a reputation for being a hard-ass. He fired his previous assistant on her first day for sending a new client to the wrong casting studio, even though it was the studio's secretary who had mistakenly given the incorrect address. Still, I wasn't fazed.

"You're good, you can talk to me," I said.

He'd gone silent, which I interpreted as him measuring me against his previous assistants. "Honestly, it's a shit show," he said, muffling his voice. "Her mom is a fucking wreck. She's holding up but it's twenty-four seven over here. So depressing."

"Well, I'm sorry to hear that. But don't worry, I've got home base covered."

"What else is going on? I haven't been in my inbox for two days and I'm starting to feel the walls closing in."

"All quiet on the western front."

"Get Kimmel's people on the line for me. I want to make sure we're all set for Bob's appearance."

"Mike, the funeral is in two hours. Be with your family. Maybe use this time to practice your meditation. That's why you took those TM classes last month, right? Take the week off and we'll block out Monday morning to do a full sweep."

"Call Kimmel."

"Happy to. Just wanted to let you know your clients understand you're out for the week. Your wife's father just died. It's *human*."

"Why are you still talking?"

"Hey, look, I was going to surprise you when you got back to the office but check this out. Brett and Linda sent huge bouquets of flowers. I think your wife will appreciate them. Sandy sent Knicks tickets. Front row, half court. Alessandra sent a case of very expensive looking Bordeaux."

"The best."

"Tim literally sent a barrel of scotch."

"A barrel?"

"A fucking barrel. Iron-cast oak. Took two guys to carry it upstairs." I heard him laugh. "They love you, Mike. We all do. Take this time to be a *dad* to your kids, like I wish my dad had been for me," I threw in for good measure. "Model being a real man, present for your family. Consider the opportunity here."

"Jesus, I should pay you for *therapy*. Fuck. Okay. You're holding down the fort?"

"Trust."

"Thank you."

"You got it."

I waited for him to hang up but could tell he was still on the line.

"What's up?"

"You like the Mets, right? Box seats on me. Call Charlie to set it up. Bring your friends, just don't be assholes." He laughed. "Let's talk about you taking over the desk full time once I'm back."

For a brief moment I felt an inkling of genuine connection.

"Mike, that's so generous. Wow. Thanks."

"Don't get all gay on me. I'm going to run. Call Bob and make sure he's got everything he needs for tonight."

I hung up, pretended to tidy something up, ate an adderall, and exited Mike's office. I closed the door behind me and smiled at Barry, Jon Rosen's assistant, probably seven years my senior, who sat at the desk next to mine. I then proceeded down the aisle and directly into the bathroom to vomit. Was I a sociopath? Was that part of the job too? Upon returning I started checking Mike's inbox incessantly like the addict I was becoming, forgot to call Bob as instructed, finally threw my hands up—metaphorically if not literally—grabbed my gym bag, and went to the New York Sports Club on Sixty-Second Street, where I worked out for two hours, which I was absolutely not allowed to do.

When I got back to 1325 Avenue of the Americas I had my reply. Or, I should say, Mike had his reply. It was from Harrison Stone. It read:

what can you tell me?

Nephew of a friend, I typed before copying and pasting the rest of my ready-made reply: Been doing Off-Broadway for a few years. JDL and I have been developing him. Now that he's graduated from college, I want to loop in all offices and do a full-court press. The kid is a star. He's got that aura. You know like when you described meeting Hemsworth for the first time? The one that got away? It's like that.

I had listened in on a conversation between Harrison and Mike two weeks earlier and thought this was a nice personal touch. I read over my response, felt good—if that's the word—about it, and clicked Send. Immediately I deleted the thread from Mike's inbox then from his sent box. A few minutes later a reply came through:

shit is he that tall?

No, probably 6 feet, I sent. Again I deleted the thread from Mike's inbox, from his sent box. A new reply popped up:

so 5' 7

No, he's legit, I typed. I flashed hot, saw all the other assistants outside the office being good law-abiding employees. I pasted and touched up the ready-made reply: Here's a shabby reel he put together: LINK. Very cute. But you get the idea. He's going to be in LA end of week. Got time?

I sent the message, deleted the thread from Mike's inbox, deleted the sent message. I clicked refresh, waited a minute, clicked refresh again. A new message appeared:

have your assistant call my desk to set it up

Immediately I ran outside. Then ran back into Mike's office. I deleted the thread from his inbox and sent box, went back to my desk, and dialed the powerful agent's assistant. I hung up. "What am I doing?" I said, loud enough for others to hear. I peppered an adderall into my hand and saw Barry eyeing me. Fuck him, I thought, swallowed the pill dry, and dialed Beverly Hills.

"Harrison Stone's office," the assistant answered. "This is Woolf."

"Woolf?" I was taken aback. Must be a lesbian, I thought, maybe an activist. "Like Virginia?"

"Yes. What do you want?"

"Hi there. Uhm. Mike Madson's office. Calling to set up a meeting for Harrison."

"With whom?"

"New talent from New York. Later this week."

"Please hold."

The room spun as the world reoriented itself around my daring. The hot chick from the mailroom, whose name I could never remember, came by pushing her cart.

"Hey, you!" she said. "Got some packages for Mike. How's he doing?"

I pointed to my headset and mouthed, "On the line."

"Got it!" she whispered quietly, cutely, and left some sealed packages and an enormous basket from Godiva on the counter above my head.

I told her to keep it.

"Really? Oh my god!"

I imagined chaining her in dog collar to bed post and feeding her chocolates by hand.

"Thanks for holding," Woolf came back on the line. "So, what's this about?"

"Harrison and Mike have been in touch over email," I couldn't believe I was saying, clutching my earpiece. "I don't know much. They're keeping it low key."

"Thank you," the mail girl said, her eyes huge and adoring. I waved her off.

"Got it," Woolf said. "If this is a talent meeting we should loop in Vin DiPiazza's office. He develops talent for Harrison."

"Great idea," I said, cursing myself for not thinking of this. Why hadn't I gone to Talent directly? Probably because they'd ask too many questions, I thought. But wouldn't it inevitably lead to that anyway? Won't someone, at some point, ask questions? I stood up, avoiding the mail girl's gaze, and sat back down, horrified at the mistake I'd made. I began to doubt the strength of my entire plan.

"Hello?"

"Yes! Can you connect us, please?"

"No problem. Please hold."

Holy hell, I had to calm down. The *point*, I reminded myself, is to get into the room with these people and show them who the fuck you are. I uncapped the adderall container, clapped another pill down the hatch. No one is going to ask questions once they meet you, they will be *impressed*. If Leo faked his way into that room, would they hold it against him?

"Yes, if he was an absolute nobody *and* working for the company he was attempting to con," I imagined my girlfriend saying. "Which is fraud. Not to mention illegal." Immediately I determined I'd never tell her about my plan, would never tell anyone. Not unless it works, and then one day I'll write about it, I thought, which felt like an empty gesture.

"Okay," the voice on the phone said. "We have Vin DiPiazza's office on the line."

"What's up, Woolf. What's up, New York. Brett here." But it could have been Brad. "What's the word?"

"Trying to set up a talent meeting for all relevant offices," I said. "Looks like Friday would be best, seeing as it's already Wednesday. New talent is going to be in town—"

"Hold on," Woolf said. "Incoming call."

There was an awkward silence. I could barely see straight let alone initiate small talk.

"So, New York, eh? I couldn't do it, man. I can't take the weather."

"It's…unfortunate," I said, hating him.

"Bro, do you know Taryn?"

"Taryn from TV or Taryn from Business Affairs?"

"I think TV. I met her at the holiday party last year at the Boom Boom Room. Epic night. What a smokeshow. You know that scene from *Shame*? At The Standard? We basically did that."

I thought to ask if he could hook me up with his drug dealer, seeing as I'd be flying out tomorrow or Friday—which meant my plan was coming together, an unfathomable concept on multiple levels, not the least of which was I had only two hundred dollars in my bank account.

"Okay, back," Woolf said. Just then an absolutely stunning actress walked by my desk led by Suzanne Leon's assistant. I made a mental note to hang around the elevators in about an hour. "So we're looking at Friday?"

"What can you tell me about the meeting?"

"Talent meeting. Harrison wants your office in on it," Woolf said before I could muster a passable lie.

"The *talent* has been in development for some time now," I added, noticing Barry listening in. I rolled my chair to the other side of the cubicle. "That's all I know. He'll be in LA end of week."

"Love me a good mystery," Brad or Brett said. "Let's loop in TV as well."

"I'm not sure if that's necessary," I said, doubting myself capable of handling so many agents at once, the complexity of my lie expanding.

"Why not?"

"Good point," I said, now growing excited by the idea of having the sole attention of many powerful agents.

"We'll have to confirm with their offices anyway," Brad or Brett said.

"Looping in Alex Bloom's office," Woolf said. "Hold on."

But I had another call.

"Hang a minute," I said.

I pressed Line 2.

"Mike Mason's office," I practically screamed.

"Where's Mike?" a woman asked.

"May I ask who's calling, please?"

"Who is this?"

"I'm Mike's assistant. What do you—How can I help?"

"Where is he?" she asked, clearly distressed. She kept demanding I tell her where he is.

"I'm sorry, are you a client?" I asked, matching her distress, hyperaware of every second I kept the LA office waiting. "I can take care of whatever you need, but first I'll need you to hold." I pressed Hold. Then pressed Line 1. There was no one there. "Fuck!" I yelled, audibly. The assistant with sharp bangs and vanilla perfume at the desk to the left of mine looked up. I knit my eyebrows and frowned in a way to suggest my suffering was significant; I'd dropped the original call.

Line 1 rang. I picked up.

"Mike Mandel's office."

"It's Woolf. What's going on over there?"

"Sorry! Had to put out a fire. It's been taken care of."

"Get it together. Harrison's going to have my ass if we don't wrap this up shortly. I've got Talent and TV on the line."

"Great, thanks. Just one second." I made sure to press Hold *then* pressed Line 2. "Hi, ma'am, sorry to keep you waiting." But she was gone. Rapidly the world crumbled around me. I imagined throngs of screeching bats, blistered wails from the dead. But it was only the phone.

Line 3 rang.

"Mike Madson's office," I answered pleasantly.

"Did a Cindy just call the office?"

"Mike!" I said, relieved I could competently pick up a phone, terrified of what would follow.

"Listen to me," he said, clearly cupping his hand over the speaker wherever he was, probably in the back of some church, or in the Oval Office giving the President the go-ahead to nuke me to hell. "Did a Cindy just call the office?" he asked very slowly.

"I don't know. She didn't say her name."

"Speak English, dipshit. Who is *she*?"

"Some woman just called and kept asking where you were and then dropped the line. I did not get a name."

"Fuck!" he shouted, then went silent. "Fuck fuck fuck!" he whispered. "What did you tell her? Think very fucking carefully before you respond."

"Nothing, Mike. I swear."

"Call her back. Tell her Mike doesn't work there."

"I…"

"Abort. Just don't do anything. Forget I called. Slut!"

"What?"

"Cancel next week's dinner rezie at Convivio."

But I'd canceled it already, I thought. He hung up. I ate another adderall and correctly switched over to Line 1.

"Hi guys, sorry to keep you holding."

"Oh, no worries," Brad or Brett said. "We were just debating the supremacy of Quentin Tarantino *over* PTA."

"Oh *lord*. Are you lost or what, honey?" the new guy said. I guessed black, his voice twangy, Southern or faux Southern, likely that of a homosexual—not that it mattered!

"PTA?" I asked.

"Oh my *GOD*," the fag said. "Are you serious right now? Is this dude serious? You're in the entertainment business and you don't know who PTA is?"

"No, I do," I said, laughing it off, not really knowing what I was saying. "I just hate movies."

The line went silent. Nervous, I thought I'd clicked off again. I checked: I hadn't.

"I'm just kidding," I said, a lie.

"I think it's a New York thing," Brad or Brett said.

"I *think* I nearly just shit myself," the fag said.

"Good," Woolf said. "That means we'll have to get this over with. *Fast.*"

"So rude," he said, pausing. "The correct answer is PTA in case New York needed an education, which clearly he does. It's like comparing Van Gogh to comic book art."

"You're so full of shit!" Brad or Brett said.

"Girl, it's not even a question!"

I wanted to vomit.

"Gentlemen, ladies!" Woolf said. "Let's set this meeting, *please*. Before you get me fired. We're blocking up the line."

Do you actually like this job? I wanted to ask, baffled, but didn't. Instead I pulled up the company directory and searched for Television agent Alex Bloom. "Monroe," I said, reading Bloom's assistant's name on the screen, "what's Alex's Friday like?"

"He's in the Valley," he said, his voice trailing. "No, no, wait, that's Thursday. Friday he's got a lunch at e. baldi."

"I love that place!" Woolf said.

"Mhm. Right by the window, bitch," Monroe said. "You know I got that hookup. You're welcome, Mr. Bloom."

"Fascinating. How about early morning?" I asked.

"Who *is* the talent?" Monroe asked. "Can we have a name?"

"It's a secret," Brad or Brett said.

"Let's just say he's the type of person PTA might cast one day," I said.

"Oh *damn*! I like the sound of that."

"Focus!" Woolf said. "Let's get this figured out."

"Guys, I need to put you on hold a sec," Brad or Brett said.

"While we wait let's lock this down," I said, rubbing myself under the desk, a nervous habit I'd had since the sixth grade when I accidentally discovered how to orgasm while studying for my social studies final exam. "We're shooting for Friday, right?"

"In theory," Monroe said.

"*Yes*," said Woolf.

"How's early morning?"

"No," Monroe said.

"Midmorning?"

"No."

"Lunch?"

"Bitch. e. baldi. Remember?"

"Harrison can't do two."

"Three o'clock?"

"That works."

"That works."

"That works!"

"Guys, I'm back," said Brad or Brett. "Thanks for holding."

"Please tell me," I said, exasperated and reeling, "that Vin is free at three on Friday," palm-gripping the head of my penis through my Levi's like a stress ball, closed-cell polyurethane foam rubber. "This Friday."

He paused.

"Yeah, sure, I'll make it work."

I exhaled.

"Oh hey!" Woolf said, but not to us. "Guys, Brooklyn just stopped by my desk. What's up, Brooklyn? We should get Jermaine from Digital Media in on this too. Harrison likes including Jermaine's office on new talent deals." The phone sounded far away as she explained what was going on to whomever this Brooklyn person was and then asked: "Does Friday afternoon work?"

A few seconds passed.

"No, I don't think so," I thought I heard Brooklyn say, my optimism plummeting.

"Fuck!" I said, far more aggressively than could be laughed off. Again the vanilla-scented assistant, whose name I never even tried to learn, looked up. My hand covered my face to communicate unutterable torment.

"Calm down, American Psycho," Monroe said.

"She said Friday won't work!"

"It's *they*," multiple assistants corrected me.

"What?"

"The correct pronoun is *they*," Monroe said, speaking the loudest.

"I don't understand."

"Brooklyn is non-binary. They go by *they*, not she."

"Is that really a choice?"

"What's your problem, bro?" Brad or Brett said.

"I, like, always forget there's even a New York office," Monroe said.

"It's cool, everyone," Brooklyn said, getting on the line, "I'm used to it. Hey, Mike's office, you misunderstood. Jermaine can make it on Friday at three o'clock. Count Digital Media in. And in the future, just try to ask a person their gender before making assumptions."

I swallowed my tongue.

"It's set," Woolf said. "Friday. Three p.m. Conference Room A."

"Hey, why don't we get MoPic-Lit in there as well?" I asked, drinking my own blood. "The talent is also an author."

But they'd already hung up.

X X X

When you wake up high, it's like waking up in a dream.

"Hi, honey," the flight attendant said, shaking me in my seat. I looked around. I was on a plane. The only passenger on a plane. "We're in Los Angeles," she said, sunlight glimmering against green iris. "Are you feeling any better?"

I wanted to ask what she meant but already I knew; I must have wandered into her memory or something. I remembered being worried about the inebriated passenger, handsome boy, whom I guided into the bathroom stall where, it was brought to my attention, he remained for many hours, unresponsive after multiple knocks.

"Is there a doctor on the plane?" I, as she, asked into the handheld microphone, maintaining a positive and friendly demeanor.

The doctor, a thin Jewish man with narrow eyes and thick brows, communicated with his gaze not to worry as I caught him check out my cleavage, disgusting thrill, as I lifted the small silver lavatory signage and slid the knob into the unlock position, an old airline trick for times like now. I smoothed over my red uniform and, bracing for the worst, opened the door and saw him—that is, I saw myself—half-asleep, half-sobbing on the toilet with his pants around his ankles.

"Oh dear," I, as she, said, judging myself for sounding like an old lady.

"Now that's a sight," the doctor laughed. "I'll take it from here."

Back in my appropriate body, I stood and wanted to thank the flight attendant for her benevolence, but speech was a submarine, something deep below the surface and untraceable. I literally could not speak, did not know how. In that moment I remembered myself as an infant, possessing only impulse and subconscious, language no more than a burp, as if a microphone were umbilically chorded to my guts, bowels, heart, conducting their inherent pulsates and whims, as opposed to a cerebral system of communication comprising words.

"Good luck at your audition," the flight attendant said, winking. My stomach gargled. I might've passed wind. I felt something like the shape of embarrassment but not embarrassment. I had no idea what she meant but her affection soothed me; I wanted to unwrap the purple silk scarf from her neck and inhale the fruit of her perfume. She handed me a backpack that reminded me of a prior conflict along with a plastic bag containing bottles of water. I uncapped one and drank and heaved and drank some more, water spilling down my shirt.

The immediate task at hand was to depart the plane. The sun susurrated through the windows like a church on high lit with mouthfuls of candles, each row a pew, and something holy did await me, some baptism of earlier regard. Only what, I did not know. Although I felt a sense of mission, I'd forgotten what it was. In my dream of myself I stood in the infinite map of possibility. The left foot goes in front of the right foot and then the left again. As I exited the plane onto the dubiously lengthy jet bridge that stretched for miles, I felt skeptical not only of my whereabouts but of having a *where* to be about. Not only did I not know where I was, I did not know there was a *where* to go, nor one from which I came. This was highly disconcerting, only I couldn't tell you why.

When I entered the big domal arena I was assured was Los Angeles International Airport, the light was spectacular. And the people! Dizzy enchanted beings that dimmed and flecked with proprietary intensity, volta energy. I put on my sunglasses, wanting to hide, but they were already on, and dropped the plastic bag of water bottles, but it was already gone.

I took in the ludicrous construction before me. The terminal's architecture seemed to be influenced by *The Jetsons*. Here we have the *super*-modern, the *super*-convenient, a world of progress made for television back when the "future" was a gimmick fantasy. Yes, the white circular lounge bar looked like an anticipative rendering of a high-tech future *if* it had been constructed in the 1960s, thereby rendering it an anachronism of the present. I smiled and nodded at the red-uniformed attendants huddled outside the gateway exit that was also an entrance, pretending they were not in fact intelligent apes with manicures, part of team *brand*. "Thank you for flying with Virgin, have a wonderful day," the words fell out of their mouths like hot foaming soap.

Do you know what I mean when I say that suddenly the world and all its inhabitants seemed like conspirators, like we were all in on one great big joke? It's as if I had walked onto the set of the absurdist comedy *This is Reality*; I wanted to ask someone, anyone, if they knew where I could find my script; I wanted to know how to play my part. Who's in charge here? What's wrong with the display? What I was seeing was like watching an old DVD on the latest HD TV, the artificial edge enhancement of the new technology playing up the sharpness of the old formatting to an uncomfortable gradation: the "film" of fiction breaks down and you are made painfully aware that you're watching actors perform on a set instead of being transported into a believable world created by their characters. Instantly it is unwatchable. Because when you peak behind the scenes, you see that there's nothing there. No deeper meaning, just a bunch of props.

"No, these are not extras," I had to coach myself as I walked through the airport lobby designed to appear like Sunset Boulevard, even though it was so blindingly clear that every man, woman, and child was playing a role. Here's the obese mid-western family from Kansas or Kentucky, one of those unusable innards, the appendix of America, waddling toward McDonald's; just as dogs often mirror their owners, these creatures looked like cheeseburgers. Or there, the stereotypical businessman, his expensive uniform suggesting a confidence undiscovered in the tub of gel smothered on his goliath head. Here's the emo teenager playing the role of "sloppy retard who doesn't give a fuck," sprawled on the ground in oversized sweatshirt, black beanie, drinking a *non-diet* Coke, just appalling. Or there, the tiny woman absolutely nailing the hypochondriac Asian tourist, N95 surgical mask covering her face and nose, cutting off all possibility of non-verbal communication, an alien robot. Look, I caught my reflection in the café's mirror, there's the fraudulent artist playing the role of "The Author," who can't narrate a coherent plot, all interior no exterior, unironically acting like an actor on his first trip to Hollywood to deepfake a group of agents into signing him and delivering his big break. You'll find these characters wherever you go, imitations of a type, the consequences of what must be a low-budget reality TV production with few resources. Around the corner I was sure I'd find the tired casting director's windowless office.

Failing to properly exchange credit card for pack of menthol Orbit, I couldn't help but ask the warm-eyed Middle Eastern woman behind the counter if this was real.

"Organic?" she asked. "Natural flavor."

"No," I couldn't quite articulate. "This," I said, pointing indiscriminately around my head like a helicopter.

"Sir, you must pay. Please slide card into machine. Slide. Not insert. Slide."

"Who is *you* and what is pay?" I tried to say. But maybe the ground split beneath my feet and I'd fallen through the cracks into an upside-down future where the past has no influence and tomorrow is always possible.

"Sir, please mind the other customers. What do you want?"

I stopped. In the absence of profundity, something about this question struck me as inordinately profound. The enormous tracks of time that had been my life until now seemed to vanish, and I remembered nothing as though I'd disappeared into the world's dream of the world.

I thought: If we do not know ourselves in the waking world, what chance do we have in a dream? No, what if I am what the dreamer dreamed of himself inside his dream? Would that not make me the narrator of the dream and not the author, whereby "author" is understood as both he who originated the dream in question and whose authorship determines responsibility for what was created?

To claim responsibility for anything in this particular moment seemed wildly inappropriate. If *I* tried to *do* anything—that is, if I attempted to assert conscious control over myself or my surroundings—I would enter an infinite void. I could barely walk, let alone architect a dream in a strange land with eidolon actors. Clearly I was a pawn in some more elaborate scheme, I determined; that my life was a simulation seemed far more plausible than that all of *this*, a neatly contained three-dimensional reality with predictable mechanics, just somehow…occurred!

I started to laugh, a bit too aggressively, and moonwalked away.

"Sir! You must pay for the gum, sir! The card must slide," I might've heard. "Sir!" But it was merely the wind.

I witnessed my character maneuver through the airport as if watching myself in a videogame. Into the densely populated crowd of strangers I went, unable to get beyond the experience of experiencing myself as a narrator of experience, not he who was having an experience. My body, yes. My hands. But who was in control, I hadn't a clue. Thus I found myself split in two: I wanted to believe I was the author of my life when really it was obvious I was just the narrator of someone else's dream.

"Well, you could say that the narrator had his own life independently and if he did not appear in the dream then the world of the dream could never exist," I said, trying to make sense of it all, having enlisted the help of some prepubescent girls with whom I was sharing the charging station. Some alien intelligence had informed me I'd soon need my phone. The vast paneled waterfall of windows looked out onto massive runways. Eagle-nosed airliners, black-tinted fisheyes, titanic ships. "Or you could say that inside the dream the narrator has no history, has no substance from which he came other than the author himself, the person dreaming the dream."

But the girls just giggled. "You're really hot," one of them said, no older than twelve, volcanic screeching in the air. I imagined Dante, the great poet, bedding his Beatrice, an infant child—and shuddered.

"Attention passengers on American Flight 232 to New York," the garbled loudspeaker announced. "The departure gate has changed. The flight will now be leaving from Gate 55."

"Yeah, you look like a movie star!" said the skinny blonde girl with so many bracelets, the courageous one. "Are you a movie star?"

"This is terrible dialogue," I imagined a publisher saying. "Very unbelievable."

But there was a poignancy. Something about the *possibility* of this exchange struck me, offering a deeper connection that I for my entire life had been trying to bring to storytelling, to writing's raw potential, a deeper purpose trying to reveal itself.

"Hi there, girls," I heard my narrator say in a way that was not at all creepy.

Through the backdrop of inertia, the sound of charring engines and hopeful takeoffs, say that it was standing there at LAX that I committed to writing the book you're reading now, a book of stories neither fact nor fiction but a proposition of possibility, whereby the author and the narrator are imaginations of themselves. I thought that not unlike the analyst or shaman dutybound to interpreting his subject's dream, the mission of the author is to write the fiction of his origins. That when writing a story, as when narrating a dream, the author is not creating its content so much as channeling, or surfing, what's already there. It's not the author's responsibility to make sense of its meaning, that's for the reader to decide.

"I'm an author," I heard my narrator say. "And I act professionally." Neither was true, but perhaps all is permitted, all is possible, in the world of dreams.

"Are you on TV?" asked the redhead, quiet until now.

"What have you written?" asked the glitzy one with sunglasses.

No and nothing yet, I could not admit. But for my entire life I've fantasized about introducing a fictional persona into the culture, massive turbulence from the sunny outside. Yes, it was in that moment that I determined I'd write the unnamed protagonist of my book, the narrator, in such a way as to confuse him with his historical author—that is, me. I'd name the narrator The Author, a cheap trick to hide the author's factual identity. It would appear as if The Author was the author of the novel you're now reading. But this would be false. The Author is a construct. A simulation. The dream of the dreamer inside of the dream. Somehow, it made sense.

"Once again, ladies and gentlemen, Jet Blue flight 217 to Miami is closing its doors in one minute," the friendly but stern airline attendant announced from somewhere. "Ticketed passengers must be on board at this time at Gate 51. Jet Blue flight 217 to Miami is at its final boarding call."

"So is he an actor or an author?" the blonde girl asked. She must have crawled into my brain, been reading my thoughts. Crayon-blue eyes, sweet dimples. "I'm confused."

Oh, sweet Beatrice, to you I dedicate this second chapter of my novel. Say that he's one to become the other, even if he's mistaken, I wish I could have said, I can only hope she's reading now.

"I'm sorry. This is *very* inappropriate," said the mother hen who'd been eyeing me from the Hudson News, coming to collect her flock.

"Very poor storytelling," again from the imagined publisher. "Pass."

"Girls, leave the nice young man alone," the mother or babysitter smiled, pheromonal scent in the air.

I want to blur the line between fiction and reality, I wanted to say to Beatrice. To get as close as possible to marrying the author and the narrator. A whisper's distance. But I don't know how. Not yet.

But she'd drifted away or was yanked out of view.

Say in that moment The Author wrote himself into existence… but then forgot.

Hovering through the airport, I determined it'd be best for my narrator to gather himself, assuming there was still a self to gather.

"Three of your biggest coffees," I heard him say to the Starbucks barista. "Iced!"

"Would you like room for milk or cream?"

"No, black," I, if I can call myself that, said, watching myself insert, no slide, my mother's credit card. I began inhaling the coffees like an undergraduate shotgun parade.

"Um, hello there," the colorful woman with many bracelets in yoga attire muttered from behind. "Some of us have places to be. Namaste."

"Sir, would you like a tray?" the barista asked, growing uncomfortable.

"No," I said, absolutely shivering.

"I just can't for the life of me understand what could be so complicated about ordering a coffee," the yoga woman said, loud enough for everyone waiting in line to hear.

"Sir, just place the card…" the barista said as the coffee spilled down my cheeks.

"LET'S FUCKING GO," I heard her say from behind, a machine gun of woke.

Which was when it hit me—assuming I can maintain some semblance of a linear narrative in a world of dreams where time is not real: a pain shot through my lower abdomen like a scorpion. Worse than that time at Noga soccer camp when my friends dared me to punt the beehive. "What the hell happened!" I remember Mom yelling as the doctor injected her son with tetanus boosters and antihistamines. "I punted the beehive," I said out of the left side of my swollen face.

This was like that, only worse. I had to piss something sinister, something molten. Urgently. I dropped everything, literally, the cold brew coffees splattering on the floor as I hurdled the yoga lady, her astonished face, and ran like Archimedes on amphetamines.

"Sir, you never paid!" I heard trailing behind me, something about "…insert the chip!" But it was only some stranger's echoed cough.

I'd no way of knowing what would ultimately subtract me back into the nothingness that had been my life until now, out of which my narrator had come, but pissing myself in front of thousands of travelers, not to mention my many *millions* of future readers, with no change of clothes would probably do it—and I did not want to find out.

Surrendering to the videogame's master controller, my narrator shucked and jived through bodies and strollers, over rolling bags and small children, around corners, across corridors, and finally into the entrance of the bathroom, absolutely sure he was going to unleash a hurricane of fury from his unfortunate cock, the buildup fissile.

Only it was the wrong bathroom.

"This is the women's room!" the yoga bitch from Starbucks yelled at him through the brightly lit mirror, the fluorescent lights. But that couldn't be possible, a glitch in the matrix. Squeezing his asshole to clog the piss from hosing his jeans, he darted into the men's room across the way, pee leaking through Italian briefs. At the wall of urinals, intense relief, joy, an infinite wealth washed over him, washed over me as I stood pissing, coming back to myself. The urine missiled against the white marble laminate. Hand on the wall before me, in the other hand a phone. I scrolled and saw text messages I'd sent myself. Directions. Reminders. A constellation of information projected before me. Simultaneously I watched in horror as showers of urea poured from my penis. Surely I'd been going for the better part of an hour, I reasoned, I was going to be late for my meeting.

Holy shit, my meeting! Suddenly I recognized myself.

But the piss! I had no power to make it stop.

In the world of dreams there is no time. What has no past can have no future. But in this world I had a very important meeting at WME in ninety minutes, according to my phone. And I was going to be late unless I stopped peeing.

Deep down I knew my fear was absurd. I've been peeing all my life, I thought to myself, at least, what, ten times per day? Twelve? In all my years I'd surely gone to the bathroom more than one hundred thousand times. Urinating usually takes about a minute to complete, at most. Given that I was halfway done—although how there was any *more* piss inside my body was anyone's guess—I'd be standing at the urinal for about thirty more seconds. *Right?*

But the guy at the urinal next to me did not respond. He just shuffled away, mid-stream, startled like a penguin. I attempted, albeit unsuccessfully, to break eye contact and only then did I realize I'd been peeing on my hand holding the phone.

"Where are my pants!" I shouted, truly terrified. But pants, along with Armani briefs, were where I'd left them, down by my ankles, collecting the ricochet of how much bodily filth.

Outside the bathroom I ordered three more coffees from the cart vendor and asked the police officer and his dog how to get to the Hertz dealership. With awesome contempt he told me not to pet the service animal, but I spoke wolf, I said, it's cool. The dog reminded me that I was hungry, so I walked over to the big sign that conveniently read *The Kitchen*, where there was no one in line. The attendant behind the counter asked what I'd like to eat.

"I'll just have a coffee," I heard myself say, crossing over worlds, having decided my face would be puffy enough from the flight, not to mention the gluten in the edibles; I'd just fast.

Which reminded me!

The edibles. New York. That was *today*, I remembered, now aware that I was tripping balls, was probably not awake inside a dream.

Which reminded me!

I was in possession of amphetamines. Enough to jetpack me back into semi-coherent consciousness in time for the meeting.

Anticipating the drugs, I began to salivate as I exchanged plastic for coffee, inserting, no swiping, to complete the transaction. But I must've gotten it wrong. Hence the yelling. But I was already back in the bathroom, inside the stall, pulverizing three pills of adderall on the toilet seat and faceplanting one hundred fifty milligrams of the designer drug so far up my nose I could literally smell my vagrant ego—not to be confused with the bronze gummy piss mapping the ledge—lost on the other side of the dream, the world from which I came I'd find myself lost in again.

Outside the bathroom, sober, sort of, I asked at least a dozen reluctant TSA employees and many more bewildered travelers how to get to the Hertz rental car dealership. "I'll sign autographs later," I said, but no one got the joke and nor did I. I was in no shape to drive, let alone be in public, but as I write this it's comforting to know that you are not identical with yourself.

How I made it to Hertz is anyone's guess. One of those cases of waking up to find yourself a passenger in life. This door led to that stranger who sent me over there where I waited in this line for that bus and so forth. But actually, I think I just hailed a cab and paid with my mom's credit card since, what the fuck, it's all just numbers on a screen.

You might wish to say that the narrator woke and the events that took place were not a dream at all. Forgive me if I quote Cormac McCarthy, whose book *Cities of the Plain* I must have portaled into while attempting to read on the plane, elements of its final chapter I've lifted for this section, but "What he saw was the strangeness of the world and how little was known and how poorly one could prepare for aught that was to come."

X X X

Hot Money, Mr. Harrison Stone, stood colossal beside the digital big-screen monitor.

"Looping in Mike from New York," one of the agents said.

"This will be—*educational*," said Mel Devine of the MoPic-Lit department.

"I should say—*informative*," said Talent agent Vin DiPiazza.

"Shit, I left e. baldi early just for this," said Television agent Alex Bloom.

The office door opened and the stylish auburn head popped in for a sequel.

"Harrison," Woolf said, "Rob Lowe is here. He says it's *urgent*."

"Tell Rob Lowe to go fuck himself!" Harrison said, tugging at the lapels of his Kiton silk cashmere houndstooth blazer.

Like some carnival circus the entire room shit itself and out came five powerful agents and one very lost author, *or* narrator, it's hard to say. Jermaine Tash of Digital Media was literally on the floor. Mel Devine fell into Alex Bloom's skinny vegan arms. Tears ran down my cheek. Some kind of laughter. Some kind.

"I'm just kidding, Woolf," Harrison said, bent over his desk, nearly hyperventilating. "Tell Rob I'll be a few minutes. We're about to set Hollywood on fire in here!"

"Go get Rob a fucking *smoothie*," Alex Bloom said.

"Oh, he loves that shit!" Vin DiPiazza said, panting with laughter. "Extra *gree-een!*"

What had been boiling to the surface popped like a spaghetti landmine. A Vesuvius of joker carnage. No, not the fire alarm, just my heart detonating into a massive black hole.

I'd been beaten at my own game. The agents had been fucking with me the entire time.

"The shifter, son!" Alex Bloom squealed, punching at his colleague. "Bro, you nearly had me in tears. I almost lost it then."

"You practically had me *puking* in my chair," Vin DiPiazza said.

"Puking!" screeched Mel Devine, who toppled over her chair in a violent crash.

"Oh shit!"

"Mel!"

The men rushed over to her.

"Quick, someone fuck me while I'm down!"

"The shifter, son!"

Amongst all the commotion, Woolf, her head still holding at the door, turned to me, sharing in a moment of solidarity, and then looked away in shame.

"May I have a Red Bull?" was all I could think to say.

The door closed and the digital mouth on the big screen,

Mike's, began spitting an outburst of threats and recriminations. All this talk about reputation, as if I had one to lose.

"You take no responsibility for your actions and their impact on people," Mike said, sitting on a porch, sunglasses on, Fort Lauderdale beach in background. "This is so fucked! I was actually considering hiring you! After repeatedly lying to me, after tricking me into believing in you, you try to use *my reputation* to support your demented dream? Are you fucking serious right now?" The screen rolled and glitched.

And then it rained. A dizzying downpour from all directions. But that afternoon you couldn't touch me. I'd woken up from a dream to find myself in the wrong life. My body, yes. These hands. But who were these people?

"You will be punished," Harrison said.

"I don't wish you well," Alex Bloom said.

"And after my wife's father just died? While my family is experiencing this *tragedy*?" Mike shouted, friendly seagull landing on the deck table. "Get out of here!"

"You should be ashamed," said Mel Devine.

"Mortified," said Jermaine Tash.

"There's only one thing worse than stealing clients from this agency," said Vin DiPiazza. "And that's trying to cheat your way in."

"That's not happening with me around," Mike said.

"That's never happening," Jermaine Tash said.

"Irredeemable," Mel Devine said.

"You will not get away with this," Alex Bloom said. "No, you are *not* getting away with this."

"Let me tell you something," Harrison said, spectacular anger. "I have killed more—"

"Harrison!" yelled Mel Devine.

"—more reputations than I've built. I will kill yours too."

"And let *me* tell you something," said Mike, the screen freezing. "I don't forget and won't forget. I hold grudges for a lifetime."

"I cherish the relationship we now have," Harrison said. "Which is no relationship at all. From Ari through my fucking mouth, you're fired."

"You are dead to me," said Mike.

"We should have you arrested," said Mel Devine.

"Instead we'll just blacklist you from Hollywood," said Vin DiPiazza.

"We'll tell this story for years to come," said Alex Bloom.

"You'll be a legend in this town," said Jermaine Tash.

"For all the wrong reasons," said Mike, practically crying, or was it the sun's glimmer reflection against the glass of iced tea?

All the more reason I become The Author, I thought, unironically.

"You'll go down in history," said I don't know who because I was off imagining myself writing this story.

"What do you have to *say* for yourself?"

All heads turned to look at me.

"Well?"

I'd like to say that when you wake up inside the dream, the joke of the world finally lands in its inevitable totality. The clarity is blinding. Humiliating. Because this sad sober life on the other side of the dream *is* the punchline—is what makes the joke so funny.

You could say that as he sat leaking vitals from a body frayed and mind disturbed, inside the rich metamorphic office of WME

Beverly Hills, the narrator did not find his way back to the author from which he came. You could say that in that moment, somewhat sobered, the narrator decided to become The Author I'd imagined. And wouldn't that be clever? Destiny delivered upside down. To wake from that world into this. But all he had forsaken, I would come upon again.

You could say that my narrator was completely fucked.

Then the glass broke. Just fell off the table. An accident. My doing. The water dribbled off the marble tabletop. The glass, the ice. They looked on, stunned. A noise buzzed and the secretary from the front desk walked into the room. Egg-blue sapphire dress and red smacking lips. Alongside was someone who announced herself as the head of HR. Behind her stood a security guard, black, enormously fat, sporting a proportionately enormous gold chain. Only in LA, I thought. Outside, a congregation of assistants and floaters and agents had gathered, looking on.

The HR woman told me I'd violated company policy by way of forgery and fraud. These offenses would be held against me, could be pursued in a court of law, and have no doubt I would be found guilty. I'd have no future in this industry. WME would not pursue charges, so long as I say nothing, do nothing, and share nothing about today's events. Just sign these documents. My firing was effective immediately. All my items in New York would be boxed up and could be picked up at a later date.

Pen in hand. Pen on table. Down the hallway, through the tunnel of desks and employees, assistants, clerks, clients. Staring, watching, talking amongst themselves. A buzz of voices. Keep looking, my friends, keep talking, that's what you do best.

Sunglasses on because I couldn't tell which side of the dream. Awake? Asleep? Awake inside the world's dream.

The following week when the story leaked to TMZ I didn't even worry because Harrison told me not to. But that's a lie. Really, pitifully, I locked myself inside an Airbnb in West Hollywood for three days straight and freebased cocaine from my burning corpse. Harrison told me to forget it, no one outside the industry will care, no one inside the industry will remember. It will all blow over soon, he promised, which, in a way, was upsetting.

But I'm getting ahead of myself.

Outside, the sun ablaze. After getting very fucking fired I stood in front of the security desk across the way from Equinox. A Bentley drove by followed by an Aston Martin. People walked by in blissful ignorance.

Walk with me, a handsome voice said. I turned. It was Harrison.

We kept walking and sat inside the nearby Starbucks.

Ballsiest move I've ever seen, he said, shaking his head.

What is this?

You hear stories from the past, legends of rockstars risking everything for their big breaks.

Is this allowed?

Tell me, was this your rockstar moment? Why did you do it?

I narrated the day's events, prior choices, all that had conspired to make today possible. He sat and considered. A woman passed by our table and smirked. I realized I was hungrier than I'd ever been. I stood to get what, I don't know, maybe some almonds.

Do you want anything?

What the fuck are you doing? Sit down. I don't have all day.
I sat.
Did you really think it would work?
I don't know.
You must have. But that would be so fucking dumb. Because it never would have worked.
Then why are we talking?
He grinned.

I'll never forget that moment with Harrison. Make me into anything you want, I said, a monster, a trophy, whatever it takes. Some people have a whole life to care about. Friends, family, adventure, love. For me there's only one thing.

He said I'd have to move to Los Angeles. If I wanted a future I'd have to be here. Where he could see me. Develop me. He'd work with me under the radar. It'd be some time until the news from today blew over but not a long time. It'd be easy to rewrite my past, my history.

I asked why he'd risk himself.

He smiled and told me he had nothing to lose. And, it would appear, neither did I. If you're willing to go this far, you've got something no one else in this town has.

What's that?

That's what I'm going to find out.

Those days. Amulet days. Days scribbled down for the history books and edited later for posterity: an airline discovery, a serendipitous seating arrangement, an overnight success plucked from the clouds. We get off on altering the pasts of our favorite heroes so as to make their ascendancies seem predestined, as if touched by god. I suppose each of us is constantly striving to reorganize chronology into some meaningful pattern, to narrate our lives in a way that makes the future dreamable.

So, what is it you choose?

I agreed to do it. Whatever he recommended.

Meet my assistant tomorrow, Harrison said. She's going to be at The Standard. The Music department is hosting a private event for upcoming artists. She'll call you tonight with the details.

I gave him my number.

Now what?

Now what?

What do I do now?

Well, you look the part. Can you even act?

CHAPTER III

the alternate enviable life of james franco

I was busy searching for cool when the casting director's assistant called my name.

The polished pretty boys, each waiting his turn, sat hunched on the old wooden bench. I stepped past the pretty boys, failing to register I was one of them, and followed the assistant down the hallway. Orange doors, whitewashed bricks, the sun blinking through sun-spotted windows.

The casting studio was an old elementary school that had been repurposed for propaganda: workshops, acting classes, casting calls, that sort of thing. Retro glass shelving units made of orange laminate and cheap wooden trim lined the hallway. But there were no arts, no crafts, no trophies. I imagined myself through twelve-year-old eyes in my awesome green-and-yellow uniform, back when time was infinite and the sad sarcasm hadn't yet registered.

"Put your headshot away. We won't be needing that."

Young babes, twenty-somethings, sat on steel folding chairs outside the casting room, a succession of skirts like you wouldn't believe. Legs you fantasized about in middle school when the thought of sex was impossible. Just dangling there, booted.

We walked inside the small sterile room, dusty white walls and linoleum tile, a closet of a classroom. Two middle-aged men and one woman in her late thirties sat huddled in the corner around a cheap coffee table. They held laptops on their knees and made estranged far-off faces. These were the producers.

"Sergio, here's number thirty-nine," the casting assistant announced.

The brooding guy in black sweatshirt, the guy seemingly in charge, stared deafly into the desktop monitor before him as faces scrolled by like cheap advertisements, headshots of aspiring actors who would never become famous. I saw him pause on my face, then click away.

"Sergio?" the casting assistant said.

"Boyfriend or delivery man?" he finally responded.

"Boyfriend."

"Goddamnit. This is the last boyfriend! We've seen enough. Understand?" He leaned back in his chair, cramped against the corner wall. "We need to start testing delivery men." He rubbed his face. "Go get a girlfriend," he said to the casting assistant.

A tripod stood assembled next to Sergio, the same kind Doug's dad brought to intramural soccer games in third grade but which my dad claimed he could not operate. Though I couldn't articulate why at the time, his excuse felt like setting fire to a great library and the histories therein contained. To Sergio's right, kneeling on the floor, the production assistant loaded a memory card into the camera. Ten feet, maybe less, separated us; I could smell the breakfast burrito on his breath. I hadn't eaten yet and thought maybe they'd serve breakfast, at least coffee, but was laughed off by the receptionist. "Breakfast," she said. "That's rich."

Fingering the adderall in my pant pocket, I mumbled hellos, vocalized a feigned gratitude for everyone in the room—for what

I had no idea, of which I had none. No one responded; no one even acknowledged my presence. I clapped the adderall and swallowed without water, god forbid any coffee.

The casting assistant reappeared. Behind her stood an ordinarily pretty blond girl. She wore a distressed skirt and white tank, modest breasts clasped inside a tan bra that showed through. I guessed twenty-two but there was a certain quality about her—like her dad had just dropped her off at daycare; I wanted to know that part of her. I nodded hello, my face distorted by amphetamines, and she looked away.

"Here's what's going to happen," Sergio said, his face glued to the screen. "After slating we're going to go for it. No script, no dialogue. Just listen and follow my directions. The client is looking for *natural*. You know, have fun with it."

"Can you provide some insight on the product?" I heard myself ask, rehearsing questions I learned at conservatory. "Client" indicated this was a commercial gig.

"What are you, an actor or a reporter?"

"I'm taking notes."

The girl laughed, sort of.

"Funny guy," he said. "Funny guy!" He stopped smiling. "Hand soap."

"Hand soap?"

"Let me paint the picture for you," he ignored me, affecting an exaggerated pleasantness. I raised my eyebrows to express mild irritation when really I felt nothing at all. "You've both just woken up," he continued. "It's morning here in beautiful Los Angeles, rise and shine. Girlfriend, you don't want boyfriend to go." I saw him swallow what he really wanted to say.

"Your action is to keep him here. A little tease, a little seduction, maybe a massage. Boyfriend, your action is to leave. But you love her so you're not in a dying hurry. Intimacy is good but keep it PG for god's sake. Nothing over the top. Nothing that makes anyone uncomfortable. We've got enough going on with all this MeToo BULLSHIT." He paused, took a sip from his water bottle. "We're all professionals here." He glanced away at nothing in particular then back to my co-star. "Girlfriend, eventually you're going to help boyfriend button up his shirt, hand him his pants, and he'll leave exiting stage right. Like I said, light and natural. The client wants it *light* and *natural*. We're looking for chemistry here. As far as timing goes, just pay attention and listen. I'll direct you through the whole thing but feel free to improvise. The client wants to see how you do on your feet." The PA adjusted focus on the camera. "Any questions?"

The camera was a mirror that dissected art from addict. Only when pointed at me could my distance from myself be described as artful, as opposed to a side effect of what some might call a minor "drug addiction," bogus term.

I looked down at my zipper, undone. Hand soap, I thought. That I'd already given up on myself was obvious.

I slated, the girl slated, and the scene would begin.

She walked to the far corner of the room, out of frame, while I unbuttoned my shirt and took off my pants and hung them on the radiator. Quickly, instinctively, I chewed one more adderall for good measure.

"We're rolling," Sergio said. "Okay, nice and easy. Boyfriend, come into frame."

"Hold on," I said, coughing. The chemical ooze had gone down the wrong hole. "Can I have some water?" I pointed at his bottle.

"Cut!" Sergio shouted. "Are you asking me for my water? Should I have my assistant order you lunch too? Maybe get you a haircut while we're at it? Jesus. Wow." The assistant looked confused. "Don't you DARE stop the tape," Sergio instructed. "Keep rolling."

"To get in character," I coughed. "My hair" was all I could utter. I pointed. "Wet," I said, trying to indicate I was *method* without sounding like an asshole, worried I was foaming at the mouth.

Sergio looked directly into my eyes, his five o'clock shadow two rotations deep. Here is a portrait of the beat-up artist well into his second decade of eating shit, I thought, seeing my life, my future, flash before my eyes. I hadn't taken a breath in a solid minute.

"Valid point," Sergio finally said. "Very *method*." He handed me the water bottle, seemingly impressed by my choice.

I cupped water onto my hair and into my mouth and heaved with redemption.

"That's enough," Sergio said, taking back the bottle. "No more interruptions. Action Jackson."

I turned to camera, winked at the producers watching through the feed, and stared out into a fictional Los Angeles made up before the actual Los Angeles contained in this gollum room.

"Take it in, boyfriend. You've just *showered*. You're feeling clean, feeling fresh. Life is good. You've got a solid job. You're a provider. Let's see it in your face. Good. You have a beautiful girl who thinks about you constantly. Good. She's right around the corner, in the bathroom, getting all pretty for Romeo. Nice. Take it in. In your face, let me see it in your face."

Sunlight poured through the classroom windows as I slicked back my hair, damp to the touch, deep pathos in my eyes. A muted orange, almost like the inside of an ancient creamsicle, flecked and chipped from the corner edges of the classroom walls painted over by a white dirtied by time. I sighed a bottomless relief.

I have a solid job, I imagined of myself, hyperaware that rent was due in a week. I've made it, I'm in the room. One audition means there are twenty more around the corner. I won't tend bar, won't serve food, won't become the cliché I fear; I'm providing for myself. I have a pretentious degree, I'm marketable; my plan B is better than most assholes' plan A. I can quit the second I decide this isn't worth it, my fingers pushing top buttons through fabric. For now I'm committed to this life. Whatever it takes.

"Why would you leave her?" Sergio said.

"What?"

"The SCENE. Not me. Play the SCENE."

In those days I'd hear strangers ask questions of me, make demands, and, embarrassed, I couldn't give them what they wanted, even though it felt like my life depended on it. I continued to attempt to button the cheap collared shirt, its holes starched over, a five-dollar purchase made at Target on my way to the audition.

"Tell me, is there anything more desirable than a beautiful girl thinking of you?" Sergio asked. "Why would you leave her, boyfriend?"

I looked at him and tried not to break character, if that's what I was trying to maintain.

"Eyeline camera."

Unsure what was expected of me and unclear how to ask, I said, "Baby, are you going to be in there a while? I'm about to take off. I've got a surprise for you."

"Nice!" Sergio said, cheap enthusiasm. "Girlfriend, come out slowly and approach him from behind. Touch his back. Boyfriend, lots of smiles, you can sense her."

I felt her approach and manufactured pleasure from her proximity.

"Off to work so early?" she asked.

"Good. Caress his back then take him from the side and tug on his shirt. Playfully. You don't want him to go."

"You want me to touch him?"

"In character! Stay in character!"

"Is that okay?" she asked me.

"Don't answer that," he snapped. "Christ almighty. Yes, it's *okay*. This is *acting*. Acting! Remember why we're here!" He stopped himself. "Girlfriend," he whispered, "touch his back and turn him profile. Now. Thank you. Boyfriend, speak."

"Big client meeting," I said, somewhat mournfully. "Wish me luck."

"With enthusiasm!"

"Wish me luck!"

"Girlfriend, say something."

"I'm sorry," she said. "I'm just." She breathed. "Oh god."

She started to respire with some sense of desperation, then began tapping her wrists, tapping as if applying medicine, some sort of calming technique. I looked to Sergio, who appeared bewildered. He whispered something to the PA, then announced,

"I want to state for the record I've done nothing wrong. No one has." He stood. "I know there's a lot of emotion here and I encourage you to use it. Find it in yourself to *use* it, goddamnit, or the audition is over. Final warning. Keep rolling!"

Without words I tried to communicate to the girl not to worry, I was safe and married to my craft, a consummate professional, whatever that meant. I pictured my final week at conservatory, the stage manager's face contorting in slow motion as she saw me snort a line the size of California before literally pushing me on stage to perform three hours of a one-act, two-character play.

The fan overhead clicked. From my periphery I saw the PA slowly try to tear open the plastic seal of packaged snack food. Sergio held his hands to his forehead and stared at the floor. The producers sat in silence. Pantless, I wondered how many douchebags pretending to be actors had already auditioned for this talentless role and felt my life drain away.

My girlfriend was retarded. I'm not making fun. Just stone-cold frozen. I pictured her as an infant, alive but incapable. "Forget the camera," I whispered, squeezing her hand. I wanted her to know that I was more pathetic than this could ever turn out to be.

"Won't you come back to bed for a minute?" she finally managed to mumble. It was awkward, not true to the moment, not at all, but it was something.

"Look," I said without thinking, searching for a way to play her ineptness to the scene's advantage, "I want to apologize," the adderall clearly kicking in.

"For what?"

"For last night."

"Last night?"

I froze. The main idea of improv is to accept suggestions and push forward. "Show through action, don't tell through contrived dialogue," I imagined my scene study instructor shouting. "Amateurs talk, professionals do!" Now I had to commit to my mistake and try to explain a "last night" that never actually happened wrapped inside of an imagined relationship that currently lacked any feeling or connection, thus further distancing me from the truth of the moment.

And what was the truth?

I hadn't heard a fucking thing from Harrison's office since nearly killing myself to move to Los Angeles at his insistence. That was months ago. Now, pathetically, I was reduced to looking for gigs on Backstage.com—college films, extras opportunities, second-rate infomercials—anything to convince myself that *this* was part of the "process" I'd intentionally designed to subvert.

"Shut the fuck up!" I shouted at the PA, snacknuts bulging in cheek. "We're trying to WORK here and all we can focus on is your mindless crunching!"

Silence punctured the room like right after a balloon pops, or that one Memorial Day party when Grandpa walked into the yard completely naked. I could feel my cheeks getting hot, the first sign of panic, a panic exacerbated by the color of my face, cherry-red splotches impossible to hide. Metal tasted in my mouth, the second wave of panic. I wanted to vomit. The burrito odor. The crunching almonds. The clicking fans. I just reamed the fat kid. I'm fucked, I thought, I can't even get through two lines without breaking down. I've upset my scene partner. The director sees right through me. Who are these mute strangers in dated suits? Harrison's dead, the dream too. I'll have to move back to New York and admit to Mom she was right, moving to LA *was* me running away. I began to cry. Real tears. Who am I kidding? I thought. I'll walk out the door and leave.

But the girl grabbed my hand. No pretense of acting, she was clearly alarmed. "No," she said. "Stop. What's wrong? Where are you going?" It worked, was working.

Sergio smacked the back of the PA's head and snatched the almonds from him.

I touched the girl's face, her dimpled cheek, and brushed away the blonde. "I'm sorry for what I said last night, sorry to have hurt you, it was wrong of me." Up close anyone looks like anyone and in that moment I was back in New York and decided to stay with my ex-girlfriend instead of walking out on a four-year relationship. "I love you so much," I said, imagining she was you. "You know that?"

The girl nodded.

"I want to make it up to you. Tonight."

"Tonight?" She smiled. "Do I really have to wait that long?"

"Good! Girlfriend, move closer. Touch his chest. If it feels right. Good. Try to remove his shirt. Boyfriend, resist."

Apropos of nothing—I'd never been on a real audition before, didn't know the rules—I took her from behind and started tickling her armpits, which had her laughing and laughing and cracking like a newborn. She slapped and pawed and began tickling me too.

"Here we go," I heard Sergio say, "this is theatre!"

"You're going to get me fired!" I said, laughing as we both looked down at my distending erection. She blinked with shock.

"Boyfriend, start buttoning up. And put on some fucking

pants! Jesus," Sergio said, ruffling his hair. "Girlfriend, don't let him go. It's like Tag! Tag, you're it!"

"I've got to go to work!" I said, snaking away, making sure my dried-out torso was in frame. But the girl intercepted my hand and kissed me like Cate O'Leary kissed me when, sitting in the boiler room of Brian Connor's basement, our friends egging us on from outside the door, she told me she'd had a crush on me since the sixth grade, that the bottle landing on her had been a dream come true. We kissed with our mouths wide open, my first French kiss, and I opened my eyes in an audition room however many years later without any friends.

"Yes!" Sergio shouted. "That's emotion! That's it!" I saw him grab the PA's shoulder, the former ecstatic, the latter terrified.

With confidence my girlfriend opened her mouth wider and slid some tongue and palmed my bare chest as I gripped her shoulder-elbow-waist, her body sinking into the moment. Why I was practically naked while she was dressed in daywear didn't make any sense, perhaps an unspoken rule of the casting world. I fondled the button of her skirt and reached down the front of her cotton panties, and she didn't seem to mind.

"Hey now!" Sergio said, leaping from his chair. From my periphery I saw the two male producers whisper something. "Boyfriend, cool off a little!" Sergio instructed. "Go get your pants. They're on the floor, there against the wall. Christ on a cupcake. Go on now!"

As I went to grab my pants, the female producer, the only other woman present, fidgeted in her seat sandwiched between her male counterparts. I felt like I understood what she wanted, though I was merely observing myself. Outside, a car alarm went off.

"What am I supposed to do while you're at work all day?" my girlfriend asked, straining to shut one of the old wooden-framed glass windows. I went over to assist and suddenly she had me pinned against the wall, her arms draped over the back of my neck. I dropped the pants and turned around to embrace her, growing somewhat nervous of her genuine enthusiasm, her latent sexiness, making sure not to fill any silences with my eyes because if I looked long enough I'd know all her secrets and that's when I'd get in trouble because, misinterpreting, she'd think me the hero when really I wasn't even in the story. We kissed like never before and never again would it happen, and for the first time it occurred to me: this must be acting.

"All right, enough of that!" Sergio shouted nervously. "Boyfriend, time to get out of here. Big meeting! Remember your action. And put on some fucking pants! Go on!"

"What are you supposed to do while I'm off at work?" I repeated, creating some distance. "That's a good question," my words cut off by interjections of her frenzied little kisses. I had to think about how to frame a response without seeming chauvinistic or idiotic—presumably I should *know* how my girlfriend spends her days. Instinctively I imagined handcuffing her to the radiator, cartoonishly dropping the key into my boxer briefs, smiling to camera, and walking out the door into Hollywood's cheerful protection. Nor can I open the opportunity for regression, I thought. Accept and push forward. Show, don't tell. Action over dialogue—

I stopped. What the fuck was happening? Confused, embarrassed, alarmed, I noticed myself *thinking* like an actor without the pretense of *appearing* to think like an actor for others to observe. This was highly unusual, very uncomfortable. "I've got a surprise for you," I heard myself say, shaking it off.

"Oh?"

"I'm taking you out on a date tonight," I said, finding my wallet in the back pocket of my pants. "Here." I handed her three hundred dollars, real money. "This is all I have on me." Was all I had, period. "I want you to buy yourself something nice. I want you to know how special you are." Then in a moment I'll never forget, a moment that would define my career, setting a precedent that would land me many jobs, my "signature move," so to speak, I broke the fourth wall, walked off our metaphorical stage, grabbed a pen clean off the PA's ear, and said, "Meet me at Spago," the only nice restaurant in town I knew by name, probably a reference from some old movie, writing it on the back of the girl's hand. "Seven p.m." I kissed her tiny fingers. "Now you won't forget."

Sergio looked astonished. The girl looked pregnant. More murmurs from the producers.

"Wow," the PA said, no mic to drop.

"Are you kidding?" the girl asked, not as my pretend girlfriend but as herself, whoever she was, perhaps my *real* girlfriend, she might have been thinking.

"Trust me."

From this period of my life, a pale blue abstraction, I can only remember moments of readymade literature, interpreting a life I'd never want to face but would instead prefer to read. A subtext of romance underscored by the despair of all time. I don't know how to describe it other than to say it's like reading a story and suddenly recognizing the protagonist is you. Only it's not fiction, it's the real thing. You read on.

As I fumbled pulling my right leg into the pants, I felt my girlfriend touch the small of my spine.

"Look at me," she said, then kissed me with the passion my poetry possessed back when I believed words could move people. "I *do* trust you. Do you trust me?"

Before I could respond, she slid my pants down to the floor, tugged them from my feet, and without batting a lash tossed them right out the second-story window.

"Oh my—" said the female producer.

"Oh no," Sergio said.

"—god."

While I knew this life wasn't real, I couldn't help but read on. I didn't so much think this as feel it in my groin, swelling to the size of a soccer trophy.

She grabbed my cock and kissed me like one of Leo's French girls and pushed me to the cold hard floor. I was on my back when Sergio yelled cut or yelled something propulsive or took the camera rogue by hand and angled it up her skirt as she crawled on top of me and we all got hired.

Later that evening we found a jacuzzi on the rooftop of a four-story apartment complex her father owned, the jets bubbling against our privates; we hadn't bothered with bathing suits. The purple heart sun melted in the distance, salt of the Pacific catching the breeze.

Rachel was religious by Hollywood standards, the type of girl who'd take half-nude photos of herself, post them on Instagram for her fifty thousand followers, and exclaim in the caption: #blessed! She described herself as "authentic." Her dad was a "major producer." And I loved her for it.

For two weeks she let me sleep in her bed. Not with her but beside her. If I got funny I'd have to leave. So I got funny with myself. She watched, mesmerized, and somehow that was better.

X X X

I was twenty-four or twenty-five, pretending to be an actor *and* a writer, as if the fraudulence of each claim would cancel out the incredibility of the other.

"I just moved from New York," I'd say, no matter how long after the fact, no matter who asked, completely ashamed to admit I was living in Hollywood, worse even, West Hollywood, the gayest place on earth. A hero's journey you'd never want to read, certainly not write.

Those days. Curled pages turned with no bookmark. Puckered lips, all smooches.

It was during this stage of my development that I routinely went to parties with Instagram models, a novel cultural phenomenon at the time. We'd refer to ourselves as friends but allow others to assume we were together, laugh when the maître d' greeted us as the "beautiful couple," that sort of thing. Though we rarely fucked, there was a tenderness, something shared but unspoken and best never mentioned.

On this particular night Rachel brought me to a hot air balloon party at a mansion in the Hollywood Hills. There, an older woman kept calling me James Franco, but she really meant

Orlando Bloom. "Hey, James Franco, are you going to shoot me with your bow and arrows?" She was a tall brunette with sharp bangs and chipmunk cheeks. "Although I prefer you as a pirate," she whispered in my ear. "Our little secret."

"Well, I did just sign with WME," I heard myself say, a complete lie, and immediately regretted it; at a place like this, I could be found out.

"I worked with Marty over there for years before the whole pedophilia thing. Tragic how that played out. His loss, right?"

We stood in the kitchen of the megalithic modern home, more spaceship than house, expansive and without boundaries, rooms distinguished by moods and modes of art instead of walls and doors. The kitchen was all window and looked out over the spectacular lullaby haze of Los Angeles, the perfect Instagram moment as the hot orange sun knotted the horizon, pink explosions in the sky. I felt rich just by participating in the view.

"Look, honey bunny, let me get you a drink," she said, literally snapping her fingers at the friendly Hispanic woman, yellow ribbon in hair, tending bar behind the marble counter as big as my apartment.

You've seen this woman in old sitcoms and soaps. You'd recognize her walking down the street, even in the colossal sunglasses she pretends to hide behind. She likes to eat at Michael's in Santa Monica on Friday nights, where she always has a table, no need to call ahead. I could tell you her name, and she'd like that, but she doesn't need the exposure. I'll call her Heather, but her name is not Heather.

Just then a very famous actor walked past me and nearly

spilled hummus on my Chelsea boots. He didn't even try to apologize. The arrogance.

"He's getting enormous, that one," Heather said, dabbing her forehead. "Major talent."

"Where are the hot air balloons?" Rachel asked, approaching from behind, phone out.

I hated her for asking such a stupid question, and in front of this influential D-list celebrity, no less. I smiled in a way to indicate, "Sorry, let me entertain this retard real quick," thanked Heather for whatever Martini rendition I was inhaling, and pulled Rachel into the bathroom to massacre three huge lines before I'd feel sick.

"Here, do you want some?"

"I've never done it before," she said, the same excuse she used for every vice I encouraged she attempt, before sneezing the coke everywhere, all over the azulene crustacean molded tile, real fossils from the Mesozoic Era, I was told, although I'm probably making it up.

"There are no such balloons but all the fat heads," I might have said as I licked the floor.

Rachel took my arm and led me to the bar in the giant parlor room. A few dudes were playing pool while the majority of the guests sat huddled on or around massive claret leather sofas and wide tufted Chesterfield chairs. One wall was lined entirely with leatherbound books, a decorative choice to admire, I suspected, as opposed to a library to be read. I wondered if anyone here had ever *actually* read a book, their heads tilted toward their designer phones with similarly strained faces, as if the burden of the virtual were a point of fashion, and I too began to scowl but not at my phone as I realized these people were my desired peers. Somewhere sage was burning.

Two Basquiats hung across from a Sylvester Stallone, a painting of psychedelic proportions. "Self-portrait," I said to no one in particular. "He paints?"

"This cost fifty grand," said the stylish, perhaps-Japanese chick to my left; she seemed to be admiring the Stallone.

"I suppose there aren't enough screens," I said, hoping for a laugh, not getting one. I attempted to study the painting alongside this woman while Rachel gathered our drinks. Feeling absolutely nothing, my typical response to "Art," I considered how many Stallones I could have bought with my fancy college tuition (about five) and which investment was more useless.

The likely-Japanese chick introduced herself, her name going right past me, and asked how did I know so and so? What did I do?

"I just signed with WME," I heard myself say, *again* horrified, *again* promising myself not to speak another word of it.

"Right on," she said, luckily not at all curious, which made me hate her. To my surprise she proceeded to strike up what sounded like an educated conversation about contemporary art, what subjects resonated with her, then about her art, where to find her online, and would I come to her exhibit in Silver Lake next Friday?

"You're a painter?"

"I'm a human being."

"Wow."

"I paint, yes. I work with mixed media, mostly canvas and collage, to create an intricate tableau of the miniature," she went on blabbing.

I nodded, pretending to listen, and mumbled something contrived about the demise of traditional tactile and analog art forms—painting and literature, primarily—their having been supplanted by the digital. "These days there's simply too much disposable art to choose from," I said. "What we once thought of as 'Art' no longer has the power to affect culture. Sadly, contemporary artists, *real artists*, are failing to maintain relevancy in the age of Everything on Demand."

"Why do you think that is?" she humored me.

"When new technologies can deliver onto a flat static medium a multimedia, multisensory experience wherever you are—in bed, at work, in transit—what would inspire you to reflect on a painting? To the same extent, why bother reading a story over the course of however many days when you can digitally binge it instead? The problem with streaming content is that it's so fucking good," I said, mimicking all the Hollywood talk I'd recently absorbed, an opinion I didn't share but nonetheless found myself endorsing.

"That's not true. Some of it is good, just like some new technologies are useful. But they can also be dangerous. Most happen to be meaningless, they contribute nothing."

"A picture is worth one thousand words, a book maybe one hundred thousand, but *Game of Thrones* will be worth one billion dollars," I said, a line I made a note to remember for later use. "Tell HBO that doesn't mean anything."

"But that's not art, it's entertainment," she said. "And that's my point."

"What's the difference?" I asked, somewhat incredulously. Why I had taken any sort of combative position was anyone's guess; I happened to agree with her.

She paused. "Art demands the audience actively participate in experiencing it. That's the only way it's meaningful. You know, tuning in versus tuning out," she said without irony before explaining how digital disposability does not concern the younger generations raised in a culture of social media, a virtual reality that's more about exhibition and exterior than artistic and cultural development. "This is a problem," she said before her friend approached, also hip, also Asian. She asked him for a glass of champagne.

"Who is that?" I asked as he walked away.

"My assistant," she said with a nonchalant arrogance I found endearing. This too I filed away for later use.

"I need one of those," I said, seeing Rachel return with our drinks. I smiled at the insinuation that Rachel was either a terrible assistant I could barely task with anything more complicated than fetching drinks or my ragdoll plaything I could do whatever I wanted with—no hint of chauvinism, just raw power—which the let's-call-her-Japanese chick completely ignored. I sipped the tequila Rachel handed me, thanked her, and did not introduce the two because I'd still failed to register my interlocutor's name. "Why is 'Art,'" I said in a way that indicated quotations, "more meaningful to the human experience than entertainment?" a question that when uttered aloud sounded so absurd, so pointless, as to peg me as a dilettante at best, a new-age woke intellectual at worst (indeed the *worst* kind of human, a West Coast phenomenon I'd only recently encountered that included but was not limited to vegans, life coaches, mystical "healers" (dubious title), and basically anyone who seriously consulted tarot cards for answers)—a projection made of me, I feared, the Japanese chick suggested with her eyebrows.

"Don't worry, I'm from New York," I said to cover my ass.

"I'm paraphrasing Lee Siegel here," she said, again ignoring me, "but for art to take you by surprise you have to put yourself in the power of another person, the artist. And yet everything in our society, so saturated with economic imperatives, tells us not to surrender our interests even for a moment, tells us that the only forms of cultural expression we can trust are those that give us instant gratification, useful information, or a positively reflected image of ourselves. And so we're flooded with entertainment, not art, which feeds our growing inability to accept any viewpoints that differ from a self-determined 'morally superior' status quo." She paused to make sure I was following, then continued: "Real art makes you feel unsafe, it takes you out of yourself. If you're unable or unwilling to put yourself in someone else's shoes, to view life differently from how you experience it, well, that's the first step toward fascism, and that sentiment, I'd argue, generally defines our culture of polarized mobs, a culture that's migrating online, shielded by anonymous monikers."

I was floored. Stunned. Clearly in the presence of an intellectual superior. Immediately I grew envious of her dexterity with and command over the finer points I had tried to communicate at the start of our conversation and, as I thought about it, in my art.

(My writing, that is, obviously not my acting.)

Rachel looked at me to carry "our side" of the conversation. Pathetically I had nothing to contribute.

"To be less political," the Japanese chick said with kindness, pandering to my mute stupidity, "what I mean is that you find yourself in the art you're experiencing. You connect with and for a brief moment can almost become the artist. An *Other*." (A word only ever used in writing, I thought, in italics no less, my self-consciousness now shrieking with contempt: this was too much.) "You live in the artist's inner world, see things a new way. In turn, you might better understand yourself and, more importantly, others. You know, develop some empathy." She smiled. "Which we all need."

"You're saying that appreciating good art can make you more empathetic?"

"In a way, yes."

"Interesting." I raised my glass along with my eyebrows and downed the tequila, considering all the authors I'd "befriended" over the years—Hemingway, Fitzgerald, Dostoevsky, Nabokov, Bukowski, Johnson, Salter, McCarthy, et cetera—an embarrassing idea I'd never share with anyone. But the author is not your friend, I thought; none set out with the aim to *please* me. Which, if I thought about it, was what made me trust the author and appreciate his work even more.

"I'm not sure if it's empathy so much as a lack thereof that draws me to my favorite artists," I said, watching as she received the flute from her assistant and tasted the bubbles, and now alive with a new sense of inner-resolve I felt capable of contributing: "Look, we're on the same team. In many ways painters and authors are facing the same existential threat." Her eyes widened. "Fuck this 'Like' culture. We can't delude ourselves into competing with entertainment. We have to offer something else."

"Oh, are you an author?" she asked, cocking her head. "What have you written?"

I felt annihilated. I finished the tequila and ordered another with soda for the road but not before "Misha" told me to follow her on Instagram, which cynically I found ironic but really I just hated myself. She shared her handle, thus revealing her name, and digitally followed me back, exclaiming she was impressed by my number of followers, many warm bodies populating the house.

"Who was that?" Rachel asked, walking me outside onto a gigantic patio that might be better described as a landed yacht, the levels to it.

"Sylvester Stallone's assistant. Here," I said, inhaling the tequila, "what do you want to drink?"

It was hard to ignore the totality of Los Angeles before us, the party's most prominent guest. The fallen lip of sun cast its bronze shadow over the city: its muscular freeways, the relic fantasy of the Hollywood sign, Downtown's lofty buildings—no greater than dim statues trailing off into the distance. Fading.

We walked down the marbled steps and stopped at yet another bar to the right of the immense infinity pool illuminated from within, its bronze floor, the glowing feet. Black marble lined the rectangular trim to give the pool an embossed three-dimensional heft. Huge bronze sculptures of lions and tigers and leopards edged the perimeter. Lo-fi house music tranced in 4/4 time over the dimming autumn sky, the entire backyard lit up by hundreds of bulbs streaming from porch to patio, from deck to yard, like fireflies. Crowds of people dressed in casual yet elegant, bohemian yet manicured attire populated the premises. An equal distribution of decades was present: twenties, thirties, and forties; probably two hundred guests or more. What we were doing here was anyone's guess. Who financed the event and why were even greater mysteries. I saw Heather beyond the pool holding a drink and talking to whomever about rich people things. She waved at me with an impish grin that reminded me of a similar gesture made by my high school English teacher who, years earlier, right outside her classroom while my genius friends filed in for first period, pulled me aside in the hallway to inform me that last night she'd fingered herself to the *aspiration* of me fucking her in the ass. Then she'd commanded ninety minutes of Victorian Lit as if nothing had happened.

Aspiration. I'll never forget that word.

The night entered its encore with a power chord of cool. The music grew louder and softer, bigger and smaller, like a sine wave, a purposeful choice I intuited as a form of sign language: Do we want a dance party? the DJ was asking. Because we could *have* a motherfucking dance party.

The hot water splashed and bubbled as I sank below it.

"Here, do you want this?" the dude asks, hot steam rising. He's an actor from a popular sitcom I've never watched whose name I can't remember, crouching over the hot tub.

The woman with whom I'm speaking licks a pill clean off his finger. She's an HR assistant at CAA, I remind myself to remember.

"Whatcha got there?" I ask, slapping at the hot bubbles.

"2CB."

"Isn't that a department store for spoiled college kids?"

He laughs or seems confused. "It's like acid but faster. Doesn't last so long. Want some?"

"No, I'm good," I say after swallowing the pink pill.

X X X

I started to melt as Heather led me through the house to find my shirt.

We went through the kitchen, past the purple rope bearing a small laminated card that read "Do Not Enter," and walked up the wide marbled staircase, its thinly twisting bronze railing, the chandelier overhead, thousands of fractals gleaming sacred codes. The top landing smelled of coconut and vanilla, candles and incense. Heather dethroned another rope that led into a bedroom.

"Do you live here?" I asked, sipping fizzy water from a glass, having no sense of whose arm, what glass, experiencing myself bathing in the liquid entering my body.

"It's complicated," she said. I hadn't the faintest idea what she meant and didn't encourage her to elaborate. "It's my husband's—" she caught herself. "I used to live here. But he doesn't anymore. Nor do I. Too many bad memories."

I watched her chest puff and dissolve as she breathed, her tan leathered skin rippling like muddy waves, saw the gaudy diamond necklace and its gold sheath held between her bosom as intensely beautiful, intensely attractive.

"Don't be sad!" I said, inflecting my pitch as if communicating with a puppy, and reached to touch the dazzling necklace, its hard smooth surface, feeling cohorts of sympathy for this poor woman, white Aston Martin in the driveway, and the anachronism she had become.

Then in the third person, on a separate screen, I watched her kiss me as if watching a movie, experiencing her proximity advancing in centimeters, in slow motion, until time paused, and as if with a remote I discovered I could press rewind—and then pressed delete.

"It's not a good idea," I said, returning to myself, amused that my consciousness was becoming something other than me, other than mine, cool water to my lips. "I'm not sober." A truth so obvious it struck me as hilarious, perhaps the funniest thing I'd ever said, so funny I literally fell to my knees.

Heather gave me a look that made me feel like a child and said, "Okay, honey bunny." Setting her flute of what I suspected was champagne on the armoire, with protean grace, unbelievably, she produced from the top drawer a white leather bag filled with solid bricks of cash, hundreds stacked upon hundreds. I couldn't believe what I was seeing, my consciousness dividing into hundreds within hundreds of cells, each with its own perspective, wax dripping from a burning candle.

"Did you rob a bank?"—a question asked seriously.

"I have a jewelry line. Some clients pay in cash," she smiled, suggesting she could do whatever she wanted in this life. "What should we do with all this money?"

Suddenly I felt very famous, suffused with a confidence not at all proportionate to my position at this party nor in this life, the universe no longer laughing at me but with me. Hold on a second, I thought to myself, trying to regain composure as my mind surfed between the many parallels of reality I'd found myself occupying. I'd never experimented with psychedelics before—not unless you count the three mushroom caps I took with Scott on that preternaturally bright and sunshiny day in the botanical garden on the eve of graduation, which was more like an encouraging portal back to childlike joy than a total departure from this plane of existence—and wasn't sure if the current drug I'd taken was safe to mix with coke and alcohol and whatever else. "But who cares," I heard my inner voice laughing, "you only have to die once." The room wasn't so much spinning as I was levitating around it; or better yet, I was occupying many positions inside the room simultaneously. But it was too much. I did not want to leave my body, did not want to multiply or disintegrate, and willed myself to stay grounded, a hilarious concept because as soon as I locked onto any singular concept, the thought would yo-yo away, each idea more like an object in the room than something that belonged to me, before it would metastasize into another idea, another object that wasn't mine, from which more would multiply.

"Is this okay?" I asked, unclear if I was speaking English.

"Look at me," Heather said, taking me by the shoulder, bringing me back to the present moment, as if there were only one. I heard the party voices coming from downstairs, the terrible electronic music from outside the window. I obeyed her instruction, focused on my breathing, looked at her intently. The color of her skin began to shadow and darken, her brown eyes appeared more like human hearts, bulbous and puffy and irregular in shape, beating forth from a cosmetic head, misshapen clay with fractures deep and scarring evident, lipstick caking like the Joker's; there'd been a shattering and the pieces hadn't been fitted back together properly.

"Yikes," I hoped I did not say out loud, avoiding her gaze, hugging away my blunder. Hugging hard. Consider the chances, I thought with revelation:

You're partying with celebrities, dating models, being chased by cougars trying every trick in the book to seduce you—and it's working. She may be on the wrong side of ugly, but she's also kind of famous. You're good, man. Trust in the process, just surrender.

Only I realized I was not talking to myself, I was speaking out loud, very aggressively. In fact I was practically pacing across the white carpeted floor, hands to my ears like the subject of *The Scream*, real "Art" in my opinion, completely losing my shit.

As soon as I confirmed I'd misplaced all faculty of coherence, had no proprioception whatsoever, in a separate window, almost like a digital popup ad, I saw a closeup of Heather's reaction, undeniably offended, and watched as I slid into frame, tackled her onto the bed in slow motion, and kissed her deeply with a passion I did not possess.

"Yes," she said. "Tell me what you really want."

"Perhaps you can imagine along with me," I said, leaving the thought unfinished. That's because simultaneously I was back outside at the party, champagne bottles in both hands, approaching Rachel and her friends gathered around the firepit, towels and blankets over their lovely shoulders, the pickings of gourmet food and snacks and drinks scattered about.

"Did you go dancing without me?" Rachel asked, standing up to kiss me.

"No." You were just so poorly written I considered deleting you, I nearly said.

"Never mind. Come say hi to Skyler!"

"Who's Skyler?"

"She's my cousin. I told you that, remember? This is her party!"

"Hi, Skyler," I said, interrupting a story. Central to the group's attention was the famous actor I saw earlier, the hummus prick, easily the most famous person here tonight. Good news, he'll be starring in Showtime's new soon-to-be-hit series, he'd just met with the producers yesterday. I said hello, pretending I had no idea who he was, pretending not to catch his name.

Imagine you're watching a movie. You're at the theater, popcorn in hand, and mid-climax, just as the story comes together, the protagonist walks off the screen and into the theater with you. Into the same world as the audience.

I knew I was still shaking the actor's hand because I was incensed, learning that this moron was getting what neither of us deserved, but I was also ducking into the back of a black Escalade at Heather's insistence, reaching for the hand of a beautiful older woman.

"Say hi to Shyla," Heather said, introducing her friend, who was already sitting inside.

"Hi Shyla," I said, kissing her hand.

The actor comes up to you, takes a seat in the chair next to yours, and starts a conversation. Soon you realize he's speaking to you not as the biographical actor you know by name but as the character he'd been playing in the film. The big screen is no longer projecting the movie you'd been watching but the encounter you're now having. The actor has been transplanted. As have you. Imagine how you'd respond when the next day you come across the actor, in character, online. He's engaging in the real world (so far as we agree the virtual is supplanting the physical): he's going to parties and tweeting about them, posting anecdotes about his life on social media, taking selfies with women and friends at bars. Images and clips are tagged and shared and take on a viral life of their own. The plot expands, his character dilates. His story, once contained on the big screen, now continues in the collective virtual reality, no longer fiction, no longer on a single screen.

Noticing Rachel's fascination with the Showtime actor, I pulled her against me with a force disproportionate to the meager impression of possessiveness I felt and grabbed her ass like the *Rape of the Sabines*, more real "Art" in my opinion, which she encouraged emphatically, palming my crotch and sending chills down my spine, which had her girlfriends gawking in affirmation, which, given her rules around sex plus all the #MeToo rhetoric she frequently quoted on Instagram, made me question what women really want.

Imagine a world in which the divide between fiction and reality has blurred, broken, snapped. That's what I want to do with literature. Just like the actor stepping through the screen like a portal, I want the narrator of my novel, whom I'll call The Author, to walk off the page.

Shyla was Heather's longtime friend. "A model," Heather blurted out, who "still has to turn down jobs left and right." She was Thai, in her early forties, though you'd never know it, and so striking it made me uncomfortable to look at her. Right then Shyla was playfully harassing the driver, a black gentleman dressed like an old-time jazz musician—classic Ray Bans on at night, black tux, black tie—who had decked out the vehicle's interior with black lights that appeared purple and blue. She was saying wild shit like, "We all have three holes. Do you play golf?"

Honestly, I think the driver was loving every minute of it. Big smiles and belly laughs. The illumined black light made his face look like a skeleton, but maybe that was the acid talking. He played it cool and even contributed:

"What do you call a black guy who golfs?"

...

"A golfer, you fucking racists!"

Amidst the laughter, my voice becoming one with the wind that boomeranged out from and in through the half-lowered window, Shyla said, "Hey, I got an even better one!" and we focused our attention on her.

"Family Matters was a good show, except for one thing."

...

"All the niggers!"

How come the most fucked up things happen when you're high on drugs? The car stopped abruptly.

If you can, try to imagine reading a novel. I know it's difficult in a world refracted by so many screens. When written in the first person, how can you tell where the author of the novel ends and his narrator begins? Who is the author? Who is the narrator? That's how I'd describe The Author: where the two meet.

"Are you an author?" Misha asked.

I want to collapse the relationship between an author and the fictional persona he creates. I want to walk off the page and into the room with you, dear reader, because you are also my scene partner.

"Okay, nice and easy. Boyfriend, come into frame."

While I'm growing more and more panicked by Rachel sharing the story of our audition and how we met, my awesome pen move, confirming me a nobody amongst a company of famous somebodies, red blotches on my face, I'm also being delivered onto the circular gravel driveway of a different mansion in a different neighborhood, all brick and lit up, exposing its vast rows of many white-framed windows.

"We're in the Palisades," Heather informs me as she hands the driver more money to supplement what she'd already offered earlier on the side of the highway, at least another thousand dollars in crisp hundreds to "keep quiet" about her "very drunk and formerly abused friend" who's seeking "aggressive psychoactive treatment." Shuffling out of the Escalade I told the driver I happened to love *Family Matters* and fist-bumped him in a way that suggested I wasn't "with" these women, we shared nothing in common, they just pay me to hang out and defile them.

As she let herself in through the front door, Heather answered without my asking, "The founder of Myspace is throwing a party. He's a good friend."

Imagine you're reading your new favorite novel. (I know, I know—but imagine.) You're tucked in bed. The lamplight is on. You fall in love with the narrator the author has written. The next morning you open up Twitter, open up Instagram, whatever the "current thing" is, and suddenly you see the fictional narrator you've been reading is active on social media. The character comes alive in the digital, is transplanted from the page to the screen to many screens. His story, more personality than plot, spreads throughout the internet at the rate at which you engage with it, becomes a multimedia experience, perhaps even an original streaming series. Not just a virtual reality but an alternate reality. No longer contained inside the author's imagination but yours too. Projected into culture, the audience projects it.

"Myspace?" I said. Time felt like a Warhol, a pop-art rendering of the real thing.

That's my big reveal. The Author is a virtual character as much as you are, as I am.

"Stop talking," Heather says to me back in her bedroom, gripping the duvet with superfluous intensity, its galactic flowers, spindles of hot light. The door creaks open, a stranger walks in and then walks out. Do I like it with the lights on?

"Never talk about my work until the work speaks for itself," I say to Rachel, pulling her aside, informing her I was leaving the party. "In fact, it's over!"—even though we weren't Facebook official.

Now I want you to imagine a world where literature can change people, can influence culture. I know it sounds crazy but it's possible. It once did, it can again. If I dare. My dream is to revolutionize the novel, now obsolete, hitherto contained within a physical book, by seeding its distribution through the communication tools of our virtual world and mapping its absorption as a multimedia experience. Perhaps I'm a sellout, but you have to meet the people where they're at.

Nothing is more unfashionable than an outmoded internet application, and yet here I was absorbed in immaculate wealth. A blend of antique and modern décor. Was the living room a museum, a country club, or an art gallery? If I were in New York I'd have assumed we'd entered a warehouse loft, the ceiling seemed too high for a three-story house, but all semblance of old-world gentility had been underwritten by a modern beachy sparkle that felt, how do I say—staged. The walls were made of distressed ebony wood, the huge windows adorned by milky-pewter curtains. Reproducible images of beaches and rivers and lakes (imitation art, in my opinion) embossed in bronze frames hung from walls made to seem timeworn; pottery holding desert plants, orchids, and cacti dressed the wooden shelving and oriental tables, also distressed. The room was spotless. It was clear that no one lived here; the house merely had the appearance of a lived-in home.

If real life has become the greatest show on earth, then "Art," real art, must flip the expectations. Since members of the audience now want to be the stars, the artist has to include them, make them characters. They must feel as if they are participating in the story. The novel must absorb them. I know I'm asking a lot of authors, to say nothing of readers, but we can't keep burying our words underground.

Walking along the whitewashed Spanish tiles, I waved at no one in particular, waved at the expensive smiles. Guests, many much older than me, stood holding drinks around the tan and black leather furniture. Soft violins played overhead while jazz music filtered in from the backyard where more elegantly dressed people had gathered. I wondered how much his house was worth, at least ten million dollars, as I tried to say hello to the handsome Myspace founder in beige blazer and collared shirt, one too many holes unbuttoned into a deep embarrassing V.

I want my work to bridge the analog and the digital, to connect the past to the future, to make for a more significant present where the audience not only becomes a character in the story but also the co-creator of the forthcoming chapters.

As I turned away from a tearful Rachel at one party, I finally caught the attention of a multi-millionaire at another while staring at his tanned and hairless chest. I tried to communicate a parallel between Tom, my first Myspace friend, a virtual persona made to promote social media, and my working concept of The Author, a virtual persona projected to defy it—but it didn't come out right because the pretentious red-headed twenty-something wouldn't shut the fuck up about his app idea, very protective of the Myspace founder's personal space. Really though, Red was just pissed because a minute earlier Shyla had dismissed his obvious overtures. It's her birthday, she whispered to me, she's feeling sexy. But maybe that was Rachel's cousin at the other party. Happy birthday, I said as I fingered her in the bathroom.

I want to deliver art as entertainment without irony, without quotations, without lowering its standards.

"Let me go, I'm leaving," I said to Rachel as she pulled at my arm, as I poured coke on Shyla's fake tits, as Heather fondled my zipper.

I know my female characters have no depth, I tell myself as I write this. It says as much about me as a person as it does as a writer.

"Girlfriend, don't let him go. It's like Tag! Tag, you're it!"

I want to become the author of my generation. I want to expand literature's peak potential, to demonstrate its significance in a world where literary authors have been forgotten, are no longer celebrities. Can't you see that we're losing our ability to express the part of us that makes us human? That language is our only hope? I want to communicate with you, dear reader, and make you part of the story even if you're an antihero born of shame. I want to spend the rest of my life trying to express with words what language cannot but if done with reverence is the closest we can get to the real thing.

"Who do you keep calling reader?"

What I'm trying to say but don't know how is that to make literature cool again we must reimagine it as a relationship. A relationship between the reader and the author or the persona he projects. You, the reader, are complicit in the story's telling. Your engagement with this story will become a living narrative, a coeval inception made by you and The Author, whom you'll have brought to life. With your participation, The Author will live on in a virtual reality we've collectively agreed is real, an alternate reality where fiction can become reality.

"I know it sounds confusing, but I believe I can pull it off. If only I just sit down and write."

"You're rushing this," Heather said. "Slow down." But Rachel, in tears, had already excused herself indoors.

We need a new type of hero, a new brand of celebrity. Post-analog, post-digital. Help me walk The Author off the page, step through the screen.

But no one was listening. And I'd lost the thread. I waved goodbye, repeating the Showtime actor's name incorrectly, saying it in such a way that its hilarity was obvious, laughing as the Escalade's window lowered into the doorframe while the paid-off tuxedoed driver drove us home from the Palisades party. Inside was silent. The fresh air whipped through my fingers as the hulking vehicle moved at tremendous speed along the cold ocean and whatever sleeps inside, the jeweled necklace of Santa Monica trailing off in the distance. But we were turning left. Back to where the night had started, back to where the story had begun. In the window's reflection I watched myself watching myself watch as the world streamed by.

X X X

I awoke in a large forgiving bed that seemed familiar.

Heather and Shyla sat at the bottom edge, speaking in hushed muted voices. Shyla was naming all the famous people she'd had sex with: Leo, Clooney, Usher, what's his name.

"Are you going to add James Franco to that list?" Heather asked, winking, noticing me awake.

Shyla laughed and said I could fuck her any time I'd like, even if she were giving birth, and then went on blabbing about […] (lawyer's redaction).

"Don't," Heather said.

"That summer at the Lake, I knew. I knew I was one of his girls in rotation but what we had was real."

"Why are you crying?" I asked, incapable of participating in any of this.

"It's really not important," Heather interjected.

"He proposed. I didn't believe him. I said no either way because I knew."

"We have company."

"He likes little boys. Which is probably why he was into me."

Heather got up to get tissues. "Clean up," she said and offered the box.

"But I should have said yes."

Delirious, I tried to rub Shyla's back, but she commanded me not to, commanded me harshly. "I'm sorry," she said. "In my culture women are designed to please the man, so when the man tries to please the woman she feels guilty."

Then she broke. Hot volcanic tears from her gut came pouring out her face. She was pregnant, she said. She mentioned the father, but I couldn't believe it. Half her age, an icon.

"He's a closet freak Christian," she said. "He won't let me get an abortion."

I considered my fingers and felt nauseated.

"Here, honey bunny," Heather said, handing me a pill. "Take this."

"What is it?"

"It's percocet. You'll want it." She also handed one to Shyla.

"Why?"

"It will help you sleep, honey bunny."

Sometime later, dark and drooling, I woke with my cock in Heather's mouth.

The moon hung tooth-crooked through what the curtain failed to reach. Shyla sat at the edge of the bed, alone. Sobbing. Was she watching? I said nothing, confused how I could get it up. I watched Heather bob her head through the darkness, her filler lips wet and fat. When she moved to get on top, it was the way she held her breath, so intent not to wake me—wide hips, the soft impale. I reciprocated the sentiment and closed my eyes and kept my palms flat on the mattress, that way we both could pretend that neither of us knew.

In the blue silence of night, when I was asleep or feigning to be, she spoke deliriously about her husband, the restaurateur turned producer turned mogul who'd swept her up at an age when you could be swept up. Back when a life could be arranged. He was much older, she said. She was a nobody then, a few appearances on soaps. He gave her everything, including her career. Memories, loved ones, everyone was watching. Then her daughter arrived and stole her body. It wasn't immediate but it was the beginning of the end. He was already old, but they couldn't get any younger. The lines he'd say. I can make you famous, I can make you famous, she kept saying. But I knew she was talking to no one.

In the morning, pale and quiet, I checked if she were breathing. She was so old that, for a moment, I imagined *what if*. I'd ingest all the drugs, I reasoned, or flush them down the toilet, or dissolve them in water and funnel the solution down her throat, and then…I don't know.

Shyla was gone. The room smelled of extinguished candles and stale champagne. What I was looking for was bunched on the floor. I pulled up my pants and did the two lines of coke apportioned on the dresser top, the bag of cash staring at me, and felt nothing.

I walked over blankets and pillows and mangled clothes, around remote controls and phone wires, to the wall-sized window looking out onto the snake-river roads of Hollywood Hills. Hazy orange morning. An hour earlier and the moon had hung in the milkblue morning lull. Not quite today and not quite yesterday and definitely not tomorrow because sleep never truly came. Standing there, I imagined seeing myself walking along the thin dirt paths and being summoned by strangers to say something brilliant, as if they'd lain in wait all along. Where they'd take me, the life I'd lead. Etched into the hills, the tributaries of secrets housed within belligerently modern all-glass Aztec mansions, renovated hutch cabins, Art Deco bungalows, however many and whatever sleeps inside. Whatever sleeps. There I am, waiting on something brilliant to say. Then I'd write it down. From that vantage, so high, you nearly forget about the Hollywood dream machine puffing smoke down below. Nearly.

Morning James Franco, she said.

All at once I felt claustrophobic, but that's not really right. I wanted to break narrative and/or delete the page. She coughed, moaned, and I didn't look. It was time to go.

Downstairs, through the main hallway, I saw Rachel standing at the kitchen counter drinking a glass of water. That she saw me was clear but what she saw was not.

What are you doing here?

I live here, you goof.

You what?

Would you like some breakfast? She cracked an egg into the pan, the smell of bacon. So, you met Mom?

Look, I want to apologize for last night.

We were drunk.

Wait—Mom?

She smiled. Mom gets close with all my friends. We share everything.

Share.

Hey, I've got a surprise for you. My shirt appeared in her lovely hand, the one I'd lost last night. Sit down, she said, let me feed you.

I've got to get going.

Eat, and then won't you come back to bed for a minute?

Big meeting, I lied.

The doorbell rang, the grand entrance hall just behind me.

Hey, can you get that?

I opened the door.

It was the delivery man.

Remember the delivery man! He was holding a package. Now what could he possibly deliver that would make this a happy ending?

CHAPTER IV

on writing

I was being fitted for wardrobe when she appeared in the doorway, tall, silhouetted, the light from outside sketching the contours of a proportionally perfect figure.

"Are you the lead?"

I don't know why but the question made me embarrassed. It was my first paid acting gig, one of those A&E murder mystery shows that only dead people watch. Still, it was something. She found a makeup stool and sat while the wardrobe assistant measured my inseam.

"I'm Madison," she said. "I'm playing your fiancé."

She was stunning. Half Japanese, half French, a legitimate fashion model. As if made to be studied and marveled. Her long dark hair cut into straight blunted bangs, the wet glimmer of lip-gloss a plum-taupe brown, her wide mouth. My god.

Look inside the studio apartment and see Madison naked on her bed, posing in obedient rebellion, her body long and miraculous. Not a single blemish. So beautiful I didn't want to touch her, didn't want to disturb the image.

For weeks she said she wanted to move slow. I was the first guy she'd been with since she broke up with her boyfriend, they'd only just separated, she thought she needed more time alone, but then I showed up and it's been really confusing and—she kept trying to explain herself. I told her not to worry, I'd wait forever.

I filled our glasses on the night table and watched her drink and kissed the wine from her lips as if taking or offering a sacrament. She closed her eyes and touched herself and told me she wanted it.

"Are you sure?"

"I'm sure. Did you bring it?"

"Yes. But are you sure?"

"Yes."

I'd never used a condom before. My first two girlfriends, spanning ten consecutive years, both their fathers doctors, were on birth control; as for the other girls, it had never been a problem. I tore the packaging with my teeth, sat back on my heels, and unrolled the silicon onto myself. Watched as she traced the indents of my stomach with her pointer finger and swallowed. Watched her eyes. She leaned back to receive me.

"Wait," she said, craning her neck.

Nearly inside her, nearly, I made myself say, "We don't have to do this, there's no need to rush." Outside, along Franklin Avenue, the pitter-patter of tires over a sewer-cap.

"Come here," she said.

I kissed the side of her neck and down her clavicle, her breasts. She sighed as I felt the softness of her lips, wet with desire, open for me, my finger inside her.

"Now," she said. "I want you inside me now," almost as if trying to prove something.

I obeyed and she exhaled as if it were the last breath she'd ever take, squeezing the back of my neck and begging me to go all the way. "Deeper," she said as I tried to find myself in the foreign object, the foreign person. "Deeper."

I told her there's no such thing as I pressed into her so hard she yelped, whimpering like a bleeding animal. A moan that sounded bottomless, like I had her in tears. She had me wanting to disfigure her. Pressing on, my body hot with sweat, the bed shook like a great reckoning, and because of the condom I could go forever; I may have, but I could no longer feel her hands on my back, could no longer sense her engrossment, and that's when I saw her face. Not that of death but of wishing for it, almost frozen with aloofness.

I dismounted immediately.

Her body had seized up like a mouse caught in a trap snapped shut. Her back arched upward not in ecstasy but as if broken. Paralyzed. I thought she'd suffered a brain aneurysm, or I'd accidently suffocated her; a series of ridiculous scenarios flashed before my eyes.

I tried to revive her—my heart, my head racing—but as soon as my hand felt her body, she screamed a gut-wrenching cry. Tears came pouring out with ferocity; she was palpitating like a birdsong of shame and grief, such violent emotion. Imagine wildlife covered in diesel fuel and filth, the horrible sounds. Her face clenched so tightly I thought her teeth might break.

She was having a panic attack, the worst I'd ever seen.

I ran naked and wildly to the kitchen to get a glass of water and now found myself crying next to her on the bed, imploring her to drink. It wasn't that she couldn't look at me—she didn't know who I was. The glass struck from my hand went sputtering on the carpeted floor. Swinging with delirious rage, she slapped my face, punched my shoulders, scratched my chest and forearms, kicking out from under the covers bunched about her legs.

"Madison, it's me," I shouted. "Madison!"

Call it love that had me consider dialing 9-1-1; call it love that gave me the strength not to. To witness her break from this life only made me want to love her more.

I told her I wished I could say something calming, to demonstrate language's peak potential. Told her I wanted to communicate worlds of meaning in one clean stanza and expose the absurdity underwriting this whole production, to expel her pain contingent on rehearsal of whatever past trauma, to help her grasp that the past cannot define her for it never happened: she can refire, rewire, reimagine her life however she wants it to go. I told her language has the power to absolve her greatest sins, those performed and received. If only I could deliver a truth so obvious she would come forth from her darkling misery and half in love and half awake see what flowers lay below her feet and weep. And I'd be there with her. I am your poet missionary, at your service. I am an untalented actor acting natural while you melt before my very eyes. I am here, I am yours, and in this moment all I can imagine is reciting by heart this very poem I wish I'd written for a time like now.

Look inside the room and see me wrapping Madison with white bedding. That's me naked and kneeling on the floor beside her, brushing her hair, encouraging her to drink from the new glass of water with my free hand while she sobs with exhaustion. The fan in the corner, the white noise. After five or so minutes the room grew quiet. She sipped from the glass and sat upright. Without transition, almost penitently, she began to speak about the photographer who raped her. She said, although not in these words—I wouldn't dare try to quote her—I know it happened, but it's like it never happened because I don't remember. I know *it* happened, she repeated, but I don't know *what* happened. What do you do with that? How can you forget what you don't remember?

"You don't have to do this," I said. "We can talk about it later. Are you in pain?"

It was my first photoshoot, she continued unflinchingly, right after I decided to leave grad school and pursue modeling full time. I arrived at the studio Downtown—

"I didn't know you went to grad school," I said, moving up to sit on the mattress. Calmness had overcome the room, was welcomed.

I was studying to be a psychologist. I loved it but I couldn't see myself at school for another three years. On a friend's dare I auditioned for a commercial and got the job. I made something like four thousand dollars. That was all the proof I needed. I decided to go for it. I deferred my second year at USC. That was two years ago.

A swarm of emotions overtook me. What we had and could have, still so new; I made new discoveries every day. I gripped her hand and said, "You're a dream. Please continue."

I arrived at the studio Downtown, she said, although again not in these words. One of those big studio lofts. Industrial. High ceilings. White walls. Exposed ventilation. The sun shone through tall glass windows. I was so nervous. This was my first big shoot. He's a real artist, a well-known photographer. I felt lucky to be there. Me in my black tank and jeans torn at the knees. My Chucks. I had my hair down. I wanted to appear casual. There wasn't much for furniture but there was this old elaborate sofa. Pink with violet stripes and gold threading along the backrest, dark brown wood. It's an antique, the photographer said. European. It's sturdy, don't worry, please sit. I remember it being the only source of color in the entire studio. Beyond the main area was the kitchen and to the right the dressing area. Music was playing. House music. It sounded like the outskirts of a river, like water trickling against rocks. The type of music you wouldn't feel embarrassed to dance to in the company of strangers. I like to dance, she said, tapping her foot, it helps me relax. She paused, took a sip of water, her big brown eyes cast down on the mattress. She said she should have known.

"That's impossible," I said. "How could you?"

He told me he was brewing tea. I didn't think anything of it. I mean, why would I suspect that? He asked me to show him what looks I'd brought. I put the hangers on the rack, unpacked my bag. He was happy with the choices. He made a few pairings and told me to go change in the dressing room. When I came out he handed me a mug of tea. Sip slowly, he said.

We worked for two hours. The light shone brilliantly throughout the room. Smokey, like it had mass. We took some gorgeous shots. I remember being amazed that I could do that, could create such beauty. My agent was so happy with the finals, those photos still land me jobs. I feel messed up for admitting that. They're like a lucky rabbit's foot, only I was the rabbit.

"Don't say that."

After we wrapped, I was in the changing area behind the curtain and all I can remember is how quickly it came over me. It was frightening how tired I felt. Like a blackout drunk, I'm told, but I don't know, I've never gotten drunk like that before. I don't really like alcohol.

I looked at my glass of wine on the night table, looked at hers.

I remember walking out of the changing room. The loft

felt huge and bright, so bright it hurt to look. I don't remember what I was wearing, don't remember if I was wearing anything, I just remember the pink and gold antique couch, its striped sofa. It's Venetian, he said as I fell onto it, the liquid music trickling through my ears. And that's the last thing I remember.

I had no response. I wanted to smoke a cigarette, at the very least take a swig of wine, but thought it would be over the top. I held her hand to offer some sense of solidarity.

When he woke me up he said it was time to go. I didn't know what was going on. The cab is here, he said, it's all packed up. Why was I in a cab? What about my car? I was going in and out. It wasn't until I was home, standing outside my apartment, when I put it together. I knew something was wrong but I didn't know what. All I could do was get into bed.

I wanted to ask how she knew but didn't want to seem insensitive or prying.

I wouldn't have paired that top and bottom together. It wasn't something I'd wear to go home. Do you understand what I mean?

"He dressed you." Just then I noticed my nakedness. I covered myself with the duvet.

His choices betrayed him, she said. She went silent for a moment. I'm sorry for what happened earlier. What am I saying? I'm mortified. It's hard to look at you. I'm so embarrassed. My mind wants to fill in the blank. She closed her eyes, tears dripping down her cheeks. When you're on top of me my imagination takes over. I can't help but see him, or my imagination of him. I lose you. My mind starts narrating a fiction I can never escape that has become my life.

"Say that again."

"My mind starts narrating a fiction I can never escape that has become my life."

"I understand."

"Do you?"

"Yes."

"How?"

It took all my strength to keep from mentioning my ambition to write this novel, how I felt too sad, too frozen to author my way out of this hapless divergence from my potential. So instead I told her about my affair with my high school English teacher, a story I'd kept secret from everyone until then, until now.

"Say that I attended what is regularly recognized as one of the top high schools in the country. A Jesuit all-boys school located on the Upper East Side of Manhattan. When I was accepted, my elementary school teachers told me it was a school for the 'gifted,' embarrassing thing to say."

"That's incredible."

"I became a bit of a celebrity around town. Adult strangers would approach me in public, congratulate me, ask me about my secret to success. Did I speak another language? Did I play a musical instrument? How many books did I read per week? Their son was in seventh grade, they wanted him to start preparing. As if I was some sort of authority."

She raised her eyebrows. Madison had this childlike quality to her, maybe because her head was too big for her body, or her face so beautiful it appeared airbrushed. I loved this part of her, loved all the parts. She was reminding me of love.

"High school was hard. It was so academically rigorous I thought I had to kill something in me to survive. A therapist called it my inner child. Call it what you'd like, but I was barely holding on. The day I saw my teacher walking down the stairwell, she was distressed, in tears. It was Ms.—well, I'll call her Brooke, but her name is not Brooke. It was my junior year. Brooke had been my freshman English teacher, easily the best teacher I'd ever had. Also the prettiest. None of us knew her age exactly, nor would she share it, but I guessed thirty and later learned I wasn't far off. At an all-boys school you can imagine what sort of attention an attractive teacher would arouse. Suddenly I had a new appreciation for literature, or maybe it was my instant crush on her. I remember being mesmerized by her knee-high leather boots over striped stockings, her pencil skirts. I can see myself, a teenager, hunched over the keyboard of a dumpy desktop computer, it's late at night and I'm writing poetry for no one but myself, believing words have the power to move people, moved to write by whatever infant muse. Although I never would have described it this way at the time, I thought of writing as a mystical experience, almost like the words were given to me, not generated by me. I received a grade of 'High Honors' in her class, a 4.0."

"That's not surprising," Madison said, smiling. She was referring to the poems I'd recently shared with her, some of which she'd printed and taped to her desk there in the corner of the room. What she didn't know was that I wrote them for someone else, I wrote them for you, but I wanted Madison to feel special and maybe old words can take on new meanings, I thought, since it's not about their author it's about their reader.

"At my high school the faculty cultivated an uncommon level of intimacy with students," I continued. "We were treated like adults, encouraged to express ourselves as equals. Teachers often took lunch in the cafeteria with us, for example. By my junior year, though Brooke was no longer my English teacher, we'd kept what was in my high school's standards a healthy and communicative relationship. As I was 'discovering myself,' embarrassing phrase, I frequently found myself inside the English department resource center, half hangout lounge, half study hall, where each faculty member maintained his or her resident desk. Brooke and I shared a playful banter. She'd tell me what bands to check out, which novels to read. She was the 'cool' teacher. I remember being amazed learning she'd read Virginia Woolf's entire library during one exceptionally cold winter month, just for fun. That blew my mind. She taught me how to fall in love with an author, to devour the author whole, to read each work sequentially in order to inhabit the evolution or degradation of the author's craft. Great literature is not about plot, it's about personality, she said. When reading you have the rare chance to portal into someone else's soul. What else could be more intimate? Vonnegut said that music is proof of the existence of god, and he's right, she said, but literature is proof of the existence of love. If for only temporarily you the reader can become coeval with someone else, someone whom through reading you've learned to love. She didn't mean the narrator, she meant the author. Because we can never truly know the people we are reading about. The narrator can never be trusted, and the author is not your friend. And yet there's a bond, an engagement through time and space. Reading is lovemaking most pure. At least I know of no gladder romance, she said. And my god did I agree."

"*Stop.* How have you successfully made my misery about you?" I imagined Madison asking.

"Is this okay? I'm talking a lot."

Madison nodded; she wanted me to continue. "I don't want to talk about me anyway."

"Are you sure?"

"Yes, really. I love learning about you." She repositioned herself and sat up against the wall.

"I've gotten a bit off track here."

"You said Brooke was crying. On the stairwell."

"I did. She was. That's when it started. It was right before we let out for Christmas break. The entire school body met for morning mass inside the huge gothic Church of St. Ignatius Loyola, one of the more beautiful spaces I've ever stepped inside. The interior is constructed of American, European, and African marbles, including pink Tennessee red-veined Numidian, yellow Siena, pink Algerian, white Carrara, and veined Pavonazzo—"

"How do you know all this?"

"Because I'll plagiarize Wikipedia as I recreate this moment for the page. Please don't ask too many questions."

"Go on."

"The great twelve-paneled bronze doors located at the sanctuary end of the side aisles. Just extraordinary. Of course at the time I didn't give a shit. To a seventeen-year-old boy, regardless of his precociousness, regardless of his intellect or general sense of wildly unfounded superiority, it was just another building I'd been told to enter, another early morning of getting up at 5:16 a.m. to catch the 6:01 a.m. train headed to Penn Station where I'd ride the C local uptown to Eighty-Sixth Street, disembark, and catch the crosstown M-86 bus through Central Park where at Lexington Avenue I'd get off and walk two blocks and finally enter the damp dark tunnel leading into the school's bricked quadrangle where downstairs I'd stumble or sprint into the locker room to do another day of school—a ninety-minute commute all in all."

"It took you an hour and a half to get to school?"

"Picture an infant dressed as an adult sitting on a train amongst lawyers, bankers, construction workers, culinary servers, a vast assortment of white-collar professionals and blue-collar laborers, the early morning riders of a metropolitan workforce, heavy brick of a book opened in his lap. He's reading Joyce and pretending to be absorbed by the writing as he imagines all the adults watching him read. He's drinking coffee to overcome mild but persistent insomnia as he makes his way into Manhattan. That was my every day, twice, once in each direction."

"*Are* you a genius?"

"No, but I love that you asked."

"Okay." She toed me with her foot. "So why was she crying?"

"Because Brooke just had her heart ripped out with no prior warning. Her boyfriend of nearly two years broke things off the night before. Christmas mass had let out and before commuting home for a much needed vacation where I'd sleep twelve hours a night for two weeks straight and still not feel caught up, not at all, I walked upstairs to the English department to retrieve a graded paper that would determine my first trimester GPA for a class led by a teacher—shit, what was his name?—known to break the spirits of aspiring writers whose fledgling egos probably needed some breaking. On my way up the school's secondary staircase, its granite steps, I intercepted Brooke coming down. She was moving quickly, holding her eyeglasses with one hand

and wiping her face with the other. She was crying. I asked what was wrong and perhaps caught off guard, perhaps desperate for distraction, I can't tell you why, she asked me to walk with her. She was bundled in a black winter coat, and though I was woefully underdressed to brave the cold, I agreed. For the next two hours we traversed the Upper East Side, through Central Park, around the Reservoir, until finally, thankfully, we sat inside an old café where she bought me a coffee and a croissant. Paleo wasn't a thing back then," I quickly interjected. "She told me about her heartache, secrets teachers do not share with students. He was her first real love, she said. She'd had boyfriends before but not like him, serious relationships before but not like theirs. They'd been talking about moving in together. She'd been dreaming of marriage. She couldn't believe it, couldn't fathom being alone and without him, the man she loved, the man in whose reflection she'd discovered new layers of herself. She needed someone to listen as she attempted to make sense of a question that had no happy answer, no happy ending—'Why?'—and I was that someone. She spoke with a tenderness and yearning, her words delivered by a sadder self, her words making to dispossess the sadness. She told me that love never dies, only dims, and once lit the flame burns forever."

"Why did he break up with her?" Madison asked.

"He said he found someone else."

"But why was she telling you?"

"I don't know." I paused. "Is this okay?"

"Yes."

"When Christmas vacation ended, when school resumed, Brooke and I began to develop a casual friendship. At first it was spontaneous. We'd find ourselves meeting over lunch, between classes, after final period, the way you do when excited about a new friend, discovering parts of yourself in someone else, experiencing those parts come alive. Brooke never had boyfriends growing up, she told me, she was fat her entire life. Even in college when she sang for a popular band. After the members kicked her out she starved herself for a month and took up smoking cigarettes. It was bizarre how many similarities we shared. I was a fat kid too. I played in a band as well."

"Really? What did you play?"

"Rhythm guitar. I also wrote the lyrics."

"What kind of band?"

"We liked to say alternative rock, but why hide it? We were a crappy emo band and we were awesome. On weekends we recorded demos and played at bars and recreational centers scattered throughout Long Island. Watching the local kids sing our songs from the crowd, I could have died. That was fame. Brooke and I were mirrors of each other. It became a common refrain, an inside joke we purposefully reinforced: mirrors. She even burned me a CD of The Velvet Underground and Nico's debut album so I could listen to the song 'I'll Be Your Mirror.'"

"I'm guessing she didn't do this for other students."

"No." I thought about it. "I hope not."

"Right."

"By March of that year I was stopping by the English resource center multiple times a day. No longer spontaneous, our rendezvous became deliberate, structured. We'd plan to meet in the hallways, walk around the city after school, never talk about anything academic. Sometimes she'd ask about my girlfriend.

Our increasingly intimate conversations soon spread into the erotic. Innocent questions like had we had sex yet?—I had, but remember, I'd only just turned seventeen—soon gave way to a more liberal type of joking, or maybe it was flirting. Why did I love giving oral? How had I learned? Where was the funniest place I'd done it?"

"Are you serious?"

"I know how it sounds but it was playful. Friends messing around. I remember when she told me about her ex, all the public places they'd had sex, how one time she'd let him put it in her ass and how bad it hurt. I had a million questions. We laughed."

"She really said this to you?"

"I'm sorry. I guess I didn't need to share that."

"And meanwhile you had a girlfriend this whole time?"

"Right. Yes. I did. She went to the local public school. We dated all four years of high school, it even dragged on into college. I had to study abroad in London to finally separate and that's where I met my most recent ex, who was visiting a mutual friend, also studying abroad—but that's a different story altogether."

"Did she know what was going on, your high school girlfriend?"

"No. Absolutely not. I never once mentioned Brooke to her, she had no knowledge of Brooke's existence. Remember, this period predated virtual reality. Digital communication was relegated to computers. Texts or calls could easily be deleted from flip phones, not that texting was much of a thing back then. Please don't look at me like that. I know I'm a bad person."

"No, you're not. I feel bad for you. Feel bad you had to manage all of this during such a stressful time in your life." She brushed my hair. "I wish I'd known you back then."

"No, you don't. I was not a nice person. From 6:00 a.m. to midnight, Monday through Friday, there was no life beyond school. The intensity of my workload broke me, or I let it break me, and my parents never intervened. At that point I was averaging just over five hours of sleep a night. Physics, Advanced Calculus, Nietzsche, Russian Lit, studying for the SATs, SAT IIs, visiting Ivies and their second-class cousin safety schools."

"That's so impressive though, don't you think? For a high school kid to treat life so seriously? I don't know anyone like that."

"Serious? Yes. Good in principle? Sure. But this was psychotic."

"I hate to stop you," Madison said, "but I really need to pee." She kissed my forehead and ran off. When she returned, she hopped into bed and under the covers like a little girl. I felt at ease if not in love with her devotion to my narration.

"How did you keep it a secret?" she asked. "Didn't your friends or teachers notice?"

"Yes and no. We learned to disguise it."

"Tell me."

"That spring Brooke agreed to direct the school play. *Romeo and Juliet.* Her dream was to direct on Broadway one day. She'd been slowly building a résumé directing Off-Off-Broadway and student productions. 'Have you ever thought about acting?' she asked. I hadn't. 'Would you?' I thought about it, sure, and decided it wasn't for me. Eventually she convinced me to be her Prop Master. 'Is that like a production assistant?' 'Sort of. You'll be my right-hand man.' 'I'll think about it,' I said. 'It'll look great on your college applications. I'll even write you a letter.'" I started to laugh. "She knew me too well. After a comment like that, how could I say no?"

"I can see where this is going."

"With Brooke's oversight I set a budget," I continued. "I bought props and fabrics and hand-me-down furniture from thrift stores, ordered costumes, did whatever was asked of me. Then my responsibilities expanded. Now I had to direct the crew, which comprised mostly freshmen, where to place what props in which scenes, choreograph the timing between acts and how quickly to move when the curtain came down, ensure the stage production team had built the set according to the schedule I'd outlined. It was a huge job. I didn't have time for it. But I took it on. How many things would I have to do out of character before I became someone else? Together, Brooke and I sat in the director's box on the second-floor balcony and watched the actors rehearse as we rehearsed acting professional. Sometimes she'd hold my hand.

"Late at night she'd call me on my awesome flip phone and ask about the timing of scene changes. How can we empower the actors to redesign the set without dropping the curtains? I want the play to move faster, I want to take this to the next level, I want to tell you things I'm not supposed to say. 'Who are you talking to?' my mom would shout upstairs (my bedroom was in the attic), and I'd lie and tell her it was my girlfriend, which didn't feel like a lie. Whispering late into the night, the things she'd say. 'I'm touching myself.'" I saw Madison blink with shock. "I'm sorry. I've shared too much."

I reached for the glass of water on the night table and drank. Madison squeezed my free hand, which was her way of communicating that what I said had not upset her. I continued:

"What happened next happened quickly. A week before the play's debut I was in Western Civ when a freshman entered and passed a note to the teacher, who announced my name. Brooke needed to see me; please meet her in the auditorium. I was confused, somewhat alarmed. I'd never been called out of class before. Craig or Flanagan or one of those guys covered their mouths and started talking shit behind cupped hands. I told myself she must need something done for the play, nothing else could explain such blatant public attention. When I entered the auditorium's skylit hall, its golden floor, there was no one there. You could hear the pigeons on the roof, or maybe they were rats. The auditorium was empty save for the chairs folded against the walls.

"'Is that you?' I heard from the second-floor balcony. 'I'm up here.' I proceeded through the closet leading to the hidden stairwell. I found Brooke in the attic, sitting on a chair. In front of her was a small night table, probably an old prop. She looked upset. I thought she was crying but it was more like she was meditating, talking herself through something. She told me to sit down. The dust, the vestiges of previous generations, nearly a century old. Along the floorboards ancient soda bottles had migrated onto wainscot dirtied with black-brown glue. We were very alone. I asked what was the matter, what did she need? Why was she sitting here? What's up? She didn't say anything, which only made me more uncomfortable; I'm sure she saw the color of my face. Then she reached for my hand and I let her hold it. As I tell you this it's like I'm remembering watching a movie of someone else, like watching myself in the third person. I felt both trapped and out of my body at the same time. This was the middle of the school day. We were no longer playing the roles of director and prop master, teacher and student, no longer constrained by separate bedrooms or computers or phones—it felt intensely wrong."

Staring at Madison I didn't want to say what happened next. Put your hand on my thigh, Brooke said, I remembered. If you move it any higher, any higher, she quivered, I'm going to come. I did not move my hand, scared of what might happen, in love with the power I possessed. "She seemed both older and younger than me at once," I said to Madison. "The silence was startling. Then a student entered the auditorium below, you could hear his rubber soles against the wood. He sat at the piano and began playing Mozart's Requiem in D Minor. Some sort of reckoning. I got up and left her there lost in whatever reverie, eyes closed behind eyeglasses."

"I don't understand. Why did she call you there? What did she say?"

"She didn't say anything," I lied. "That's the point. She just needed to be with me."

"She was in love with you."

"Maybe. Maybe you could call it that."

"It's obvious."

"That's when the jokes began. My peers suspected something long before she had called me out of class, but that was the tipping point. What had previously been neatly contained was now bleeding outside the lines for others to see. 'What's it like fucking the teacher? Does she let you put it in her ass?' Word spread around the student body. Younger guys revered me like a hero. Seniors publicly anointed me their superior. Walking through the hallways was like evading paparazzi. No one took the claims seriously—it was all a big joke—but it was relentless, and I was alarmed."

"So what did you do?"

"I admitted nothing, of course. Brushed it off like they were assholes. 'You don't know what you're talking about'; 'The play's a bitch and demands all of my time'; 'You're just jealous it'll look sweet on my college applications'; 'I'm sure you love getting off to the thought of me screwing the teacher'—I dispatched any defense the accusation called for. I could not, would not be found out.

"A few days later, two days before opening night, Brooke was late for rehearsal. When the female actors arrived (we'd held auditions at the neighboring sister schools), they said they'd seen her inside the principal's office and she looked hysterical. I ran out the auditorium into the school's historic foyer and up the senior marble staircase to see inside the office, but the door was closed. I don't mean to compare myself to you," I said to Madison, "our experiences were nothing alike. But I know what you meant when you said the exhaustion came on so suddenly it was frightening. Instead of my autonomic nervous system activating in self-defense, you know, fight or flight, it shut down as if I were already dead. I was absolutely certain we'd been found out. This will be a huge scandal, I imagined, I'll be kicked out or, worse, arrested—no Ivy will ever consider me. My world felt on the verge of total collapse. I remember finding myself in the bathroom in front of the toilet, unsure what my body needed to disgorge, tears or vomit. I was so fucked up I eventually walked outside without telling anyone and flagged a yellow cab and had it drive me all the way home to Long Island, something I'd never done before, during rush hour no less. I paid with my mom's credit card, or maybe it was the spare hundred-dollar bill I kept in my backpack—I can't remember if cabs took cards back then—whichever it was, I was only to use it in case of emergency.

This felt like an emergency. Although I probably told my mom there were train delays, track issues at Penn."

Now I did take a sip of the wine, did not care how melodramatic it seemed, and when it touched my lips I downed the glass entire.

"Here's where it gets fucked up," I continued.

"Oh, only now?"

"There had been a scandal. But it was with someone else." I refilled my glass, emptying the bottle. "The faculty discovered that Brooke had recently been in a romantic relationship with a former student who was now a sophomore at NYU." I paused, let this information sink in. "They had begun their relationship *after* the student graduated from my high school, Brooke argued; he was legally a consenting adult. But it didn't matter. That she had once been his teacher, and not very long ago at that, was a clear violation of the school's conduct policy, to say nothing of its principles. Brooke fought through tears as she admitted this to me over the phone that night, mortified less by her behavior than how I'd respond. 'Why aren't you saying anything? Please tell me what you're thinking.'"

"Hold on. You're telling me she was with *another* guy from your high school?"

"Guess who'd just broken up with Brooke when I found her in the stairwell after Christmas mass? The story comes full circle."

"It was him."

"When Brooke described her ex, I always pictured a man. Someone with a career, maybe an academic. But he was just a kid. She never once hinted at his age."

"How did the principal find out?"

"Apparently," I sighed, "one of the guy's friends informed the school without his consent. The friend thought it was the right thing to do. I don't know the full story because after that I more or less cut off communication with Brooke. She kept apologizing, promising she'd wanted to tell me about him but didn't want to scare me or whatever. It didn't matter because no matter what she said it wouldn't change the truth."

"Which was what?"

"I was number two."

"I'd like a drink now."

I handed her my glass of wine.

"It gets better. Or worse. Brooke was fired, or no, she was asked to 'resign' at the end of the school year. She would fulfill her duties for the remaining months. I think the school wanted to do whatever it could to prevent a proper scandal from leaking, make it seem like the decision was hers. This was *not* the sort of thing that happened at an institution of its caliber."

"I'm sorry but I'm having a hard time listening to this. It's breaking my heart."

"I can stop."

"It's just a lot." Madison closed her eyes. I held her hand. Then she asked, "So what happened next?"

"Well, I did the play. I had to. It was the right thing to do. On opening night a freshman crewmember forgot to place the bench in Romeo's opening scene, but otherwise it was a success. It had a weeklong run and even Rudolph Giuliani came to see it. Back when he was New York's hero. After we wrapped, I was so busy visiting colleges, taking the SATs, SAT IIs, studying for finals, it was easy to keep distracted."

"But weren't you hurting? I'm hurting just listening."
"Hurting? No. Not really. I didn't have the time."
"How?"
"Nothing had changed."
"*Everything* had changed."
"Not for me."
 I could tell she was getting frustrated.
"What happened to Brooke?"
"She got a job at another prestigious high school in Manhattan. Became the head of its drama department."
"Are you kidding? She continued teaching high school boys?"
"Yes."
"And you didn't do anything about it?"
"What could I do?"
"Tell the faculty…your family…anyone!"
"I'm not finished yet."
"Oh fuck." Madison never cursed. "I don't want to know."
"Really?"
"Of course I do." She drank the wine, downing it.
"Are you sure this is okay?"
"Go on."
"The last day of final exams was also Brooke's birthday. We hadn't talked in nearly a month. For some reason, call it delirium or desperation, I texted her happy birthday as I exited the building on my way home for summer vacation. That night Brooke reached out to me over Instant Messenger—remember AIM? She thanked me for thinking of her earlier and expressed sorrow for not seeing me to say goodbye in person. Then in a moment

I'll never forget, a moment etched into my memory, she invites me to come to her apartment for dinner the following night 'to make it up to me.'"

"Stop it."

"And I accept."

"No."

"'Since we are no longer, technically speaking,' she wrote," I said to Madison, "'in a student–teacher relationship.'"

"Stop."

"'What do you want to do?' I type, press Send, wait.

"A minute later she replies: 'What do YOU want to do?'

"I don't know what came over me, I think I gave myself permission to stop giving a shit, tired of being so responsible, exhausted in general, but in a moment wildly out of character, at least at that point in my life—I hope this isn't hard for you to hear, but it's integral to the story—I type: 'I'm going to fuck you.'"

"And what did she say?" Madison asked, slight tremble in her voice.

"'Yes, please.'"

There was silence.

"Why are you telling me this?"

"Because this is something you need to know about me. The next night I drove to the nearby train station and parked my car and walked up the steps of the raised platform and waited for the train to arrive, the train that would take me to Brooklyn. I remember the big yellow lights pacing through the dark, the warm damp summer evening, the train muscling to a halt as it approaches the platform, the breaks screeching, the muffled whistles. The train doors open and an overwhelming sense of dread comes over me as I walk forward. 'Beware of the closing doors,' the stern but friendly automation says. I see my reflection in the window of the door across from me, a phantom in the night dark. I'm seventeen and about to participate in the most scandalous event of my life, a fantasy come true, if that's what it was. Do I dare? The train doors close like a seal of victory and the train pulls away. Only, without me. From the concrete platform I watch it go into the night. Then I walked back to my car and deleted Brooke's number. And that was the end of the affair."

Madison stared ahead with a vacant expression, then stood and walked to the kitchen. She was naked, let herself be naked. Minutes passed. I didn't know how to interpret this; I was about to call for her when out she came holding the second bottle of wine, uncorked, and tilted her neck and arched her elbow and drank, a move wildly out of character for her. Something thrilling in her defiance. I wish I'd had my phone on me, I'd have told her to hold just so and taken her picture and saved it forever, maybe make it the cover of this novel, at least this chapter. She passed me the bottle and I drank and watched as she found her thong, unbunching it from itself, and slipped her long legs through. On the bed she covered herself with the blanket.

"I have so many mixed emotions right now."

"Maybe I shouldn't have told you," I said.

"I always want you to tell me the truth."

"You might not like what you hear."

"Promise me."

"Okay, I promise."

"So that was the end of it?"

"There's one more thing. But I've been talking for a while."

"Tell me."

"You're not tired of this?"

"You must."

"First, come here."

She came over and kissed me, her lips tasting of wine, and held the bottle to my mouth. I drank and smiled, our lips, our tongues, purple. She brushed my hair from my eyes.

"The following year, my senior year, it's the third or fourth week of school," I said, "and I'm called into the student counselor's office. We met regularly for college admissions preparation, but something is different. Her desk, usually strewn about with student files and sticky pads and spread-open Kaplan books and college pamphlets, is clean. Somehow I already know what's coming. She tells me to sit down. She asks if she can get me anything to drink, any water, but before I can respond she blurts, 'I want you to know you've done nothing wrong. Absolutely nothing wrong. You are safe.'

"I raise my eyebrows as if to say, 'Go on.'

"'It has come to our office's attention that last year Ms.— [Brooke] was spending a great deal of time with you. Is this true?'"

"Here it comes," Madison said.

"'Yes,' I confirm, nodding at Madison. "'I was the prop master for *Romeo and Juliet*.'

"'Can you share what your relationship was like?'

"I don't know exactly what I told her, but I'm sure I elaborated in painstaking detail, as I was wont to do, the totality of my duties, the intensity of learning a new skillset during the hardest academic year of my life, hoping she'd express an easy sympathy that at the very least would confirm I was neither crazy (this school really was insanely demanding) nor retarded (I was not orders of magnitude dumber than my peers), which always proved calming. But she doesn't. Her eyes, her expression, they don't seem to register reception of my blabbering. Or maybe she was just tired of hearing it. She asks a few questions and it's clear she has no idea what my relationship with Brooke was really like.

"'What is this?' I ask her. 'What's this all about?'

"'It's come to our attention'—she keeps repeating the phrase—'that [Brooke's] relationship with you went beyond the bounds of appropriate behavior. Our office has discovered certain things about her past and we are taking this claim very seriously.'

"'What claim?' I ask, eager to play along.

"'Some students,' she repositions herself, 'from last year's play have expressed concerns.'

"'What concerns?' Now I'm truly pissed. 'What have they told you?'

"'Believe me, this is very difficult for me to ask of you,' she says, her voice inflecting down a register. She's noticeably upset, her eyes glistening. '[Brooke] is a dear friend of mine, we still keep in touch. This is not easy for me. I'm simply gathering information.' Her face reddens. 'I need you to know that whatever happened, *if* anything happened, was not your fault. You are by no means in trouble. By no means. It's the opposite. I'm here to help you.'

"It's funny," I said to Madison, "my initial reaction was rage. Rage I was put in this position. Rage one of my peers had told on me. Weren't we supposed to be brothers, men for others? Weren't we supposed to act like adults? Who rats on his brother for screwing the teacher? Is that what being a responsible adult is, pandering to the institution? Not having the balls to address me directly? I could have destroyed this woman, the school, Brooke, the geek who tattled; I could have raised hell and threatened to tell the authorities, whoever they were, and demanded reparation—but I didn't. Instead I kept my cool, and keeping cool I look the student counselor straight in the eyes and say:

"'This is pretty funny actually. A total misunderstanding. Was it Jefferies who approached you?' Jefferies was a disgruntled upperclassman who, at this point, had already graduated," I said to Madison as an aside. "He thought he should have been Romeo, but Brooke cast him to play Mercutio instead. He and Brooke had a falling out over the matter. If this doesn't reek of high school drama, I don't know what does. As I explain my interpretation of the situation to the student counselor, I conclude by saying something like, 'Look, [Brooke] was very close with a number of students. And they all happened to have been involved in her productions. And the majority of them happen to be gay. Obviously no one ever suspected anything *untoward* of her in those relationships—they'd never been reported as *inappropriate*. But with me it's considered inappropriate.' Now I'm direct, stern. I say, 'I am offended you'd take an upset former student's claim seriously, offended you'd have me respond to lies, and frankly I'm embarrassed for [Brooke] that you'd consider her capable of whatever abuse of power you're suggesting.'"

"You defended her?" Madison said, raising her voice. "Why would you do that?"

"Because this wasn't right either. I wasn't going to put Brooke's fate in the hands of some board. She was my friend. That's what I've been trying to say. The whole thing felt so normal. Yes, it got weird, but she was my friend. What was I going to do, tattle and let the school annihilate my friend and her reputation? It didn't seem right."

"I can't believe you still don't think she did anything wrong!"

"Was it really so wrong if I wanted it to happen? She was thirty-two and I was seventeen. You might say she held all the power and abused that power. No doubt if the roles were reversed, if she were a man and I a girl, 'he' would likely be arrested, maybe thrown in jail, and I would hopefully have a book deal exposing my victimization. But it wasn't like that. The suggestion of victimhood is absurd. I wasn't a victim. *You* were a victim. It's unspeakable what that criminal did to you. But me? I played along."

"He is a criminal," Madison said. "And so is she! I don't think you understand that. She took advantage of you, and others. Who knows how many others."

"You're wrong. No one took advantage of anyone. Or maybe it's more accurate to say that we both took advantage of each other. Isn't that what all relationships are? She made me feel good during the hardest year of my life. I can't express how valuable that was."

"But that's what predators do! She manipulated—"

"No, yes, I mean no. Look I ultimately had to be the adult in the room, but I *always* had to be the adult in the room. Don't you get it? That was my fucking job."

"I'm sorry," Madison tensed. I must have gotten loud. "But if you don't think she did anything wrong then why are you telling me this?"

"I don't know. Because it's a good story."

"Is that all this is? Is that all it was?"

"I'm sorry for raising my voice," I said and placed my hand on her knee. "I just wanted you to know that I can empathize with you, that on some level I understand what you went through, but I didn't mean to suggest that our situations were the same or the outcomes comparable."

"You're allowed to feel however you feel. You're right, it's not a comparison. I'm glad you told me. Have you really never talked about this before?"

"No."

"Not to anyone?"

"No, but when I walked out of the student counselor's office, I promised myself that one day I'd write about this experience, and when I did, I'd know I was a real writer."

"It's life-changing."

"But it wasn't. That's what I'm trying, failing, to say. Nothing about me had changed, maybe apart from my weight—I probably gained fifteen pounds that year because of the stress. But it did feel significant, something worth writing about. I thought if I wrote about it, I'd discover why."

"Have you?"

"What?"

"Written about it."

"No. Not yet."

Having projected myself into the future, dear reader, I'm now looking back and making good on that boy's promise. Outside the cabin, down by the creek, the frogs croak. My only audience.

Silence punctuated the room. The whirring fan. A car alarm sounded outside.

"You loved her."

"No."

"You did. That's why you're telling me. You feel safe."

"I didn't love her. I loved what happened. Loved that it happened to me." I pulled from the bottle of wine, a cheap cabernet, but everything was expensive in those days.

"You know," Madison said, "for the past few weeks I've been asking myself if this was a good idea. I've been questioning myself: maybe rushing into a new relationship isn't wise. Especially when so much hasn't been resolved with James. He keeps calling and sometimes I answer." She smiled, or frowned, but not timidly, and looked me in the eye. "But then tonight happens and my worst fear comes true. I thought I'd rather die than face you seeing me like that. It's a nightmare. I have nightmares about getting close to someone, nightmares that person would see me like you did and be horrified, and I'd have explain myself, and he'd think me damaged or broken, and—"

"It's okay."

"James and I didn't," she paused. "We never—he's very religious."

"Oh."

"You're the first."

"Ever?"

"Since the thing."

"I see."

"I've never had to talk about this before. I met James a few months after it happened and his rules were fine by me."

"I understand."

"But then tonight. With you. My worst fear comes true." She grabbed my hand. "You don't understand how important this is." She kissed my fist embalmed in her grasp. "You helped me see that the fear is worse than what actually happened. The way you responded—I know I hit you and I'm sorry—you're so gentle, so good to me. Instead of reacting you got vulnerable. Thank you. Thank you, I mean it. Listening to you tell your story, I know why we met. You're here to help me heal. I met a good guy. You really are a good guy."

I didn't know what to say.

"If you hadn't shared your story, I wouldn't have told you what I'm about to tell you now. I feel messed up for saying this but I stuck with modeling because I thought if I could get through that experience then I could get through anything because I'd already been through the worst. In a weird way I'm thankful it happened. And now, even more. Because it led me to you."

She stretched across the mattress and kissed me with the tenderness of someone who means what she's doing. We kissed softly, sweetly, and I rested my forehead in the curve of her clavicle. We held each other like so. Eventually I took another swig of wine and passed the bottle to her.

"So, you're writing a novel?" she asked, wiping her mouth.

"It's complicated."

"What's it about?"

"It's about an aspiring author who avoids writing his novel and goes on to become a famous actor instead."

"That's funny."

I purposely failed to mention I hadn't begun writing the book yet.

"How does he become famous?"

"You'll have to read the book."

She kissed me and said she will, she can't wait.

"Should I put the story about the affair with my high school teacher in the novel?"

"Yes," she said. "Yes, I think you must."

"Okay."

"Just promise you won't include the part about me."

Funny to look inside the room and see two recent strangers meet, come together, embrace, the worry of sex vanished from possibility. And how comfortable they feel. Madison took a shower, so did I, and clean, a clean that water cannot dispense, we laid in bed together watching *Who Framed Roger Rabbit?*, one of my favorite movies, on her laptop. Her long legs jerking every few moments, she was soon asleep.

Thinking over my story, I supposed I did sound like a good guy. Only it wasn't the full story.

Because I did step off the platform, did wince as the mechanical doors pressed closed before my face, did see the train pull away—but while driving home in my dad's Infiniti, which I was allowed to drive on weekends, I realized I'd made a mistake.

So I drove to Brooklyn instead.

Speeding along the Grand Central Parkway, Shea Stadium in the distance, all blue and lit up like a space mall, I cherished my first experience driving beyond the imaginary limits of Long Island and into the "City." I was only seventeen but I felt immortal. It took three wrong exits and two gas-station employees to get me there. As the car crept into the crowded neighborhood, the streetlights bronzing the brownstones and eateries and shops whose charm derived from their anachronism, I imagined looking back on this moment from some distant romantic future—and immediately slammed on the brakes.

Pedestrians had crossed the street. They were waving at me to stop. Nervously, I waved back.

Parking proved difficult. After many random left and right turns, I found a spot on a block featuring an elevated pink neon sign that read "SODA." Somehow Brooke was already there waiting for me by the mailbox. How did she know where I'd park? I can see her now, her arched eyebrows, so hopeful. Outside the car, she pushes me against the open doorframe, her mouth open, and I'm kissing my teacher. Was I surprised? I didn't so much ask myself as experience the essence of the question spread throughout my body. Quickly the facts of my life rearrange themselves around our coupling, my tongue licking hers, my tongue catching the crown of her teeth. She takes my hand.

It's a warm summer night, surfaces glistening from an earlier rain. People walk the streets in teams and crowds. A group of smartly dressed hipsters stand smoking cigarettes in front of some storefront's spray-painted steel roller shutters. We pass them and turn the corner, and there against the brick stoop Brooke pulls me against her. No light overhead, we lurch in the shadows, which she must have preferred because now my fingers are inside her, smooth as a baby. She's so wet it takes my breath away.

She leads me inside the classic prewar brownstone, upstairs through the careening narrow stairwell, and into her modest apartment that smells of milk and lavender. She looks at me, looks down at the hardwood floor, and does not flick the light because she says she's nervous. "I can't, we can't," she keeps saying as she walks me to her bedroom, as I kiss her neck from behind. Her hips in my hands, now I'm removing her top. "We can't do this."

Oh, no? I take her hand and make her feel it, hard and getting harder. She groans. That's right. Let yourself be taken by a teenager. Obey as he pushes you down on the mattress. Find your courage. Show him what you really want. Stockings on, stockings off. Unbutton his jeans and finish what you started. Climb on top, snake free from your bra. Rage and sit down on your throne. Make him your king. And fuck me like you've won.

The following few weekends she thought getting drunk might help.

I remember the inscrutably old Korean woman, amaranthine, who operated the corner market with bright yellow signage, commenting on the attractive couple while Madison, dressed in sweatpants and T-shirt, who didn't like to drink, asked me which whiskey she should try.

It didn't work. Didn't help. It wasn't her. I couldn't do it. It isn't real, I said. It will always be a problem. But she wanted it. She said she'd do anything. She'd get drunk and kiss my stomach and tell me she wanted to try again, wanted to make me feel like I'm her man and only hers. My cock in her mouth, whatever it takes. But it didn't feel right. No, but she'd do anything for me, anything. She'd already set up a meeting with her agent. I'll help you write your novel. Write about the teacher. You're so good, if not you then who can? Who better? Yes, darling, and what if words could disappear the past, could make miracles believable? And I just follow my senses onto the page and through the page and into the room with you, a reader who holds my life in her hand. But I want it, she says, kissing me, fellating me, posing like a ragdoll the way she does for famous photographers, one of whom will rape her and get away with it and ruin our relationship, the music on, liquid music running like river water to which she can dance and careen and forget herself, forget what's going on here. I want to take and hold your heart the way a great artist needs. I want you to come in me and only me and no one else; I want to be your woman, not your girl—said drunkenly from two meager pours to an unreliable narrator who hadn't yet been written by an author who is no more than a figment of his imagination. It's a fantasy, I say. It isn't real.

No, what are you doing? she asks as I stride to the door. Black Levi's, black T-shirt, Chelsea boots. I wanted to appear casual. Her humble apartment, not much furniture but for the bed and desk housing some of my poems that would soon be torn down, the rolling hanger rack dangling practically an entire department store.

The door opens. The threshold. The hallway.

She runs to me. Where are you going? No, please no. I walk through the hallway and down the stairwell and irresponsibly, half-drunkenly, drive home to my apartment in West Hollywood instead of my parent's house in Long Island, not at all disturbed by having just cheated on my girlfriend with my teacher—because in this alternate reality that lives on the edge of fiction, a world no one knows unless you read it, I suffer no consequences. Rain on the window, the cinema of rain falling hard as I pull into the driveway and sneak inside through the basement door. The sex was great; the sex was underwhelming. Two bodies fishing. Fun while it happens, boring when it's over. To culminate in one buffoonish grunt and gasp. Pull out fast; yes, sure, on the belly.

I thought if I kept behaving out of character I'd become someone else.

Did it work? Did I do the right thing?

Here's what I know for sure. Now that the cat's out of the bag, no matter how many layers of anonymity I've sheathed this novel in, you'll know it's you when you read it, dear teacher. And the pain you'll suffer you'll never forget.

That night was the last I saw Brooke. The last I saw Madison.

CHAPTER V

f. scott

F. Scott Fitzgerald died on my street, coincidentally, however many years ago. In the apartment of his lover, Sheilah Graham. 1443 North Hayworth Avenue. A few steps from my front door. He was unemployed, a drunk.

I got out of my car and walked up the driveway toward the back of the property.

Jo was pumping heavy metal and sweating bullets and playing the electric guitar, but it wasn't plugged in. It was late winter and hot like never before. The heatwave that had annihilated the rest of California had finally hit Los Angeles. Jo saw me come in and kept going, head demented like a mannequin's, attached but not connected, eyes fucking juiced. I could smell his hair from where I stood at the threshold of this—what would you call it?—garagehouse. He lived in a detached garage that at one point had been repurposed into a small cabin-like domicile. Bare wood showed everywhere, nails stuck out from corners.

I needed a guy. Since moving from New York, I'd never settled on a guy, and maybe Jo would be my guy. His place was only a five-minute drive down Fountain Avenue toward Hollywood. I got his number from a girl I met on some matchmaking app that pairs users based on respective levels of desperation and/or self-indulgence. Oh, digital romance, to you I owe so many confidences. Her eyebrows looked lifted from a Salvador Dali painting, so material as to seem fake: thick, dark, and never-ending. I honestly hadn't felt that kind of longing since I was twelve and discovered masturbation and also the language of angels. White noise trumpet godspeak. I pursued her relentlessly for her eyebrows—not to mention her two hundred thousand Instagram followers—sending sweet little texts plucked from poems I'd written long ago when I still believed poetry had the power to move people. I swiped right, hard.

After I made all sorts of promises I'd never know how to keep, she agreed to meet. With the help of my riotously gay neighbor, Minh, a four-foot-ten Vietnamese fashion photographer who regularly shot for *Vogue* and whose opinion of trendy cocktail bars I considered more reliable than those of internet dorks obliged to leave reviews on Yelp, I chose what he described was a "lowkey" speakeasy in Hollywood. A mistake, I learned, because immediately upon entering I saw the flamboyant pink leather booths, the assembly of muscular legs in booty shorts, some studded leather vests. Heads turned. I texted Minh, threatening him with violence, and he texted back saying I should come home so he could suck me off like snarling dragon. I turned off my phone and considered leaving. But the eyebrows, I reasoned, and didn't.

The plank above the bar referenced Prohibition-era cocktails, attics of history that our ancestors drank for motives other than their names: Hanky Panky, Gin Rickey, trendy hashtags for millennials to promote a nostalgia unfelt for a time forgotten save for its drinks and *Boardwalk Empire*. I stood at the bar and watched the two fags next to me post a selfie to Instagram, the massive wooden menu featured in the background—#datenight, *click*—and considered the fictional struggles of my seizured generation as opposed to the actual struggles of prior generations during, say, Prohibition, when scrolling through freezeframes of other peoples' posed lives until your head blew up might have gotten your head blown off, certainly your ass kicked, at the very least you'd have been treated as a threat to society, a drain on the collective.

I flatlined my third absinthe-mixed Monkey Gland, which tasted terrible, a color-dyed rendition of a dead frill, and then ordered another while I waited for my date to arrive. It was getting late and seeming more and more likely I'd been made a fool. The waitress, a heartbreakingly young girl who, without the uniform and California's working regulations, would not pass for a day over sixteen, came up to me all by my lonely self; I'd drifted over to the pink gay booth at some point. She asked if I wanted another absinthe "on the house," and boy did that make me feel wonderful. I said thanks, or said nothing at all, and asked for a cigarette. I followed her into the coatroom and ten minutes later came out smoking.

I'd never been fellated inside a public establishment before, I don't think, certainly not a gay establishment, and that it was performed by an employee, questionably underage, on the clock seemed...illegal, like prostitution. Maybe it was. The lights had faded to dim maroons of amniotic shadow, my private corner of the lounge smelling like the inside of a new car upon my return. I drew on the cigarette, did not give one single fuck about smoking indoors, and sat down. Or maybe I passed out. Because when I came to, or remembered where I was, there sat my date in the booth across from me. She was smoking a cigarette, *my* cigarette. How long had she been sitting there? To my surprise she looked dumpier than her photos had suggested, heavier than the disputably anorexic girls I tended to go for. But my god, her eyebrows. Thick schools of unspoken language, every love poem therein contained, slightly mannish but not. She was Israeli. Her name was Dani. I fell in love with the last six inches of her.

"What did you order me to drink?" Dani asked, stubbing the cigarette on a napkin. Just then, the waitress arrived with my absinthe. I said I'd ordered her an absinthe and then ordered another, promising myself I'd not tip for the free drinks, the free fellatio, anxious I'd incur more overdraft fees, god forbid some sort of lawsuit, and winked at either of them.

"I've never done this before," I lied, referring to meeting someone from Tinder or Fucktrust or whatever.

"I have."

Over the next hour the two of us had nothing to say and said as much. If afterward a friend had asked how it went, I wouldn't have been able to report a single fact about Dani other than:

1. She hated absinthe, and

2. She distrusted I was not a homo.

"So what, are you a homo that likes girls?"

My intuition, that departed faculty, suggested this was not going well. I would order many more drinks, not knowing if I'd have enough money on my card to pay for them, and at some point we went outside to smoke her cigarettes (I didn't have a pack, was trying to quit) and talk about the artistic merits of influencer marketing, Dani's new side hustle, but really I just listened to her yawn. Sprawled before us was the fallopian rodeo of old Hollywood smoking vintage out the gutters of hundred-thousand-dollar rides shit-storming down Hollywood Boulevard. Prompted by nothing I pulled her against me, anticipating I don't know what, and to my amazement she sucked my tongue right out of my mouth and moaned like I was inside her. I knew then we'd be friends.

We dated, if that's the word, on and off for a few months. She'd given me Jo's number and now I was at Jo's. I'd come to buy a month's supply of adderall, and maybe some coke, and maybe some molly.

I stepped inside and tried to shut the door when a cat scurried between my legs. I buckled my knees and looked to Jo, but he was busy heavy metaling, so I let the cat go outside. The room was proportionally tiny and set up as a living room. There was a couch, a small table, a television, some books, and a few guitars mounted on the rosewood walls. No windows. Vials and containers of all shapes and sizes lined the bookshelves. It smelled of pasty mustard and weed, ounces of the stuff littered all over the place, bagged but mostly not, ground up and stored in the crevices of opened books, scattered on the table, packed into bowls burned however long ago. The heat was excruciating.

Jo finally acknowledged me and asked if the cat ran out, cursing like I should have known better. I tried to keep it cool and mentioned how I loved the exposed wood, is it just this room or does it extend beyond? He said he slept in the room over there, he nodded, through the bunker.

"It's cool," I said. "Reminds me of my cousin's treehouse when I was little."

"It's not a fucking treehouse."

"Right. It reminds me of a boat, like a cabin in a boat."

"Fuck yea. I fucking love boats, dude. I had a boat when I lived in Boston and it was a sad sad day when I had to get rid of it."

"You had a boat?"

Jo got up to put down his guitar and frowned in a way that looked like a smile, like when a vegan tells you how you can save the world by not eating meat, his unblinking eyes big and glossy. He looked about thirty but it was hard to tell: bearded, of Indian descent, marvelously thin. His shirt on the floor, even with two fans pumping from either side of the room he was dripping like a boxer. I considered shaking what I imagined would be a clammy hand but didn't know if social convention applied when engaging a drug dealer.

"Yeah, I went to school in Boston," he said. "Well, not *in* Boston, but nearby."

If you're from that sort of upbringing, which I am, then you know, as any asshole knows, that "near Boston" means he attended Harvard. The insouciance of his tone inculcated all sorts of judgments I'd be forced to wield and now wielded, I had no choice but to despise him for having gone to a better school than mine. I did not shake his hand. Serendipitously the music stopped playing, the gelatinous chug of guitar and double kickdrum ceasing altogether, which delivered an uncomfortable silence. I felt as though he could hear my thoughts and immediately thought to stop thinking them, just like Mel Gibson in that god-awful chick flick with Helen Hunt, which I'm embarrassed to admit I've seen twice. I made an attempt at speech, opening my mouth and piercing my eyebrows as if in deep contemplation, superficially demonstrating an attitude of mastery over a world of conversational topics to choose from, capable of synthesizing any such-and-such impression of whatever into communicable language simple enough for this dickhead to chew on—just give me a subject, or better yet *don't*, I came for one thing, buddy—suggesting ever so slightly that both Harvard and drug dealers were beneath me, that the pairing of the two was sad and hilarious. But failing to organize anything intelligible, I gave up and said, "I don't know," even though Jo had said nothing that would elicit a response. He farted into one of the fans and rubbed the sweat from his arms against his thighs, limbs flipflopping like fish quickening to suffocate.

"Jesus," he said and did it again.

I too started to wipe myself and said something unoriginal about the heat, something pathetic like, "It's a scorcher out there!"

The smell of mustard. The farting fans. I wanted to die. I've failed, I thought, I can't even buy drugs from a drug addict. My drug dealer is smarter than me. All is referent to failure. I'll just turn out the door and leave.

"What do you need?" he said, thank god. "Here, take a seat. Relax."

I sat down on the couch and pulled myself together, whatever that meant, and told him what I wanted. "A month's supply of adderall. And maybe some coke. And maybe some molly."

"A month's supply. How much do you weigh?"

"I don't see how that's relevant."

"I'll eyeball it."

Jo walked to the back corner of the room housing all the drugs and started opening cannisters, juggling items. On the coffee table directly in front of me, his phone made a loud dinging sound, the blue light flashing. He asked if I knew Dani, the girl who told me to contact him—my *girlfriend*, one might say, although I'd never say it.

"Yes. In fact she's waiting for me now." A complete lie.

He ignored me, or didn't hear, his attention elsewhere; really though, he looked like he was just staring off into space. The phone dinged again, the blue light flashing. I told him we had dinner reservations in about twenty minutes at SoHo House, somewhere I'd never be able to afford, but he didn't flinch at the trendy namedrop. Hatred swelled in my biceps, my knuckles, my molars. He said he'd known Dani for years, she called him all the time. This was perplexing because she never had any money; now I understood why.

How did we meet, he asked, and immediately I regretted telling him.

"Really? Man, I'm just tired of being the initiator," he said suddenly, heatedly, with a vulnerability that only best friends share. Shocked, I was certain he would elaborate and made no effort to encourage him to. "It's like, okay, equal rights, feminism, whatever that means. Women should be doing half the work. Are they? I don't know. Maybe they are and I'm not interesting." He walked toward me but carried no drugs and my heart sank. "But gender politics is all the rage right now, and while I firmly agree with the core issues involved, I'm not convinced that the contemporary discourse makes any goddamn sense whatsoever."

I reached for my back pocket and offered him a cigarette as he sat down next to me.

"No, man, I don't smoke," he said, which made me hate him for making me hate myself for being addicted. I promised myself I would quit at the first of the month.

But now the predicament: was I permitted to smoke or not? I opened the pack of American Spirits and put the cigarette to my lips with a nonchalance that invited Jo's refusal should he want to ruin this for me and let it hang there almost like a point of fashion when—

"FUCK," he said, jolting from the couch like the revolution of death I'd been waiting for, practically screaming, "SERIOUSLY, man. FUCK. I mean, I WOULD say that I'm a feminist were it not for the fact that I don't think that word refers to anything constructive anymore."

I picked up the cigarette from the floor, along with my pride, his sudden histrionics having dropped me to my knees, and imitated listening while I inspected whether the drop had rendered the cigarette unsmokable. It hadn't. I raised my eyebrows and tilted my head, again bringing the cigarette to my lips, nonverbally suggesting I was going to smoke it if it was cool with him. Was it?

"For example, this hyperbolic MeToo rape talk," he said, ignoring my good manners. "Yes, rape is a huge issue. Let's not trivialize it by trying to define it so loosely as 'woman sort of doesn't want it, guy is a little pushy' and then drops it is *attempted rape* for fuck's sake." I did not like where this was going. "Because no, it's not. That's taking advantage of the stereotype that women are *not* in control while men *are* in control *and* need to read women perfectly at all times."

"Fucking identity politics," I said, having no idea what it meant, and reiterated all the drugs I needed, how the maître d' at Soho House was always a cunt about timing, and did he mind if I have a quick smoke while I waited? He said he was on it and blatantly failed to acknowledge my request. The phone made another dinging sound, Jo turned to look. Fuck everything, I thought, jamming the cigarette in my mouth. I flicked the lighter until the smoke burned blue, sucked the log like his mother, and waited for my drug dealer to put a gun to my head and end this sorry delusion.

Would you believe me if I told you that the room shook? Just flat out erupted. The screaming of grown men, drums hammering at impossible speeds, guitars blazing like plane engine turbines. Hell stacked hell. So loud you couldn't hear my bitch shriek. I hit the ground hard, my hands clenched over my head like a war pose.

"Oh shit. My bad, dude!" Jo shouted over the music, fumbling with his phone. "Fucking technology." The room went silent. "Damn, that shit gets loud! You need a hand, comrade?"

I was on the floor, possibly in the fetal position, as Jo helped me to my feet.

"Do you know what I mean though?" he said, crouching alongside me.

"—No," I said, relieved to still have my life, my precious face, feeling its actuality as I nursed the cigarette. Smoke seething out my nose.

"Rarely have my go-for-its failed, but sometimes they have. Was I being rapey in either of those scenarios?"

"What?" I said, hyperventilating. "What scenarios?"

"Was one instance more rapey than another on the basis of the outcome? When the woman initiates is *she* being rapey?" I thought of Heather. "I mean, really, I'm not saying we need a national dialogue on how much it sucks as a man to be expected to approach women while simultaneously being expected to know that you should *NOT* approach. But—fuck," he said, looking defeated, "it's just so confusing." He sat down on the couch and didn't offer me a seat.

The phone dinged again. Fuck it, I thought, this is never going to happen. I was halfway out the door when from under the couch Jo pulled out a mirrored platter. On it was a mountain of coke, and I mean a *mountain*, a few lines already divided and canalled away from the motherload. Jo did a line and offered me the metal straw. "To fortify the relationship, man."

You know you're addicted when every problem in your wasted life promises to retreat forever if just for one sniff, like a virus experiencing itself will never crave to be cured.

"Well. Just to be polite."

"It's really good shit."

It was.

"I'm just saying," he went on, unfortunately, "maybe the shriller voices, the types that always end up dominating the conversation, need to be more visibly reined in by more moderate voices because it ends up coming across as this oddly entitled princess talk that makes shit more confusing."

I sat down next to him as if this were our lifelong ritual and railed another line without asking permission, which only in retrospect seemed questionable. I grabbed his sweaty disgusting shoulder, winced as if I too were suffering a similar angst—which wasn't exactly untrue; our issues with sexual predation seemed to stem from comparable, albeit contrasting, experiences—and searched for something profound to shut him up and, ruffling my hair, found it. "It's like a huge metagame of the very social dance we're supposedly critiquing," I said. "Self-victimization is a drug, man. It's addicting."

"Yes!" Jo said, jumping up to high-five me, which he completely whiffed. "Yes. You fucking get it. *YES.*" He did a line and passed me the straw and said he'd get those bagged up for me. I felt like Goliath before he met David and took out the cash and threw it on the table next to *The Untethered Soul*, which in that moment I did not find ironic. I opened the book at random and read:

> You're sitting on a planet spinning around in the middle of absolutely nowhere. You're floating in empty space in a universe that goes on forever. If you have to be here, at least be happy and enjoy the experience. You're going to die anyway.

I closed the book and watched Jo reach onto a shelf and grab a giant white pharmaceutical container that called to mind protein powder, the size of the thing. He took several small plastic baggies from a dispenser and proceeded back to his "office," the couch, to do the math and apportioning. His phone dinged again and I imagined watching myself pick it up and throw it out the window that didn't exist.

"Now, granted, it's important to understand that my critique of the other extreme, the Chauvinist Bro, is much harsher," he said, but I'd stopped listening. For the next however many minutes I nodded along and smoked a cigarette and rocked the guitar, unplugged, punking away, eyes fucking juiced, which Jo encouraged with tremendous enthusiasm. Finally he handed me five little baggies with six adderalls each, two baggies of mdma, and two baggies of this epic coke that had me tolerating hanging out with a drug dealer with self-esteem issues for what must have been an hour. When I heard him say, "Of course it's very possible I've been letting this get to my head in recent months because of my solitude," I knew it was time to go.

Without transition I opened the door, paused dramatically as if in the audition room right after the asshole says, "Whenever you're ready," and, one more ding sounding from the phone on the table, my final cue, having no idea what I'm going to say, said, "Essentially you're suggesting that women need to take a more proactive role in courting. Insofar as we are equal, women often take for granted the skewed social dynamic resulting from an outmoded patriarchal system in which men always made the advances and weave it unknowingly into their feminist discourse, which precludes a clear avenue toward resolution." Before he could jump in, I raised my finger, took a deep breath, and said, amazed, as if watching myself from an imaginary podium, "This is a controversial opinion since the contemporary discourse essentially claims, firstly, that no problems that appear to be male originated may be solved with greater female responsibility and, secondly, that men are inherently incapable of meaningful critique against feminist perspectives. As I see it, you're now forced into a deadlock where you neither feel comfortable advancing your position nor acting upon it, and your best course appears to be one of self-improvement—hence *The Untethered Soul*—so you can better determine the proactiveness of women at large while working on attracting one to you who vibrates at, shall we say," I powwowed a pill straight down my throat, "a higher frequency. You know, someone more on your level."

No more words. He shook his head with the sort of disbelieving pride you see from a parent watching his child take its first steps, those big beady eyes marveling me in their ecstasy, imagining a plurality of futures of equitable plausibility all equally exciting. He told me to wait a minute, libidinal charge in the air, and after rummaging under the sofa came up with another baggie of coke and slapped my hand with it.

"This one's on me," he said, gripping me and declaring himself my "guy," from here on out he's got all the fun I'll ever need, just reach out whenever, we should hang out regardless, and for a brief moment I thought he might hug me. I felt exhausted.

Outside inspired imaginations of sweatshops and steamships, the nightdark air doing its best impression of an oven. Not humid, just humiliating. The stillness of it. You could hear the crickets panting. Sweat rolled down my face like somebody else's tears as I made my way along the brick walkway toward the driveway. Another guy stood in front of the garagehouse or whatever you'd call it; he looked bored, slowly orbiting a spot he'd picked on the ground as if no one were watching. I'm watching you, my friend, am still watching you, and will we meet one day in heaven, tender and blessed? I guessed Russian but that could have been my imagination at work, movies I'd seen. He was tall and stylish, wearing a leather jacket and black boots, his slicked blond hair coming undone in just the right places, handsomely disheveled. He might have been the best-looking man I'd ever seen. Immediately I felt inferior and gave him *the nod*, intimating subtly that I would slit his throat with indiscriminate butchery if given the chance. He pretended not to notice, thereby exacerbating the complex I'd created between us. That I now had to walk past him to exit was nauseating and in a moment of unforgivable weakness I blurted out that it was good to see him, which didn't make any sense. He nodded, sort of, or raised his eyebrows, or turned his back to me and lit a cigarette. I had the audacity to ask him for one when we both heard Jo shout through the wall that it was cool to come inside. He walked past me and even in his absence I could smell his cologne incubating prettily in the stillborn night exhaust.

I picked up what he'd tossed, the smart orange burning hot, a menthol, I discovered, and laughed at his offensive cigarette preference. Feeling better about myself, I took a drag, which triggered a latent excitement about the transaction I'd just executed. Inadvertently and undetected, I'd given Jo a hundred dollars less than we'd agreed upon, if "agreed upon" was the appropriate phrase: his prices were a fucking rip-off, the markup close to three hundred percent the going rate. I wanted to kill him for that fact, but somehow this was sweeter. Upon exiting, in my right pant pocket I found the original five twenties I'd been carrying before stopping at the bank to get more cash, which I'd thrown on Jo's table. That my mistake was authentic nullified any sort of remorse or fear for having wronged Jo. If I were found out my apology would resonate organically, stupid word, from a dormant honesty the texture of which I'd previously rubbed upon the original moment of discovery. The script already memorized, my lines learned, some improvisational pandering, a loaded pause or two—I *am* an actor after all, god help me—of course he'd understand, he'd be sorry he brought it up. Or fuck him, I thought, I'll just keep the money and never see him again.

But I knew I was incapable of such heroics.

I fingered the baggies, massaged each pill, and thought about all the mornings I'd never see and all the nights I'd pretend to be enveloped by my "work," fastidiously writing away like a man possessed, the author of my seizured generation, a millennial identity crisis boiling rapidly to unprecedented sublimation.

Laptop open, Microsoft Word in view but never in focus—I'd much prefer to rabbit hole the Mets or UFOs—the same boring pages staring at me from the novel I submitted my senior year, an embarrassingly stylized neoclassical bildungsroman absent of trajectory, rewritten countless times with no clearer end in sight. I could recite the opening lines in my sleep: "The sun was brilliant, having risen at a quarter past six and shining well into noon through the sliver of window the bedroom curtain failed to reach." I wanted to be like Fitzgerald. I'd start chapters in big voice, with poignant self-reflective lessons to be learned later on. I experimented with form like in *Paradise*. I lifted lines from *Gatsby*: "In my younger and more vulnerable years my father gave me some advice that I've been turning over in my mind ever since" became "Father once told me that a man is only as good as his word until he forgets and then he's only as good as his imagination." This is how I'll hook you with Book II, I'd tell myself.

Who the hell are *you* and where is Book I?

That I was a fraud was undeniable, I didn't care to pretend otherwise. That I understood myself to be the living protagonist of my own fiction and structured my life according to the densely progressive present of my future writing—what you are reading now—toward an undefinable tragedy, hailing to almighty "experience" as pardonable cause for multiple addictions, stupid word, and neglecting to correct myself as I was—an imposter of imagination in a story I could not and cared not to finish—was something else entirely: post-fraudulent, or…completely fucked.

I opened the plastic seal of one of the little baggies, put the oblong-shaped pill into my mouth, chewed the chemical burn, and swallowed.

Walking down the long driveway, I saw lights from inside and stopped and stared blatantly into the brightly lit dining room window of whoever's house this was, the lord property to Jo's vassal, the menthol hanging from my lips, coolly smoking another man's trash. Blood brothers for life, trash-flavored trash. A man and woman in their late forties, Caucasian, whom I took to be husband and wife, sat at a rectangular wooden table. Before them stood a much older couple, whom I suspected to be the man's parents. It was the way he looked at his elder, how only a son could judge his father. The younger couple sat on the same side of the table and were holding or petting each other's hands; it was done lovingly but more so out of a mutually distracted rhythm of concern, their expressions staid and unflinching, drained of something vital, eyes pinned to the man's father. The father looked old and sorry for being old, some sort of glassjaw trepidation in the way he bent his head; it was what he did not say, I told myself. The smoke puffed from my lips and I did not care to hide. I stood looking on.

The father held a glass in his right hand that my imagination filled with scotch. As he spoke he never once took his eyes from the glass nor did he sip from it. Just held it and waddled its contents. His wife, the mother, kept shifting her attention from the father to their son to the son's wife, her old leathered elbows jutting out worriedly as she gripped her hands for mercy before her very chest, as if molding forgotten prayers into the shape of a heart to replace the one that had just suddenly burst. I imagined the worst: the father was about to die, imminently. Cancer of the lungs. Cancer of the head. Dishes sat stacked at the far end of the table, wine glasses and water glasses and some other glasses scattered on the table. It was about eight o'clock and I hadn't eaten, some food still on the plates. How would it taste knowing you'd soon be dead? I imagined I was inside the room situated at the right hand of the father, a member of the family, imagined I was his son learning that my father was soon to die, furious he couldn't look me in the eye as he told me. Some sort of secret shared between us the culprit of his shame. An affair, multiple affairs. I had a half-brother that Mom didn't know about, a lowlife scumbag burnout who still depended on Dad for money. Mom's going to find out about the bastard in a matter of seconds. The jig's up.

Then I realized *I* was the fictional bastard looking on from afar, perpetually tucked away behind a mirrored window, a symptom of delusion, voyeur to my symptom.

Here I am, I would say as I stepped through the front door of my false family, I wouldn't even knock, and from the shadow's edge of their conceited pity I'd bow my head and channel Auden, reciting by heart the stories I'd have written had my life been good. Then I'd crush an oblong-shaped pill in my mouth and swallow.

It was time to go.

I made my way toward the bottom of the driveway when an expensive-looking silver Audi peeled in and nearly took me out if not for the obnoxious blue high beams spotting me through the dark. Hip-hop reverberated from inside the car and literally shook the ground, the heavy bass. Outside smelled like weed, but that couldn't be possible, I thought, the windows are sealed. I walked by and squinted but only saw my clownish refraction in the tinted black window. I kept walking and noticed two more cars, a Range Rover and something else, parked in the street, headlights on. None had been there when I'd arrived. The orchestra of engines hummed in unison something like the refrain of a horror film, a prelude to storming, the headlights on and unforgiving and not asking for forgiveness. I checked the time and couldn't believe it: what had seemed like days was merely a '90s sitcom, twenty-five minutes at most.

I wondered what the family of the dying man thought of the party organizing outside their home, and at such a tragic moment no less. Then I considered how often this sort of gathering must occur, perhaps every night, and could they really believe that Jo had so many friends? What was the family's relationship to Jo anyway, I wondered—they obviously weren't related, was he just renting? Then it struck me: the family must be in on it. How could anyone be so ignorant and an operation of such rapid turnover go unnoticed? I thought about the prices Jo charges, Harvard, my hatred of vegans, Heather raping me, Madison, the whole holier-than-thou shtick about cigarettes, and, outraged, considered vandalizing their home in protest, my imagination going wild over how I'd pull off such a heist, anger swelling, until I forgot the exactness of each of their faces and could no longer imagine a family of actual individuals but only the virtual concept of "Family," some vaguely American commercial rendering crowded around the dinner table, holographic blips of my own uninvited family members entering and absorbing into the gross collection, and I no longer cared what they thought of Jo or his feeders or me and let them die away to where they'd always been.

I squinted at the headlights of another car pulling up before me. The menthol had extinguished some time ago or fallen from my fingers, I don't know—doubly departed. I walked across the street and opened the door of my shitty Mazda, now leased, which I could barely afford given my hard stand against service jobs, and got in. I sat for a few seconds and considered eating all the drugs and driving fuck-all-to-hell toward Santa Monica, where my mother lived and nearly died in a lie I told a sweet lady to avoid getting arrested for DUI on my third day in LA, a glimmer of hope then, now entropy; I could zoom straight off the Pier like a videogame. I wanted to call Mom and apologize for putting her life in hypothetical jeopardy, even through this blurred wall of fiction. Really though, I wanted her to know that while I wasn't suicidal, I wasn't *not* suicidal either; I couldn't imagine living like this much longer, would chew off my very own head to get out of this trap. I pulled out my phone, which spilled the baggies from my pocket, and used the screen's blue light to find them on the car mat. I let out one pathetic sob, the world shrinking to its horrible conclusion, when a ding sounded, a text message. It was Jo. I owed him a hundred bucks, did I already leave?

I drove away and saw in the rearview mirror a Mercedes pull in, replacing me.

X X X

Dani and her eyebrows came over that night and together we shared a baggie of mdma.

Dani was your prototypical gypsy girl found hanging around Venice, the only partner (besides Madison) with whom I'd ever considered using a condom, but didn't. Since I didn't have it in me to travel to the westside, it was common to find us strolling up and down Hayworth Avenue together, soft breeze at sundown, unseasonably warm winter, gawking at what looked like wedding trees shedding bouquets of purple vaginal trinkets. "These flowers look like pussies," she'd say, giggling, a running joke that never got old. Through the pleasant sound of sprinklers we'd hear the blue hum of television coming from inside the small hut apartment across the way, see the same woman with the same Chihuahua approaching, and in the same way of making salutations Dani would bend down on one knee to kiss the pup hello, talk about her basset hound Roger, who had his own Instagram account—revolutionary at the time—how I *had* to come to her place for once and meet him, and sure, sure, meanwhile I'm just swaying on my heels, too high to speak, too pleased to care, mesmerized by the green cacti, the dragon flowers, the white bungalow apartments that looked like tiny homes of Disney characters. Stoned, very stoned, on this particular starless evening, I gripped Dani's hand and raised her from the ground and never mind the dog, I beckoned and kissed her with a tenderness that emotes better in writing. Do you know what I mean if I say that suddenly the world was pure romance, an exhilarating pattern of inexhaustible fascination? It was like seeing the solution before the problem and not the other way around. In that moment I wanted to sound my barbaric yawp over the roofs of Los Angeles, to write volumes upon volumes of what cannot be held, to incubate the minds of so many readers with novel ideas that might drive those brave enough to produce such great works of art they'll weep with confusion over what came over them, what came out of them, not knowing from whence it came, but of them, some, perhaps you, dear reader, will trace their genius back to first reading me, to the relationship we developed; for as long as it's taken me to write, I hope this moment may live on in your memory, hope you're experiencing now what I was experiencing then: that everyone should be in on the secret. It was during these vintage LA moments, so high you'd forget your life was a tragedy dressed in sarcasm, that I'd allow myself to appreciate living in Los Angeles—yes, even West Hollywood, so gay you had no choice but to shave your chest—that I'd consider myself fortunate to be alive and sniffing this wild dream, imagine holding a needle that sewed together in happy coordination life's every thread of circumstance into a rich tapestry of meaning, call it destiny, that could only ever result in fame.

"Can you believe F. Scott Fitzgerald died on my street?" I asked as we walked, stopping in front of 1443 North Hayworth, thinking back to when I seriously imagined myself capable of displacing him. I was already older than his most productive years. "Maybe it's a sign."

"Who is F. Scott?" she asked.

Did I mention that Dani was an Instagram model? This too was of interest to me. These were the early days of social media when a hairdresser who styled the heads of a few reality stars could quickly build a sizable audience of her own: nearly two hundred thousand followers, *real* humans, I was assured. How was this possible?

Because, as I was soon to learn, users of these new social platforms proved desperate enough to compulsively monitor the lives of other more attractive people who weren't exactly famous (because fame is too alienating) but weren't *not* famous either (because we need something to aspire to). Thus emerged "social influencers," the cultural phenomenon we're now all too familiar with, of whom there were relatively few at the time. Whereas previous generations of self-made celebrities commonly attracted the attention of the masses by creating or delivering *something* of cultural significance, influencers managed to capture the world's attention by focusing exclusively on themselves. Utterly brilliant for their utter lack of brilliance, these people created a multi-hundred-billion-dollar industry by contributing absolutely nothing of value.

Thus I found myself a selfie of the artist as a young man leeching the followings of woke sluts who timed the talentless technology of social media perfectly. I knew absolutely nothing about the *INDUSTRY* but was confident that chasing auditions without credentialed representation was as useful as doing copious amounts of drugs and *not* going to auditions—a method I'd tested vigorously. Since Harrison and Woolf would not respond to my emails, nor return my calls, and had informed security I was banned from WME's Beverly Hills office, I was becoming more and more frightened that my gambit for instant fame was losing merit. This left me in a rather unenviable position: I was committed to a year-long lease in West Hollywood with no lifelines, no connections, no money to speak of, no humility to *ever* consider service jobs, and absolutely no desire to act. My being an actor was, after all, an act to establish myself as an author—*The Author* of an entire generation, no less—a tall order for any mortal man, let alone one who wasn't writing.

Clearly I was fucked up, deeply lost.

I didn't so much think this as avoid it, snorting lines of mdma while Dani jerked me off. With her free hand she worked on building my Instagram account. Growing my followers would be easy, she said, she just had to promote me on her account to get things going. "Like three to five times a day," said seriously. While "we" did this, she explained, she'd simultaneously orchestrate an aggressive photo-posting campaign on my account, also three to five times a day. "I can shoot you on my iPhone. Some old school filters will make you look dark and mysterious and fucking hot," she said. "You can add your poetry or whatever in the captions," the only strand of this ploy that got me excited. "No one will read it, obviously, but you'll come across as all artsy and shit," piquing my interest. "That will distinguish you from all the other *boring* models out there." I agreed, unclear if she was poking fun at herself. "We'll batch shooting and get a week's worth of content done in a day. It'll be super dope. And now we'll have so many photos of us!" said with a genuine enthusiasm that made me nervous. She kissed me and I flinched, maybe from all the molly.

But she wasn't done.

To round out our "growth strategy," embarrassing concept, Dani would kickstart "share-for-share" groups she'd find on "underground apps" like KIK, where five to ten accounts would aggressively cross-promote each other's posts all day long; this would create a false sense of virality among their followers that would manufacture real virality through the algorithm. "One of my friends, she's a fitness model, a badass bitch, taught me how to do it," Dani said. "It's how I've grown my account so fast. I'm already on my phone all day, it's so easy."

I felt disturbed if not horrified. This all seemed like a tremendous waste of time, not to mention a preposterous amount of work, if you could call it that. Plus, I hated social media, had never engaged with it for personal use (the only thing less appealing than watching other people stage their "authentic" lives was staging my own), and felt immortal resistance to promoting myself in a public-facing way. I imagined Holden Caufield, or a hallucination of Holden, setting fire to the digital grid of phonies.

But I wanted *not* to hate social media, I reminded myself, drawing heavily from the joint Dani and I shared. Harrison *did* say, "In today's landscape, having a strong presence on social media is *essential.*" Exposing yourself would be a big personal breakthrough, I thought, the molly definitely kicking in—a necessary step in your professional development. The Author needs to be *seen.*

Dani agreed. "Why wouldn't you? Don't be gay. You can make a shit ton of money. Brands are already reaching out to me to wear their shit. It's so dumb, it's great."

I considered the opportunity. I'd be trading my last shred of self-respect for imitative popularity, something I'd always wanted but would never dare admit. But at what cost?

I'd have to consume *many* more drugs to feel comfortable with this plan, I reasoned.

"Pass me the coke," I said. She did. "I'm in," bumping the right nostril. "Under one condition," bumping the left. "You'll have to handle everything for me. I am...incapable."

"That's what I've been saying!"

She seemed so happy she started bouncing on the bed like a toddler, which reminded me of that time in middle school I kicked Doug off my trampoline and broke his ankle.

"Come down here," I snapped like my insane mother. Dani fell on the mattress and got on all fours. "Fine, let's do it," I said and offered to pay for her services with the money I'd soon have thanks to the robbery I'm about to narrate, but Dani said no, that's what girlfriends are for. I had no idea what she was talking about and didn't say anything more on the matter.

On my bed we watched the neighbors across the alleyway fuck like rabbits, my bedroom window seeing into theirs. The mystery unveiled. No more mysteries. Clumsy half-naked Latinos gripping at the throat. He wore baggy red basketball shorts pulled down to his knees and she didn't take off her shirt. He had her from behind and right as he was about to come, I shouted out the window, "I'm pregnant!" and closed the blinds and hid under the covers. After two bottles of wine Dani and I might've fucked as well. I can imagine our legs falling off the mattress like we had to have it. Sick little puppies. In bed that girl suffered nothing; her father would be so proud.

Later I determined that watching a man come was the saddest thing I'd ever seen and asked Dani her thoughts on the matter, but she was already asleep. So I got up, dressed, and knocked on Scott's door to see what he was doing. I entered and found him sitting on his bed holding a gun.

Or maybe it didn't happen like that.

Maybe Dani hadn't come over and that was a different night and I've got it confused. So many windows to see through. Maybe I came home from Jo's and walked straight into Scott's room and found him holding a handgun, hunched over his mattress inspecting its configuration. A live gun. Two cartons of bullets and the black rubber briefcase opened next to him. He took a drag from the joint dangling in his lips and with an affectation of machismo uncharacteristic of his personality waved me over from the threshold of his doorway, where I stood stupefied, staring at my roommate holding a gun. Presumably *his* gun.

It's likely I then proceeded to launch into a longwinded and abusive tirade against Scott, intentionally infusing the situation—he had seemingly purchased a death weapon without consulting me—with hyperbolic severity, as if my politics demanded it, as if I claimed allegiance to any set of politics ever, and out of obligation to convention, to the Left's tireless efforts to increase gun control and tame the havoc violence maiming our nation's spirit and safety, not to mention my deranged sense of superiority over the apartment, I called to Scott's attention that it was *this* type of behavior that made him a shitty roommate, no less a menace to society, which I'd no longer tolerate.

I grabbed the gun from him, gripping the cool metal barrel, fingering its grooves, and immediately felt my cock move. I'd never seen a live gun before, let alone held one. With tremendous energy Scott leapt forward and reached for the gun, shouting with clownish horror, "No!" while in jest I pointed it to the side of my head and then pointblank at his face. I nearly pulled the trigger when he swarmed me. Backtracking into the hall, I ran wildly through the apartment reciting spaghetti-Western zingers, irresponsibly waving the gun and pretending to shoot shadow villains before he tackled me to the floor, locked me in an armbar, and punched my shoulder until it turned purple. I'd never seen him so angry, huge veins milking from his skull, he was practically weeping, trembling and cursing me to places I'd never heard of. I asked why he was crying as I saw him fumbling to lock something on the weapon—the safety, as it were.

"You fucking idiot. You fucking idiot. The gun is loaded. You fucking idiot." Panting, out of breath, crazed. "I was practicing how to load it. You fucking idiot. You fuck." Drool hanging from his lip. Then quiet. When he managed to get to his feet, it seemed like there was nothing left inside, as if he were already dead and now had to deal with maneuvering this tired trap of a body around the apartment. Turtle-like, he shuffled through the living room and into his bedroom. Those were real tears.

The kitchen light went on. I thought I'd be nice and pull a beer from the fridge for Scott. It was so hot I grabbed a second bottle and immediately judged myself for the gluten. The apartment felt as though it was crying, possessing an air of misfortune that for the rest of the night, no, year, would describe every shadow, rattle, and creak.

"The ghost is back," I shouted, but he didn't laugh, and neither did Scott.

Outside beyond the cracked kitchen window I heard Los Angeles on fire, sirens and engines summoning blind dates from imaginary places you'll never know. I took the beers to Scott, ducking under the Mauritian beads through his doorway. He sat at his desk watching a video of a middle-aged man from Middle America, thick goatee coming in hot, holding a gun for reference and talking about guns. "The Glock 19 is a nine-millimeter compact in the Glock family. It is carried daily by law enforcement and military professionals in addition to law-abiding citizens *like you*," the man said, pointing at me through the screen. I put the beer in front of Scott and tasted mine. He paused the video and didn't look up.

"I don't think we should be roommates any longer," he said.

"Go on."

"You could have killed me."

"I could have killed me too."

"Fuck you."

"I didn't know."

"Yeah, you didn't know."

"Yeah, I didn't know," I said, annoyed at the game I was encouraging. "Why the fuck do you have a gun?"

"For when shit hits the fan," he said and took a swig. "Which will be soon."

"What are you talking about?" I asked, judging him.

"There's going to be a revolution," he said, judging me.

I made a face suggesting, I hoped, the shape of skepticism, or my opinion that he was a lunatic, or my attitude that his decision to purchase a gun was congruous with his behavior in general, which tended toward obligatory hastiness and was inspired by an extreme-Leftist rebelliousness in the name of revolution, which, he failed to see, was as conformist as the institutions he condemned and as predictable as the media he despised. Naturally he'd call me a dick for thinking that of him, and I'd call him a dick for thinking he thought he had to.

Scott was the sort of person who, despite having a fridge stocked with premium groceries, would go dumpster diving as an act of "protest," fabricating empathy for those less fortunate by salvaging expired trash and later fabricating an eagerness to eat it; the sort of person who had the nerve to regularly say things like, "Couch-surfing and rotating guests are part of my fluid mobility and restless curiosity"; the sort of person who'd buy a gun and then claim he was too poor to buy groceries—hence the dumpster diving. That he came from affluence (his father, a retired surgeon turned day trader, drove a fucking Bentley) all but negated every effort he made to convince otherwise. A self-projected paradox, predictably unpredictable, he was my best friend, I guess, or something like my best friend. We lived together our senior year and a few years later moved to Los Angeles at the same time for independent reasons, figuring we'd join forces and relive the "glory days" I'd never experienced.

What else can I say about Scott? Like many of our former peers in their mid-twenties, recent graduates from compelling institutions, he'd convinced himself that more school was the answer to having no answer to the question: What are you going to do now? He enrolled at UCLA and committed to its five-year anthropology PhD program, hoping, I guess, that the titular trophy would award him options he didn't currently enjoy. It didn't make any sense: he'd never taken an anthropology class in college, and I frequently made it a point to call out the bankruptcy of his pursuit. Fuck you, he'd say, at least stalling is better than choosing the dead-fucking-wrong path. How's acting going? And back and forth we'd go, lamenting the tragedy made of our wasted lives.

Amused, I threw Scott's portion of the drugs on his desk.

"Oh, word! Did you meet the new dealer? How was he?"

"Dude, the guy's a fucking basket—Wait, shut the fuck up. Tell me why you have a gun."

"I already said why, you heinous dick. Shit's going to hit the fan before there's any sort of overhaul to policy. We're going to force the overhaul. Now I'm ready."

"Who is we?"

"California is all dried up, man. The ice caps are melting. Step outside and tell me global warming isn't real."

"Not again."

"Water is going to be the most valuable commodity in the twenty-first century. I'm telling you we live in a bubble. But it's all dried up and soon we the people," said without irony, "will need to drink."

I attempted to make a joke about how, come Judgment Day, I'll expect to find him alongside "the people" outside our front door, weapons in hand thanks to his dad's credit card, conniving to raid his former friend's fresh groceries from Trader Joe's—but while considering how to connect the joke back to dumpster diving, I just gave up and said I was going to write, an empty gesture, and turned to leave.

"Wait a second!" he yelled, holding up a baggie, dangling it like a precious jewel. "Don't you want to test drive?"

He knew I was powerless.

Powder poured on the paperback cover of *The Road*. I took out my license and chopped the mdma and coke into four beige-chalked lines and rolled up one of the twenties I still owed Jo and railed two of them. The hot chemical sneeze shot so fast up my nasal cavity I could feel it in my feet. Boy was I juiced. Oh boy, oh boy, oh boy. I tossed Scott the twenty and kissed his forehead and said I was sorry for nearly killing him. He did the other two lines and said if he had to die by fire he'd want me shooting. And that's about when we both heard me say we should rob Jo.

"Who is Jo?"

"The drug dealer."

"We should rob the drug dealer," he said mockingly.

"We should rob Jo."

"Rob Jo, the drug dealer."

"Stop that."

"I can't see how robbing him is going to contribute to any sort of social justice."

"That's because you didn't have to suffer through paying for this shit."

I was kidding, of course, or was I? I proceeded to explain how Jo operates by himself completely alone, citing his many feeders in luxury vehicles, my umbilical soulmate the Russian, and the four other cars as proof. Not to mention the deluge of text messages.

"I was there for twenty minutes and his phone practically blew up."

Scott looked at me doubtfully. "What's with you always wanting to rob service providers? First the sushi delivery guy and now the drug dealer."

"Okay, fuck you, we were high and it's a good idea. The sushi guy carries a fat wad of cash. All we'd need to do is have him deliver to another apartment in our building, someone we knew wasn't home, and when he rang the bell, we'd clock him from behind. No one would know. There aren't any cameras in this shithole. Obviously we'd wear masks."

Scott dismissed me and defensively I admitted I'd never done anything like armed robbery before, had never even shoplifted, but I was serious all the same. We had a gun now, all we had to do was show it. As I kept talking I triggered something like a latent note of inspiration, the thyroid of creativity I'd been searching for my entire life. I realized I was not kidding, not kidding at all—a critical turning point in this stage of my development. I thought, quite seriously:

To solve our money problems, which were such that we had no money at all (Scott was a PhD student "pursuing music," pretending he didn't come from wealth, and I was an abject failure pretending to be an artist), we should rob Jo.

"I will not be reduced to waiting tables and tending bar, goddamnit! This is a good idea," I saw myself say as I gazed at my reflection in the window before me.

"Stop looking at yourself," Scott said. "You're full of shit. You'd never go through with it, you'd pussy out as soon as we got there."

"I have never in my life been more serious than I am right now," I said, grabbing his chest, twisting his shirt. "These are the facts: he's a drug dealer, he's hooked on everything he's selling, and he's got no protection." All wild speculation. "How's that sound to you?" Before he could respond, I gripped his shoulder with a strength that surprised even me and said, "The idiot went to Harvard and is now a drug dealer. How much more fucked can you get?"

Scott flinched, looked a little frightened. "But robbing the guy? I—"

"Don't interrupt me!" I slapped him. "I'm on a roll! On any given night he could have up to three to five grand on him, and that's not even considering whatever he made the night before." An unfounded projection, entirely made up. "You think he pops into the bank on his way to yoga in the park every morning? No. Fuck no. And the best part is," I said, holding both of Scott's cheeks in my balmy moisturized hands, "he can't call the cops because guess what? *He's a motherfucking drug dealer.* Fuck this guy, he charges to the moon, and he's got it coming. And fuck you too, I haven't even mentioned all the drugs."

"All the drugs," he repeated.

"Which we can sell."

"Which we can sell."

"For thousands."

"Thousands?"

"Tens of it."

"What are you on right now?"

It was then that I remembered, assuming it was the same night, all I'd ingested in the last few hours and felt surprised because I'd forgotten I'd taken anything at all—which meant the coke or molly must have kicked the adderall into overdrive. I was ecstatic. I threw the rest of the drugs stashed in my pocket on the desk. Teeth on iceskates, I told him about the treasure of adderall, the mountain of coke, the containers of prescription drugs, the impossible quantities of weed, which, pointing to the joint I had found on Scott's desk and was now lighting, was much better than this shit. From his laptop Scott turned on and turned up the track he said he'd been working on "all day," which I sincerely doubted but was in no mood to argue. He asked what I thought and I said it was the best thing I'd ever heard, that it defied description, the contradiction of African tribal chants and warehouse synth pop forensically dissecting the other into an angular call and response of neon green and maroon. Wow, he said. Wow is right. I asked what he called it and he said Wet Hot Friendship and that changed everything. Then, in a moment of euphoric genius, I texted Jo and asked what else he had. Five minutes later I got a response:

"He's got molly, coke, xanax, and a higher milligram version of adderall too," I said, reading the text, bobbing my head, grinding on Scott.

"Get the fuck off me!" He pushed me away.

"Which he must have forgotten to tell me about! That's crazy, you should have SEEN the size of the bottle, man. Oh shit!" I read on. "He can get acid on demand as well! Just let him know!"

"Fucking demand the acid."

"Why? Acid is cheap. We won't make any money from it."

"I *want* it."

"Fine, okay!" I said and texted Jo. I typed something like how sorry I was for the money mixup, it was an honest mistake, I loved him forever. Then danced around the room and picked up the gun and said, "Let's just go now. The guy is hopped up on so much coke he's out of his fucking mind. He's talking about raping women and masturbation. I'm talking therapy, man, he needs a therapist. He's broken. He's sweating like a sweatshirt in a sweatshop, he's sweating like a J.Lo music video. It'll be so easy, man. Let's just go."

"Hold on a minute."

"This is an act of revolution!"

"Shut the fuck up and give me the gun. If we're really going to do this then we have to be smart." He paused. "Give me an adderall."

"Take them all," I said, throwing him the baggie. "We're practically rich!"

And then took one myself.

X X X

Twilight hour, the early-morning yesterday.

Together on his bed. Heroes of fortune literally swimming in it. Double-fisted. The money on the mattress, more than I'd ever seen. I guessed fifty thousand but Scott counted twenty. Well, what the hell, I said, I'll take twenty.

Help me with this, he said.

Tell me how you remember it, I want to write it down. No, don't ever mention it. No one can know. We can't tell a soul. I'll swallow the gun.

Fuck it. We'll figure this shit out tomorrow, he said. We could have upwards of another fifty grand here, shit maybe more, if we sell the drugs. We'll need a distributor. He handed me a pill. Take it, I'm having one.

Where's the money? Where's the money? You sounded like you'd done it before! I know, I know, the fucking cat, man. I know. Look, I *know*! I went a little overboard.

It's fine, I think.

Let's talk about the cat, just for a second. Does it make me less marketable?

Here, do you want some vicodin?

I know you think I'm some sort of monster or something but I fucking hate cats, dude, I'm allergic to them. Blame Jo, man. That fucking—like he wouldn't even say a fucking word. And don't get me started with you!

Take one, it will help.

Fuck off.

What?

I don't like downers.

Why?

Bad experience. Bad bad bad.

It's not a downer.

What is it?

It's like contained laughter and it's always funny but only you know it.

Oh.

It's like, you know when you're on coke and it feels like you're superman and you can repel bullets and they just fly off your chest? This is like you're superman but you absorb the bullets and pass them through undeterred.

Cool.

Like instead of rushing to say everything you already know the right thing to say.

I get it.

Yeah.

Well, give me one.

The morning sun had forgotten itself or taken the day off and nighttime would last forever. Dark. Still dark. The type of dark you thought would never come. In my room I pulled the covers and found Dani asleep. Asleep no more. Where have I been, she asked. Where? I kissed her forehead and scooched her over and went to bed a millionaire.

X X X

What I haven't mentioned, what I can't admit, was the girl. On the other side of the garage, through the bunker, was a girl. She was no more than five, maybe six. She sat cross-legged on a simple ugly mattress, the sheets bunched around her. One pillow. There were no feathers but I saw angel wings. In her lap she cradled a stuffed animal, a silly cat. But I couldn't. I couldn't look. The passive voice I prefer to remain, passive to the consequence of whatever happens. That the girl saw me was clear but what she saw was not. A glass of water. Can I have? Please don't, I said. The realer you are, the farther into fiction I sink. I dream of her.

"Of course all life is a process of breaking down, but the blows that do the dramatic side of the work—the big sudden blows that come, or seem to come, from outside—the ones you remember and blame things on and, in moments of weakness, tell your friends about, don't show their effect all at once. There is another sort of blow that comes from within—that you don't feel until it's too late to do anything about it, until you realize with finality that in some regard you will never be as good a man again."

F. Scott. Died a loser but forever my hero.

CHAPTER VI

meta lit

I opened the Microsoft Word document and began reading the nascent draft of a story I must have written in New York sometime before I'd burned my brains out, a story I had no memory of writing.

It began with a car crash. My narrator was late for something, although in this early draft I hadn't established what that was. The woman whose car he hit was a high school teacher. She'd just found out her husband was cheating on her with a student, a ponytailed junior who routinely came to their house for tutoring. The previous afternoon the teacher headed home early and saw it all—not just the infidelity, but the illusion that her life was good. Shattered, she'd spent the whole night driving up and down the 405 hoping she'd fall asleep at the wheel. Now she was headed to the Getty, determined to jump off one of its peripheral cliffs.

Enter my narrator. Driving well above the speed limit and directly up her ass, he slams the brakes but not in time and rearends her bumper, inadvertently saving the teacher's life. They pull over to the side of the highway and their ensuing exchange reminds her that she has a reason to live; he sparks in her a dormant sexual charge long forgotten. Or maybe it was revenge.

The day before I'd found an old external hard drive which, clicking through a bunch of random folders, one named *meta lit*, led me to the Word document now opened before me. Was it pride I experienced while absorbing my narrator? Who was he? From whose dream? As I read the prose, I could identify what can only be described as my voice, or style, which was confusing because as far as I was concerned, I had no voice, had no style. The trashed novel I wrote in college read like Fitzgerald parodying Hemingway; it might've passed as satire if it first passed as legible. But this newer writing was different. It was fast, aggressive, funny, irreverent. It made me feel dirty, my only reaction to "Art" that feels authentic. What's more, I liked the direction the story was taking, although I couldn't tell you where it was going nor how it would end. But I had the thought: *I might have the beginning of a novel here.*

It was now or never—I simply had to write. But first I had to walk the dog.

Roger the basset hound looked at me with skepticism in his big droopy eyes. Without thinking I swallowed an adderall and anticipated it hitting by the time I returned.

Roger pissed and shat—I didn't have a bag!—and was a good boy.

Back at my desk I clicked into the Word document, intending to advance the story, but knew I wouldn't be able to write in such a messy room. First things first, I decided to make my bed. Feeling satisfied, *dare I say* accomplished, I realized I hadn't given the apartment a proper cleaning in months, maybe ever, and was certain the concept had never once crossed Scott's mind. I found Windex under the kitchen sink, grabbed a fat roll of paper towels, and proceeded to spray and wipe every exposed surface in my bedroom: the desk, the bed, the nightstand, the dresser, the room's many mirrors, the bookshelf, the tops of books where dust had coagulated into thick gooey mass, the bathroom sink, the toilet bowl, both its seat and rotten underbelly having collected so many dry tears of vagrant piss, crumpling and tossing dozens of sheets of paper towel into the wastebasket and discarding its effects into the kitchen trashcan. Pleased, I popped another adderall (I'd commit to sobriety tomorrow) and found myself eagerly if not manically wiping clean the surfaces of every piece of furniture throughout the entire apartment, and now with rabid exuberance I knew I'd have to mop every speck of each room's floor no matter how long it would take, no matter the sacrifice, to give myself the satisfaction of finishing the job, any job, even if it was the *wrong* job—and did.

Thus the day went: instead of rising at 6:30 a.m. and meditating as the sun drew pink and orange glints over blue smudge, then writing undisturbed until lunch when I'd walk two miles up Nichols Canyon Road, projecting myself into futures capable of possessing any one of its modern Mediterranean palaces, and jogging back home through Runyon Canyon, then writing until early dinner when I'd take another walk before settling down for the night to read a physical book, one of the dozens I'd bought on Amazon and never touched, successfully cycling one entire day without addressing my phone, a first in ages, a monumental feat, and prepare myself to repeat the same "perfect day" tomorrow—I woke up at 8:00 a.m. to Dani asking doggy favors, fell back asleep until 9:00 or 9:30 a.m., forgot to meditate, broke sobriety and took drugs while blindly probing social media on my new iPhone, which I did not keep turned off and in the top right drawer of the living room's red hutch to remove temptation, walked Roger, took more drugs, occupied more phone time while obsessing over my number of followers, supposed real people Dani had duped into following me with whom I shared no connection and offered nothing more than soft pornography and distressed designer art (whitewashed poetry, blackhole feelings, staged spontaneity: the world to come), and cleaned my apartment as if *MTV Cribs* was coming to document my awesome life.

But—if I can say—the apartment looked immaculate. Just spectacular. Notice the shimmer of sunlight through the living room blinds reflecting off the polished hardwood floors like train tracks. I checked my watch: more productive in half a day than I'd been all year. I lit a candle and stood proudly over my empire of ridiculous results.

Now I was ready to write, but then came one of those moments.

I was sitting at my bedroom desk when Scott opened the door. "Oh, you're home."

"Come here. What the fuck is this smell?"

"I cleaned."

"No."

I ran into the living room. "Roger!" The little guy had shat and pissed everywhere. Oh my god, what had he done. "What have you done!"

I cleaned the mess, walked Roger, and texted Dani that her dog was in the proverbial doghouse since I had no doghouse. She said she'd make it up to me at dinner tonight, come meet her in Venice. I sat at my desk, sulking, chewing myself out for once again backsliding into a relationship I wanted nothing to do with but was terrified to end given her ties to Jo. Really though, I was only pretending to sulk about Dani because I was actually sulking about my failure to write, a defect I could no longer avoid even if I tried, it was staring me in the face.

I opened Microsoft Word and continued to read the nascent draft I'd discovered earlier and half-cringed, half-marveled at my writing—cringing for being affected by my own prose; marveling because in that moment, like many moments, I was dumbstruck that I'd once written anything at all. That I had gave me hope I'd write again. I lit a cigarette and thought it rather bizarre that the car crash mirrored an event that had actually happened on my first trip to Los Angeles, the story that begins this novel. I'd written that first draft, what I was reading now, at least two years before my actual accident as described in what would become "Wet Hot Famous." What could it mean?

Originally I'd been under the influence of Denis Johnson, whom I'd discovered soon after graduation and whose first story in *Jesus' Son* features a car crash. His style had me believe I could write the novel you're reading now. Just like my first reading of *The Sun Also Rises* made me believe I could write the college novel I trashed.

But maybe it was something more mysterious than that. Perhaps the narrator of my story and the voice inside my head shared no distinction, shared the selfsame history, their timelines ultimately converging on the page. Perhaps my fate had been sealed long ago and the only way to break through, so to speak, was to crash the fucking car.

X X X

Later that night, Dani and I sat outside a belligerently trendy vegan restaurant frosted over in distressed white.

Dani was telling me all too proudly about how much weight she'd lost since changing her lifestyle, taking my advice to heart, while I judged out loud the industrial ceilings, bronze pipes, brass casings, exposed wood, many hearths, falling plants, blah, blah, blah—I guess it really was a beautiful space. It looked like a horticultural arts and crafts shop, or a yogic nursery school; no, it looked like Tinkerbell's home: touched but untouched. Under the flutter of tiny lights and so many candles, we finished two bottles of vegan wine and after dinner—Dani offered to pay, and I let her—went to a roving party behind Abbott Kinney. A number of shops, connected by their shared alleyway, conspired to keep their backdoors open and free wine flowing while partygoers tried on vintage hats, vintage leather jackets, vintage T-shirts, and other vintage finds in front of vintage mirrors. There was no ocean breeze on this night but the ocean curlicued its infinite dance not far away.

Inside Dani's hair salon—notice its chic white walls, the woven dream catchers dangling from overhead, the black-and-white photographs of wolves in the wild, of digital wolves in the digital wild—I drank whatever was offered and held my breath while Dani held my hand. Then came the catcalls, lewd misogynistic offerings made by a woman dressed in black. It was the salon owner, Dani's boss; Dani wailed. This woman might have been beautiful, she wore a cowboy hat and sunglasses under the dark sparkle of night and, I had to hand it to her, she made it look good.

She reminded me of a lover I'd have in the future about whom, through the privilege of authorship, I can now reminisce: it was the way she smelled my neck, obscene gesture, like some sort of animal summoning; how she'd inhale my scent like a shewolf and whisper silent demands in a language I'd never understand—no one has tried to love me more, and still it wasn't enough—and that's what the salon owner was doing now, sniffing me up with feral perspicacity, her big diamond eyes peeking over silver rims of tilted shades, fine wine aged to acid. I felt something like the vague shape of thrill, maybe its skeleton, but no thrill. This woman, early forties I guessed, was Dani's mentor; she had helped Dani get her shit together. Dani hadn't gone to college, had barely completed high school, and with few prospects had vagabonded her way through life before embracing her tonsorial talent.

"I remember this gypsy girl hanging around the boardwalk, cozying up to the street artists. Her drawings were good," the salon owner said. "But she needed some direction, more like a good spanking!" They both laughed onanistically and rubbed each other's elbows.

Dani was no academic but knew how to survive, which was more than I could say for myself, and quickly learned how to game the social media algorithm I never cared to understand; in less than a year she'd amassed over one hundred thousand followers. This caught the attention of the salon owner, whose name I missed, who leveraged Dani's chops, and soon the salon was featured on some E! television program where circus clowns dressed as middle-aged women abused the insane privileges of our extravagant economy. I often wondered how cockapoos and designer dogs descended from wolves, it seemed impossible, but then I saw the women featured on this show and understood the power of compounding degeneration.

The salon owner loved Dani, and Dani seemed to love spending time with me, which at this stage of my development, before there was any coattail to ride, I couldn't understand.

After reading my horoscope and nodding her approval, the salon owner said, "So you're the actor," to which I said, "No, I'm the writer," and Dani laughed and said, "No, you're not." I lit a cigarette and smiled with my eyebrows, wishing them both dead. Then the salon owner asked if we'd heard about the afterparty at the famous artist's house overlooking the Canal. No? It was a sex party. Did we want to join?

(You know where this is going.)

I'd never been to a sex party before, didn't know what to expect, but I imagined one endless hall of rooms featuring rich and chiseled patrons cloaked in Venetian masks riding each other like teenage Balrogs, a Dionysian rollercoaster.

As we entered the elaborate three-story beach bungalow turned modern glass chalet, its angular perforated façade, I pressed the door shut behind me, blocking the view from the street, embarrassed someone might see inside. Dim lights. Puffy terracotta tiled floors. Tall windows stretched to the ceiling made of wooden beams and carved arches. The beautiful architectural details presented the hallway and living room area as an old Spanish chapel. It only took one glance to see that inside the home looked absolutely nothing like you'd expect from outside. Even more disorienting, each room had its own distinct style: the bathroom was classically Victorian, adorned with pewter tub and toilet and hanging chandelier; the dining room sparkled like a freshly polished 1950s diner, peak Americana, notice the red leather booths, sky blue tables, black-and-white checkered floors; the kitchen appeared as if you'd entered an Amazonian jungle, the island counter chiseled from a massive tree stump, huge swaths of plants and vines covering the walls, the appliances lined in Bengal bamboo, the sink spouting like a waterfall, the ceiling made of slate to mimic the sky. Walking through the house I couldn't stop rubbing my eyes, I thought I was losing my mind. Perhaps I was already tripping—but no, that hadn't happened yet. It was as if aliens had picked from an elaborate architectural menu with no care for tradition or consistency.

I continued through some stray hallway and stopped to regard the huge canvases designed to look like concrete slabs that hung on the walls: muscled splatters of acrylic, spray paint, charcoal. Each canvas slab told an episode of some greater narrative featuring a zoo of wild beasts of all shapes and sizes dwarfing man, or the suggestion of man no matter how disembodied, in prayer, hands up to the gods. Imagine cave paintings had been found in a pre-historic or, better yet, post-apocalyptic subway station—that's what I was viewing. I felt high, I felt high not at all. If I had any money, I thought, I'd ask to buy one, and years later I did; in fact I'm staring at it now: maroon-black and navy hunt of paw trails, a blood march of humanoid skeletons feasting on themselves: *Beast Be Kind*. Throughout the extraterrestrial home's eclectic and synesthetic rooms, dozens of paintings like these slabs were hanging on the walls or leaning up against them from the floors. Hundreds of sculptures of all shapes and sizes populated the shelves. I touched the football-sized bronze statue of a dolphin, then a butterfly, this here mantis, an octopus, and I couldn't tell what this one was—

"That's a remnant orb from a spacecraft," the posh chick with hair under her armpits said about the object held in my hand. "You can feel its pulse if you hold it to your heart." I nodded and slowly stepped away.

A few dozen or so people stood at the edges of the vast living room area; large canvas drop cloths covered the floor and the room's furniture. Nude women smacked themselves with body paint and rolled around on ancient scroll-like parchment paper while others painted portraits of what looked like, well, "This is my pussy," the small-breasted revolutionary with crooked teeth said. A few heroic-sized men with long beards and even longer—never mind—stood dazing about, completely naked, staring at nothing.

The owner of the home, the famous artist, was an older man in the last quarter of life; his mustache was exhilarating, a touch of Dali, a touch of Teddy Roosevelt. He and his wife, much younger, probably mid-forties, were naked in the jungle kitchen and kissed me hello. It was kind of endearing, kind of repulsive. They told us to make ourselves comfortable and suggested we disrobe; there were bins for our possessions located in the backyard and upstairs where the "matrimony" was taking place (that's a direct quote). They passed around an easter basket filled with cannabis edibles, mdma, and chocolate-covered psilocybin mushrooms while talking about simulacra and simulation and how all artists are merely chasing the wind. I grabbed a handful of drugs and ate them without discrimination. Dani told me to slow down while the artist's wife laughed; they were rolling hard, she said, purring glossolalial yumyums, as she and the artist touched each other and expressed arousal while we watched.

Upstairs on the spacious veranda were mattresses and daybeds and lounge chairs. Boxes of condoms. Despite the generous burning of incense, the smell was vigorous, like that of a gym over a holiday weekend. Small groups of humans, mostly malnourished or bowlegged, middle-aged, had chosen their sections to make love, which was what everyone was calling it. This made me uneasy, only I couldn't tell you why. Inside each band of orgiers—and that's what it was, live performance art, sort of like this novel—certain select persons would have their turn while the others encircled and held tight the "container" (kill me), caressing each other and talking about god knows what. Whatever music was playing from the surround-sound speakers was swallowed by the cacophony of moans and grunts and slapping thuds. There was nothing sexy about this, nothing sexy at all. Without transition Dani began to kiss me passionately, then included the salon owner, and the three of us sort of fell onto an enormous beanbag. "Isn't she beautiful?" Dani said about her mentor, but before I could respond the two of them helped each other's tops off and laughed with excitement while embracing. The salon owner asked if I was ready and, boy, what a question. The whole thing felt staged, like middle-school truth or dare—everyone knew how the game would go—only kissing had been exchanged for coitus. Intense shame spread throughout my body as I lurched to take off my pants; I wasn't sure if I'd be able to perform.

Look, I know what you're thinking: Do people really live like this?

I can assure you they do; they're just not your friends. Most people hate being alive and will try anything to make it more compelling. Or maybe I'm merely speaking for myself.

That's why you could find me lying naked on a beanbag kissing the breasts of a salon owner, her leathered nipples betraying her disguise as someone younger, with whom I felt a kinship, while Dani, hunched over, tried to fellate me. Only I couldn't get it up. And here's what I really meant about the shame. Because in that moment, clearly tripping off the twisted energy of our environment, not to mention whatever stacking of psychedelics she'd consumed, Dani told me she had hooked up with Scott.

"What!" I practically shouted, pulling back her hair, which she seemed to enjoy. "When?"

"I've been waiting to tell you. We had a moment and I went with it."

Part of me was furious. The other part relieved. Now I had an excuse for my flaccid embarrassment. But the furious part was in overdrive. I wanted the salon owner to disappear, to let me self-destruct like the petulant child I was, but she'd already gone off with some other guy who looked like Val Kilmer's Jim Morrison, only taller and built like a wide receiver. Suddenly I felt a terrible longing. He was astonishingly beautiful, and his size, my god, as thick as a can of red bull. I hated him as I watched the salon owner mount him, searching for holy matrimony, her hand between her legs, and, finding it, exhale obnoxiously. Intense jealousy coursed throughout my body.

But actually it was intense nausea. The mushroom cocktail mixed with Dani's admission was making me dizzy, but it was more like dizzy had become the world, as if my inner voice was outside of me. I was experiencing reality as a sine wave of dark energy as opposed to a collection of particles suggesting solidity, experiencing language as the aftermath of a collision of random shapes with no organizing principle as opposed to parts of speech signifying meaning. Dani snapped me out of it. How many did I have? How many what? Mushrooms! I ate four eggs, I think, I don't know; I was so hungry after dinner, I need protein! But I was only supposed to have one! She looked shocked if a little scared. Then the ceiling caved in to reveal the cyclone helix of some other world, a dystopic sound bath of hornets buzzing. Now I was completely outside my body, or I had no body at all; that a "body" is something one "has" occurred to me (bodiless) as hilarious. Do you know what I mean if I say it was like remembering myself in the womb, a fetus feeling itself come alive? What I'm failing to describe was like that but in reverse: I was dying, this much was obvious, only death was not the conclusion but the encore, Dani the only thing tethering me to this world. I knew I was in for it.

I'm sorry, she said, my mind snapping back into coherence, her words no longer sounding like hot foaming soap. I thought it'd turn you on. Turn me on! Fuck you, you never pay me attention. I do so much for you. I wish you looked at me the way Scott does. What are you saying? Maybe I can be the apartment slave. Was she being serious? Was this really happening? I'm way too serious, she said, I never have any fun. This was bad, I determined, my soft cock pathetic in my freezing hand. I was smaller than I'd ever been. Existential dysfunction. See the audience exsibilate the poor actor, who is not a writer; off the stage he goes.

Warning. There is the possibility of life-threatening rising seawater washing inland. Winds of one-hundred-fifty or more miles per hour will come from the southwest then the west. Be prepared to evacuate. The night sky shone over us, the twirling incense, the beads of rustic necklaces bouncing into puddled crescendos, hypnotic tremulants of sad spirits speaking through the fairy godmothers of Venice. My life was on the cusp of never getting worse.

X X X

I found myself puked up on a large mattress, catatonic, surrounded by faces expressing concern. They looked like they'd been praying over me, like I'd been raised from the dead. I knew I had battled these people earlier, each in some meaningful way, and lost. The room was dark, dimly lit by glowing orbs spread about the windowsills. But that was just my eyes buzzing. Upon closer inspection, they were merely candles, some pink crystals, burning incense. Dani leaned over and said to the others, "He's awake."

"What happened?"

"Dude, you freaked the fuck out," Scott said. "Completely lost your shit."

Then Dani: "First you were grabbing Camila and…"

"It's not important," the artist's wife said. "You had a bad trip."

"Scott!" I yelled, trying to move; I could not. "Why the fuck are you here? Who is Camila?"

"I'm Camila," the salon owner said, peering over me. White silk pajamas, loving smile. "You know that."

"I'm so…" I said but didn't know how to finish the thought. I looked at Scott, felt intense anger. He and Dani were holding hands.

"My boy. You saw the truth of the world and the truth is frightening," the man said. It was the artist. His mustache.

"You're safe. Stay still. Here," the artist's wife offered the glass of water. "Sip slowly."

"Tell me what happened," I shouted, casper rays of light crawling on the walls.

The artist's wife touched my shoulder and with her free hand raised her finger to her lips. "Mindful now. We're still in ceremony," she said.

The others looked at each other awkwardly. No one wanted to speak first.

"It's not important," the artist said. "We gave you something earlier, something potent, to calm you down. You're here now. Everyone's gone home."

"You were a king at war, like a lion on the Discovery Channel," Dani said, "attacking a heard of water—"

"It's h-e-r-d," I said. "Not h-e-a-r-d."

"Buffalo," Camila said.

"What?"

"Never mind," I said, confused why I was seeing Dani's words flash as text messages before my eyes.

"Those paintings were old and meaningless anyway," the artist said.

"You kept asking, 'Where's the script? Where's the script?'" Scott said.

"Did you two fuck?" I asked, dexterity returning, language possible. Peeking under the sheets I saw I was wearing white linens, clothes I'd not come with, clothes I'd never wear in normal life. Their choices betrayed them.

"Where's the script?" the artist repeated and massaged his chin.

"Like we're in a movie and the whole thing is staged," Scott said.

"Isn't that obvious?" I said, exasperated by everyone talking over each other.

The artist laughed. "Oh now. That's rich." He stroked my hair. I froze in terror. Where had his hands been tonight?

"Why don't the three of us talk about it later?" Dani said. "I have feelings for you both."

"I can't deny the connection, man," Scott said.

"Slow down," I said to everyone and no one. "You're making it difficult for my readers."

"Have you ever read 'On Exactitude in Science' by Jorge Luis Borges?" the artist asked.

"No. But I've always wanted to read him. I've bought his books on Amazon—"

"You really should," Scott said. "Start with *Labyrinths*."

I gave him a glance suggesting murder.

"May I?" the artist asked, placing his thumb on the center of my brow, my "third eye" he or Dani or anyone at such a gathering might say, although I'd never say it, and proceeded to tell me about Borges' very short story about a great empire that created a map replica of its geography that was so detailed it eventually became as large as the empire itself. Lifelike, the map would be expanded and deleted as the empire conquered or lost territory. Years later when the empire crumbled the map was all that remained. The artist said he'd read the story as a young man on a *bus*, pronouncing the word, but only that word, in French, right before he and his friends tripped balls at the Louvre. It was his first time taking psychedelics. After months apprenticing with his mentor in Amsterdam, the young artist successfully smuggled magic mushrooms into Paris in his socks. The four young lads met at a nearby café, ate the mushrooms, drank coffee, smoked cigarettes, and went off to have an adventure. Soon after entering the Louvre, the young artist quickly grew convinced, almost psychotically so, that his life was a movie, the false film of reality so utterly clear that he couldn't help but spend the next few hours trying to persuade his fellow actors—that is, every guest at the Louvre, including the security guards—to break character and stop pretending. "We don't have to pretend anymore!" he told the museum attendees, he told me. Predictably, he was asked to leave. Outside, although the famous glass pyramid hadn't yet been built, he remembers the majestic courtyard as if it had. Having lost his friends, the young artist made his way to the café, where the four of them had planned to meet in case they were separated or *expelled*, the artist said, laughing. He spent the rest of the day feverishly drawing on dozens of napkins image after image of a snake eating its own tail, or was it a snake with two heads eating themselves?

The artist composed himself for a moment, realizing he'd opened up too many threads. What was the point he'd originally intended to make? Why was his thumb on my forehead? These were important questions. "I apologize," he said, shaking it off. "I think back to that moment and I portal into the meta-awareness of my life changing. Because in the back of that café, amongst espresso saucers and bottles of beer and so many napkins, I found my inner eye."

"Inner eye?"

His thumb seemed to sear through my skull, it felt like my brain was orgasming. Immediately I began to spiral. I shut my eyes.

"Breathe through it," I heard the artist's wife say.

"He's going back in," I heard Scott say, as if on the far side of a tunnel.

"Do not laugh," I heard Dani say, which made me love her, "he needs this," which made me wonder what she meant.

"As a young artist I suffered from paralyzing self-consciousness, an intense fear of my ego," the artist said. He was speaking like a prayer, as if delivering a sermon to our small group gathered on the massive bed. "I was afraid that my desire to become an artist was a plea for attention, that I was screaming for attention. But, as I learned, this was the fear talking. What I want to say, no matter how cliché it sounds, is that an artist's job is to wear himself inside out, to connect with that visceral thing that's part hate, part love, all survival, man's primordial language, the only thing that's to be trusted. It's inside each of us. Some call it intuition, some an antenna, I call it my inner eye. It sees the truth from the inside out."

"Like a snake eating itself," I said.

"Or a snake with two heads eating each other."

The artist removed his thumb, and my eyes must have rolled into the back of my head because all I could hear was my voice saying, "Wow, oh wow, oh wow," as time and space dripped away like circles in water that got bigger, not smaller, into waves. I felt nauseous.

"Here," the artist's wife said, touching the glass, reminding me of the water. "Drink," she said, guiding it to my lips. I sipped from the glass and passed it back, not knowing how, having no proprioception of my hands.

"It sees the truth, but to fully come alive it must share the truth. Do you understand?"

No one said anything.

"At any rate I got off easy that day," the artist continued. I leaned back into the pillow, his wife guiding me down softly. "In fact it was a great day. There in the café I met my first wife, a small American girl with curly blond hair. She was curious about the chaos of napkins before me. 'You must be a great artist,' she said. She seemed so unassuming, but in truth she was a sorceress."

"Like you," the artist's wife interjected, speaking to Dani, who stoically meditated into the acknowledgment.

"This woman had answers to questions I'd been asking my entire life," the artist said. "She showed me the answers inside myself, helped me understand that certain answers can only be derived or summoned by the dedication of a good woman. I loved her so very much. She had my first child, and she was taken too soon." The artist's current wife rubbed his shoulder and kissed behind his ear. "My love," he said. "If not for Leighann," he continued addressing us, "I wouldn't be sitting here with you nice people. She's why I came to America, was what led to my discovery, my notoriety. To you, my love," he said to his wife. "Well then, where was I?" His wife handed him the glass of water from which he drank and handed back. "Yes, of course. This is what I meant to share all along. Back at the Louvre, my friend was taken by security and offered to the police and thrown in jail." The artist laughed, pinching the bridge of his nose. "My friend," he said, snorting, "my friend seemingly decided to rewrite the day's script as a heist film! I am serious. He took off his shirt, wrapped it around his head like a mask, and attempted to steal the *Mona Lisa*. Can you imagine? Of course he was immediately sacked by the guards, well before he could figure how to detach the frame from the wall. I share this with you," he said to me, and directly to me, "because I know what you mean about the script, how tripping on mushrooms can make the world seem like a movie in which everything is staged. But here's where the story gets trippy, very trippy indeed, I'm still unclear to this day what really happened. Because, if you can believe it, my friend was a professional actor who at the time had just finished shooting a film in which he played a thief who'd orchestrated an historic heist from the Louvre. In my memory, I can't distinguish what actually occurred from what I saw in the film."

"No," I said.

"Yes," he said.

"Maybe you were an actor in the heist movie too," Scott interjected.

"Or maybe you never went to the Louvre that day," I said. "Maybe you watched the film and the drugs made you think it was real."

The artist blinked in a way to dispel shock. "It's not impossible," he said, appearing moved if not conflicted. Finally he smiled at his wife then the rest of us on the bed and said, "This is fun."

"What happened to your two other friends?" Camila asked.

"No one knows. I never saw them again. Darling," he said to his wife, "can you please put on some tea?"

"Yes, we can all go downstairs in a minute. Let's give her a bit more rest." She was petting Dani, who had drifted to sleep curled in the artist's wife's lap.

"You have a magic touch," Camila said to the artist's wife. "It must be a motherly thing. Dani didn't know her mom. This is the first time I've seen her submissive."

Scott looked at me, smirking as if to say it wasn't the first time *he'd* seen her submissive. I determined I'd substitute the water in his bong back home for bleach.

"Thank you," the artist's wife said to Camila. "This is my gift. It's why we host these events. Modern life is robbed of ceremonies. This is our contribution," she smiled.

"Thank you," the artist said to his wife. "Thank you, all of you, for joining. For contributing. What happened tonight was sacred in its own way. You are moving through a darkness," he said to me, "do not be afraid." He paused. "Allow me to return back to Borges, if you'll entertain me." The others sat looking on and nodded. "The philosopher Jean Baudrillard was a good friend. I don't suppose you know his work, but Jean believed we live inside the map of Empire that Borges wrote about. The map is a simulation of reality where the citizens of Empire spend their lives ensuring their reality is properly circumscribed and detailed by the mapmakers. And so it is reality, not the map, that is crumbling away from disuse."

"The medicine shows you the fiction that our lives have become," his wife said.

"The medicine?" I asked.

"The mushrooms," the artist, his wife, and Camila said in unison.

"Society has replaced reality with symbols and signs, simulacra that are not mediations of reality nor even deceptive mediations of reality since they are not based in a reality nor do they hide a reality, they simply hide that nothing like reality is relevant to our current understanding of our lives," the artist said.

"When you eat the medicine, it can be intensely uncomfortable to see the world for what it is. Intensely uncomfortable," the artist's wife said. "But it is necessary for where you are going."

"Where am I going?" I asked.

"Only you can know. You must draw your own map," the artist said.

"Please drink," his wife said, tipping the glass of water to my mouth; I was sweating. "The medicine is known to call forth traumas, those first memories or ideas that expose the illusion of reality. What did you see that caused you so much torment?"

"When you say torment."

"Forget what I said," she repositioned herself. "Please, share."

It was in that moment I remembered smacking Jim Morrison's doppelganger over the head with a huge canvas painting. I more or less shook it off.

"I don't know how to say it."

"Try."

How can I say that none of this is real unless I write it down? Impossible to capture, the ambition is a nightmare. It's easier to project you, dear reader, than to look you, bad actor, in the face. Here on the page, this is what I dream about. This is me narrating my fiction as I live it. This is me in the glass shower masturbating in public. I can dress down, ante up, go out however I like.

No one told you to read it.

CHAPTER VII

health coach

I was so beat up pretending to be an actor and a writer, a parody of the artist as a young man in a virtual wasteland or whatever the fuck this is, that I never finished telling you about the robbery.

Well, what to say? We took everything I'd witnessed, imagined, and more. Tubes and containers and cases of prescription pills stocked on shelves, inside cardboard boxes and cartoon lunchboxes, hidden under the couch; adderall, more adderall, uppers, downers, zingers, doozies; ziplock bags, freezer bags, countless tiny baggies filled with white powder, beige powder, yellow powder, coke, molly, whatever; two huge bricks of marijuana rolled in clear sandwich wrapping, fastened by rubber bands; sheets of acid shoddily coated like floral mandala jigsaws sheathed in aluminum foil; huge green pills as long as my pinky (I dream of you). I imagined what the crusaders felt a million years ago, the untold treasures before them. Hellish liquidation. Scott aimed the gun while I seized the drugs. He did the talking since Jo knew my voice. "Where's the money?" he kept saying as I packed our ancient L.L.Bean backpacks with narcotics and designer drugs. One, two, three, four to the brim. It must have been a hundred times he said, "Where's the money? I know you've got the money in here. Where the fuck is it?" But Jo couldn't keep his head up, couldn't stay out of his dreams. He just sat on the couch slouched over himself, his brown body exposed in tighty-whities, waddling back and forth, humming, almost in prayer. He appeared to be crying—was he crying before we'd arrived?—his eyes big and sick-looking like he'd seen something far more terrifying than we could ever deliver. In his lap he held an orange striped cat.

"Where's the money?" Scott barked. "You've got ten seconds to start talking." He widened his stance, tightened his grip of the Glock 19. Trigger pull, 5.5 pounds of hard American. I went over to Jo's desk in the corner, opened some drawers, and found what must have been two grand in twenties and fifties. I showed Scott the loot and nodded let's get the hell out of here.

"No! I know there's a shoebox in here," he said. "Every drug dealer keeps his money in a shoebox." He had this deranged look in his eyes that even the pink ski mask could not hide. I didn't know what he was talking about, he sounded insane. Then Jo started cooing an aboriginal mantra, nonsense syllables, and my face began to itch. The room was a furnace. There was a tap at the door then another at the side panels, and Scott whipped around like a car flipping into a parking spot with the gun in his hand. What the fuck, it was only the sprinkler! We really need to go, I motioned. Jo wheezed, laughing like he knew we were frauds. I touched Scott's shoulder, gave him the thumb.

"Inside this garage, there is a shoebox," he said, "and inside the shoebox there is a fuckton of money. And that money is mine." Scott's aggression was worrying, paternal. He took Jo's face in his gloved hand and pistol-whipped him like Jenny, my babysitter, hot on my ass. I nearly screamed. Poor Jo, a sad pile of discard, one hand clutching his face, the other hand clutching the cat tightly against his meatless chest.

Scott jammed the gun into Jo's temple. "Where's the money? Where's the shoebox?"

Then Jo came alive, his huge marble eyes. "That's a good question!" he said, looking psychotic. "I don't even know what money is!"

"You have ten seconds to remember," Scott said, clicking the gun. I was impressed; I guess he *had* been practicing. "Ten!"

"What the hell are you doing?" I whispered. "We're making out like bandits."

"Nine, eight…" Scott counted, ignoring me, a live gun pointed at Jo's head.

"Twelve thousand years ago a comet struck the earth and killed ninety percent of the world's population," Jo said, practically seething. "These were advanced civilizations more powerful than ours, utterly obliterated."

"Seven, six…"

"What are you going to do, shoot him? Come on." I gave him a tug.

"Within the Great Pyramid, inside the King's Chamber, there are five more chambers elevated three hundred and fifty feet above the ground. Each built with granite beams, roof and floor, each beam weighing seventy tons." Jo's laughter was terrifying. "That's ten elephants! And there are hundreds of them! Tell me, how is that possible?"

"Shut the fuck up! Five, four…"

"Violence was not part of the plan," I said, then realized we had no plan.

"No ramp could fit inside. No number of slaves could lift that shit. We think our ancient ancestors were idiot cavemen. What a joke! The ancients knew of abilities we've long forgotten. Psychic powers of the mind. Telekinetic powers. Telepathic powers."

"This is getting weird. Let's get the fuck out of here."

"Three…"

"Time is a flat circle. It's not even real!"

"Stop that! Two…"

"You're making me very uncomfortable."

"Shoot me. Go ahead. It'll just come back to get you too."

"Where's the money!"

"Fucking shoot! My life is worthless anyway. Shoot!"

"I'm telling your parents."

"One and a half…"

"Shoot!"

"I'm leaving."

"This is your final warning."

"Pussy!"

"The shoebox!"

Without thinking I grabbed the gun from Scott and considered, or realized I'd forgotten, all the drugs we'd ingested that night. (Jesus, was this really the *same* night I first met Jo?) We should definitely get out of here, I thought, watching Scott wave his hands "No" like a mental patient, my eyes buzzing like sawblades, some minor part of me alive to discern the precariousness of our situation: Scott edging up against homicide, Jo begging for it, a firearm in my unlicensed hand, illegal drugs in our system, many more in our possession, an intense desire to take off my clothes and dance the night away. This is highly unwise to hang around any longer, I determined, very unsafe—

Only I determined this *after* I'd already committed to expediting our growth strategy by taking possession of the cat. Or shall I say I shot the cat to hell through the cushion crushed against the couch to muffle the sound? Desert dry air in a land with no rain. I wished I had a knife to sever its tail. Like a rabbit's foot, I'd say to curious parties, wearing it around my neck while I wrote beautiful stories like Hemingway in Paris. When the gun went off, Scott hit the deck like a Harlem breakdancer, ducking, swinging, bracing for cover, madness in his movements.

"The shoebox!" I grunted, doing my best impression of Batman, feeling invincible. This was easily the best role I had ever played.

Stunned, Jo pointed to the little cubbyhole above the doorway that led to the back bunker of the garage.

"I always thought *shoebox full of cash* was a literary motif of socioeconomic privation popularized by rappers rather than a literal device of economic transference," I said later in Scott's bedroom after we'd walked home under moonlight morning dancing in each other's arms. Actually, I had to drag Scott out the door and logcarry him down the driveway and order a Lyft with money I did not have, money I'd subsidize with my advance from the robbery. I'll never forget the image of Jo holding his exploded cat as we exited into the dead of night. "I was wrong," I said, removing the Nike shoebox from my high school soccer duffel bag, then the Reebok shoebox.

When I poured the money on Scott's bed, it was more than I'd ever seen. I guessed fifty thousand but Scott counted twenty. Well, what the hell, I'd take twenty.

"We could have upwards of another fifty grand here, shit maybe more, if we sell the drugs," he said. "We'll need a distributor."

Then he handed me a pill and we lived happily ever after.

X X X

It was spring semester and the days got longer and the nights longer still.

Scott had somehow demonstrated he was fit to teach Anthropology 101, a decision endorsed by the UCLA faculty. To say it another way: in pursuit of a PhD he had no intention of completing, in a subject he'd developed no prior competence in, at a reputable institution that costs hundreds of thousands of dollars to attend, in a galaxy exactly like our own, Scott was considered credible to educate over one hundred students about *anthropology* and in some minor though likely forgettable way make an impact on each of their futures.

The escalation of his academic responsibilities sent Scott spiraling. How many times would I have to listen to him say he was going to quit academia altogether while pacing our newly furnished living room, promising no one but for the lithograph of the cow jumping over the moon that he was ready to double down as a music producer and tour Europe like he'd always dreamed? The first step to letting go is admitting words are powerless.

That was right about when Dani intervened. Together, she and Scott conjured their brilliant plan to sell the stolen drugs, deflating in value by the day thanks to my "bad habit," to his students—a turning point in my development. My *big break*, one might say. Only not the kind of break I envisioned when

I'd torched my life and moved to Los Angeles nearly a year ago. Given my direct access to bounteous quantities of highly addictive drugs, I could now empathize with some of my favorite artists who'd killed themselves from overdosing—only I was no hero, no great artist, no Hemingway, no Hendrix, no Heath, no headstone whatsoever, the clock keeps ticking: nothing.

It was during this phase that I too began to spiral, not out of control but out of a world in which the idea of control is understood. Words lost meaning—but not only words, my belief in words. Not only was I not writing, I no longer related to myself as someone who aspired to write. The former ambition that had underscored my sense of self and reality's range of wild possibilities—though at times depressing, though at times disorienting—at least contained a semblance of hope and futurity that were no longer present. Experience had compressed into a flat band without emotion. Call it an identity crisis, but that would presuppose the subject's ability to self-identify. I had no words to describe myself, to describe my experience of self. I hadn't transcended language and its pure potentiality, I'd descended into an autistic void removed from language and meaning altogether.

At first this was freeing. Untethered, I no longer felt compelled nor restricted by previous desires or lifelines. My past was mine but was no longer possessed by an idea of me, an idea of mine. I held no attachments and thus could move about freely with no internal compass, no set of organizing principles. Since my relationship with myself no longer obtained the subjunctive, I could participate in the ridiculous reality unfolding before me in the same way I could watch a movie, feel loosely interested in its protagonist and his pursuits, and just as easily turn it off without experiencing any sense of loss. At the same time, however, I felt, if that's the word, a limitless emptiness, like I'd been reborn as a lab rat in a lightless closet forever dark. World of no world. Only amphetamines could unlock the door.

That's why you could find me at the back of Intro to Culture and Society every Tuesday, Ray Bans on, gifting sample baggies to jocks and sorority babes and stoners, anyone who took Scott's class to fulfill a requirement, which was basically everyone. "Text 310-749-4955 with 'looking for teaching gigs' for the best party supplies this side of the 405," I'd hear myself say, so drugged I'd lost the ability to narrate my own experience.

To fulfill our orders, Scott cut a side deal with Dani, whom he claimed he loved, which drove me insane. It's not that I felt anything for the girl—I mean, sure, I thought she was attractive, our short-lived tryst dug the death cold out of me, the sex a portal riant and screaming with desire; it wasn't love, it was fuck, and it was good—it's that Scott had no problem potentially compromising our relationship over her. How we came to it, I don't know, I think it was because of her social media prowess, but somehow it was decided that Dani would manage "operations" while I nodded along not really believing any of it. The two of them purchased a burner phone for twenty bucks, as demonstrated on *The Wire*, which Dani handled, while Scott continued teaching and I stood in the back of the lecture hall, goodie bags in hand, mentally rehearsing lines from Tony Robbins' *Awaken the Giant Within*, reminding myself there was a reason to live.

Orders came piling in so fast it felt scripted. Dani would cross-reference each request with its referral source, gather the drugs from the off-site storage unit we rented, and make the delivery. This typically happened inside Fat Sal's near UCLA since, according to Dani, it's safest to sell drugs in public; no one wants to make a scene or do anything stupid. I had to hand it to her, with Dani's ingenuity and persistence, we looked like we knew what we were doing. Maybe we did. Maybe this is what college prepared us for. We worked overtime to develop a customer-friendly experience that rewarded loyalty—I'm talking reference codes, referral incentives, big-spender prizes, a minimum transaction threshold of five hundred dollars: the works. Our internal rule was *Leave No Trace*, a nod to Burning Man, which I hated, which meant no texting, emailing, or calling; no saving digital files or using public Wi-Fi; no doing anything that could trace the three of us to each other, UCLA, or the drugs. For twenty percent off the top, access to whatever drugs she wanted, and what was trending toward free room and board, Dani did a remarkable job running sales and putting together handwritten spreadsheets. She was punctual and professional. She even enlisted the services of her brother Kyle, who accompanied her on big deliveries for an extra seven percent.

    I met Kyle once at the In-N-Out on Hollywood and La Brea. He wore a black tank top, his muscles huge and beautiful. "You're late," he said. "I already ate. I got us four Double Doubles and a few orders of fries." He pushed over my dinner. "It was fifty bucks." There's no way that was right but who was I to argue. "Here, do you want these? I don't eat bread. Or fries," I said. He laughed, not kindly, and said, "What are you, gay?" I'm not sure our relationship ever recovered after that. Anyway, Kyle provided Dani the token threat of violence should shit ever go down. Which it never did. Privileged college kids only know how to attack or defend with their parents' money.

Our plan worked, was working, because every Sunday evening Dani would deliver our weekly earnings in sealed busting envelopes. As the semester rolled on, the envelopes grew fatter and more numerous. I bought a steel safe on Amazon, one step above a shoebox, because I felt superstitious about depositing drug money at a bank, like an alarm would go off. Really though, I was terrified of my mom; pathetically, she still had access to my online account, and I'd been poor for so long there'd be no way to explain the excess money. (Citing "commercial jobs" would only invite further questioning and I was in no shape to lie about it.) So I kept most of my money in the safe. Then we three would snort lines so thick my nose would bleed from both holes like a cleft faucet and, hanging upside-down on the living room couch, you could hear Scott reprimand me for dipping into our stash.

On one such night I was going on about moving back to New York—an empty threat I'd wield to feel significant, a significance that never arrived—because I could not shake the sense that I was being followed. "You need to relax," Dani said. Why at that moment she was slathering glitter on my face, applying eyeliner, was anyone's guess.

"I told you to quit it with all the uppers," Scott said. "You're going to owe us money if you keep it up. No one is fucking following you."

"Whatever you need to tell yourself to feel better," I said, pinching my eyes, motioning for Dani to stop.

"What are you talking about?" Scott said. He sat on the hardwood floor, a few envelopes filled with twenties and hundreds and the leatherbound ledger book beside him. Some bottles of beer. He'd just gotten his knuckles tattooed, the plastic wrap dressing his hands. Eight symbols total of ancient hieroglyphics, but I couldn't tell you why nor what they meant.

"You don't think someone, somewhere, wants their shit back?" I sat up on the couch. "Jo's a pawn. We're going to get killed for this."

"We've been over this before, many times," Dani said calmly, placing her makeup kit or whatever on the coffee table, modern, red-glassed. A baggie of coke and its speckled remnants. "There's no way Jo knows it was you."

"That's not the point," I snapped. "It wouldn't take too much digging around town to trace the drugs. Just follow the money." I rose and grabbed the pack of cigarettes on the coffee table. The room was dimly lit, made brighter by the muted television.

"Can you not smoke in here?" Dani asked. "I have a cold."

I laughed at the lunacy of her ask—she didn't seem to have a problem *snorting*—and lit the cigarette and blew the smoke in her face.

"Don't fucking do that," Scott said. "What's wrong with you?"

"What's wrong with me? I'm selling drugs to college kids with my loser roommate whose entire life plan hinges on his inheritance once daddy dies, who somehow couldn't put two and two together that fucking a girl his supposed best friend was dating might upset him, regardless of what his friend felt for her!"

We both looked at Dani, who looked away.

"Take it back," Scott said and stood to face me.

"I can't believe this is my life. Can't believe I'm doing this with you people."

"Shut up and take it back."

"I'm hyperventilating at every siren, sprinting into gas stations to hide from the asshole across the street, the car slowly rolling behind me, the helicopter in the sky. It's relentless. Being alive is like being dead, only worse."

Enraged, he asked me if I'd told anyone, if that's why I was freaking out. It's the only way we'd be found out, the only way this thing fails. Did I? Tell him if I did. Questions no longer posed as questions flying out of his mouth as accusations. He came closer, the veins milking his forehead.

"Scott, calm down," Dani said.

The next thing I knew I was on the floor. Like the world had hiccupped and time vanished and the crack of the floor was the crack of my head, my jaw dislodged, Scott on top of me barking that it was *my* idea to begin with, *he* was getting us out of it, he's the most exposed, it's a risk he's willing to take, do not fuck this up for him, tell him the truth. There we were, two Sisyphuses rolling around, and all I could do was laugh. Now Dani was covering me, her body a shield.

"Are you okay?" she asked, after guiding me to the couch, a plastic bag of frozen vegetables from Trader Joe's on my cheek.

"Jesus, I hit you," Scott said from somewhere, pacing the room. "You're freaking me out! What have you done?"

"The first rule of Fight Club is you don't talk about Fight Club," I said through the frozen plastic. Dani pressed against me on the couch, holding the bag to my face; her perfume reminded me of Hollister, the smell of teenage virgin sex.

"Have you told anyone or not?" he said, inspecting his knuckles with exaggerated concern.

"If you're Marla Singer, which is a near perfect description," I said to Dani, "Scott, do you think you're Brad Pitt or Edward Norton?"

"Stop it! Shut up!" He took the carton of cigarettes and threw it across the room.

"I think Edward Norton."

"Please," he said, as sober as I'd ever seen him, "before you drive me fucking insane, please be serious for a minute."

"I haven't told anyone anything," I said. Which was true, I think.

"What about N—"

"Don't say her name."

"Do you two still talk?"

"Only in my head."

"So, you haven't told anyone?"

"You know what I think?" Dani said, caressing me on the couch, brushing my hair. "I think you're both hurting. I think you need some relief."

"Then give me a fucking cigarette."

He came over to the couch, bent before me, and handed me a smoke.

"I haven't told anyone."

"That's good," he said and lit me up. He lowered his head into Dani's lap and sighed with exasperation. "Look," he said, staring down into her black nylon leggings, his world before him in its unfortunate mapping, "once we've cleared our overhead we'll have enough money to do whatever we want. I won't have to teach. You won't have to act." He looked up at me, my best friend of how many years, and still I couldn't tell you the color of his eyes. "I'm going to produce an album and put a tour together. You can write or whatever." Dani held me close, held Scott close, her hands on our cheeks. The night a daze, cloudless. A TV going from some other apartment, gayboy Minh upstairs stomping through the ceiling. We sat and huddled there for a long time, but Dani's hand was cold and Scott's knuckles bleeding and just then I noticed I'd lost a tooth, left bottom canine.

To no one in particular, the cigarette burning on my lips, I said I wasn't reading anymore. Kafka said we ought to read only the kinds of books that wound and stab us. If the books we're reading don't wake us up with a blow on the head, what are we reading for? We need books that affect us like a disaster, that grieve us deeply, like the death of someone we loved more than ourselves, like being banished into forests far from everyone, like a suicide. A book must be the axe for the frozen sea inside us. But I couldn't find a single book that could give me that. Not one. I'd lost my last remaining dependents. What then?

But I don't think anyone was listening.

From inside the vintage trunk positioned under the French window, Scott produced the volcano smoking device he reserved for special occasions, turned it on, and let the balloon fill with vaporized cannabis. I was inside the kitchen when rubbery EDM music started playing from our new surround-sound stereo system, a business expense. My head felt like a balloon, floating from one moment to the next, bewitched by its own absence of thought. Dani removed her tank and kicked off her leggings then pushed Scott to the couch and straddled him. I pulled from the bottle of whiskey, accidentally smearing glitter in my eyes, and turned away like I'd been made privy to some secret thing.

By this point Scott had ripped three bags by himself, his face looking like it'd been run over by a tractor.

"Come over here," he called and turned down the volume. I walked over. "Here." He handed me the envelope holding his weekly earnings. Dani scooted off him, her tan legs bare, indents of her body bare. "I'm sorry," he said. "I want to make it up to you."

"It's fine, I liked it," I said, standing by the couch, not really knowing what I was saying.

"Take it."

"Ok." I put the envelope in my back pocket.

"I want you to kiss Dani," he said, his hand awkwardly on my elbow, the music still going. "She and I have been talking about it. It's what she wants and I'm willing to try it."

I looked at Dani, who raised her magnificent eyebrows and shrugged her shoulders, taut and tanned, revealing all the weight she'd lost, her breasts cupped by a bra that held no mystery. I looked back to Scott, his eyebrows curious. I found the whole thing sad, but really I felt nothing at all. But Scott wouldn't leave it alone. I guess he wanted to prove to someone, I don't know who, that he was the type of person who could exist in a consensual three-way polyamorous relationship with his best friend. When I asked him why, he mumbled something about dethroning the dominant politics of monogamy, or protesting our Protestant programming, or expanding his romantic availability, but he was so high it was hard to interpret what he was saying—not that it mattered because he was so clearly full of shit.

"You'll regret it," I said, trying to do the right thing.

"We won't." Scott stood, putting his arms around me.

"What are you doing?"

He tried to kiss me.

"Stop it! Get away."

Then Dani came from behind and whispered something I'd never be able to repeat and licked the back of my ear, sending a cold tickle down my spine. She removed my shirt, helping it over my head, and turned me around to kiss me, which I did not reciprocate until she bit my lower lip, reached under my briefs, and fine, now the three of us are bare naked on Scott's bed and I have her from behind while she takes Scott in her mouth, and despite the coke, despite the white noise numbing my inner world, I'm throbbing like a warlord captured and noosed and hanging before his people, grunting his final breaths before his neck snaps, cursing the world and shaping it in his image, penetrating madly as Scott, limp as an invalid, tells us not to, we have to stop, if he can't perform then neither can I, and sure, brother, sure, let's just listen to her begging for what you cannot deliver, let's just focus on the beads of sweat coagulating on the small of her back, dripping down her plush little ass, which I thumbed and gripped and, gripping, came like my life depended on it, or had already gone.

x x x

It was seven or so in the morning when some drunken lunatic stepped onto Fountain Avenue and laid his hands on me.

And perhaps he was not drunk, but I certainly was.

"Dude, are you a trainer?" he asked, clawing at my naked skin. I'd sort of spun out onto the street. It was quiet, the pink sun massaging the clouds. I could see him eyeing my wet heaving torso, and I ignored this man, ignored his outstretched arms wanting what of me, and kept running, only then realizing I'd been running for some time now.

"Slow down, Brad Pitt! What do you do? Pilates? Acroyoga? I've seen you at Muscle Beach! What, too in the zone to answer?"

I'd come from Beverly Hills or Hollywood Hills—last night I'd traversed many terrains. I wanted to tell him I'd just been raped for the *second time* by a woman approaching my mother's age and needed a minute to put things in perspective. Did he have any downers, maybe a spare shirt?

"Fuck. I thought you were a trainer, maybe one of those influencers. Was going to ask what's your secret. No one has veins on their stomach like that. Man, get lost, you fucking junkie!"

Now I felt compelled to correct him: I was addicted to amphetamines, *not* heroin; I'd never stoop so low—and would he like to come over and blockparty some drugs I robbed from a local drug dealer? But thinking it over I figured I'd only confuse him, let alone my readers, not that I had any, and began to panic because I could no longer distinguish fact from fiction, meta from morph, and which sounded sadder.

But a white Range Rover drove by. The back window rolled down and a handful of young girls, their lollipop heads, catcalled me, which was not uncommon at this point in my development. I kicked off my boots and resumed the chase I'd never catch, arms churning like two pistons, doing my best impression of Robert Patrick in *Terminator 2*, running through the orchestra of foliage, the coastal sage scrub and chaparral and so many trees —eucalyptus, pine, walnut, oak—sprouting wildflowers that spattered the greenery with specks of golden orange and purple buds and strange floras that looked like pelicans or toucans, so dizzying and beautiful. I heard trumpets sounding through palm trees, saw birds cartooning into this world like looneys, front doors open and housewives waving me inside. I shut my eyes, the cool breeze against my face, the oncoming traffic just beyond the scare.

But a honking. The windows closed to black tints and the big bloated vehicle sped away while the driver from behind honked frantically at the animal running in the middle of the street. I woke in my bed a few hours later in last night's pants and dirty socks, no scars except for blackout memories that do not heal.

I got out of bed afire with thirst and brushed my teeth over the yellow-tiled sink. In the kitchen I made a pot of coffee and lit a cigarette, a rebel in my own home. Browsing my email, still nothing from Harrison, I trashed the notices from Backstage.com (I swore I'd canceled my membership) and ignored the auditions my commercial agent had set up for me.

Some months back, when things were nearly looking up, Madison had floated the idea of introducing me to her agent at Wilhelmina Models. The better part of me said no, don't confuse looks for talent, that would be the worst offense. The better part of me was right, but the desperate part of me won the debate. Actually, there was no debate: as a model I would be paid to pose, no pretense of craft required. Scanning me from head to toe, her agent said I was too short for fashion but if I grew a mustache I could pass as a young Johnny Depp; she could work with that. She took me on as a commercial client. The next day I stepped into a casting office that felt more like a debarred pediatrician's waiting room. I swear, no amount nor clever stacking of drugs can soothe the embarrassment of walking into a modeling casting call—and believe me, I've tried. Sitting by the water dispenser, a black dude dressed like David Bowie, perhaps even prettier, nodded at me in solidarity. I could have kicked him in the teeth.

I already know what some of you are thinking: it's because he's black, I must be some kind of racist. No, it's not because he was black, it's because he was a raging fag.

As if this association wasn't humiliating enough, I also needed polaroids. According to my agent, we needed to fill my "look book"; she'd set up a photoshoot for me. I arrived at the Culver City studio sometime late in the afternoon, unfed and reeling, and it wasn't going well. Leo, the photographer, kept telling me to stop biting my jaw. "It's all in your eyes. Tell the story with your eyes." His attractive assistant, Chloe, whom I took to be a prop, offered me a joint to relax. While I cannot recall with a shred of accuracy the events that followed, I swear it was Leo's idea to dress me up in fishnets and cowboy boots and pose me for hundreds of, shall we say, *indelicate* photographs, which, months later, I'd have to pay so much money to disappear I should have just hired a hitman instead. You'd think buying back the rights to intensely homoerotic photographs of yourself is as low as it gets —wait until you have to go on a mad hunt to remove them from the internet, where my likeness was being used to catfish horny bottom boys on gay dating apps.

Perhaps I need a manager, I thought, standing in my kitchen and staring into the black void of my wasted existence, the black coffee—but the thought went nowhere. There was a text message, in fact there were many text messages, from Liz reminding me to bring candles to class today. Instead of responding I opened Instagram and saw that my follower count had grown since last night. I read a message from a health brand congratulating me on our partnership and welcoming me to the team, then read another from Dani saying she'd organized an influencer marketing deal for me: I was now the public face of an online nutrition company pioneering a tasty new type of collagen. I exhaled, the smoke curling my face. This news seemed strange, if not unbelievable, because later that day I had a meeting at Equinox to sell the last of the drugs. I allowed my mind to wander.

Thanks to the dozens of thousands of *likes* my shirtless photos generated on Instagram, some part of me thought FITNESS might fit the bill for an easy, mostly talentless line of work that suited my highly educated skillset. Perhaps adopting a more health-conscious lifestyle would help me overcome my addictions, I daydreamed, or at least some of them. Maybe I should seriously apply for a job at Equinox, I thought. Given my recent financial success, wouldn't it be smart to generate *more* income? I could do some honest work, learn to sell, gain experience, you know, shit my grandpa would encourage. Anything is better than serving rich people food, I had to remind myself, thinking back to those two desperate weeks I worked at the Four Seasons in Beverly Hills, so hungry I stole the scraps off half-eaten plates. It was a good job if you knew your life was over.

That is, of course, until you fuck the bride of a $500,000 wedding reception on her big night in her penthouse suite without wearing a condom. (I don't mean to brag or anything.) Shortly after orgasm, one of her bridesmaids found us together in the elaborate bed—ivory framed canopy, Egyptian cotton sheets, courtyard view—passed out and naked and sucking each other's thumbs like neonates. The news made shockwaves through the hotel network like a screeching virus. You should have seen the husband's face as he charged down the hall, a raging bull of violence, the things said about me, the fists you threw, like you could somehow touch me, like it would change anything if you could. I was promptly fired and forever banned from the premises.

Those days, lacerations on the page. But whose dream are you reading? From what head? But those days were over now.

Relieved, somewhat, I went into the bathroom and turned on the shower and got inside holding my coffee. I sat on the dirty tub floor and huddled over myself and cried demonically for six minutes straight, water pooling and diluting the black inside the mug.

"Oh hello," Dani said a minute later, opening the shower door.

I looked up as she stepped inside.

"Where's Scott?"

"It's finals week," she said. "You know that."

One minute I'm waterboarding myself, the next minute I'm caressing or being caressed by my best friend's fake girlfriend, who thinks she's my girlfriend, in the shower.

But I wasn't in the mood.

I grabbed a towel, stepped around her wet body, and slipped through the hallway into my bedroom. At the dresser I let my towel drop and pulled out the free briefs I received from that embarrassing Calvin Klein rip-off job and put them on.

"What the fuck?" I heard from behind.

I turned around. Dani stood at the threshold of my bedroom doorway. Her lean shoulders, full tits, the slit of her vagina plundering me.

"Can you please put on some clothes, *please?*" I asked.

"Are you serious? What, now you don't want me?"

I sighed in a way that suggested infinite torture and opened the closet door and retrieved my private collection from the safe; I noticed I was running uncomfortably low. At my desk I emptied a baggie and cut four lubricious lines with a credit card. Dani stared at me while I rolled up a hundred and offered it to her.

"It's like twelve o'clock. You're crazy."

"Suit yourself," I said, vacuuming all of them.

"Talk to me," she said.

"We shouldn't do this anymore. Sneaking behind Scott's back."

"It's not sneaking. We're working through it."

"Fucking when he's not home is not working through it. Have you told him?"

"I will when he's ready." She came over and kissed the top of my head and rubbed my shoulders, her nipples erect as my tongue glided over them.

"Maybe don't." I dabbed my gums with the remnant coke. "He's got a fragile ego."

"Yeah," she sighed, "but a thick cock."

"Okay, I need to study my lines." A complete lie. "I have class soon."

She looked dismayed, maybe hurt. "We still owe Kyle two grand. Can you please get that to me before you leave?"

I rolled my eyes with a dismissive nonchalance that suggested my impotence in the shower was her fault, not mine, much like paying her intimidating brother was a nuisance, not an arrangement I recommended. I lit a cigarette inside my room, something I never did, and told her I would. "Now, can you please close the door?"

Alone, I proceeded to check inside the safe for the second

of twenty-one times that day, my OCD approaching psychosis, and counted my small fortune. For the next hour I crafted a carefully worded email to my psychiatrist in New York with the hope that, sight unseen, just because I'd asked, he'd prescribe me vyvanse, which is like adderall only longer lasting. Now that our "team" had sold most of our "product," god help me, I needed to replenish my personal supply. I wrote:

> Hi Dr __:
>
> I read <u>the article</u> you suggested about the harmful, potentially deadly effects of vyvanse. Quite horrifying indeed. It pinpoints my problem with relying too heavily on medicine—hence why I've decreased my SSRI intake since I strongly believe I don't need it any longer. Plus, they prevent me from ejaculating (!). To the same extent, I don't believe I *need* vyvanse to function. However, I do think it would help correct my sporadic motivational issues that have recently proven more damaging than distracting.
>
> The few instances I've tested vyvanse, thanks to generous friends (hah!), have helped me put my sprawling ambitions into organized practice. This is why I feel it could do me well. Ultimately, I know my success hinges on maintaining a healthy lifestyle. I just want to be productive and do good work at an age when I should be doing good work. I want to not forget I'm the author of my life. I'm seeking your help to tap into my full potential. It's your call. I'll respect your decision.
>
> Thanks and best–

Pleased, I pressed Send and refilled my coffee mug two more times, the least offensive vice in a life fueled by addiction. While scrolling through Instagram and harassing vegans, I remembered

I had to get going: today was a big day. I got dressed, packed my workout gear, packed the collateral, and found Dani in Scott's bed on her laptop.

"Tell Kyle thank you," I said, tossing the envelope containing two thousand dollars on the navy fluid-stained duvet. "We won't be needing his services anymore."

"What? Why not?"

"Final delivery today. Big order. I'll tell you about it tonight," I said and shut the door.

I just had one quick stop to make on the way.

X X X

The struggling actor is a danger to society, much like the bastard son of the King—the illegitimate heir on a mad hunt scheming for fame.

Raised with all the trappings of privilege, he eats at the same table as the royal family, drinks from the same golden goblet, is granted comforts and access and notoriety. But deep down he knows his life is a fraud. Where for others gratitude would beat thick with blood, for him there is only darkness. These are not his people nor this his home. An alien in alien land. Yet such heartbreaks pale in comparison to the death-savage torment he cannot come to bear, the tragedy made his fate: he will never be King.

So then, the killing.

After a lifetime spent self-mutilating, the illegitimate heir must learn to feed off others instead. One by one he will eat his prey without your even knowing. He will bleed you out slowly over time and drink your blood. A vampire, he will hang in the crooks and know your every secret. He will make you his friend, make you feel loved, wanted, appreciated. Your trust he'll twist out of you. He will ask for many favors and be charming about it. You will believe in him, root for him, ask for nothing in return. "Just don't forget me when you're at the top!" you'll say, and though he'll laugh to suggest he won't, inwardly he knows he will—and relishes it. Over time he will raise an army of sycophants, lovers and losers mesmerized by his royal ties, his stunning claims. You'll want to be one of them. And if somehow you don't submit, he will blackmail you into his engine of doom.

The day of reckoning. When it comes and the King chokes his final breath and the question of succession is posed, the illegitimate heir will strike with heinous savagery, will show no mercy, will do whatever it takes to make himself legitimate. He will bite, slice, and crucify any detractor, will cannonball all representatives of the established order who deter him from actualizing his dreams. If he must, he will raid, steal, pillage, and plunder from the very people he's supposed to protect, supposed to love, his friends, his supporters, murdering mad with indiscriminate butchery. Glory is all that matters. Hot blooded fame.

The struggling actor who's taken the leap and can't take it back is much like the illegitimate heir slavering for the throne. Though he might look good on the outside, like someone who has his shit together, you must not be fooled—for he contributes absolutely nothing to society (unless you consider stealing his parents' money for acting school and/or competing with first-generation Mexicans for service jobs a *contribution*). A spiteful villainous creature who cares for nothing but his own advancement, the struggling actor will do whatever it takes to get ahead. Mostly he will lie, his deadliest weapon.

The struggling actor will lie to make you believe he's royalty when really he's just a fucking bastard. So if he pays you attention, *beware*: you're already caught in his handsome web. Because when that rare and treasured acting role comes his way, no matter how small the production, no matter how deeply you believe in his love for you, or yours for him, one callback from a casting director is all it will take, the struggling actor will gladly nuke you to the ice circles of hell to get the gig. You will not be remembered nor even forgotten because you never meant anything to him to begin with. You were used. And he'll be gone. Never to be heard from again.

The life of the struggling actor has no relief. Because deep down in his gut where blood and bile share no distinction, where love and mercy stink like shit, he knows that even on the lottery chance he does make it big—fame and celebrity and whatever fantasy—he'll still be dead inside.

Struggling actors, poor and feckless, are what give Los Angeles its bad reputation. A town of liars, connivers, tricksters, and jokers. A shiny collection of prom kings and queens from every town across America fending for themselves for the first time. Imagine hordes of house pets sent into the wild; when out come the wolves, their paws trampling the mud, there will be blood.

Take pity, but take cover. They're doing what they can to survive. Whoring in the name of art, perpetually one paycheck away from impoverished. Someone's dinner, someone's dessert. Cannibals on the hunt for the next juicy neck to suck, shamefully aware they're no more than mosquitos quick to be crushed by much bigger hands.

In many ways living in Los Angeles is like living inside social media: an alternate reality comprised of exhibition and surface with little room for artistic development or contribution, where struggling actors freely lie to themselves by hypnotizing your attention instead of doing the fucking work.

At the Beverly Hills Playhouse you can find large swaths of such struggling actors, which was exactly why I enrolled however many months ago.

Whereas in New York students go to acting school to study and perform theatre, in Los Angeles struggling actors treat each class more like an AA meeting, which makes sense since all struggling actors are addicted to themselves. When packed in groups their collective illegitimacies magnify their individual delusions; the addiction becomes enabling, the depression darker. But always with a smile.

:)

I parked my shitty Mazda on Robertson Boulevard and didn't put money in the meter because I was only going to be a minute. I lit a cigarette and walked through the courtyard toward the theatre, past the tall hanging tree giving shade. Some struggling actors were sitting outside with scripts in hand and books opened on benches, water bottles uncapped and granola bars unwrapped, suggestions of work being done but no actual work. I knew their faces but not their names because straight from the jump I determined there'd be no one of use here.

"What's up, stud lightning!" the fat guy said, a thirty-six-year-old class clown. The others sat huddled and smiled; some nodded hello. I thought I caught one of them checking out my

Instagram profile on her phone, but then again I always imagined I was being watched.

Liz came running up to me, brushing away the cloud of smoke. "Thank god!" she said, exasperated but bubbly like a right-to-do midwestern girl. She was dressed in 1950s Americana regalia. "I've got the stage all set. I've been trying to call. Where were you? We're up now! Do you have the candles?" But before I could respond she said, "Don't worry, I brought extras. And I have your sports jacket. You left it at rehearsal last week." She smiled and sort of raised her eyebrows, making an embarrassing reference to the moment our characters kiss. "Are you ready?"

Just then the instructor, tall and handsome, walked outside and asked, "Has our star arrived?" He was forty-seven but looked thirty. A decade earlier he had co-starred in a TNT show that got canceled after one season. Apparently that was all the credentialing one needed in this town to make preposterous claims like, "I'm not teaching you how to act, I'm teaching you how to be a *human being*." I knew he had it out for me.

The struggling actors stood to make a circle. I was being ambushed, swarmed on all sides. Panicked, I saw my resolve slip out from me like a belly wound. I sucked on the cigarette and looked at my watch: I was already twenty minutes late for my meeting with the Playhouse office manager. I'd intended to quit the class and get next month's tuition back. "You see, I need to move back to New York. It's my mother, she's just been diagnosed with cancer," I rehearsed many times on the drive over, emphasizing my struggle with the words, prepared to make a scene—once again lying at Mom's expense to suit my narrative, for which I no longer felt remorse.

By now a sizable crowd of struggling actors had gathered in the courtyard. Some even began to clap. Confused, I could see they were *genuinely* excited for Liz and me to perform one of the most overplayed scenes in the history of drama school: Scene Seven from Tennessee Williams' *The Glass Menagerie*, which I'd completely butchered in class two weeks ago. I was not prepared for this. Someone placed a hand on my shoulder; it was Todd, the stage manager, an Irish-American dude from Pittsburgh. "I'm really looking forward to seeing what you've done with the character," he said, smiling, no trace of irony in tone. I had no idea what to make of this.

"Curtains down in five minutes!" the ageless instructor shouted.

The world quickly shrank around me. Liz grabbed my hand. "Put that out and come on! Let's use this energy for the scene," she said, leading me toward the theatre. Obediently I tossed the cigarette into the world's baggage, and together we went through the small hallway, practically galloping up the stairs and into the backstage area. The poorly lit dressing room smelled of moldy damp wood, was filled with antique props and thrifty costumes, unfortunate details reminding me of the joke my life had become. Tara, a middle-aged housewife who thought she'd be an actor now that her kid was heading off to college, stood there also outfitted in 1950s costume, a full-skirted circle dress and ridiculous shoes.

"Tara is going to play Mrs. Wingfield," Liz said. "You know... my mother...in the play." She smiled, showing her big teeth. "Now, before you protest, I'm *aware* the three of us have not rehearsed together, it's a shame you were late today, but Tara and I *did* manage to squeeze some time in, just like we'd agreed, and anyway she's going to close out the scene with us." She paused as if I'd have something to say, which I did not, and continued: "In my opinion, your interaction with Mother is absolutely necessary to show the full arc of my character's pain. Remember Jim—is it all right if I call you Jim? It helps me live into my character—when you see Mother, all you want to do is *leave*. Any awkwardness that arises between you two due to lack of practice will be perfect for the moment as you rush through your actions toward your exit. Of course, I don't want to *tell* you how to act, you're already so incredible, that's just what I think! Make sense?"

"Hi!" Tara said. She'd just gotten a slick boyish haircut that framed her thinning face. "I'm excited to work together."

"Would it be all right with you if we record our performance?" Liz asked. "I have Paul filming on two phones outside. I can edit the best clips and it'd be so amazing if you share it on your Instagram and tag me, but we can talk about that later."

"Curtain down in three!" a voice shouted from the auditorium.

"It's *time*!" Liz said, delighted.

I walked on stage, the black curtains hiding me from the audience, which had been repurposed into a makeshift living room, dimly lit: a couch, some candles in the middle of the floor, a table set with glass figurines in the corner.

Tennessee Williams introduces the play with Tom, the protagonist, recalling the sad impoverished years of his life spent caring for his mother, Amanda Wingfield, and sister, Laura, before he runs away to pursue his dream of becoming an artist. Because the play is based on memory, Tom cautions the audience that what we see may not be precisely what happened. I was playing Jim, a "gentleman caller" invited by Tom to placate his mother and wow Laura, a fragile girl who'd grown up with illnesses that isolated her from the world.

In that moment, unrehearsed and stone-cold sober, I was confident that what was about to happen was *not* what Tennessee Williams had intended.

I glanced around and saw that I was alone on stage. I have one chance, I thought, and took it, running like a bastard in retreat through the side stage and out the Actors' Only door. As I turned the final corner, freedom in sight, say there was an earthquake, but no, it was just my heart. Because there stood the instructor blocking the exit.

"I thought I'd find you heading this way," he said, beautiful five o'clock shadow darkening his chiseled jaw. "You know," he said, lingering on his words, "when I was your age, I minimized my acting because of the drama in my life. I was friends with Johnny Depp and his crew while they were making money on TV and buying bars and clubs. I rode their coattails like I was in on it, and they let me ride for free. Life was fun. And fast."

I knew where this was going, braced myself for endless torture. He continued:

"Oh, I was doing plenty of acting, *outside* the theatre, *outside* the casting rooms. I was acting like my life was worth a damn. Then there's someone like Brad Pitt, a terrible actor, just awful. He'd leave a homerun networking dinner with some bigshot producer just to come to class. He'd leave commercial shoots if they ran overtime to meet with his scene partner to rehearse. And they *always* ran overtime. Do you understand?" I considered if I could take him. If it came down to it. He was a good four inches taller than me, all legs. "When Johnny started landing movies I was no longer invited to the party. I lost ten years of my career because I'd been acting like I'd made it. In reality, all I did was con everyone into believing I was an actor, mostly myself. Well," he paused, "every con is eventually found out. Life got hard. That's what led me here to the Playhouse." I'd kick out his knee, I determined, then headbutt him in the nose. He'd never suspect it, would drop unconscious in a heartbeat. But instead, he dropped into a lower register to say, "To hell with your hurt, man. Go for the art. Art is not just about you, it's about the *possibilities* of you," a line I'd heard him repeat in class while I wrote poems about my ex-girlfriend, poems I'd never share. "Your ego is worthless. No one cares about your problems. No one out there in the audience. Not me. Not your scene partner. The director doesn't care. The critics. All we want is the result. Got that? We care how you take your problems and go to war with them." I was prepared to swing if I had to when with a friendly smile he said, "Don't be me. Be Johnny." Now I felt compelled to listen. "Well don't be Johnny *now*, he's completely lost his mind. Be Johnny *then*." Still listening. "Don't be humble. That's not you." I hesitated, felt a warm choke in my throat, his charm tentacling around my insides. "Be the dirt. Be the pirate only your whores get to experience." A little excessive. "Be the killer who wants to slit my throat with his keys." I hadn't considered *that*. "Bring it into the scene. Bring the dirt and the smut, bring your cock into it. Be the star you can't avoid. But don't play the star. That's who you are. *Be* the star. In the dirt. Grounded. Do you understand?"

I knew I was being played. Knew I was under the influence of an expert bastard. But I didn't care—I loved the acknowledgement.

"Look," he said, "there are two ways an actor can go. One is that of the poser, the indicator, and the other is that of the honest actor who tries to live the experience of his character. I'm here to help those in the latter group. It's your choice," he said, stepping out of the way. "Which are you?"

"Jim! Where are you, Jim?"

While I knew this life wasn't real, I couldn't help but read on. I walked back to the stage through the side door.

"Oh good, there you are," Liz said. "I've put the two glasses of wine on that block over there," she nodded. "Remember to take them with you as you enter. Here's your blazer," she said, handing it to me as she made her way to the middle of the room, transitioning into Laura, where the scene would begin. I smelled if there was alcohol in the glasses, hoping there was. There wasn't. I put on the sports coat and, as if it were that easy, wishing it was, became Jim.

"Curtains up!"

Instinctively I reached inside my pockets for adderall but remembered I was out. I stood paralyzed. The curtain rose. Thirty or so shadowed faces looked on at the elevated stage. Rows of burgundy fabric seats. The lights on me. I took the glasses of play-wine and walked through the improvised hallway. I paused dramatically as if I had something to lose, reminded myself I'd already lost everything, could not believe I was going to do this sober, truly a first, and having no idea what I'd say, said, "Hello there, Laura."

In the middle of the room, on the floor just before the couch, she sat up nervously. I entered. "Hello," she said, faintly, clearing her throat.

"How are you feeling now? Better?"

"Yes. Yes, thank you." *[Her speech at first is low and breathless from the almost intolerable strain of being alone with a stranger.]*

"This is for you. A little dandelion wine." I extended it toward her with extravagant gallantry. *[JIM's attitude is gently humorous. In playing this scene it should be stressed that while the incident is apparently unimportant, it is to LAURA the climax of her secret life.]*

The scene unfolded with disregard for authorship and stage direction. I bastardized my lines, spoke over my scene partner, switched this section with that—and I did it spectacularly. I owned my every action, embodied my character; I disarmed Laura, made her feel appreciated; I knew my lines well enough to call her an old-fashioned girl, to call her Blue Roses, to coach her through her inferiority complex. The words flowed through me. I studied her glass collection, I swayed her to waltz, I twirled her to music I hummed from my belly. I was embarrassed, I was confident, I was goofy. I was worried I wasn't a good person but wanted to show her I could be, no acting required. I was the dirt in the sky, or the cock in the star, whatever the instructor had said. She laughed, she fell over, I helped her up—authentic moments, scripted but unrehearsed. I was there with her. I was Jim. Which meant this never happened.

I told everyone at the Playhouse I was an entrepreneur, the owner of a profitable online business that funded my artistry. "We sell party supplies," I'd say if asked, insinuating nothing, laughing at the strangeness of my career. "Mostly to college kids. It's a long story." I credited our success to our small but dedicated team, a leveraged sales system, some viral campaigns, and minimal competition. "It's been a wild ride!"

"Everybody excels in one thing. Some in many! Take me, for instance. My interest happens to lie in electro-dynamics. I'm taking a course in radio engineering at night school, Laura, on top of a fairly responsible job at the warehouse. I'm taking that course and studying public speaking."

"Oh!"

"I guess you think I think a lot of myself."

"No-o-o-o!"

"My agent thought acting classes would accelerate my career," I told my classmates. "I'm also a poet," I added for good measure, but only after the confidence with which I spoke about my business reoriented their projection of me from "douchebag fuckboy" to "powerful titan." "You can follow my work on Instagram." Astonished, they thought my large following was one of the most impressive things they'd ever seen, Instagram being so new at the time. "Wow, people actually *read* your work? That's amazing." I must be "super successful" was their conclusion, "extremely productive." My enthusiasm to pursue and integrate multiple interests into a financially successful and socially profitable personal brand was "something to aspire to." The word "genius" was used.

Then in what seemed like practiced succession I spun Laura into the table that housed her glass menagerie, her hand brushing the figurine unicorn which fell on the floor. She gasped with horror as she saw the crown had broken off her favorite piece.

"Is it broken?" I asked.

"Now it is just like all the other horses."

"It's lost its—"

"Horn! But it doesn't matter. Maybe it's a blessing in disguise."

"Still I'm awfully sorry that I was the cause."

"I'll just imagine he had an operation. The horn was removed to make him feel less—freakish!"

My classmates treated me like a celebrity when I told them I'd recently signed with Wilhelmina. Modeling was a short-term strategy to monetize my personal brand while I built up my acting reel; my agent at WME approved. I encouraged their gaping murmurs, their embarrassing conduct, because now my social distancing could be interpreted as an artist savant's removal from himself as opposed to the consequence of what was (at worst) a minor drug problem.

"In all respects, believe me! Your eyes, your hair—are pretty! Your hands are pretty! You think I'm making this up because I'm invited to dinner and have to be nice. Oh, I could do that! I could put on an act for you, Laura, and say lots of things without being very sincere. But this time I am. I'm talking to you sincerely. I happened to notice you had this inferiority complex that keeps you from feeling comfortable with people. Somebody needs to build your confidence up and make you proud instead of shy and turning away and—blushing. Somebody, ought to. Ought to —kiss you, Laura!"

I can't pretend that when I kissed Laura I didn't mean it. Because when she clutched my chest and tried to remove my sports coat but stopped herself, I wanted her to keep going. I heard sighs from the crowd, wishing we would. And when the instructor prematurely yelled, "Cut!" and the audience hailed us with cheers, we did not stop because her tears were real. I silenced the crowd, directed down their applause; I need quiet, I gestured, to tell Laura I was engaged to Betty. I broke Laura's glass unicorn and her spirit too. I broke both. I cried as well, having never cried on command before, I didn't even have to try because seeing into her eyes I could no longer escape myself. Which was fine because I was Jim. When Laura's mother entered the stage, and I rushed to leave, she didn't know how to interpret what had happened. And nor did I.

Because by finals week we'd sold nearly seventy thousand dollars' worth of "product," ludicrous expression, after what I'd ingested, which was a lot. Today I was about to sell the last of it after I walked off stage for the last time. I don't know how to describe it—it's like you're acting in someone else's story and suddenly recognize the protagonist is you. Only it's not fiction, it's the real thing. What you think, what you've always thought, appears on the page. Confused, you read on, but you already know the lines.

"It's been a wonderful evening, Mrs. Wingfield. I guess this is what they mean by Southern hospitality."

"It really wasn't anything at all."

"I hope it don't seem like I'm rushing off. But I promised Betty I'd pick her up at the Wabash depot, an' by the time I get my jalopy down there her train'll be in. Some women are pretty upset if you keep 'em waiting."

"Yes, I know. The tyranny of women!" She extended her hand. "Goodbye, Mr. O'Connor. I wish you luck, and happiness, and success! All three of them, and so does Laura! Don't you, Laura?"

"Yes!"

"Goodbye, Laura," I said, taking her hand. "I'm certainly going to treasure that souvenir." I looked at the broken unicorn in my hand, brushed the wet from her cheek. "And don't you forget the good advice I gave you." Defying Tennessee's directions, I kissed her again with whatever love was in my heart and turned to leave. "So long, Shakespeare!" I shouted at the hushed audience to a make-believe Tom. "Thanks again, ladies. Good night!"

Ducking jauntily out the door, stage right, I rushed out of the theatre. The crowd erupted as I exited the building and sprinted through the courtyard and down Robertson Boulevard where I found my car. Inside, sweating or crying, I sat for a few seconds and considered what had happened. For the first time in my life I felt like an actor. Enjoyed it even. Truly a disturbing thought. I let out one pathetic sob, the world reorienting itself, the light drawing away along the edges, when a ding sounded, a text message. It was Liz. Where was I? It's time for notes. Instructor told the class it was the most courageous performance he'd ever seen. I did a keybump, drove away, and saw through the windshield a parking ticket, marauding me.

X X X

I was on my way to Equinox when I spotted two black SUVs hot on my tail.

I turned down an alleyway then again onto a new street. I parked my car at random and ran inside the nearby Starbucks to shake the bastards off. In the bathroom I harassed myself with cocaine, lukewarm water, and more cocaine. Refreshed, if you can call it that, I changed my clothes and proceeded onward. I asked the talkative barista for an iced coffee and swiped, no, inserted my card to pay and forgot what I was doing and sprinted outside and practically tossed the cold plastic beverage to the homeless guy blowing bubbles from an empty Windex container. Trenchcoated, shoeless, sockless, his hair wild, this man was deranged; I think he even called me a fag. Given my black lululemon spandex capris and army-green tank top, wardrobe choices that matched the personality of the character I'd now be playing, his assessment wasn't far off. I popped on my Ray Bans and, from the backseat of my car, swapped the duffel bag carrying my clothes for the duffel bag carrying the drugs. The door shut, the car lock sounded. I turned to the homeless guy and said, not unpleasantly, "Biohacker, bro. Keep it clean," as I walked in the wrong direction to Equinox.

There were many moments in those days like that one, days delivered without transition, where this morning was yesterday and yesterday never happened and so on.

The Beverly Hills Equinox was conveniently located in the same building as WME, a happy coincidence, really. I made my way past the dark marble slabs, up the steps, through the glass doors, and into the porcelain marbled hallway. The same heavyset security guard sporting the colossal gold chain over blue uniform sat at the luxurious kiosk. I feared he would recognize me from that harsh moment nearly a year ago when, fresh off the plane, I'd made a spectacle of myself in front of WME's finest, a time before I knew how to deal with Harrison's pitiless rejection—if you consider binging on drugs you stole from a drug dealer *dealing*. It demanded all my strength and one percocet not to jumanji over the guard, rush up the stairs, and throw myself at Harrison's rich Prada ankles. I nodded, or hid my face in my phone, or curled up in a ball and rolled inside.

I'd never been inside an Equinox before. On the one hand I felt like vomiting, just a tablespoon of grey heat, like every neuron had decided against my best interest to torch its jelly shell and smoke signal for Harrison's attention, he was so close. On the other hand I liked the idea of Equinox because it made me feel elite. If not for the metallic machines and zip-churn of treadmill, you wouldn't know if the attractive hostess would greet you with designer clothes, designer lunch menus, or designer art imprints—but surely you'd know you were in the presence of *Design*.

The workout area was unbelievably polished, the ceiling unbelievably high, the windows unbelievably bright; the white marble that went from wall to wall looked like freshly fallen snow or an artist's trendy rendition of freshly fallen snow. Money walked around in expensive clothes. Women yapped away on treadmills like they owned the place, defying the "No Cellphone" signage. Middle-aged white men made exercise moves like hunks of cheese, slyly surveilling young babes through an elaborate reflection of mirrors. Gays wearing headbands pumped away on ellipticals like jackrabbits. Abercrombie models strolled around like royalty in sleeveless tees, each admiring his own chiseled chest, his angular jaw, each of whom I sized up with conspicuous revulsion; I checked in the mirror: my face was more angular. Crystal doodads decanting the presence of human sweat hung all over. There was a wanting in the air, not to be confused with citrus aloe vera aggressively ventilating throughout the club.

At the front desk the hostess gave me the fakest sweetest greeting I'd ever heard. Early twenties, blond spiky bangs, sides and back pulled into a bun, she looked exactly as you'd expect of someone in her position: retarded.

"Hi there! How can I help?"

"I'm interviewing to be a health coach."

Only then did I notice the cigarette smoking from my lips. Noticeably caught off guard, the hostess didn't seem to have a pre-packaged reply for such an entrance. Shocked by my blunder, I crumpled the thing and tossed it behind me while the poor girl fumbled with the keyboard, scribbled on a sticky pad, picked up and put down the phone. Wanting this to be over as much as she did, I assisted by asking for the general manager and made sure to punctuate the name of the D-list celebrity, Heather (although her name is not Heather), who had referred me and whose instructions I repeated precisely: the general manager told her to tell me to say I was here for an interview. Exuding an air of superiority incongruent to checking in at a gym but which felt entirely appropriate given the pomposity of this one, I couldn't determine if the hostess paused and raised her eyebrows, impressed by the namedrop, or if I merely wished she had. She told me to wait a moment, she'd be right back.

Britney Spears cooed from the speakers overhead, or it could have been Rihanna, or Ariana Grande; I don't know who was popular at the time, it all sounded the same. Despite my artistic elitism I noticed my feet tapping along to a chorus that seemed to devour the song entire. Staring off at the main workout floor, I realized there were few if any teenage girls present; able-brained adults appeared to enjoy this music, an idea I'd never let materialize before. I considered the interchangeability of pop music, its sly capacity to intoxicate diverse demographics across time and space. I imagined *Pop* as a machine, a technology of utility to score the soundtrack of consumerism: it both decorates the backgrounds of large public venues and occupies the forefronts of people's attention, often bringing strangers together to dance, sing, fuck—at bars, clubs, concerts, whatever. Like a pendulum, the more people that feed it energy, the more powerfully it sways.

I thought with real marvel:

Perhaps the producers of *Pop* are making a claim against art altogether, an "Art" so devoid of artfulness that only in its engineered absence can it be described as artful. In this light I grew appreciative of *Pop's* design, not to be confused with its sound, in the same way you appreciate what the nerds have created with their billion-dollar apps. In many ways they are one and the same, pop music and social media: sticky webs of absorption made to seem consensual, where you're more than likely participating without choosing to participate; it's harder *not* to participate. People think they are acting on personal conviction when in fact they're following the will of the cultural pendulum fed by the corporate machine.

I suppose that's my rebellion, I mused; my art has nothing to do with *design*—clearly—or inclusiveness—even clearer—as a new song, indiscriminately hip-hop, played overhead. That's exactly why you could find me at Equinox with ten thousand dollars' worth of prescription drugs in my possession, mumbling along to an R&B and hip-hop playlist aggregated by iTunes, pretending to know the lyrics but only knowing the one word I could *not* say, eyebrows pierced as if experiencing a deep pathos while I ventriloquized a lifestyle comprised of fucking bitches, selling drugs, and making money—which, only as I read this, can I sympathize with myself.

"Right this way," the hostess said.

I followed her callipygian tush into an office that reminded me of a modern art exhibit, an overt rendering of the digital in analog. Everything seemed designed to scroll through or disassemble: shelves and desks composed of white particleboard, black laminated melamine, no trace of "work" ever having been conducted in these parts. I sat down, instructed by the hostess that her boss would be with me shortly and would I like some pomegranate green tea while I waited? At the same moment the rapper Rick Ross grunted "I'm a boss" through the overhead speaker, profound girth in his voice. The synchronicity was startling, the significance astonishing. Impulsively I thought of the security guard outside; I saw him become Rick Ross, whose real name is William Leonard Roberts II, not because they're both enormously fat black men (I mean, probably a little) but because Rick Ross worked as a security guard before becoming a famous rapper. The light in the room suddenly shrank to a particle, like a dying star extinguishing to its natural conclusion, as I saw Rick Ross accomplish through hip-hop what I wanted to achieve through literature: become a character who transcends the limitations of his former pathetic life and shifts the culture with his celebrity. He's Rick Ross, but he's not *really* Rick Ross, he's William Leonard Roberts II—and yet, maybe now he *is* Rick Ross, an imagination of himself. Just like The Author.

At once I felt shocked but shattered, encouraged but conquered. What happens to a star when it dies, where does that energy go? Suddenly my lifelong dream revealed itself to be no more than an unoriginal rendering of a project perfectly executed by an obese rapper—by all famous rappers with ridiculous monikers, now that I thought of it. I tried to shake it off, but who the fuck was I kidding? I just want to be famous like every other asshole. I am nothing more than a predictable product of the pendulum I've spent my entire life condemning. My quest for fame has no artistic merit, just pretension. My literary ambition is no better than a preposterous rally cry in a world where language is eroding, an illiterate wasteland perpetuated by culture's addiction to shitty pop songs and social media. I give up, I thought, I've got no choice but to take this job prospect seriously.

Thus I prepared myself for the deal I was about to execute. In theory, I was ecstatic. For many weeks I'd been eagerly anticipating this very moment when I'd sell the last of the drugs, collect my final big payday, and get out of "the game" I was woefully unfit to play. In actuality, I was terrified. Now I'd have to decide what to do with my life, an existential Rubik's Cube I'd failed to solve so many times before, a failure that ultimately landed me in Los Angeles and, pitiably, this very chair. Naturally I regressed into a college senior, experiencing mammoth hatred for everyone I knew who'd landed cushy jobs at investment banks, consulting firms, who were genuinely excited about medical school, psychology graduate programs, whatever the fuck. I lowered my head, keybumped some coke, and thought to myself, face in hand:

Those people hate their careers as much as you hate their careers; the difference is that they put up with it. Relax, you've got money now. You can start again. No more acting as an actor. No more acting, period. That life is over. This past year has been humbling. You're ready to take responsibility for your actions, intentionally design a future, build yourself up.

Yes, but *how*? Instinctively, unfortunately, ideations about law school occurred to me. I pushed them aside. You're allowed to pursue your dreams and be an author, I told myself. You're allowed to figure it out on your terms, your timeline. There's no rush.

Don't be an idiot, the other part of me, the rational part, thought. You'll never write a word. You blew up your life and moved to LA on a whim and what have you accomplished? It's time to return to New York, be present for your family, repair things with your ex, overcome your addictions, grow the fuck up. But was I *really* addicted, some hollow part of me wondered? My entire life had been a performance; now I was performing a satire of the artist as a young man who doesn't have his shit together, who because of multiple "addictions" has absolved himself of personal responsibility; it's theatre, *technique*. In fact, I'm *proud* of my commitment to the role. Obviously, I'm in control. I'm choosing hell for the sake of experience, which will help me write. When I'm ready. Stay in Los Angeles, I told myself. You have permission to be a normal dude with a normal job who goes to the beach and enjoys it without irony, develops a healthy tan, maybe starts a meditation practice, eats avocados. You *deserve* to have some fun, not take life so seriously for once.

"There's my guy," said the voice from the threshold of the doorway, interrupting what felt like a personal breakthrough. It was the general manager. He was the most structurally beautiful man I'd ever seen. His muscles were spectacular, his skin tan, his charisma saturating. In his office anything could happen; if he'd asked me to go down on him, I might have. But what am I saying?

"Don't mind my hands," he said, walking over. "I've been training clients all day. I like to work out alongside them."

"Yeah, I hate when that happens," I said, shaking his hand, something a drug dealer would never do, indicating I was above all that.

"Did my assistant get you some green tea? Theanine and caffeine, good for the nerves." He reached over me to press the speaker button on the landline. I don't know what came over me, I had the impulse to kiss him, but didn't. "Jamie, some green tea, please. For our guest. Thanks."

"Great."

"I hear you know my client," he said in a winning way. "She's hardcore."

I pictured Heather riding me reverse cowgirl after lacing my wine with pain meds, the half-conscious bob and lilt. Pictured designer bags filled with money.

"She's filled me in," I said, a response vague enough to suggest I understood his intentions if not the entire innerworkings of his operation when really I had no idea whom I was dealing with nor why I was dealing with him.

"Menopause," he said, shaking his head, which caught me off guard. "Women over fifty struggle so much with their weight. Adderall is the only thing that predictably works." He walked behind the desk and sat down. We sat in silence. I am not sure if it was his general discomfort with the situation or pity for my mute awkwardness, or if radical transparency was a tactic he used to bridge our aloofness and make transacting smoother, but when he finally began to speak, I had to shake myself free of my self-absorption to grasp what he was saying. The women in this club are going to get their pills no matter what. They're so wealthy, most keep their psychiatrists on payroll. Some don't want their husbands or doctors to know, so they come to him. They trust him. It's a special relationship, that between a coach and a client. He spoke with what seemed like genuine care and concern. "I'm probably the only man in their life who really understands them." Then he reached across the desk and rested his hands on top of mine—and it was in that moment I knew this man was a real psychopath. "At the end of the day, I get results."

The hostess, Jamie, walked in and handed me an iced tea.

Theanine, I thought.

"Thank you," I said.

Suddenly I felt very sober.

He asked her to shut the door on the way out, which she did, but he got up anyway, betraying his previous composure, moving with an intensity one might call threatening.

"I appreciate you going the extra mile," he said, locking the door. He looked through the blinds. "I don't normally expect someone in your," he coughed, "line of work to be so amenable." He turned toward me, his face softening. "Heather said you were trustworthy."

I removed my sunglasses, hoping to communicate whatever he wanted to believe.

"Do you have everything I requested?"

"In the bag," I nodded.

"Excellent." He walked back to his desk. "Ten grand, was it?" He kicked an Equinox backpack from behind the desk into view.

"Is it okay to do this in here?"

"I mean, we're not trading sex favors. Just give me the bag and I'll give you mine, champ."

"Can I see inside first?"

"I'll show you mine if you show me yours."

A vague thrill shot down my spine. I ignored it.

"How did you get into fitness?" I asked stupidly, awkwardly, attempting to divert the confrontation.

"It's reductionist to call my work 'fitness,'" he said with a gentle pretension, unzipping his backpack and confirming the money was inside. "It's far more transformative than that." I raised my eyebrows and felt my cock chub as he reached over and looked inside the duffel bag cradled on my lap. He nodded in approval and leaned back in his chair. "I have to hand it to you," he laughed. "The outfit is spot on. You certainly look the part. A little thin, maybe. What's your body fat? Seven percent? I can usually eyeball it. I'm hovering right around five myself."

I didn't know how to respond. Why did I love receiving his approval?

He told me he was building a health coaching company, an online membership site complete with digital programs. He's bootstrapping the operation. Equinox was just his day job. I told him I was writing a novel, what you're reading now, which I hadn't started yet. Something about this exchange struck us both as hilarious. Everyone in this town is just trying to make an honest living, posing as one thing to be something or someone else. Looking down at my ridiculous attire, I said I'd like to be considered for a full-time position at Equinox. I even handed him my résumé. He was practically in tears.

"What is this?" He handled the laminated document. "Man, you're really taking this fake job interview seriously. It's just a front." He glossed over the text. "Mensa? WME? You went to *what* school? Are you fucking with me?"

"No. I'd like to be a health coach."

He stared at me with a detached nonchalance that suggested

mine was merely one of many ridiculous requests he's heard that day—I can only imagine, given his clientele. The silence in the office punctuated by the bubblegum beats from the main workout area approached intolerable.

"You want to be a health coach," he finally said, looking dumbfounded if not amused.

"As part of our deal."

"You're a," he leaned forward and whispered, "drug dealer."

"I'm an entrepreneur."

"Oh boy."

"I think you should consider what I'm proposing."

"Or what," he laughed, "you're going to blackmail me?"

"Not unless you try to blackmail me."

He smiled. "Why would I agree to this?"

Because soon the water will dry up and there's going to be a global energy crisis. Because working here, I'll have a good excuse to stalk WME whenever I want. Because I'm trying to get my life in order—I wanted to say. Instead I said, "Because I'm giving you the deal of a lifetime. Because if you ever want to transact again you can explain I'm on payroll. Because influencer marketing is proving to generate *ten-x* the returns of traditional advertising channels, and I can help you grow your personal brand. Take your pick."

"Slow down. What are you talking about?"

"Are you connected to Wi-Fi? Here, give me your phone."

I pulled up my Instagram account and handed it back. As he studied the screen his face grew more and more concerned.

"How do you have so many followers?"

"That's not important. The right question is do *you* want that many followers?"

He thought it over.

"I also have sponsorship deals with health brands," I threw in for good measure.

"Do you even have a PT certificate?" he asked. "Company policy."

I gave him a look suggesting that to deny a drug dealer, even one as unsuspecting and metro as me, a double entendre I purposefully wove into my layered character, could only result in harrowing violence.

Ten minutes later the papers were signed. Jamie would be following up about the company's training program. I nodded along as I removed from the duffel bag's side pocket the half-pound of coke I'd brought in case he wanted it, which, thankfully, he did not, and put it down the front of my spandex to make my bulge look superhuman. I passed him the duffel bag. He handed me the Equinox backpack. "Welcome to the team," he said, tossing me a shirt from inside one of the desk drawers. Then he produced a raw stick of butter from the mini fridge beneath his desk and bit directly into it. He was keeping his keto fast going, he said. "Don't worry, it's pasture-raised, grass-fed."

Many years later I was not surprised to learn that an internet celebrity health coach took a group of unsuspecting clients to a cabin in the woods a few hours outside of Los Angeles and ate them alive. It's a good thing I never showed up for my first day of work.

Making a beeline for the exit, I literally ran into a brunette smokeshow with shapely tits, sharp bangs, and tattoos covering the left side of her body. She stumbled back and dropped her green smoothie on the floor, spilling some on her clothes. "Don't mind that, they'll mop it," I said, snapping at the girl behind the front desk like I owned the place. I opened my backpack wide enough for the smokeshow to see inside, handed her three crisp hundreds, texted myself from her phone, and told her to buy a new outfit before I nearly vomited. "Give me a call sometime if you want me to take you to your favorite restaurant."

Sprinting out of Equinox, I felt immortal. The automatic doors opened and the preternatural breeze took my sick away. I saw adrenals of light colliding into miracles out of thin air, saw the building blocks of life reassemble themselves into loving transports.

The days of desperation, that life was over.

I thanked Rick Ross for his contribution to culture, my art, and the possibilities both express, and stuffed a twenty inside his styrofoam cup, which I had failed to notice was piping hot. But it was no matter, he could get another one; I had so much love to give. I didn't even curse the elegant marbled WME mural as the security guard shouted for the dumb motherfucker to stop.

Strolling down Beverly Hills, I imagined licking ice cream cones made of money. Then I popped inside Gucci to buy a new suit because I could, paid in cash because I was rich, and let the saleswoman sell me perfume that I'd gift to Dani for all her help. Upon exiting, a red-headed stranger and her necky over-the-shoulder husband approached and asked if they'd seen me in anything popular, if I was that guy from that show. I smiled and deflected, but she wasn't convinced, and in that moment, dear reader, neither was I.

As I approached my car, I noticed the bum soundly asleep, dreaming bum dreams, the plastic Starbucks cup still half full. I unleashed the sizeable ziplock bag of coke from my spandex and placed it under his arm. Could that life be over now too? I got into the car and just as quickly got out and hustled over to retrieve the coke before he woke or anyone noticed, laughing at my gaffe like the ending credits of a primetime sitcom. In the window's tinted reflection, I saw my ancestors' wildest dreams.

When I arrived home later that evening Scott was in the living room. On the floor. In front of the couch. The lights off. A candle before him. Dimly lit. He was crying.

What's the matter?

It's over.

What is?

Dani broke up with me.

Uh-huh.

It gets worse.

Oh no. I ran into my bedroom. The safe was gone.

She stole the fucking safe! I yelled.

I know. She took mine too.

What the fuck!

She told me you tried to fuck her!

No, this is not happening.

Did you?

Who cares!

He sucked through tears. She's blackmailing me. She said don't come after her or she'll show UCLA.

What? Show UCLA what?

That I was selling drugs to my students. She has evidence. Videos. Photos. On her phone. I don't know.

Did she say anything about me? Does she have videos of me? I don't know.

Maybe when you think of Hollywood you imagine billboards promising not just the good life but the *best life*. On a sunny afternoon you can count by the handful the number of Bentleys on any given intersection.

And the people. My god, the people!

Is it time to call home and say I've made it, I'm finally famous? How the world is filled with such extraordinary people and I'm finally one of them?

* * *

Hi Dr __:

I hope all is well with you. I'm writing to let you know that the vyvanse is working fantastically. I feel my mood, motivation, and general outlook have improved. I don't use it every day, only when needed. The only problem is the dosage. I find that one pill (50mg) doesn't work. When I do need to use it, I end up taking two pills. I've already gone through my month's supply as a result. I don't want to take too much, but taking too little defeats the purpose. What do you suggest? Thanks–

* * *

Hi Dr ___:

Following up here. Thanks.

* * *

My apologies for not getting back to you sooner. It's been a bit hectic here. My mother, who is 92 and lives in South Africa, fell and broke her hip. At the hospital, they discovered she has cancer. I have been preparing to fly back to aid her but then got into a car accident myself. Nothing serious, just a few scratches.

In any case, 100 mg is an excessive dose. They do make a 70 mg. It cannot be called into the pharmacy. I can mail it to you. What is your address?

CHAPTER VIII

dmt and chateau

Chateau Marmont is Hollywood's apocryphal fuckchild. Hadean nights turned Holocene days. A big jeweled rock on a famous boulevard housing secrets since before movies could talk. It is the ultimate Hollywood landmark because it sells itself on a story larger than life, no knowing what's real and what's not.

I told the hostess I'd left to buy cigarettes, the bouncer said it was cool.

She glanced up, phone in hand, its blue crystalline screen piercing the night. Clipboard on the valet stand. "You've already been inside?"

I nodded, lying, the cigarette dangling from my mouth. I'd just come from Jo's.

There was no one around, the back entrance quiet compared to the shitshow out front. All night the streets complained under the pink purple dark. The helicopters overhead ripping down Sunset Boulevard. The traffic. The police diverting it. Raging fans thronged like street addicts, knowing not for what nor whom they raged. The press, the media, a medusahead of urgency. Hot mics, cameras rolling.

"I'm in the movie," I said. The wind picked up.

It was just before autumn, Hollywood having returned from its summer glamorama. As for me, I'd fallen out of time. Sparks shot and clicked and kept clicking as my thumb peeled against the metal grate. The empty sparks showed and clicked through my fingers.

"Here," she said, quick to produce a light. "Mr.—remind me your name?"

You needed an invitation to get in. Invitees were mailed golden credit cards that served as tickets. There was no re-entry. Off in the distance under a dark awning of manicured shrubs—succulents and cacti, some palms—two hotel waiters sat watching me, their ties flapping in the wind, the wind gusting through the branches.

"Been trying to quit," I said as the cigarette took flame, her hand nearly grazing my cheek. "Thought I could make it through the night." I exhaled, smiling. "Guess not."

The hostess opened her blazer and revealed a pack of Camels in her inner breast pocket, her immaculate cleavage. "Don't be hard on yourself," she said in solidarity. "I'm trying too. Failing."

Keeping a secret in Hollywood is like getting dateraped by a movie star. Management denied the party was happening until the day of, when red carpets were rolled out at 7:00 p.m. Once news broke, the press bumrushed the scene. Wax-embossed letters were slipped under the doors of hotel guests who hadn't been bought out for the weekend: the front entrance and driveway would be closed at 3:00 p.m., management explained. Alternative routes to get in and out of the building were provided along with a gift basket containing a free dinner voucher, a bottle of Chateau Mouton Rothschild, and, it was rumored, an eighth of Cali Kush. Workers were told the event was being hosted by a "world leader." You could not buy your way in.

"Dad smokes those," I said, referring to the Camels. It could have been any brand. "Well, he did. Before—" I coughed.

"What?" the hostess asked, fingering the pack's edges. Cream, maybe pink, fleck of polish.

"I just got back from New York," I said, looking off to the side. "The funeral—"

"Oh my god."

"No, no."

"Oh, honey."

"It's fine."

"I'm so sorry."

"Don't be," I said, exhaling the blue velvet smoke into a night remembered in no particular order. "It is what it is."

"How did he," she paused, "pass?" She leaned closer.

Well, my father had been sober for twenty-three years when he overdosed on vyvanse and killed himself, I wanted to say. Or was it that he confused my prescription amphetamines for his anti-nausea medication, selfsame container, selfsame surname, and drove his car into the furnace face of an oncoming pickup truck? Just spazzed out! It was the first time I'd visited New York since moving to Los Angeles over a year ago; I thought I'd go home and tell everyone how much better I was doing.

Look how much better I was doing.

"Lung cancer," I said, taking a drag of my cigarette to punctuate the complexity of my tortured state.

"Fuck."

There was no parking on the premises. For guests who preferred anonymity, their escorts were instructed to drive past the front entrance and go to the service entrance at the back of the hotel, where paparazzi and media and "journalists," laughable description, were barred. A Rolls Royce came up the sloping gravel through the purple night, a gothic machine, its headlights lecturing the awning. Burnt sand, long drapes. The castle just behind. The celebrated people and the people they keep on payroll. The door clicked. Like snowfall in summertime a famous actress slid by and up the stairwell into the stone archway, no need to confirm her name.

"I'm really sorry," the hostess said. "You look so familiar, but I need some verification." She rubbed her forearms, the night unseasonably cold and getting colder still. "I'm embarrassed to ask."

"Don't be sorry."

"Oh my god, I am!"

"You're fine. What do you need?"

"The gold credit card. Your invitation."

I patted my pocket, my eyes widening. "Shit, it's inside. Along with my jacket and wallet."

The wind picked up. The hostess quickly glanced behind her. Slight shiver. "Some form of proof then," her eyes pleading, offering promises.

I produced my phone and paused to look up at the sky. Then something funny happened.

X X X

Jo was heavy metaling on his silver Ibanez, unplugged, while I played air drums and counted how long I could hold my breath.

The room was hot, stale. It smelled like a porn set, the aftermath of many hours of deep penetration. Two fans were going from each wall, oscillating back and forth. My shirt on the floor, still I was dripping like a boxer. The lights bright, the smell of sage profound. A burning bundle of leaves wafted from a ceramic bowl on the carpet next to a framed portrait of Jo's dead cat and two, maybe three bouquets of dead roses, brown and grey and withered. A memorial had been arranged with some sense of care. But I couldn't look. Weed and mustard smelled from the corners. Mold.

I'd been going on and on about how one day I'd write a novel about an aspiring author who wrote his narrator into a metaliterary hero—transubstantiating from typeface to flesh, from prose to man—only he fucked it up and became an actor instead. But even I was tired of hearing myself talk.

"Read me your quote again," I said.

Remember Jo? He was a spiritual healer now, ready to take his message public. Phone in hand, I was in the middle of helping him make his first inspirational post on Instagram. Jo palm-gripped the neck of his guitar and said, "If you're at your emotional edge, go ahead and jump." Watch as he brooms the long dark hair from his crumpled brow, shimmies slightly under the weight of his tawny tunic. "We repress, deny, and dismiss what's truly coming up for us out of fear of losing control. But the obstacle is the way. What imprisons us directly points to our freedom."

"There you go," I said, setting the phone on the coffee table. "It's live."

Jo was so excited it reminded me of one of those nature shows where the mother doe gives birth standing up and out from the slop emerges some lion's next meal. We high-fived and caught only the bones of our hands. Jo lifted his guitar high toward the wooden ceiling and continued to shred while I banged on the table, banged on my knees, hallucinated seeing myself bodysurf over cauldrons of raving fans, hot omen of my life to come.

After a few minutes of this, Jo's phone made a dinging sound, its blue crystalline screen lighting up. I felt my heart flutter, hoping it was Cash.

"Shit. No luck tonight," Jo said, reading from the device. His guitar hung dumbly from the strap around his neck. "Cash says it's impossible to get in without an invite. Industry chicks only."

I'd been sober from the hard stuff for one month and the flatness of the world seemed prophetic, Dostoevskian—like the whole thing might snap at any moment. Sober, I thought there might be more to life.

There wasn't.

I hurled myself across the room toward the dresser and shoveled enough coke to make a sandcastle in the middle of the silver platter, then proceeded to snort the entire pile.

"Brother, don't!" Jo said, concerned or affecting concern. He lumbered over, the neck of the guitar slapping his torso. He took the platter away from me and said, "We already had one scare tonight. Plus, this stuff doesn't exactly grow on trees."

"Actually," I said, knitting my eyebrows together as if in deep meditation, "it does."

Laughter trampolined from two heads colliding as I handed him, could've stabbed him with, the metal straw, the laughter suddenly sounding very far away. I couldn't tell if I wanted to kiss him or bathe in his blood when I felt my heart pause, just stop dead in its cage. I knew something was off because I experienced laughter not as a sound but as a pulse, as if encased in a pillow, the echo of many laughters billowing from my vocal cords, around my body, then around many bodies, in luminous harmony; no, it was more like one laughter occurring now in the present and in many pasts. I experienced time slow to a pause and solidify into a physical mass, a shape, experienced myself floating above it, looking down on myself as I heard my voice ask, whimpering, "Did you write that quote for me?" Higher I went. From an infinite perch I saw my life as a collection of episodes, scrollable selections as if featured on Netflix. At will, I could zoom into any episode and enter the memory as if reliving it, and just as easily zoom out.

Here I'm standing in my parent's basement on Candle Street, opening the acceptance letter from my prestigious high school, slight tremble of hand as I read and reread the opening sentence, laughing the way I laugh when alone, uneasy of my own joy. Now I'm on the London Eye with you whom I'll never name, glass bubble ascending in rotation as you tell me you don't want to go back to Barnard, Westminster Abbey in my periphery, a city of windows aligned in perfect precision, laughing because of the obvious tourist trap we'd found ourselves in, laughing because we were twenty-one and in love, real love, for the first time, and what's more beautiful than when sad news is only sad because of the intensity of your happiness? What's more hopeful than promising to write letters from abroad and actually making the effort to write them? Now it's the morning after we drank his dad's entire bottle of Bombay Sapphire, my first black-out drunk, I'm fifteen and Doug is asking me if I blew him last night; he's joking but he's not, and I'm laughing it off, swearing I'd never tell...Happy moments, mostly. Then I tried to enter the ancient memory of fishing off the docks in Greenport with my father, I'm five or six, the only phase of my life you'd catch me wearing a baseball cap, when the screen glitched and froze into a flat band of pixels and particles, dogged paralysis, cold halo around the edges. I felt nothing. I felt everything. I held out my hand.

"I wrote it for you," I heard Jo say, taking my hand, speaking as if from a foreign room, a different time, "but I also wrote it for the collective you, the universal you."

I began to cry, choked and silent tears. Because I knew. Here I was with no stories to recite, none written. Typed tears in Garamond falling from a face I'll never describe, chose not to describe. Deleted memory. Fade to blinking cursor.

"Give me the fucking platter," the last thing I remember saying.

X X X

"I heard the prince rented out the hotel for the weekend," said the stylish gentleman, late forties. He was dressed in a beige tuxedo with black trim, no tie. A studio head, I gathered, he possessed the aura of someone who used his power for sexual favors and got away with it.

"The *entire* hotel."

"It's true," the tiny pop star said, big eyes and convincing lips. "He bought out every room, and I mean *every* room. My team put the deal together."

"Ah. Remind me, who represents you?"

"I heard that too," from someone else.

"Management would never allow it," the woman to my left

said, winking. Early to mid-sixties, jet-black hair streaked with silver, she was of an older generation of new money.

"You mean would never admit it," the studio head said. They all laughed.

Some prince of the Saudi royal family, a trillionaire, was financing a new film. Something about fracking in Bahrain, black market oil, and the CIA. The news was very scandalous around town, very political. James Franco was set to star in the movie, I think, but it could have been Ben Affleck. Many celebrities would join us tonight at Chateau.

We sat in the expansive lobby retrofitted like a palace salon with large round tables and magnificent sofas. The band played a peculiar blend of classical and eastern, jazz and mystical. Everyone talked of the famed hotel. French gothic. Thick muddy walls colored flushed-nude canary and burgundy carpets. Massive chandeliers hung from raftered ceilings. Newly upholstered Arabian drapes of black-and-gold damask; blood-red-and-cream silks hung overhead. The wildest imagination of an old-world carnival tent. Pewter-and-orange-speckled kilim swathed the walls. Wax dripped from hundreds of burning candles into bronze alhambra. Black lanterns with Moroccan fretwork. Gold lanterns. Jeweled lamps. Lights dimmed to produce a darkness. Inside, all was permitted.

"Are you staying overnight?"

"No, I live in town. Are you?"

"No. Clive and I are over in Brentwood."

"You?" the pop star asked me.

I was rolling or reeling so hard I couldn't talk. I frowned in a way that suggested my bastion in the Hills eclipsed this shithole.

"Anyone?"

All shook their heads: No.

"I stayed here once, back when I was living in Paris," the blond actress said, sipping champagne. "When I arrived, there was this old gentleman who greeted you, if that's the word. He was like Alfred the butler, you know, in the Batman films. No, he was like Oscar Wilde. What an inspiring performance. Like he was merely tolerating you. Because didn't you know how lucky you were to be coming to a place as wealthy, as storied, as this one? And yet it was not unbecoming. It was really quite charming."

A waiter approached our table. He was ambiguously tan and lanky with long hair in a ponytail and he didn't smile and he didn't frown. From behind him emerged two brown servant girls dressed in black leather wetsuits and hijabs carrying buckets of ice before them like their very own hearts. One was short and chesty, the other was not, and out of some cabalistic sense of obedience not once did they acknowledge each other. They set the buckets onto the table, and the waiter carefully placed a bottle of expensive vodka as big as your leg into each to chill.

"The prince wants to mindfuck Hollywood," the older woman with streaked hair said.

"He succeeded," said someone across the table.

Arched windows looked out onto a grassy courtyard that lit up like a movie set, a roving museum where more money than Disney-god walked around the damp grass and admired itself. Notice the relatively delicate, relatively thin yet visible brushstrokes, the open composition of light play, the inclusion of movement: here and there, the impression of someone important. Outside blushed as when immediately following rainfall. Inside smelled like an ancient bathhouse, woody and balsamic. Bottles and glasses clinked and emptied. Wine flowed. Voices poured.

Two more servants, or whatever you'd call them, issued forth with pitchers of orange and cranberry juice, tonic and soda water, eight tumblers total of decade-aged cabernet and chardonnay. Two other servants poured the vintage Dom Perignon into our flutes. I downed mine entire and asked for a top up. Lately I'd been drinking with unparalleled aggression. For the past year I'd exhausted myself pretending to be a miserable artist and now, fully aware the dream was dead, was no longer pretending. Most of my favorite authors were drunks, I reasoned; maybe they were onto something.

"I heard the hotel is haunted," the Italian director said.

"No more or less than Hollywood."

Everyone laughed in a way that suggested we were better than normal people; I was practically on the floor. A famous British stage actor came over and said hello. I rose and made introductions, even though I had no idea who any of these people were. The model girl to my right gushed and the stage actor looked at me and, after a short beat, transferred his hand to hers as if performing a transaction, it was so precisely executed. Lights poured upon the table. There was a click and flash from beyond and then another. Photographers scurried about capturing moments supposedly worth remembering.

"Where are *you* staying tonight?" someone asked the stage actor.

"Why here, of course."

A few notable celebrities, one extremely famous, came and went. I befriended both a fashion designer whose clothes I'd be buying from major retailers in less than a year and a well-known

DJ who had just completed his first residency in Vegas. When the latter asked how the *project* was coming along, said with a wink, I had no idea what he meant—maybe he saw into my sad sunken eyes and was mocking me, The Author buried alive in his casket of a book, its cold empty pages. Or maybe he simply mistook me for someone else; that was happening quite a bit tonight.

"The prince wants to show the West that he and his people are coming to Hollywood," the older woman with streaked hair tells me, bidding to strike up conversation. "New players in town."

I'd seen this woman before; I thought she was a news anchor back when she had normal hair, but she could have been the President's wife. "To the prince," I said, raising my glass. Something about this struck me as hilarious. I grabbed the woman's thigh to balance myself and produced the paper tissue from my pocket, unraveling its contents in my hand: molly and vyvanse and whatever else, probably viagra. I nodded along as she counted out loud the number of celebrities walking about.

(Years later, after I'd been banned from the premises, I learned that this woman *was* management.)

I swallowed the pills conspicuously in a way that suggested advil.

"He wants us to know he's into all the great things of the West," the older woman said, loud enough for the table to hear. Then, leaning over: "Got any of that for me?"

I smiled and kissed her with a passion incongruous to the moment, a non-sequitur wildly inappropriate given the circumstances.

"Oh dear," she said, touching her lips. "Yes, please."

She adjusted her lipstick with the help of a pocket mirror in her purse. I handed her a pill of I don't know what and sprawled back into the myth of my existence. Silently I sat chewing myself.

"Oh look, he's coming," someone, maybe Paris Hilton, said.

A group of Saudi bridemodels filed down the winding stairwell in somnambulant procession. Dressed in split-open abaya gowns, nocturnal red-and-bronze netting, bare shoulders, bare legs. Syncopated steps, one by one. Sparklers spat outwardly from their delicate hands crisscrossed in each other's arms. The ringleader, a dude in black vaquero garb, black masked. Behind them followed the prince, his elegant white robe, his head lowered, shrouded.

"Shit," the handsome studio head said, amused. "He wants to compete with the studios."

"Be the bridge to Hollywood from the Middle East."

"It will never work."

Yes, it would, I want to say from the future. But I was off to find Woolf.

X X X

Earlier that night I'd arrived at the garagehouse with no sense of the night to follow, no plan for tomorrow.

I walked in and shut the door and thought maybe I'd entered the twilight zone. Vials and containers of all shapes and sizes lined the shelves along the far-side wall. It appeared as if the drugs Scott and I had stolen months ago had been replaced. By whose doing? With what financing? Jo was cat-cowing in the middle of the living room floor just before the coffee table where Scott had lost his shit. The place had been done up. Electric guitars hung on the walls: Les Paul, Fender Jaguar, Rickenbacker, some others. Huge desert plants and cacti in mauve clay pots lined the perimeter. There was a record player, one of those classic 1960s Pierre Bartet consoles that my grandparents owned. Had it always been there? The room was hot, the old fan going stochastically. Sage and weed produced a horrible holy smell, ounces of the latter littered the coffee table. With one long exhale Jo straightened his arms and swung his ass up and back into an elegant downward dog. He held the position as I waited with a patience I did not possess.

I needed a guy. Since selling all the drugs, I'd never settled on a new guy, and maybe Jo would be my guy again. Personally, I was willing to look past the whole "robbery" and "murder" thing. Seeing as I had no money, a persistent theme in this phase of my development, I agreed to help Jo build his Instagram account—perhaps my most embarrassing confession to date. In exchange, I'd have access to free drugs and whatever wisdom Jo had to share. Soon I'd be coming over every night.

"Greetings, my brother," he said, swinging up to his feet, wiping the sweat from his brow. He hugged me hello. "It's so good to see you. How long has it been?"

"Hi. Yes. I don't know."

He stared into my eyes. "A few months, at least. So much has changed."

He could see I was upset.

"What's wrong?"

"May I?"

"What's mine is yours."

I walked to the couch and from underneath pulled forth the

platter of coke, placed it on the coffee table, and kamikazed into the giant pile like a tyro surfer into a hundred-foot wave.

"I'm so tired of being called the bad guy," we both heard me say. "It's like, okay, you want me to be 'transparent' and 'vulnerable,'" said using air quotes, "but only so far as it's exactly what you want to hear." Shocked, I was certain I would elaborate and made no effort to stop myself from doing so. "Women love to cast men as emotionally unavailable but only because they can't handle what we have to say."

"Slow down, brother. Slow down." Jo relit the extinguished sage and breathed it in, offering to cleanse me with its magic powers. "May *I*?"

"No, man, I don't cleanse," I said, brushing him off, not really sure what I was saying. "It's like, no shit I shut down and close off. I'm wrong if I speak and selfish if I don't. Every conversation turns into managing her fucking feelings."

"What? Who?"

"First of all, I didn't even *know* we were dating. I thought she was my fucking *assistant*. Then she fucks my best friend! Girls in this town are insane."

"Brother, calm down," Jo said, breathing deeply as if to absorb my upset. "This is why, amongst many reasons," he laughed desperately, "I have chosen the path of celibacy."

I rubbed my gums with the remnant coke or whatever was on the table and lit a cigarette without asking because after you've jammed a gun in someone's face, even if he didn't know it was you, the thought of asking permission for anything seems lower class.

"Why don't you tell me what happened?" Jo said, placing the burning sage inside the bowl next to the cat memorial.

I pulled out my phone, tapped into my text thread with Dani, scrolled up past her latest texts threatening to reveal everything to Jo if I didn't take her back, and began to read:

"'Oh, a text message breakup! Really? Wow. I was starting to learn that you can't hold me or care for me in any real way, but this is downright disgusting. WAKE. THE. FUCK. UP.'" I spoke in a lurid staccato, making sure to emphasize each period. "'I would never feel the need to spell this out to such an asshole but in this instance it's necessary. You do NOT get to treat me or any woman this way. You do NOT get to come into my life, pierce my heart, pierce my body, feel me surrender to you and love you, only to completely fuck off when things get messy.'"

"Who is this?" Jo asked, sitting down on the couch, newly upholstered.

I was embarrassed if not terrified to admit it was Dani—remember, she and Jo were friends. His face contorted into a shape approaching disapproval, and, stimulated by the coke, I felt the need to explain myself. "I did it over text," I said, "because last night she said she never wanted to see me again and then spent the next hour crying and asking if we were broken up." I took a drag from the cigarette. "You don't ask if you're broken up if you're not broken up!" He waved his hands to lower my voice. "I texted her in the morning to confirm that we were *not* together because we were *never* together, and I didn't want there to be any confusion over the matter. You know, put it in writing."

"You've been together for this long?" he asked. "Since I last saw you?"

"We were never together!"

"Right."

I read on:

"'You partner with a good woman'—*partner!*" I practically shouted, "'who day after day gives herself to you. Her love, her time, her creativity. In service of whatever you want. And how do you respond? You constantly let your triggers take over and leave her feeling unwelcome. Shut down when she needs support. Seduce, penetrate, only want convenience, and then you leave.'"

"Hey man, this feels like a betrayal of privacy."

"Okay, where do I begin?" I said, breaking character, nursing the cigarette, the smoke curling into my eyes. "First of all, I'm pretty sure she was following me."

"Following you?"

"Yes. As in stalking me."

"That can't be," Jo said, deeply confused, his insane eyes. "Are there women who do that?"

"You tell me." I began to pace. "She lives in Venice but then *randomly* runs into me in West Hollywood? In Beverly Hills? At Equinox when I'm in *business* meetings? Oh, you shop at *this* Trader Joe's? Café IF is my favorite coffee shop too! Don't worry, I know plenty of guys who go to tanning salons. Come on! That's a once in a lifetime kind of probability, not once in a week."

"I don't know…" he said, trailing off. "Maybe there are and I'm just not that interesting."

I could see I was losing him and tossed him the phone. "Here," I said. "You read."

He fumbled the device and raised it to eyelevel, mumbling, "'Seduce, penetrate, only want convenience, and then you leave.'"

"Read it out loud!" I shouted, waving the cigarette, reveling in the performance of losing my temper. Again he gestured to lower my voice. "Go on," I said.

"'Now I see that I didn't vet you enough to make sure you were safe, and that's on me,'" Jo read Dani's words, repositioning himself on the couch. "'But you outright dishonored me. All you had to do was learn how to comfort me when you made a mess, learn to make some compromises. I know you're just going to read this message and think I'M the problem, I'M the bitch, it was MY fault what happened with Scott and the money,'"—I winced—"'but that's on YOU. You have serious ISSUES. You're so fucking cold. You just ruined something with a human being who believed in you, who was genuinely willing with her heart open to create something incredible with you…'" He stopped and said, "Man, I can't read this. This is brutal."

"Read it!" I shouted, then realized I was shouting. "We'll work on your Instagram as soon as you're finished. I need perspective."

I need to call out the inherent complication of performing this for Jo *without* saying what really happened: Dani stole the money to make a point; she wanted me to commit to her. Fine, so I took her back. (I was desperate!) But the relationship felt intolerable, I just couldn't do it. Meanwhile Scott was furious at me, convinced I'd forced myself on Dani. *That* was why she left him—it was unfathomable that she was playing him, playing us, the entire time. For weeks our home was divided by a cold and barely civil war, only the Israeli-Palestinian conflict rivalled its intractability. Sadly, pathetically, without Jo I had nowhere else to turn. (And I never did get the money back.)

Reluctantly Jo picked up the phone and, dear reader, he read on:

"'It didn't have to be hard. But you made it so fucking hard. Like it was all such an inconvenience. Then you toss me away like some Tinder slut. Just because you don't know how to use hashtags and hate social media doesn't give you the right to disrespect me and how much I've done for you. Good luck getting famous when you can't even post a fucking selfie.'"

I cringed, wanted to press delete; Jo had to believe I knew about *growth hacking*. I made a face to imply that she was full of shit, jealous of my number of followers. Again I felt compelled to explain myself. I said, in so many words, that things got weird, obsessive even. Forget that she screwed my best friend, all she cared about was managing my online identity and used it as a convenient excuse to make her life all about mine. The entire relationship felt staged, every authentic moment nullified by having to capture and post it on social media. Here's us eating sushi on a Wednesday afternoon, I re-enacted for Jo, crushing the baller lifestyle. *Snap*. There's you drinking your coffee, thinking of something brilliant to write. *Snap*. Here's us driving up PCH, my man is always making time for me. (Your *man*?) *Snap*. There's you crying at your desk, so poetic. *Snap*. In your workout gear, so hot. *Snap*. Babe, take off your shirt for this one. *Snap*.

"No baller lifestyle. No poetry in my morning coffee. Not your man!" I said, looking for sympathy in Jo's gaze, finding none.

"'You are disgusting,'" he read on, looking me straight in the eyes with a loathing that cannot be manufactured. "'You did not deserve my pussy, did not deserve my love, did not deserve my brilliance. I have never, EVER given anyone my rage like this before, but you DO fucking deserve it. I hope this message serves you in the future, you fucking cunt,'" Jo said as he threw the phone at the couch with superfluous intensity, consumed by a commitment to the performance that undoubtedly I provoked. But there was more.

I picked up the phone, invested in completing the virtual argument I started, and read aloud:

"'You literally lived into your character, The Author, who you won't shut up about but can't even write. I hope you don't because he's the only person more self-absorbed than you. And you've become him. Congratulations on your life's ambitions coming true. Fuck off,'" I said as Dani to myself to Jo. "'Seriously, just do what you do best and fuck off.'"

I tossed the phone to punctuate the conclusion. And where was my sympathy?

Jo cursed and screamed and curled into the corner of the couch—no, he stood and grabbed its armrest to stop himself from hurling, what, maybe the phone at me. But that's not right either. I expected Jo to explode like the rage of death I'd been waiting for, but he didn't say a word. He just walked over to his guitar and picked it up. The silence was terrifying. Finally, after strumming a few pickless chords, in a remote and flaccid way he said, "You think you have all these problems," lifting the strap over his head. "But your problems are luxuries. You have so much love thrown your way you don't know how to let it in. You're oblivious."

I guess you could say my drug dealer was also my life coach. Because in his or the platter's glossy reflection, I began to doubt myself, began to doubt the credibility of my misery.

Yes, I was poor, but up until graduation my entire life had been paid for by my parents; if ever I was in serious need I could always move home or ask for financial support. Yes, I was depressed, but only because I hadn't self-actualized by my mid-twenties—plus who isn't depressed? Sure, I worked astonishingly hard at school, drove myself insomniatic in a twisted bid for undefined success, but I'd never known *real* suffering. Until recently my greatest heartbreak was the death of my childhood dog Rex, who lived to be sixteen and was put down gently. Okay, fine, maybe I was an addict, but that's because until this year my life had been so predictably boring, so normal, I felt I needed a chemical excuse to provide what reality could not. No doubt I was alienated from my family, resented having to raise myself and be my own authority at far too young an age, but that's because my parents worked full-time white-collar jobs to provide me with everything I wanted, every opportunity, including an elite private education. So Mom and Dad were spiritually absent and culturally oblivious, so they contributed practically nothing to my personality apart from a biochemical proneness to anxiety and addiction—they were there for every soccer game, every award ceremony, every graduation. Mom loved me so much she even put one of those horrible bumper stickers on her car: My son is an honors fag or whatever.

Was this not the curse of privilege, ridiculous phrase? Here I was, lamenting my designer life marked by consumption and self-absorption, completely incapable of putting anything together without the help of Google; meanwhile the solution to all my problems was handed to me on a silver platter—no, not the coke; I just needed to sit down and fucking write.

I thought with actual horror: Is my projection of The Author just one big cry for help?

Here I was modeling my entire life on a character that only exists in my imagination, waiting for the day my life would prove compelling enough to write about it. Meanwhile I hadn't written seriously since college, and could I really consider my senior thesis project, a failed novel that was at best a rip-off of *The Sun Also Rises*, at worst a rip-off of *Tender is the Night*, serious writing?

I shuddered. The truth hit me like a Dylan Thomas obituary: roistering, wasted, and doomed. I'd become a parody of a writer with writer's block, only I wasn't a writer and my block was the backbone of this pitiful novel's entire plot: my narrator's twisted ambition to become an actor, which he hated, instead of an author, the only thing he claimed to love, who one day, despite his drug-induced delusions, wakes up a celebrity and writes the great work of his life, becoming a figure of possibility for an entire generation.

I railed a line so fat I cried. That I was a fraud was undeniable. That I understood myself to be the living protagonist of my own fiction, pathetic. That I impaled myself with a senseless amount of drugs to both avoid my fraudulence and in a perverse way feed my virtual narrator's baseless drive toward fame could only be described as schizophrenic.

I'd become a caricature of the artist as a young man. Dani was right: I'd become a caricature of The Author, a character I'd probably never write. I'd become a caricature of myself.

Which was when I snapped back to life, sucking for air. The white of the room condensing into grey matter, shapes with depth, Jo's slender brown face, so many whiskers, colors returning. I must've blacked out because all I could hear was Jo shouting,

"Holy shit. Holy shit." I saw my shirt on the floor, what looked like vomit. "Holy shit."

"What happened?"

X X X

I was getting jiggy with Will Smith or Steve Urkel on the dancefloor when I saw or remembered seeing the text from Woolf.

The underground garage had been repurposed into a pop-up nightclub. An unlikely space for a dance party. Low ceilings, no windows. Big columns bore years of mechanical musk, the smell of gasoline. Teakwood and tobacco candles inside hundreds, maybe thousands of lanterns lined the perimeter of the garage to metabolize its presence, surely unsafe. It was a type of dark that makes you feel dirty.

In the middle of the underground was a platform slightly raised to make a stage. Steve Aoki or some goblin stood in the DJ booth off to the side, the music so loud, so dumb, you thought your head might shoot off. Hands in the air. The clichés unforgiving. The smiles, the sweat. The bass exploding from the overhead speakers; the crowd cheering along to comets colliding into pop songs. It sounded like the inner world of a computer, its seizure dreams. From afar I thought I saw Woolf, her sleek auburn hair, buzzed sides, and nearly tripped over Channing Tatum doing the worm as I hauled myself in her direction. She walked with a bounce, like a bunny, unaware of her importance.

I made sure to keep cool as I danced through the swarm of famous people, shaking hands and patting shoulders like this was my normal life. Over the horrendous din I could hear next to nothing but smiled and nodded at the actors, rappers, pop stars, models, talk show hosts, startup geeks, media heads, NBA players so tall they triggered a latent inferiority complex which I swallowed along with whatever pills remained in my pockets, and continued shuffling through the interchangeable mashup of celebrities when the music stopped and scores of servers raced into the crowd like professional tennis ball kids holding flashlights and champagne bottles and plastic cups. The underground was so dark you couldn't see the person next to you. A terrorist could have wiped out half of American culture in one notorious inferno, a twelve-figure ransom. After a few staid moments and some harmless groping, the stage came alive, lit up like an invasion, its floor paneling a pattern of LED-squares, white beaming lights. A troop of women, nude but for their pasties, appeared in carnival burlesque regalia like a dada punking of the classics. Sparklers shooting from their vaginas as they performed a faux striptease. Music blasted. Amazed, I walked on.

But I walked directly into a dance-off. Before I knew it, Nicki Minaj or whoever the hell is grinding against me while I'm twirling her in circles while a famous Late Night host is smacking my ass like Jenny my babysitter. With a hard jerk, I'm pulled forward into a pirouette, the floor dizzying below me, a small crowd forming to keep me perpendicular. Hollers and cheers. Kicking outwardly, my left foot matching Nicki's, we kind of snaked and coiled into and out from each other before the bass dropped and scattered into a seizing trap beat, clapping hi hats, echoed decay, lasers firing, her hips going psychotic. I was on the floor heel spinning around myself in a circular maze, mimicking the bebop kids I used to watch at Grand Central Station, mimicking badly, when, what the fuck, now I'm up doing the crip walk alongside a famous pop star who's sold over a dozen million albums, rotating over the heels and balls of my feet like I'd been given the code. Together we led a flash mob parade through Hollywood's belly underground, the music so loud it dominated all else and the lights miraculous spindles of color and mad darkness flashing. So disorienting that when Harvey Weinstein took my face in his hands and whispered in my ear—notice the dry and cracked lips, avoid the smell of garlic—I thought I might've misheard him. I can't hear you, I mouthed back, staring into eyes absent of reflection. Come to my room, he said, or something about the death tube, or goodnight moon—I didn't understand, nor did it matter. You'll never remember this, I said. Either I'll never get published or your life is about to end. Then I let myself fall backwards into the thunder and lights, or shall I say I dared to leapfrog over Lamar Odom to get on stage? I must have because while crowd-surfing over a sea of celebrities, a cauldron of raving faces, my erection profound, I could finally relax. I'd been absorbed.

Later I found a handsome Middle Eastern man at the urinals.
"How does your night go?" he asked, zipping up.
"I just had a baby chicken stuffed up my ass," we both heard me say. I needed to put things in perspective.
But he just shrugged. "Praise be to god, I feel good," he said and flushed.

X X X

Palo Santo, sage, sweat: toxic staples of fear and loathing in Los Angeles.

The garage seeped in red. The air hot and heavy. No light from outside, no windows. The sprinkler outside tapping against the paneling, Madonna's "Like a Prayer" playing softly from the record player. See Jo dance in a circle around himself as if performing a powwow. The weight of his tunic too heavy for his ecstasy; off it comes. Bare brown skin, bony ribs, pink-lit prana. A maroon carpet newly laid because of my doing, a different time, a night poorly narrated but not remembered.

When he sat down, he told me his life was over the moment they entered the room. They stole everything. The drugs, the money. Who they were, he didn't care. They were a gift. He opened his eyes wide like moons full of it, as if he were asking something of me, but I couldn't look. For weeks he dreamed or half-dreamed of a snake eating its own tail, but that's not right, it was more like a snake with two heads eating themselves. (How did I know he would say that?) And his cat. They killed his cat. It was his fault, he said. What they delivered was the consequence of his own choosing.

What he hadn't mentioned, what was difficult to admit, was his daughter. Sweetie, don't worry, they're my friends, he lied. We were only roughhousing. How do you explain to your little girl that her pet had been blown to hell? Like a cartoon but not a cartoon. That she saw what happened was clear but what she saw was not. What stories does she tell herself? Who can say what's in her head? What's fact, what's fiction? Another's memory has no witness. She's only but a little girl.

"Where is she now?"

"Back East with her mom, the cheating bitch."

Then Jo told me about the money, how he'd saved enough to start over. He's a guitar teacher; he also fixes guitars. He runs his own business, Jovan's Magic Guitar Shop, through which he launders his drug earnings. It's all cash, all legitimate. He has enough money to buy a home and build a studio. His boss promised him more protection. They can't touch me, he said, but they took my daughter. He's not a liar, he said. He's a lot of things but not a liar. He'd been lying to himself for far too long. No more. His new life was beginning, had already begun.

"I know my life's purpose now. I am here to shepherd lost souls into their spiritual awakening. To help them choose themselves." He paused and leaned forward. "I see myself as a spiritual healer. A teacher of many."

"An influencer," I said, wishing this all would end.

"Thanks to you." He smiled. "Deep gratitude for helping me spread my message."

"Like a child, you whisper softly to me," Madonna sang chalkily from the old speaker. From the floor Jo continued petting my hair as I laid on the couch. He'd wrapped me in a blanket. My shirt was ruined.

He told me to come to the floor, he had something for me. A message. A download. We were going to discover my portal. He crossed his legs and assumed a meditative position.

"Close your eyes," he said.

Some part of me knew that some part of Jo knew what really happened the night of the robbery, that it was me all along. So this is how it ends, I thought, kneeling and closing my eyes.

But it was not the end. Jo held my hands and walked me through a guided meditation. I won't even pretend to remember what he said nor convey with any shred of accuracy the ideas put forth. He called himself a channel, a correspondent. He appeared to me like a waterfall, something you'd try to capture on camera but could never capture; no, he was the digital blip in the photograph, in the background what appears to be a UFO is merely a ray of light refracted around vagrant splatters. But maybe. Transfixed by his own galactic rapture, he talked about the godforce, talked about portals. Portals are mystical locations scattered across the globe, often concealed or unfamiliar to the naked eye. They manifest in various forms. Sometimes as a holograph revealing a floral archway or vapor drizzle drawing into itself through a wormhole. Sometimes as circular orbs, like hovering ringlets in the sky, or the dimples of a lucent rain on a calm windless lake. Still often they are right in front of you, assuming the dull shape of life's common occurrences. The key to connecting with your portal is realizing that it already exists inside you.

He told me to align my vibrational resonance with that of the portal. To call it in. As you release the deceptions of ego and magnify your awareness, you can become your own portal to a new life through a clear channel. The godforce is the energy available on the other side. I wanted to leave. Sit down, he said. The godforce is the all-that-is, a radiant super-energy composed of thirty-three energies hugging together like DNA. The godforce is a spiraling portal that allows you to transcend the limitations of the physical world. But you must make an effort, make it your purpose. The energy doesn't just pick you up like an Uber. You must stretch yourself. You must expand yourself into its dimensions and align to its vibration. Are you ready? Am I ready?

The better part of me wanted to tell Jo I'd killed his cat and swam in its blood—but the addicted part of me needed free access to his bounty of amphetamines and whatever psychedelics he'd surely been macrodosing to talk with such wild confidence. I acquiesced.

"How do I find my portal?"

"You have to call it in."

"Call it in?"

"Call it in."

"This is so LA. I can't."

"Quiet the mind. Let go of the ego. Imagine your portal. Hold it in your mind's eye. And that's the *secret*," he said with a mesmeric hissing that made me drop into a seated position on the carpet. Hypnotized. My body, yes. These hands.

I allowed myself to meditate over the mystery of the world. I imagined not death but death's captor. Helical moaning in the yawn of a rifle. Thus we sat, my hands in his, the record player no longer playing music, only the sound of static. Then the phone dinged. I tried to match Jo's breath. But the phone dinged again. Livid, I opened my eyes. There on the coffee table, Jo's phone made another loud dinging sound.

"There it is, the third calling." Jo nodded. "Pick it up. What does it say?"

"It's Cash," I said, reading the screen.

His eyes lit up.

"Who is Cash?" I asked, handing him the phone.

"My boss. He promotes for the big venues in LA. Then we have this, our side hustle. We cover all corners of the market."

He smiled, the light reflecting from his teeth. This guy really is a genius, I thought, conceding if not lamenting his Harvard education. "A lot of celebrity clientele. Looks like I'm going to have a few customers soon. There's that big party."

"What party?"

"You don't know? Practically all of West Hollywood is shut down for it."

"I have been…fasting."

"Seeing as you're an actor, I can't believe you don't know about it."

"I am not an actor! I'm an author," I choked. "Aspiring author."

"Yes. Beautiful acknowledgment."

"Where is the party?"

"Chateau Marmont."

"Is that the weird Scientology building on Sunset?"

"It's a hotel. Not Scientology."

"Oh."

"Where John Belushi overdosed. It's famous."

I looked down at my hands held within his. He squeezed.

"Don't you see?"

"What?"

"How the universe provides?"

"What are you talking about?"

"The phone rang with a message for you."

"The message was for you."

"The sun rises in one place and sets somewhere else, and if not for eyes it'd be hard to believe it so. And that is the point. Because the sun does not move at all."

I leaned back, uncomfortable by all this guru talk.

"I think we found your portal," Jo said.

"You're saying a private party at a famous Hollywood hotel is my portal?"

"I'm simply reflecting what occurred. Miracles are all around us."

"Can Cash get me in?"

"I'll text him."

I lit a cigarette and immediately texted Woolf.

"Brother, I've been meaning to ask," he said. "Do you mind stepping outside to smoke?"

X X X

Me: you need to come to chateau

Woolf: Who is this?

Me: are you kidding? please tell me you're kidding

Woolf: You need to stop texting me

Me: i can get you in

Woolf: Bullshit
How did you get in?

Me: maybe if you fucking responded for once you'd know shit I'm sorry
come I'll get you in

Woolf: How?

Me: you'll be my date
i'll say you're my agent

Woolf: That's funny

Me: it shouldn't be
i have Newman for you
wtf news*

Woolf: What?

Me: are you still at WME?

Woolf: What do you want?

Me: you'll have to come if you want to know

Woolf: Are you really there or is this bullshit?

Me: yes really here

Woolf: send photo

Me: can't no phones
literally texting through sealed plastic bag

Woolf: If you're serious, I'm impressed

Me: i am serious. will you come?

Woolf: You're a liability
Yes, I'm at WME

Me: great, see you soon?

Woolf: I can't believe I'm saying this
I'll be there in an hour

Me: make it two
we could be Hollywood's next power couple

Woolf: You're an idiot
And I'm not your agent

X X X

I was in the service elevator searching for Woolf while this Victoria's Secret model was going on about DMT.

"Our shaman is coming tonight," she said. "We're holding ceremony."

How embarrassing, I thought. But that wasn't all. I'd recently masturbated to this woman on multiple occasions. I was ashamed, like she could sniff out a pervert, but not ashamed enough to ask if I could join. She said of course, all are welcome. There was a bodyguard off to the right and another behind me. Large men dressed in black. Sunglasses on, indoors, at night.

The clunky doors opened and together we walked into an ugly darklit hallway. Two Disney boys were kissing each other outside a hotel room. Next to them, unperturbed, two young girls—"Youtubers," the model mentioned, whatever that meant—sat buried in their phones. I wanted to say something profound about the alarming societal imperative to self-lobotomize via surgical screens, how the digital delusion in which we're all participating scales well beyond the younger generations, that just because *Mom* doesn't know how to upload photos to Facebook directly, might accidentally post private messages on your public wall, does not mean she hasn't crossed over—but I was nearly run over by Pharrell and Steve-O racing go-karts. I jumped to the side, holding the model for dear life, and was told hands off by one of the bodyguards. Unperturbed, she kept talking, making wild claims about the "Medicine," punctuating the word like a proper noun, saying all politicians should be mandated to take DMT or ayahuasca or at least mushrooms before taking office—it sounded very convincing. But before I could respond, we were already there, wherever we were. She opened the door and inside the penthouse we found the Venezuelans, seemingly awaiting my arrival.

"The Author!" Julian said, brushing long curly hair from his face. He finished tying his robe and gave me an affectionate hug hello, the gold chain around his neck stabbing my ribs, his hair smelling of pomade and protein. I was taken aback, felt a bit scandalized; I thought maybe he was gay but that wouldn't explain my half-erection. I don't know why but I attempted to kiss him in the European style to disengage but I didn't fully commit and caught the edge of his mouth. He laughed and waved his finger. From the threshold of the balcony entrance, across the living room, his brother Gabriel turned to view me. Shirtless, he looked like Christ on the cross if the tables had been turned, as if satirizing the rotting soldiers hanging by nails, his massive arms spread against the French doorframes inviting the wind to blow against his body, his knuckled abs. A force of nature.

"Our star," he said, no trace of irony. The pearl lights of West Hollywood necklaced the dark in the distance.

I didn't know what to make of this nor how I knew these people. For a moment I thought maybe the brothers had seen me perform downstairs in the garage and were making fun. But that didn't make sense; I hadn't been underground yet even though I remembered the night as if I had. I wanted to meditate on the absurdity of telling a story in which its movements are narrated not so much out of chronological order but *outside* of order itself—like a broken timepiece, its logic you think you understand even though the timing is off; only later you see that it's not the timepiece that's broken, it's you.

Julian handed me a drink and told me to relax. My attention was overwhelmed by the large common area adorned with expensive but worn furnishings and vintage fixtures: the grand blue velvet couch (maybe it was satin), mahogany fireplace, wall-to-wall glass windows, the light from illuminated billboards on Sunset Boulevard filtering through the sheer curtains. An array of emblematic ephemera chronicling Hollywood's eras had been preserved to create an ageless experience, a portal into another time, an alternate dimension, a literal hall of fame.

"This room was Howard Hughes' hermit lodge," one of the chicks on the couch said. She'd heard he'd hid unfinished reels in the vents. "Want to try to find them?"

The other one disagreed. "No, this is the room Greta Garbo lived in."

Julian took me by the shoulders and showed me around. The penthouse was populated with stylish men and women, late twenties to early forties, many of whom I'd seen before in movies, on TV, online, those sorts of people. They were his friends, Julian said, nodding to a few well-known passersby; by their lukewarm reactions, it was clear he used the word "friends" to describe many people. He and his family visited LA frequently, he explained as we walked outside onto the massive balcony. The air was chilly but the heaters and lanterns lining the perimeter created a warm filmic atmosphere. I felt like I was inside a holy temple standing above hidden treasures, not outside an obnoxious hotel, a jeweled spectacle for all to see. A group of Venezuelans stood smoking by the ledge, talking at impossible speeds. "Come meet my family," Julian said. They possessed the air of people who smoked on many elegant balconies. A dazzling array of necklaces and bracelets, rustic yet elegant attire, elaborate tattoos. I intuited a deep and tested bond; they'd been places together, seen things, more nights than mornings but the mornings too. They knew how to keep secrets from the outside but gossiped relentlessly inside. I can't pinpoint why but they gave off the impression of a cartel.

I made sure not to stare at anyone in particular as I made pleasantries and snuck peeks at the Victoria's Secret model's impossibly long legs. She was the brothers' blood cousin, I learned. Her mother had died when she was just a girl; Julian and Gabriel thought of her as a sister. Gabriel walked over and explained that Taita Richard would be arriving shortly. Then, as if initiating a dance, he casually snapped his fingers at the service girl standing near the door—a move I remembered to file away for later use—and she disappeared and soon returned, handing me a warm mug. Gabriel told me to drink the tea, it would prepare me. For what, I wasn't sure. I smoked a cigarette, drank the tea, and made friends with the family of people I could barely understand, convinced they were the entitled children of drug kingpins. I felt a little terrified, a little turned on.

Eventually I realized I hadn't urinated in hours and hurried inside to find a bathroom, which took some maneuvering, but finally I found it, and a minor thrill of accomplishment spread through me. Only it was locked. I waited and meditated over the art on the wall, some pastel Warhol knock-off, although, who knows, maybe it was real. I had the thought, Is that all art is—something you hang on walls? Which reminded me of a line from my favorite Hemingway short story ("That's all we do, isn't it—look at things and try new drinks?"). Minutes passed. I had no idea how long I was standing there. Time felt like a Warhol, a pop-art rendering of the real thing. The pain was horrendous. I considered pissing in the kitchen sink or maybe the spare closet at the other end of the hallway and almost went for it when the knob turned. I held my breath, a ridiculous response, and some dude and a very famous pop star walked out. She smiled an inscrutable smile, the coolness of someone who's never had to explain herself. Immediately I fell in love, a love confirmed by a prior lust; I frequently Googled her name and saved sexy photos of her on my iPhone. It's clear I use the word "love" to describe the way I felt about many women. She kissed me hello, which didn't happen, but I imagined it in a way that felt like remembering. The dude was shirtless, expensively tattooed, clearly wasted.

I am embarrassed that I am not kidding when I tell you he held a stack of hundreds in one hand as casually as the beer bottle he held in the other, laughing like he'd just gotten his dick sucked. Maybe he had. What a thought. He hugged me hello, kissed my cheek, said I don't know you or who are you or something about the death tube, and I mumbled something incoherent about how crazy the night was, it was good to see him, thanks for the bathroom, and rushed inside and fumble-locked the door without clean transition, barely missing the back of his necklaced head. I sat, peed, hopefully inside the toilet, and proceeded to pass out—but it was more like passing *through*.

Because as soon as I heard the knocking at the door, I walked straight out of the bathroom without doing any coke, which seemed significant, and entered a jungle or forest or some mixed media of the two. Clearly I was still inside the penthouse, but I was also outside, not outside Chateau but some *other* outside. The ground was soft and damp like volcanic ash, the lights aggressively dim. Painfully obvious shamanic music was playing, which I found endearing, which meant something inside me had changed. Walking on, I canvassed the new terrain, the cool earth in my paws, intuiting the syntax of the moon's reflection through the window. It spoke to me of impact, of worlds colliding, and even though I didn't understand, I thought I did. I came in contact with ancient memories from before the language of man ruined animals. Something primal, something righteous. I stalked on and saw my reflection in the sliding-glass door; what I saw was a flicker, a ghost, of what seemed like a wolf, and I was pleased because I had always related to myself as such. But what I did not understand, not then and not now, is that a lone wolf unto himself is a hologram, a suggestion of something remarkable but only a suggestion—because a lone wolf is a dead wolf unless he finds his pack. And then there's me, and I just want to eat you, dear reader, you mythical creature.

The party was over; the partygoers had been replaced by spirit animals. I stepped on a rabbit, but the rabbit was a girl, and the girl was Lindsay Lohan. She rubbed her ankle and scolded me sharply, and I'm so sorry, I said, mumbling a forced apology, considering whether I should bite her throat. Would you believe me if I told you that a dozen or so celebrities were present? Global personalities. How many hundreds of years of solitude were gathered in one apocryphal room? Yoga mats had been arranged in a semi-circle spanning the living room floor. Pillows placed on top. Blankets. Miniature wastebins. Hushed lighting. Wax shadows. The world had become eternally weird.

I walked toward Julian and Gabriel, making sure to remain bipedal. They were talking to the Victoria's Secret model and the tatted dude I'd encountered outside the bathroom.

"Who's your pretty friend?" the dude asked no one in particular. He didn't wear sunglasses inside but struck me as someone who would.

"This is our new, how do I say, creative partner," Julian said energetically.

"The talent," Gabriel confirmed.

I had no idea what they were talking about but hugged the tatted dude with great affection, kissing both his cheeks effusively, behavior wildly out of character for me.

"What did you give him?" he asked the brothers. But they just laughed, or I didn't hear them. Because there on the counter, say I noticed twin leather duffel bags filled with rubber-banded hundreds. Say I saw a handgun.

"Taita Richard has arrived," Julian said. "He is in the master getting ready."

"Are you prepared for the DMT?" Gabriel asked me.

"Cash, come smoke with me on the balcony," the model said to the tatted dude.

"Cash?" I said, spellbound. Then to the brothers: "What's DMT?"

"I was telling you about it on the elevator!" the model shouted as she disappeared.

"The god molecule," Julian said staring into the holographic universe of my lupine eyes.

"Tonight," Gabriel said, stoic and staid, "we portal."

X X X

I was already on stage when the prince appeared underground—a critical turning point in my development.

The crowd of famous faces before me, the burlesque dancers off to the side of the makeshift platform, their feathered wings craning against the low garage ceiling. I realized I'd been talking at the microphone for quite some time already. With what I thought was masterful lucidity and cadence, especially given the cornucopia of drugs I'd consumed, an impossible calculation, I found myself narrating the opening act of the first chapter of what would become this novel, an antihero's journey, so to speak, when at eighty miles per hour I'd driven my rented Mazda into the back of a moving Volkswagen while jacked up on an indiscernible amount of cocaine to keep the previous night's roll going before getting on a plane to New York in less than an hour. I paused to catch my breath. The crowd stood watching, mouths agape in all the handsome heads. The music had quieted to little more than static feedback from the microphone in my hand.

With rapturous aplomb that can only be described as operatic, I performed my performance of lying to the driver of the vehicle I'd hit, an innocent middle-aged woman whom I arbitrarily named Bev for the sake of narration, while standing on the side of the 405, her fender a bit bent out of shape—"Nothing serious, I can assure you!"—inhabiting both characters and delivering a subtle yet poignant metacommentary on the disconnect between one's internal experience and social self-presentation just like Ben Lerner does in his novels, who to me, writing in the future, will become a literary model, whose books I'll read and reread so many times his authorial voice will permanently change the voice inside my head, whose books I will consciously and I will unconsciously lift from and transpose lines of prose regurgitated through my narrator, who is an alternate version of me, like a collage.

The famous faces looked on, curious if not rapt. I demonstrated the crumbling of my inner world while at the scene of the crime, using the pacing and valance of my speech to exaggerate my anxiety: I could be accused, found out, or, god forbid, arrested for DUI—all valid and appropriate outcomes, none of which I was prepared to accept. But it wasn't my fault! My mother had just crashed her car in Santa Monica, I was racing to her rescue. "They" said she might not make it. I described the delicate balancing act of seducing Bev while eliciting her sympathy. How I needed her to believe in the possibility of a fairytale ending in which not only did my mother survive, but with her complicity Bev might receive a lavish, perhaps erotic, showing of gratitude from a certain late-night gentleman caller who was enamored by her massive heart, stimulated by her largess, could look past the extra thirty pounds, that she was twice his age. Had I mentioned I'd twice been raped by an older woman, much older, the *same* woman—some of you ladies in the audience are probably wearing her jewelry, paid for in cash—or is that not relevant to the story? What about my affair with my high school English teacher? I know I have a rather complicated relationship with intimacy. Don't worry, Mom was totally fine. In fact she was safe at home in New York celebrating her birthday. What can I say? To all my older gals with your wet lashes and dying wombs—do you still love me today?

I had half the crowd, the men, in tears, a laughter so loud I imagined someone would come and hand me a golden trophy, perhaps the golden credit card I never received in the mail. I know it sounds like I'm kidding, maybe you think I'm a professional comedian here to entertain you—I agree, my life sounds like a joke—but what I'm telling you is true, these are the facts. Why does everything in my life seem to live on the border of its opposite? I tried to explain that this story too is one where opposites come together, look at one another, are reflected in one another's tensions and resolve themselves without resolution. Only I didn't know how. I'm not sure what to make of it, but I think I've got the beginning threads of a novel! Do you know what I mean when I say that real life has become the greatest show on earth?

The energy of the room shifted. An intoxicated pulse. Chatter and whispering rising like a wave from the back of the room. In the following decade, I said, we will spend the majority of our lives hooked up to screens, will become addicted to watching the lives of other people, *you* people, parading in alternate realities. The media will sensationalize news while our politicians weaponize language to make reality appear like a streaming television series, each day a new episode with an even crazier twist. In the name of social progress and radical equality, we'll use language to segregate and splinter our differences. The social internet will resemble a medieval map not unlike Borges' where anyone we don't know or who doesn't espouse our ideology is considered the enemy—giving up basic freedoms and privacy to soulless institutions whose policies advertise no care for public good, whose only agenda is to produce a great fucking show. And no one will do anything about it because we are all guilty, are all addicted to the endless feed, the global screen.

We've made the world a parody of itself, and inside this parody we're all looking for meaning, but there's no meaning to be found precisely because we've stopped believing in the truth of words, so we create new words, and we're fucking it up. I cried with a passion I manufactured, which when manufactured became felt, reveling in the power of my performance. Real life is now the show and we can't stop watching because we're all day-players, or wish we were, which must be why so many young people aspire to be influencers, influential for being themselves. Absurd because being yourself is a birthright; it should not be considered extraordinary or supernatural. And then there's you, the old guard, I pointed, famous for playing someone else. Not absurd because in this autistic town, here in this very room, you'll find pedophiles, rapists, criminals, racists, gluttons, addicts, cowards, all variants of moral retards—and we celebrate you, aspire to be you. Boo all you'd like. I know I'm just as bad, but at least I can admit it.

The noise from the crowd was now deafening, but I waved away the noise. I said I refuse to live in a culture that values attention over significance, a culture predictably trending toward a singularity when "art" and "ad" will share no distinctions, when artists become self-obsessed ambulatory advertisements of themselves who create content, not art, as quickly as possible to be liked or followed. You are not artists, you cartoon gurus, and there is nothing authentic about instructing people how to live their lives when behind the screen you're no better than the rest of us. It does not matter if your social self-presentation is a stock photo of the good life, being liked by screen addicts is not an accomplishment.

The tungsten lights shined down on so many faces I'd seen on so many screens. And I am one of you, I said, or will be. That's why I can say what I'm about to say because I'm also one of them, a loser on the outside looking in who got inside. Ridiculously, I wanted to quote Beckett and say perhaps that's what I feel, an outside and an inside and me in the middle, perhaps that's what I am, the thing that divides the world in two. Mic in hand, the lights hot on me, I wanted to stand tall and soliloquize my illusory torments and ask who will be the heroes, the real artists, in our seizuring new world? Who will rip rhapsodic and speak out of line if all incentives point to promoting the line? I'd love to be the one, I wanted to say, a new kind of literary hero romantically rooted in the past yet relevant now. But I don't know how to break through and make myself heard. I'm losing hope. I don't have faith. Literature is dead. Nobody reads. But still—if I imagine a world where I can't write, or imagine a world in which what I've written won't be read because no one will care to read it, a world where influence has little to do with talent, is not at all concerned with contribution, a world fast approaching, I would inhale all the drugs and never wake up.

I guess that's my fight. It's why I'm here on this metaphorical stage. I'm no poet, no hero, I offer nothing new, no original ideas. I stand crooked and crippled on the shoulders of giants but maybe I can remind you of something you've forgotten. Perhaps that's my contribution. It's embarrassing for me to say this, I want to sound more intelligent, be less direct, less ribald. I want to be your philosopher king and in one clean stanza deliver you from stupidity—but I'm not, and I can't. Words do mean something, in fact they mean everything in a world where everyone has a say. Will you take me in your hands, earmark the pages, write in the margins? I hope that my failure to be original, to be a serious author, to say nothing of my failure to be a good person, can serve as a model for serving no model at all. Write or perish. Read or abort. Save yourself from feeling incapable. Perhaps it's the ultimate act of service, an antidote to universal deafness—if you want your voice to matter, then do yourself a favor, do us all, and shut the fuck up. It's better to say nothing until you have something to say.

Failing to heed my own advice, I practically moonwalked my way to the other side of the stage and hilariously concluded my rant with Bakhtin, the Russian philosopher and literary critic who wrote about the utopian ideal of the carnival, which through its temporary dissolution of conventions generates threshold situations where disparate individuals can come together and express themselves on an equal footing without the oppressive constraints of social objectification: the usual preordained hierarchy of persons and values becomes an occasion for laughter, its absence an opportunity for creative interaction. How could I not laugh while pointing out the irony of discussing literature, radically unpopular, and literary theory, radically useless, in a garage full of Hollywood megastars with a lyrical genius that must have seemed practiced, surely commissioned? Here before us is a great artist, a special talent, I projected the audience projecting me in their collective amazement. Perhaps tonight, this story too, is a carnival. What do you think?

Before I could ask if Mel Devine or any of the agents who tried to rope me off from my own story were in attendance, before I could tell them to take a good look at the dark star of self-absorption they'd missed out on, how that day at WME could have been one written for the history books and edited later for posterity, before I could spill the beans on Harrison and blackmail Hollywood into submission and demand my absolution, someone took me by the arm. I expected to see a security guard, perhaps a police officer come to arrest me for DUI in a story that happened hundreds of pages ago, an ironic ending to my storied performance—but no, it was one of the burlesque dancers; notice her unbelievably long eyelashes, her glinting tiara. She wore a surgeon's coat over lingerie, and I didn't know why but she seemed familiar. Yes, it was the woman I was following earlier, the one who walked like a bunny, whom I must have confused for Woolf. Just then I noticed I'd been leashed to her the entire time, the leather strap around my neck. And that's when I noticed the spectacle of the prince approaching.

The crowd gave way. The prince sat fatly on a throne too large for the underground, a cavalcade of slavedriver coryphées carrying if not dancing him toward the center of the platform. He was fitted in a white ankle-length thobe with long sleeves, a silken shroud covering his entire face. The lights were blinding. The crowd remained still. There was no music, no noise whatsoever save for whispers and murmurs. They waited. I waited. We waited as one breath. The prince sat still, silent, hooded like a seraph Nazgul, as if delivering a life-changing prognosis. Would Mom make it? Would I? Then the surgeon woman snapped her fingers, the prince stood erect, his servants unveiled his face, and with no transition whatsoever, out of my ass came a baby chick wholly intact.

I suppose that was the big surprise. Because all along I'd meant to find my pants and why in god's name someone was taking my temperature anally. What could it mean? I guess that's the point I'm trying to make. This novel is a story about a story that might be worthy of being a novel, but when you try to get to its center and uncover who I am, you end up squinting at a refracted image of yourself; the joke's on you. The signifier is not coeval with the signified, whatever that means. Or maybe my life is just that meaningless.

But say there was an eruption. A gasping frisson from the celebrity crowd pushing up against the velvet ropes. See drinks spill and maudlin mouths agog. See Harvey grinning from ear to ear. See the author of this novel come alive as The Author, a container of experience made to bedazzle and shock and disappoint. In that moment I knew my purpose, knew who I really was—forgive me if I repeat myself, I've been doing that a lot lately—a type of dark that makes you feel dirty.

The surgeon woman handed me the chick bobbing its pretty birdy head, and I met this gesture with silence, the crowd mad with excitement. I held my silence and bowed my head and kneeled to offer the chick to the prince. But he did not take it. Looking up I saw wonder in his eyes, softness in his chiseled face, was that eyeliner augmenting his gaze? Some suggestion in his wink? The moment of reckoning. The crowd on fire. Was it time to call home and tell Mom I've made it, I'm finally famous? It must have been. Because the prince took me by the shoulder with one hand and with the other raised the golden chick high above him like some immaculate conception for all to see, all to marvel, and under the din of revelation among the celebrities clapping and howling, the strobe lights sputtering, in my ear he whispered his room number, and I knew then we'd be friends. And the crowd went wild.

XXX

"Give me the fucking platter."

The butler handed me the platter filled with five flutes of champagne.

"One for you, one for you, and the rest for me," I said, laughing with my new friends, two brothers, the Venezuelans. We were standing inside a hidden sunroom in one of Chateau's bungalows located in the garden off to the side of the main entrance. "I'm just kidding," I said to the butler, inhaling the glass of champagne. "You can take the platter with you."

Outside, occupants of the garden bungalows had gathered on their patios, drinks in hand, feet bare on the manicured grass, heels off. The moon shone through the branches. An up-and-coming actress was bathing her terrier in the pocket-sized pool. The noise made by the party beyond the French doors beat around us. No one would sleep tonight. Inside our little canopy, a few personalities sat at the table behind ours sipping wine. The lighting was warm and dim over an abundance of floral arrangements.

Say I found my portal. Because all night I'd been having the same conversation about the death of authorship and, by analogy, the death of cultural free will.

How exactly we found each other is unclear, but the brothers and I were deeply offended that a handful of social media "stars" had been invited to the party. This is no place for imitators, we agreed, taking great joy in pointing out the paradox of these peoples' privilege:

Since the use of phones was not permitted, how will their fans know they're alive?

Naturally I was happy to overlook the minor footnotes that I had not been invited, had no business being here whatsoever, and had somehow managed to build a large social media following of my own. Nor did I know anything about the Venezuelans or their connection to the industry. It's not the kind of thing you ask, a major faux pas: at exclusive events you simply assume everyone is invited; not knowing someone's identity is a sign of your ignorance, not their fraudulence—a sort of invisibility cloak I'd wear on many future occasions. It was clear the brothers were extremely wealthy given the flippant way they spoke of vacationing: I'd have to come to Ibiza with them next summer, I'd love their villa in Monaco, et cetera. They appeared to be of a noble class who never worked but loved to talk about work, for whom work is done. I was enthralled.

"Are you saying that literature is art at its most intellectually demanding?" Julian asked at one point, trying to make sense of the various tangents I'd taken us on. He placed his hand on my chest, which a few moments later I realized he had not removed.

I took out a cigarette and placed it on my lip, forgetting the one that was already there. "I'm saying the absence of authorship in our culture represents an intellectual deficiency in our art. I fear this to be the prequel to the privation of cultural free will," I basically repeated myself, putting out the original cigarette, offering my pack to the brothers. Gabriel produced matches and lit us up. "Sadly," I said, "contemporary artists, *real* artists, especially authors, are failing to maintain relevance in the age of Everything on Demand."

I saw them mouth the phrase like it held weight.

The air was fresh and cool with the aftermath of rain. Across the lawn, inside the main lobby, the band played acid jazz renditions of pop songs. Throughout the night I repeatedly found myself amazed if not overwhelmed when spotting the original artist of whatever song was being covered; I imagined producing work so popular that everyone knew it by first impression, work so popular it was selected to entertain Hollywood elites and pop stars at international parties—and my head practically exploded.

"Give the internet to every philosopher throughout history and show me what they *did not* write," Gabriel said in a way that demonstrated he understood my point.

"Would you like some?" Julian offered me a small glass vial of cocaine.

"Yes, please. Can you?" Julian held my cigarette for me. I turned and bumped the powder into each nostril and handed him the vial. He handed me my cigarette, then turned and snorted the excellent cocaine himself. I waited to continue, then said, "Is it crazy to say this?"

"It is not crazy," Gabriel said, pouring the coke on top of his clenched fist. "It is brilliant."

"No, you didn't let me finish."

"Ah," he said, snorting like a coming bull.

"And thank you." I took a drag of the cigarette. "I was going to say, as sad as it sounds, in this day and age reading is a defiant stand against mindlessness, an antidote to addiction. It's why literature is so important. There's a dedication when reading, a romance in one's relationship with the author. Our culture is missing that in its art. We have too much access." I wiped the remnant powder from Gabriel's mustache, which he appreciated. "While reading you get to canvas the inside of an author's thoughts," I said. "What could be more intimate, more moving?"

From inside the lobby, across the lawn, the guests cheered loudly. Julian looked at me, again doing the thing with the touching. "I love to read," he said, a hollow admission. "But you are having me embarrassed. I do not read enough."

"It is true," Gabriel said. "We learn to be unfocused and prodigal. Is that the right word?"

"It is a good word, an interesting choice!"

"Thank you. Yes. We are wasting our god-given gifts."

"That's exactly the problem. Don't you feel like no one actually *knows* anything anymore?" I huddled close to the brothers, lowered my voice. "What celebrities are actually celebrated for their intellectual contribution to the world? What are they contributing other than a romanticized reflection of their insane privilege?"

"What is the solution?" Julian asked, mesmerized.

"Make good art," I said and flicked the cigarette, its red embers scattering on the floor, indoors no less, to punctuate the suggestion of profundity. Then I asked, "What are you two working on?"—another turning point in my development.

With gusto Gabriel described their many-yeared quest to sell the working concept of a film loosely inspired by their childhoods, a film that would rival *The Godfather* in its scope and impact, an epic drama that follows the rise and fall of Pablo Escobar, who becomes a billionaire through the production and distribution of cocaine, featuring the notorious drug kingpin's feuds with drug lords, DEA agents, and opposing political forces. They were looking for a major writer to attach to the project. Would I happen to know of anyone?

I heard myself laugh and said, "You realize you're describing *Narcos*, don't you?"

Gabriel cocked his head. Julian turned to his brother. They spoke in Spanish.

"Can you say again?" Julian said. "We think we not hear you."

Buzzing from a shockingly small amount of cocaine, I told the brothers that soon Netflix would turn their brilliant concept into a streaming television series, one of its first major franchises. They looked furious.

"It isn't true," Julian said, spitting. "Netflix does not produce original content."

But it was true, or would be, and the company will.

"You speak lies," Gabriel said, no longer friendly. "How is it I never hear of this?"

Because I'm reading to you from the future, I might've said.

Julian shoved me, accused me of "being a lying," mixing up his English. "He wastes our time," he snapped at his brother.

"What are you saying?" Gabriel said.

"I'm saying no one is going to back your idea because it's already in development. But hold on!" I winced and held my hands to my head, I thought he might strike me. "I've got a better idea."

"Go on," Gabriel said, unmoving, merely inches from my face.

"Hemingway." I swallowed, slightly nauseated by the smell of his breath. "Imagine a film about his early years in Paris as described in *A Moveable Feast*. It's never been done and I'd like to see it and I know I'm not alone."

"I love Hemingway," Gabriel said, deadpan.

"Think about it," I went on, pushing thoughts of either kissing him or slitting his throat aside. "Despite the online memification of his personality, there have been no good films made about Hemingway or the figure of possibility he represents for our far-more-lost generation." I produced another cigarette, having lost count of how many were going, and accepted the match from Gabriel, cupping his hands, captivated by my monologue. I turned my head and exhaled. "I envision this to be the story of his origins. A hero's journey of authorship. *We* probably wouldn't be able to get the rights to the work, not without years of headaches, so we could base the character on his likeness and keep him anonymous." This really was a good idea, I thought, having no idea where I was going with it. "We will call our hero 'The Author.' It's Hemingway but it's not Hemingway. He'll be an unnamed protagonist. It worked in *Fight Club*." I bumped more of the incredible coke, Julian keying the coke to my nose. Gabriel smiled through his cigarette, a twin flame to my own, the two practically touching, we may as well have been smoking each other's smoke. "The film will be about craft and celebrity back in a time when celebrities were worth celebrating. Hemingway's cult of personality, his heroic machismo, his rise to literary greatness sells itself on a story larger than life. Just like Pablo Escobar," I said, the brothers' exhilaration palpable. "It's the perfect Hollywood story."

"My god," Julian said, wiping back his long curly hair. He turned to Gabriel. "This is—"

"Genius," Gabriel finished his brother's sentence.

They asked me if I was an actor, I looked like one. Titillated, I mentioned I was being considered for a role in the prince's movie. Saying it made it half true. That's why I was here tonight, I was supposed to meet with the prince. (A lie but a lie unprovable.)

"How come we've seen you in nothing?" Gabriel said.

Because I was not interested in fueling the Hollywood dream machine of shit recycled shit, I told the brothers. I'd been waiting for the perfect role that does not compromise my ethics and artistry. I refused to participate in the commodification of art, even if my career suffered in the short term; I'd rather die. I knew my principles would pay off in the end. The brothers thought my determination was the bravest thing they'd ever heard. I was destined for greatness was their conclusion and I encouraged more of that sort of talk. I emphasized that I was hard at work on a novel, acting was more like my day job; I have a degree in modernist literature, I could help write the script. They glanced at each other, blinked with avid excitement, and, dear reader, I thought they might suppurate.

A server walked into the moonlit sunroom. Gabriel waved him over. Flutes of champagne were passed around. Julian produced his phone and demanded the man put down the tray and take our photograph, defying the rules forbidding the use of phones. The flash went off, the moment memorialized. He said one day when we're famous we will look back on this photograph and the memory it contains and remember how it all began—and he was right; in fact that's what I'm doing now, only it wasn't so happy after all: Harrison made me let them go, which is a kind way of saying that Legal stealth-bombed the shit out of them, the brothers didn't know what hit them. But I'm getting ahead of myself: that's a story for Book II. In that moment all was happy and hopeful. We drank champagne and made plans, and I determined I'd delete my Instagram immediately.

"You are The Author. In our movie," Gabriel said, taking my shoulder. I was around Hemingway's age at the time of his Paris years, was I not?

I was. "I am," I said. "I'm also signed by WME." Why not? "If you are serious, I'll bring it to my agent," a ludicrous suggestion. "She'll be here soon." Which reminded me—Woolf!

Julian gripped Gabriel's shirt, half-unbuttoned, the stylish cotton linen bunching against his many necklaces, his dark coiled chest hair. Then he gripped mine and nor did he remove his hand.

"We are serious."

"We will produce this film."

"You are The Author."

"To The Author!"

They raised their flutes in unison once more.

"Where did you get this amazing coke?" I asked, raising mine. But they just laughed.

"My friend," Gabriel said, "that is mescaline."

X X X

Taita Richard put the mouthpiece to my lips and told me to hold it forever.

N, N-Dimethyltryptamine, or DMT, is an entheogenic substance used in various indigenous cultures, most notably Amazonian shamanic rituals involving a brew called ayahuasca, to induce "nonordinary" states of consciousness for the purpose of engendering spiritual development in sacred contexts, I later read on Wikipedia. Other means of absorption, such as vaporizing, injecting, or insufflating the drug, can produce intense hallucinations for a short period of time, usually less than half an hour, although the experience can seem to last many lifetimes, as I was about to learn.

I was not convinced that a penthouse suite at Chateau Marmont could be considered a "sacred context," although most Hollywood dickbags would, and I was fairly certain that our urban shaman, "Taita" Richard, a middle-aged black dude from Harlem who moved to Los Angeles in the '90s to pursue a commercial acting career, was neither Amazonian nor trained by Amazonian shamans and thus not at all qualified to safely administer such powerful psychedelics, despite his Burning Man regalia, despite referring to drugs as "medicine," despite the palo santo wafting from his necklace censer like an easter priest, and I was absolutely positive that I was radically incapable of any sort of "spiritual development"—but I inhaled anyway.

As I held it forever, the night rewound, but not just the night: my encounter with the Venezuelans, entering Chateau, dancing in the uncommon rain, driving home from Jo's after I twice nearly overdosed in a daze so dark I couldn't distinguish street from sky, believing I'd died, seeing my life pass before my eyes in moving frames, texting Woolf, breaking up with Dani, who wasn't my girlfriend, breaking up with you whom I'll never name who could have been my wife, boarding how many planes from and to New York and all the messes I'd made, driving into Bev's Volkswagen hybrid, driving to Brooklyn to come on the belly of my high school English teacher, driving out to Greenport with my dad as a kid, where every summer we'd fish for fluke or bluefish from the docks and throw them back into the Peconic Bay, a choice that described Dad's personality perfectly, which was upsetting to me, catching a jellyfish that one day when Dad was napping and I'd determined not to throw it back, I was probably five or six years old and not sure what kind of fish had an umbrella for a head and red trailing tentacles, medusa of the sea, inflictor of unheralded singeing pain: my hands, my arms, my knees; screaming for Dad to come save the day, which he never did—all the way back to the jelly womb (do you know what I mean when I say I remember feeling trapped?) and furthermore to the end of times where the future resides, when I'll steal lines from my favorite authors to write this novel and transpose lines from previous chapters to write this final one, a night that represents the conclusion of an era but was just another day in the life of the artist as a young man at the end of empire at the dawn of virtual reality shot through a wormhole into the alternate universe you're now reading.

"Oh my god."

The onset was rapid. The terror unpredictable. By the time I exhaled it was as if I'd sublimated into a vapor ghost of myself, but not just myself, of everyone gathered in circle, as if I'd parallactically tentacled onto ten yoga mats and we became one selfsame demented energy. The super-feeling was too much. The decision to flee came suddenly. Or, better yet, I shrieked like my wan soul had been cut from the empty place next to my tarred and speckled lungs and now had to deal with the pathetic creature from which it was determined to escape. The dark of the room fell into the shadow of another darkness. A winter cold swept through. I heard Taita Richard, his holographic body, telling me, "Stay with it, brother. Stay with it."

I opened my eyes as he held me down.

"Do not resist," he said. "Go into it. Go deep."

But I did not want to go deep. Going deep seemed like a death sentence, not a spiritual awakening. I could not help but notice the celebrity participants writhing on the ground, each surrendering to or fighting back whatever flavor of existential release: panic, ecstasy, despair, mercy. Their cries became my cries, and then I too was experiencing each of their crises. The room was spinning, but it was more like I was falling out of time. I tried to hold on to reality, determined I preferred life delivered in three dimensions. I kept my eyes open despite Taita Richard insisting I go inward, go deep. Then I went all cross-eyed, my vision fracturing. Any particular face or object I'd lock onto would seem to age or oscillate without transition, as if holographic blips of film had been transposed and overlaid to create a collage of spiraling perspectives in one single frame. That the majority of my fellow journeyers, embarrassing word, were famous actors had me thinking I was watching a retro horror film, poorly edited, and this was the penultimate scene when everyone drank the kool-aid and thus came the rapture.

"Close your eyes. Stay with it."

That I could not do. I stood up suddenly, which felt like dropping through a trap door into a basement below a basement, casket black. I was freezing, I was shivering. Intense nausea, my stomach in skeins. My vision of Taita Richard blurred as did all reliable proprioception as I landed into a pool of uncannily soft sheets. The echoed sounds of rainforest playing from surround-sound speakers absorbed into my consciousness like raindrops, each drop an ocean. Falling forever. The suffocation was total.

I closed my eyes. I was in it now whether I liked it or not, portaling into the womb of a jellyfish torching itself alive. Electric circuitry, thin film of panic, the universe scattered on its marble underbelly. Frisson. Veined. The end of times was hardened wax under molten wax burning bright in its candle casing seen through two snakeheads, one dancing, one not. One snake, two heads, one hungry, one not, eating itself alive. Into the blinding light. A spiral cornucopia of every color known to man and unknown to man, orthogonal circles made into dyads, triads, piano frequencies where shapes make sounds and sounds carry matter—is there a word for that? Magnetic river, like how the ancients moved megaliths. A flash of orange turned to flame and drizzle and then negated all at once, color dissolving into a mandala of sepia crawling zygotes, and with another flash, a caesura, however brief, before explosion: the birth of the sun, the death of the sun. Hieroglyphics in the night sky, sacred patterns made of stars, no moon, no hand to hold. A codex. What does it read? I heard my ancient ancestors speak to me in deep-bellied singsong, a language more like humming before humans had words, pre-grammatical, when we communicated in complex patternings of emotions like birds do talk: a transmission, mesmeric hypnosis. I felt held. I felt judged. Tell me what you see, my ancestors said but not with words. Tell me what you see.

How can I describe it? Imagine you are viewing a classical painting from the Renaissance abstract into modern art. See the emphasis on simplicity, proportion, clarity of structure, its formal perfection disassociate as when a kaleidoscope rotates, the symmetrical figures pulling out from themselves into asymmetrical shapes like ripples of lucent rain on a calm smooth lake, the colors bleeding into pulsing puddles of dexterous patterns and discordant lines; now before you is the representation of form, the suggestion of story, the possibility of some deeper meaning that only you, dear reader, can interpret. A Michelangelo becomes a van Gogh becomes a Picasso becomes a Pollock like progress in reverse. A murderous splattering contained but not contained in one single frame but also many frames. Sometimes they appear as circular orbs like hovering ringlets in the sky. Then you realize you're not witnessing a work of art abstract before you; no, you are the abstraction: your personality, your history, the people you know and love, everything you've collected, experienced, and assembled into one complete memory-awareness that codifies your identity, all that which makes you *you* abstracts in a rapid entropic vortex toward obliteration through what I can only describe as the death tube. The black hole of consciousness. White shock of apocalypse. What could be on the other side? It is clear. My god, it is clear. You know you are dying, death is fast approaching. What do you do? You desperately try to hold on, your ego begging to stay as it is, believing it is, you are, something whole, intact, special. This is an illusion, just like Hollywood with all its ropes. Just like this book. Your identity is an illusion. You will die soon. You will die. What are you going to do?

I opened my eyes. Throughout the room some journeyers were purging into waste buckets. The smell was vicious. To my right I saw the suggestion of Gabriel, sepulchral, lying still as a rock. To my left Julian making shapes with his fingers above his head and cooing like a baby. He turned and looked at me or the grim reaper haloed above my head, his huge psychotic eyes, and kissed the air in my general direction before portaling back into whatever funerary fantasy begot him; I'll never forget his shrieks. I thought of Jo, how I'd never forgive him for sending me here, wherever, whatever this was, whose hair I wanted to twirl like I did Mom's when I was a baby boy and too scared to walk into nursery school without her. Mommy hug. I saw the shape of Taita Richard, his many bald heads, walk around the room in deep affected prayer, spraying a floral mist over seizuring bodies, bending down to palm the chests of terrified idols gasping for something unutterable, trying to make sense of a loss that has no language, only sound. Surrender to the medicine. Let it teach you. Then I saw Harvey Weinstein sit up from his mat in abject confusion, embarrassed look on his face, and terrified I closed my eyes, confident I was already dead.

The medicine is not a hallucination but a window into dimensions that our normal perceptions cannot see, Taita Richard said, although not in these words. Say yes, my children, and surrender. The medicine gives you what you need not what you want. Surrender and say yes.

I surrendered. I didn't have a choice. Which was freeing in a way. Into the blinding light I experienced the night abstract into a pile of pieces like a puzzle that hadn't been fitted together properly, like the shape of this chapter. I experienced the weight of responsibility to try and fit the pieces together, to make sense of something that has no meaning. If you are no longer witness to yourself, do you cease to exist? How many things would I have to do out of character before I become someone else? I realized the question I'd been wrestling with for so many years did not make sense. As my personality dissolved to disappear altogether, a rapid fragmentation into an impossible scattering of nonsense, I—if I can call it that—understood that our personalities are narratives narrated by a malleable consciousness, a flimsy author who can never understand himself because there is no self to understand. I thought if identity is that fragile, if my personality can blast into incalculable shards of memories and impressions without any central unifying actor, then isn't it possible I can come back as whomever I choose? 'Tis a consummation devoutly to be wish'd. To die, to sleep. To sleep, perchance to dream. Cosmically fucked into the great unknown.

I felt ecstatic. Everything in my life up until now could be erased. If I chose. And then it became abundantly clear:

In order for my project to work the author and his narrator must become one selfsame "I." For the past year I'd confused the narrator of this book that hadn't been written with the author of my life who wasn't going anywhere, hoping fiction would overwrite reality. I thought of Oscar Wilde who opined that "Life imitates Art far more than Art imitates Life." I understood that if I'm to write myself into existence, I the author have to eat the narrator to become The Author. Only then can I form an authentic relationship with you, dear reader—my only hope for redemption.

What you're experiencing is evidence of the eucharist that guarantees life after death for those who dare to drink from the oversoul of the universe, Taita Richard said. The holy grail and its miraculous contents have never been found until you experience the medicine. Say yes. Surrender.

The moment of reckoning. More purging from the famous Others, guttural and tormented. I had one choice to make: I could choose to become The Author, or I could choose death.

History is a lie. Long before our historic texts begin, well before the ancient Egypt we think we know, the earth sheltered an even more magnificent civilization, Taita Richard said. An advanced civilization rivaling our own that was so completely eradicated twelve thousand years ago that virtually all signs of its existence disappeared, leaving behind the subtlest whispers of clues. What could have been the cause? Some natural disaster as devastating as a hundred nuclear bombs, such as that of a comet strike, perhaps the hand of god. Alas, this civilization emerged from shamanism, had evolved beyond the brutish standards we over-impose on the ancients. With technologies as impressive as our own, albeit very different. Alien in a way. These people held deep forgotten wisdom. Possessed of twelve senses they cultivated powers of the mind and spirit that we dismiss. What you might call woo-woo.

Then the bells tolled. Say that I found myself, or a vision of myself, standing at the outskirts of an altar on which stood a massive table, white cloth laid over finely chiseled and gold-bespeckled wood, populated by my favorite literary authors—most dead, some not. The room seemed familiar, empty save for the large gathering at the center. High ceilings, yellow-laminate wooden floors, the checkered wall-sized windows and the light pouring through. It had been years, but I knew I was standing inside the auditorium of my elementary school, an old gymnasium repurposed into a small theatre. Imagine something like da Vinci's *The Last Supper* transposed over Raphael's *School of Athens*, where all classical elements had been exchanged for a gaudy '90s Long Island Catholicism. There I was, an outsider beyond the frame looking on at a gathering of literary heroes in council on stage, my back turned to camera, my back turned to I, The Author's, witness gaze.

The authors were silent. No one spoke a word. Hemingway and Fitzgerald sat at the center; to their left: Dostoevsky, Tolstoy, Nietzsche (whose narrator I considered literary performance art), Wilde, Woolf, Joyce, Proust, Kafka, Camus, Graham Greene,

Nabokov, Kundera, Marquez, Borges; to their right: Faulkner, Didion, Hunter S. Thompson, Bukowski, Vonnegut, Pynchon, Percy, Salter, Denis Johnson, McCarthy, Bret Easton Ellis, David Foster Wallace (whom I admired out of obligation but whose writing I hated); I'm not sure why he was present, this was supposed to be my dream.

All were silent. No one spoke a word. Then something funny happened. I heard my mother's voice recite my favorite bedtime poem just as when I was a child:

> Goodnight room
> Goodnight moon
> Goodnight cow jumping over the moon

The authors looked at each other, some seemed slightly confused. Then a small laughter produced from the center and dominoed outward from head to head and quickly spread throughout the group. The poem continued as my omniscient mother read aloud:

> Goodnight friends
> And goodnight pens
> Goodnight Grandma and Grandpa
> And goodnight Dad

I could sense but not see a wave of transition, the celebrity participants inside the penthouse mumbling themselves back into consciousness. Transplants of laughter and gratitude and crying from the room beyond whatever world separated me from theirs echoed like a tidal chorus, an underbelly current that spilled into and fed the intensifying laughter inside the author-filled hall like a whale cry, a hydraulic melody over which Mom's voice carried in singsong prosody:

> Goodnight Rex
> And goodnight desk
> Goodnight books
> And scary nightmares

I remembered back to when, as a child, I would repurpose the famous children's poem after my mother tucked me in bed, making the words make sense to me, for me, making the poem my own. Then Oscar Wilde—arguably the first influencer, famous for being famous before contributing anything to the literary cannon, a feat I both despised and admired and knew I'd one day emulate—stood among the laughter and commotion and recited rather ridiculously:

> Goodnight houses on the block
> And goodnight to all my loved ones
> Goodnight animals who sleep outside
> And goodnight pets who sleep inside

Say when Taita Richard announced it was time to open the circle to share what we had experienced, to integrate, that the auditorium erupted. All the authors apart from Nietzsche (obviously) were roaring with amusement, clearly laughing not with but at me as I tried to explain that I'd forever thought of my life as a collection of stories, a loosely threaded novel without transition between the chapters, something like what you're reading now, how it was up to me to write about it and capture the essence of my time, but I couldn't do it, I needed their help—as Mom, Wilde, the famous celebrities inside Chateau, and the celebrated authors sitting at the altar of my imagined trial sang:

Goodnight light
Goodnight dark
Goodnight dreams
Please be good

I saw my past: I was no Oscar Wilde—if life imitates art then my life is at best an emo song, something too embarrassing to share. I saw my future: what I saw was a dream, some epitaphic fantasy without predicate when I'd become a celebrity author who defines a generation. Then the authors' laughter became the laughter of the agents inside WME's office the day I was fired, a relentless bludgeoning. Say yes. Surrender. You know you're fucked when the only thing more terrifying than dying is the idea of coming back.

I'd never write, I determined, while I alone finished reciting the poem's conclusion:

Goodnight sky
Goodnight God
Goodnight Mom
Now please close the door

Because the choice was obvious: I chose death.

On cue, Hemingway stood and pointed a shotgun directly at my chest and said I could never resemble his likeness. Then he pulled the trigger, and as the bullet entered my heart the only thought I had was that these people are not and will never be my friends.

Inside the Great Pyramid there are five chambers above the King's Chamber, each made of granite beams, ceiling and floor, each beam weighing seventy tons, equivalent to ten large elephants. Elevated to the height of three hundred and fifty feet above the ground. How? No ramp could fit inside. No number of slaves could accomplish this task in such close quarters. The ancients knew of abilities we've long forgotten. Psychic powers of the human mind. Telekinetic powers. Telepathic powers. We can awaken those techniques again. The power is inside all of us.

Then I purged.

When I came to, I dreamed I was looking right through my eyelids. But her pussy smothered my face. I guess I've finally found Woolf, I thought to myself. Time had skipped, the tracklist played out of order. But it wasn't who I thought it was. A tourniquet made of the sheets. Twisting infantile gagas, manic erotica. And nor was her friend shy. All pelvis pressing down into eternity, cleaving herself ragged. Potentate on her throne of fuck.

What is your language? What language do you speak? Now scissor yourself.

There, from beyond the threshold, a kaleidoscope of astonishment. Mesmeric are the voices, the people watching. You are not to record this, the stern one says. Bermuda-blue ringlets, sepia stagecoach, sapphire wallpaper. Lights on, lights off.

I had her from behind now. Wild thrust of capture, worlds colliding. Moon in moon. Buoying like circles in water. Two sisters in a maze of themselves, goliath breaths from such small bodies. Panting, panting like she'd been buried alive. Whiplashed. And the crowd of voyeurs, a parallax of encouragement. Lights on, lights off.

Holy shit, someone says. Holy matrimony, the stern one says. But why? But why? Oh god.

Focus on the task at hand, he tells me.

In her mouth, she says in her mother tongue and rolled over her friend in garter thong, face down crying mad like a rape victim begging for more. Imagine snakemouths squealing like some incensed medusa. This tongue to lick that tongue. This tongue to—

Finish the task.

I saw not death but death's captor. Helical moaning in the yawn of a rifle. Light bloomed like light to a newborn spilling onto hospital bedding while I made my departure from one world to another, white hot, liminal, lime-cream mosaic. An usher of pearls made into a crown to suck down and swallow and gasp.

X X X

Dear administrators of the Nobel Prize, I deleted from the Word document some days later.

Please allow me to thank you for your attention since no one reads anymore in a world filled with so many screens. For my entire life, I fantasized about the possibility of my fiction becoming nonfiction, how the line between imagination and reality would unblur into the selfsame story. It was a long time, too long, that my dream cowered in fantasy. I made nothing of myself, was no one.

But then something spectacular happened. You *became a part of the plot.* For my project to come alive, The Author had to break through the fiction. As a caterpillar transforms into a butterfly, imagine a two-dimensional character in print grow flesh and blood and walk off the page. Because of your participation, The Author is real.

Just as had been written, just as I'd written it. You learned to love him as you read him, as you watched him become the star you read. You need not concern yourself how it happened: your reading was, is, the chrysalis.

I'll leave you with this quote by James Salter. It summarizes my life's ambition:

"There comes a time when you realize that everything is a dream, and only those things preserved in writing have any possibility of being real."

Dear reader, dear friend—thank you for reading.

~~the end.~~

Oh, but I nearly forgot.

At the backdoor entrance, when the hostess asked to see some verification, I had to laugh. Because wouldn't you believe it, it started to rain. An ocean of warm bullets smacking fat against the cement. Like a portal had opened to rinse and deliver me from myself. A flooding. Calm lover in a world with no screens. I reached out my hands to grip what cannot be held, can never be held, and let the rain lick my face. See his white teeth wolf through the dark. Some silly kid after all. Some kid.

Get inside! the hostess called, practically begging. The bar towel in my hand, the attendees drying me off. She handed me my phone sealed inside a plastic bag. Pink porcelain polish. Bracelets that tinker and chink. The blue light flashing. Who could be calling at a time like now?

Through the plastic I managed to answer hello as I walked like Liotta through the kitchen's crypt corridors toward the main lobby, listening to Jo recite some inspirational quote while I died in his garage and was reborn smoking vaporized DMT inside Chateau Marmont—the most Hollywood story you can ever imagine but never read until now.

And then the director yelled cut and I awoke in a dream staring at myself in a makeup trailer full of my fans.

the end.

EPILOGUE

yikes

The first surprise came the following morning. Woolf stood over me, her pretty mouth instructing me to shower and meet her downstairs for coffee. We had a few things to finalize before she left. I didn't know what she meant but knew she meant business and reluctantly unleashed myself from the plush duvet.

Jesus, she said. She turned and faced the curtain and unsheathed whatever contraption held back the preternatural sunlight, so blinding. Put on some fucking clothes.

She was right. I was completely naked.

Well, should I shower or get dressed?

The door slammed.

A Bloody Mary, please!

Rinsed of whatever degradation I invited the previous night, having tested all the lovely soaps, I walked into the living room that smelled of mud and stale champagne and extinguished smoke. Half-empty bottles and bunched-up phone cables and pillows of all sizes, some women's heels, a domesticated fowl beanie baby. What a mess. I grabbed my pants and searched the back pocket for cigarettes, found a pack, and lit one. I walked over to the small French window that looked out onto the hollow glamor of West Hollywood, some billboards. On them I imagined my face, huge and seraphic, and knew I was seeing a reflection of the future. I cracked the window, the smoke snaking away.

Downstairs, celebrities walked about the courtyard in bathing suits and sundresses and polo shirts. Waiters in white tuxedos and white shorts moved about graciously. Fabulous people waved at me dressed in someone else's tunic; I seemed to have lost my shirt, a common theme of this stage of my development. I waved back and my third eye blinked at all the bright shining lights. California would burn in a few weeks, several massive wildfires catching in the north and then, to our disbelief, in the south. Hundreds of acres, thousands of homes, how many animals—all decimated. But you couldn't touch us inside Chateau.

I found Woolf sitting outside on the garden patio; behind her, a magnificent buffet. She looked up as I sat down. A coffee pot and three plates on the red-checkered tabletop. I poured myself a cup. She lowered her sunglasses and waved at the pretty group at the accompanying table; notice the sides of her head shaved like a punk rock barbie doll, her blonde hair streaked dark and dark undercuts. I've been meaning to contact her people, she said about the actress smiling back. She sipped from her cup. Red lipstick kiss the seal.

How are you feeling? she asked. Before I could respond, she said that after this she was heading to the office to start drafting the agreement for signatures. She wants this done by Monday.

You work on Saturdays?

Are you serious?

I sipped the coffee and listened to her talk while considering if lox and avocado would sit well after the apocalypse I'd swallowed the night before.

We'll have to be smart about planning your shooting schedule over the next eight or nine months, she was saying. Was I happy with my rates, did I have any questions?

I had a lot of questions but before I could betray myself she asked sincerely if first we needed to talk about what happened. We're about to enter a professional relationship and last night definitely crossed some boundaries. She had no intention of being in the room, it just happened. What I did in my personal life was not her business—unless I fucked it up and then it was her business. Did I understand?

I felt excited, a little scandalous. I assumed she meant we'd slept together and was a tinge remorseful I didn't remember. I tried to play it cool and said I was surprised about last night as much as she was; I hadn't heard from her all year.

Yeah, well, we didn't expect TMZ to break the story after you were fired. I mean, who cares about some nobody assistant being a crazy asshole? I cringed. Still, she said, we had to disassociate.

Why? I read the blurb like five hundred times. My identity was kept anonymous. I'm still doing that now.

She shook her head. Doesn't matter.

If only you knew what I had to do to survive this year. I could write a book about it.

Stop feeling sorry for yourself. She sipped her coffee. It's pretty funny, actually.

What?

You're a bit of a legend at WME. Assistants still talk about the "great con" that almost was. She said it like announcing a Broadway spectacle.

Go on.

For all the horrible things assistants have to endure in this industry, your story offers some sort of relief. Or retribution.

I loved this. My demented quest for fame that resulted in my firing now served as a model of possibility for demented assistants who pretended their lives were best spent landing assholes like me roles in movies.

Does it offer *you* relief? I asked, raising my eyebrows in a way I hoped would intimate oceans of intimacy.

No, I've been promoted. I'm a junior agent now.

I took out my pack of cigarettes.

I noticed we slept in the same bed together.

She rolled her eyes. Are you ready to have this conversation? Drink some coffee. You look insane. Why are you wearing that?

Just then a very famous actor shouted my name and congratulated me for the performance of a lifetime last night underground. Funniest thing he'd ever seen, I played the room like a maestro. Those were his words. I stood and we embraced. His fame was shocking. He couldn't wait to see me in the movie, he said, he'd heard the big news. I had no idea what he was talking about. Really though, I think he just wanted to see Woolf. With his arm around my shoulder, he asked if they could have a word in private.

She looked directly into his gaze and they shared a silent moment only permissible after having battered each other naked, I intuited. He walked to her side of the table where they spoke in hushed grownup voices while I mimed surprise at whatever pressing business I imagined was occupying my phone's screen; use of phones was now allowed, according to the signage.

He shook my hand goodbye and said with what seemed like

genuine enthusiasm that I should come to his house party next week, just text him. Incensed, I did not save his number.

What the fuck was that?

None of your business. The coffee cup touched her lips.

I thought you were a lesbian!

What are you talking about?

A waiter came by and asked if he could get me anything. I needed a minute to put things in perspective. No, wait, a Bloody Mary, please. Vodka *and* bourbon. Extra spicy.

Does the gentleman like olives?

The gentleman loves olives.

Very well.

Woolf's phone rang, the blue screen flashing. Something something on the patio, she said; I couldn't really hear. I will say, she said, placing the phone on the table, I'm impressed by your following on social. That will be helpful if we have to pitch you to the board and get you off the blacklist. I am *not* impressed by all this modeling shit, however, it's gross. You'll be typecast. Only women can make the leap. You'll need to fire your agent immediately.

Hold on. Did we really sleep in the same bed last night?

You've seriously got two seconds to pull it together. I'm here to talk business, got it?

I *thought* you were a lesbian!

She looked at the menu, which was a kind way of saying I should go fuck myself. I'm going to get the omelet, she said.

This was too much. I reached for the pills in my pocket, but there weren't any.

You still haven't told me how you know him so well.

Who?

'Who' he says. The prince.

The prince?

She took off her sunglasses as if to get a closer look. Iceblue lavender. It was hard to take myself seriously in her gaze. You're fucking with me. She kicked me under the table. Stop fucking with me, I'm too tired for sarcasm. She downed the coffee in her cup and poured more, eyeing mine to see if I needed a refill, which I found touching.

Of course we all *know* him to some degree—

First you don't answer your phone. Then the prince's cavalry comes down to let me in. I thought I was being abducted, his security is special forces. Then there's you running around the lobby with the prince on your back, piggybacking him legs akimbo like a little boy. And then the threesome with his wives! She paused as if I had some sort of explanation.

In that moment I remembered piledriving two foreign women like we were professional wrestlers, coming in one of their mouths, and watching as she spat into a champagne glass, which the prince downed entire.

Yikes.

Yikes? The prince wants you in his movie now.

I laughed. Oh sure, that's believable. I raised my hand like an asshole to let the staff know I expected my drink.

The air outside was cool and clean, as if summer had swallowed itself for autumn's return. The breakfast smells were both delicious and nauseating.

Woolf took a long sip of her coffee, tipped the sunglasses over the bridge of her nose.

I had to broker the deal for you while you were passed out naked in his bed. You wouldn't stop reciting *Goodnight Moon*. Hands down the weirdest moment in my career, maybe my life.

What are you, my agent now?

I don't think you understand what's going on here. You are going to be in the prince's movie.

Shut up.

What is wrong with you?

You're joking.

I'm trying to talk terms with you so I can get to the office and put this deal together.

I'm going to be in a movie, I said. The impossible light dimming.

Why else would I be sitting with you?

I glanced away, hiding my hurt.

Look, we've got something here. That's what I'm trying to tell you.

We?

I'm going to run point, but ultimately Harrison and I will tag team.

You talked to Harrison.

He's very impressed by what you've pulled off this year. He wants to tell you himself. After this we should get in touch with Julian and what's his brother's name again?

Gabriel.

Gabriel, right. I know the perfect director for *The Author*. I'm excited.

The Author?

That's the name, right? Of the movie you're producing? I think it's a good idea.

I said nothing, could only stare at the famous people eating egg whites and avocado toast at the tables surrounding us.

Fine. I think it's a great idea. You're a pretentious prick, aren't you? What's not to love? *Midnight in Paris* was fantastic. I think *The Author* has legs. Roman will love the concept, he's a huge Hemingway fan. It's good timing too. He's blowing up after Cannes and needs a new project. He's very fucking selective. Very. We'll sell him on the concept you pitched me last night.

I lit a cigarette. Who is Roman?

The director. We rep him. He's a good friend. Dude, are you going to offer me one or what?

I handed Woolf a cigarette, leaned over, flicked the zippo and lit. I wanted to touch her cheek and tell her I trusted her but thought it would be over the top.

Your managers said you came up with the concept?

The brothers.

Yes.

They're more like my partners. Investors. I had no idea what I was saying but it sounded good enough. I paused to take this all in. So—we really didn't have sex?

She kicked me under the table, hard this time.

All right, all right.

I'm going to need you to send me whatever contracts you've signed with them. Harrison despises managers and refuses to share duties. We need to see what we're dealing with. Can you do that for me?

They're not my managers.

She nodded along, ignoring me, and showed me the digital manuscript she'd been reading on her phone. I've been wondering, she said, why don't you use quotations at the end of your stories?

I don't know. Because I wish I could be like Cormac McCarthy but don't have the courage. Or maybe because everything collapses in the end.

Well, this time is different.

I wish I could quote you on that.

The second surprise came when Harrison appeared. Sunglasses on. Argyle vest. White collar touching up against his beard. Sunglasses off. He nodded. I stood.

I thought I'd never see you again.

He smiled brilliant drools of money.

Looks like we can do something with you after all, he said.

I was just saying, Woolf said to Harrison, she said to me, I have to hand it to you. In one year you've landed two movies—one potential blockbuster and one art piece with festival potential, if Roman greenlights it, which he will—a producer's credit, maybe a writer's credit, an impressive social following, and business partners, she knew to say, who seem committed to financing your career if not your lifestyle. That's pretty good.

That's pretty good? I repeated.

Harrison sat down and nodded at the waiter, who placed before me a highball glass filled with red juice and vegan accoutrements and hot flavors I'd never be able to describe.

Just a coffee for me, Harrison said.

And you, ma'am?

I'll have an omelet, thanks. Hold the toast.

Sir?

They looked at me.

Well, Harrison said. What do you have to say for yourself?

Glad I'm not writing my novel anymore.

acknowledgments

The chapter "The Talent" playfully engages with text from Hunter S. Thompson's *Fear and Loathing in Las Vegas*, published in 1971 by Random House. Pages of the penultimate section of the same chapter repurpose dialogue and quote a passage from Cormac McCarthy's *Cities of the Plain*, originally published by Knopf in 1998.

In the chapter "The Alternate Enviable Life of James Franco," the character Misha repurposes a passage from Lee Siegal's article "What The Critics Failed to See in Kubrick's Last Film," which appeared in *Harper's Magazine* in 2017. Its anachronistic reference in this novel reflects the book's unstable blend of fact and fiction. The same section of this chapter riffs on ideas put forth by Bret Easton Ellis in his book *White*, published by Knopf in 2019.

The closing page of the chapter "F. Scott" quotes a passage from F. Scott Fitzgerald's *The Crack-Up*, which appeared in *Esquire* in 1936 and was republished by New Directions in 1945.

Pages of the penultimate section of the chapter "Health Coach" quote dialogue and passages from Scene Seven of Tennessee Williams' *The Glass Menagerie*, which premiered in 1944 and was republished by New Directions in 1999.

The chapter "DMT and Chateau" repurposes a few lines from Shawn Levy's *The Castle on Sunset*, published in 2019 by Doubleday, to describe Chateau Marmont. In the same chapter, the character Jo uses ideas and phraseology introduced by New Age philosopher Stuart Wilde in his article "Tolemac," which appears on his website. Similarly, the character Taita Richard uses language and concepts expressed by Graham Hancock, particularly in *Fingerprints of the Gods*, published by Crown in 1995. The same chapter quotes briefly from the children's poem *Goodnight Moon* by Margaret Wise Brown, originally published in 1947 and now owned by HarperCollins.

Thank you to all the masters mentioned herein, my only teachers.

Thank you to Daniel and the Meta Lit team for delivering this book to the public under unusual constraints; thanks for having the balls. As for everyone else, those of you who are supposed to have my back: Fuck you, kindly.

about the author

The Author's lawyers and agents have demanded he not release this scandalous tell-all, in fear of one of their biggest talents being canceled. Thus, to satisfy the wishes of his representation, the author of this book has decided to keep his identity anonymous. His team has worked overtime to bury all associations made in this book to its author, including names, dates, locations, timelines, etc. Hence, "The Author."

Made in the USA
Middletown, DE
06 April 2025